I0699289

THE SEER

Also by Nathan Manioci

Demonic War
Nightwalker

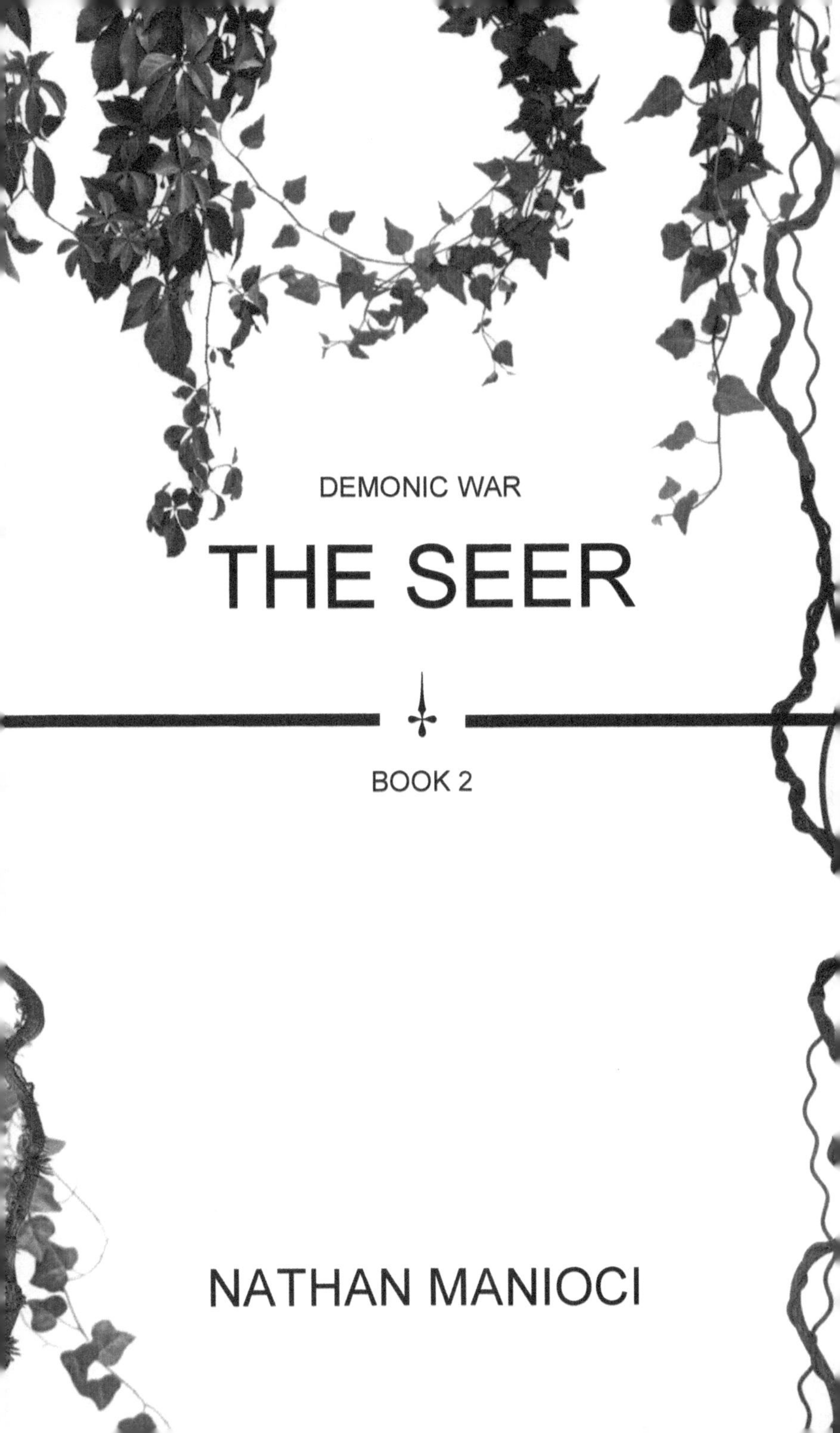

DEMONIC WAR

THE SEER

BOOK 2

NATHAN MANIOCI

Names: Manioci, Nathan
Title: The Seer/Nathan Manioci
Summary: The stones have been found and Algiroth has been defeated, but the mission isn't over yet. Ren and the others must return to his home world, Nexus, in search of information on how to remove the stones, all while dealing with his rapidly dying relationship with Kelsey.
Identifiers: 979-8-9886716-4-0 (Paperback)
Subjects: / CYAC: Vampires – Fiction / Magic – Fiction / Monsters – Fiction / Adventure — Fiction

Library of Congress Cataloging-in-Publication Data is available upon request.
ISBN 979-8-9886716-3-3 (Hardcover) — ISBN 979-8-9886716-4-0 (Paperback) — ISBN 979-8-9886716-5-7 (eBook)

First Edition

Printed in the United States of America

Visit us on the Web!
www.manioci.net

For all those who feel enslaved to their positions. The future is what you make it.

THE SEER

Montac Desert
VESTA
Yaman
Wolfsbane
Ramuse River
Theinsford
Norshire
Crdy
Veil
Talos
Darrat
Cas
Iona Sea

Mountains
Quin
Bayrock
Seidra
Arden
Avoline Ocean
Dridia
Shadowierre Forest
Clode
Shail

One

Aftermath

R en walked the battlefield. Smoke rose into the air and disappeared amongst the clouds. Bodies lie covering the ground. A thick coat of blood sploshed beneath his boots, seeping into the soles. There was so much destruction. So much unnecessary death.

Even as one who takes lives, Ren still viewed death as a cost only taken when necessary. Life was still worth keeping. But this, this was entirely *unnecessary*. Just senseless death that should never have occurred. Worst of all, it had to happen in the human world.

This kind of thing was precisely what he had been trying to avoid. He wanted to prevent any battles from occurring in the human realm. It would leave them exposed, as it had, and reveal their existence to the world. He should have known better. Trying to stop three armies that were dominant in the human world from clashing was just wishful thinking.

Ultimately, no matter what they did, their battles would have escalated, and the human world would have succumbed to the fighting. The war would have broken through the barriers of their worlds and consumed this one. It was unfortunate that the human world had to be the middle ground between them, the battleground where it all would take place.

Now, they were exposed. The existence of monsters had been revealed and spread across the world in but a single day. As it stood, Ren doubted there was very little they could do to stop it. There would always be some who refused to believe, only accepting it as a mere ploy. Alas, too many people within the city had seen the army of shades marching to war. A mere staged event wouldn't force the evacuation of an entire city.

Ren had the strongest feeling that everything had gone according to Algiroth's plans. That everything had fallen into place so perfectly to lead up to their reveal was too much of a coincidence. He bet even the pope was part of Algiroth's plans.

What a complete mess. Ren had no idea how they were going to fix this. Was there even a way to resolve it? It had gotten thick real fast. He just didn't know what to do. His head felt like it was about to explode.

Ren took note of their injured and the damage. One-quarter of their side was dead, and over half were injured.

Most consisted of ordinary citizens, monsters that supported Trinty but had no direct involvement. People who had chosen to fight of their own free will. Those willing to support the cause. And among those, three of their own. Members of Trinity.

They gave their lives for peace, but Ren wondered if this battle had really even accomplished anything other than exposing their existence and getting their people killed. Algiroth was dead. They had defeated one of Verin's four generals. But Algiroth could easily be replaced. No doubt another general would take over soon, and they'd be no better off than before.

Rather than contemplate the unpredictable and dwell on it, Ren settled on focusing on what was in front of him and returned to his tasks. He had taken it upon himself to continue providing aid and help heal as many of the injured as he could. His next patient was a nearby soldier who was lying against a tree. A gash cut through his armor, and his arm was broken.

"Prince Nightwalker," the soldier said, recognizing Ren immediately.

"Don't talk; save your strength," Ren said back.

"It's not as bad as it looks," the guy said. "My armor stopped most of the attack, so the gash isn't that deep."

"Yes, that appears to be the case. The problem is your arm. It's definitely broken. You're going to be out of commission for a while."

"Bha, one arm is the least of my concern. I'll be alright. It's nothing I can't handle."

Ren was met with cries and then groans from the man as he set his arm. Holding his hand out, golden light covered him. It held for several minutes, casting a warmth over the wounded soldier. Then, it disappeared.

"I've healed your injuries, but that's all I can do for now. Our forces have set up an ICU tent and medical tents on the West side of the park. Head there. You can eat and rest to help regain your strength."

"Will do. Much appreciated, Your Highness."

Ren helped the man to his feet and watched him shuffle away before heading off to help more of the injured. He found a group of three people limping toward him and ran over to them. They were all beaten up badly. After using some of his magic on them, he directed them to the tents.

Ren wondered where Marcus and Kelsey were. He hadn't seen them since the end of the battle. No doubt they were around, helping out the injured like he was. There were still many more to treat. It was a good thing his vampiric powers had already healed all of his own wounds.

Using his vampire powers to sense blood flow, he found two people about one hundred yards from him. One had a regular pace, so he guessed they were fine, but he could barely sense the other person. Their blood was slowing down, and fast. He had to get to them before they died. Whoever the other person was that was there could help him carry the person to the ICU.

He ran toward them, uncertain of what he would find. Unobscured by obstacles, Ren saw the two people well before he reached them. One lay on the ground, the other leaned over them. He could see a faint glow and feel the pull of magic. Healing magic, but Ren could tell it wasn't very potent. They might be out of magic.

The person in better condition was dressed in silver armor and covered in dirt and blood. From behind, he could still see the glimmer of their long copper hair.

Ren stopped as soon as he recognized them. Memories of the fight with Aligroth and immediately after surfaced, but he immediately pushed them aside and took a deep breath. This wasn't the time to be worrying about his own problems. Right now, helping the injured was his priority. The situation with Kelsey would have to wait.

Kelsey saw Ren drop down next to her.

"Ren. Thank goodness you got here when you did." She seemed focused on the injured person herself. That made things less awkward.

"Let me take a look," he said.

Ren examined the injured warrior. They, too, were female. Her breathing was faint underneath her helmet, so Ren removed it.

"I've been trying to heal her, but it's not working. I can't draw any more power from the stones."

"Perhaps they've reached their limit," Ren said.

He put his hand over the wounded girl's stomach. "Her injuries are numerous but not life-threatening. The problem is she's lost a lot of blood. We need to close her wounds and get her to the ICU."

Kelsey put her hands over the woman and tried more healing. Ren could see the sweat dripping down the side of her face. She was giving it her all. She was pushing herself to try and do everything she could.

"Kelsey, that's enough. It's obvious that you're out of magic. A spell is pointless to use if it doesn't have any effect."

He reached out and grabbed her wrist. Suddenly, the green and blue bracelet around his own began to glow. Then, the stones around Kelsey's wrist started to glow. The light and intensity of the healing magic grew. Ripples of golden energy swam across the woman's body. They watched as her injuries healed. Her cuts and gashes closed, and her scrapes disappeared.

Kelsey stopped the flow of magic, and both the glow of the stones and Ren's bracelet disappeared. She looked at him like she had no idea what just happened, but Ren wasn't so sure himself, though he had an idea. The bracelet around his wrist wasn't actually a bracelet. It was a magical artifact that had transformed into one. The official name for it was the Sacred Key. Similarly, the Sun and Moon Stones had secured themselves around Kelsey's wrist, at the apparent behest of her unable to remove them. It was a significant problem they would need to deal with after they dealt with this whole mess.

"Come on, let's get her to the ICU," Ren said.

"Can you carry her?" Kelsey asked. He nodded in confirmation. "Okay, then I'll leave it to you."

Ren picked the girl up, sliding her close to him. She rested her head against his chest, and they headed for the ICU.

"So, do you have any idea what that was?" Kelsey asked him. "It was like the stones got a major power boost as soon as you touched me."

Ren nodded. "I have a theory," he said. "I think the stones have a limit to the amount of power that can be drawn out."

"But I thought they were supposed to be all-powerful."

"They are, but you can only draw so much at once. The stones must regulate the amount of power they give so they don't kill the person using them. Remember, by themselves, each stone holds immense power. But, only together is one able to access their full potential. Consider the consequences otherwise. The stones chose their wielder, yes, but that doesn't mean they'll always be someone extraordinary, especially you, a human. You have no abilities at all. Just imagine what would happen if you immediately used the full power of the stones."

Kelsey didn't like the way Ren said it, but she knew he was right. His theory made sense.

"The same scenario applies to Heaven's Blades as well. Our weapons can read our magic and our hearts. They can immediately tell how powerful we are. Some don't even require physical contact if they and their wielder are strong enough, like Shadow Hunter and I or Glorious and Marcus. Together, they regulate each other for maximum effect. Without the other, there would be no limiter, and the user would destroy themselves."

"And the key?" She was, of course, referring to the Sacred Key.

"It must be the link between the stones and their user. As you've seen, the power of the stones isn't limitless, at least not now. At your current level, with all you're able to draw out from them, the power of the stones is eventually used up. It's essentially the same as anyone using up their strength after hard work. The Sacred Key must draw out more energy from the stones, unlocking their extra power as required. In that sense, the key is quite literally that, the key to using the stones. Without it, you cannot draw out more of the stones' power beyond your limit."

"We still don't know why they chose me, though," she said.

"That's what we intend to find," Ren said back.

They walked into the ICU tent. It was packed full of injured. The few specializing in healing magic were running rampant, trying to help everyone, but there were so many injured, and more just kept coming in. It would have helped if those who brought them knew healing magic, like Ren and Kelsey, but they needed more healers. If those searching for the wounded could heal injuries as soon as they were discovered, the chances of survival were greater.

Ren sat the injured woman down on her backside against the wall.

"You should be alright since we healed most of your injuries, but you need sleep."

He stood up to leave, and the woman grabbed his hand. She looked at him with fear in her eyes, though not directed at him. Ren gently placed his hand over hers, and she visibly relaxed. Afterward, he exited the tent with Kelsey.

"Come on, let's go help more injured," Kelsey said. She grabbed his hand reflexively and pulled him along. He didn't even bother trying to pull his hand away. It was easier to just let her lead him.

As they walked, Ren continuously searched for the flow of blood. He finally found two signatures directly ahead of them.

"Kelsey," he said, squeezing her hand to get her attention. She stopped and looked at him. "I'm sensing two people up ahead."

"How's their condition?"

"It doesn't appear bad, but we won't know for sure until we reach them."

They let go of each other's hand and ran to the two people Ren had sensed. One of them was a heavier-set man. He was covered in sweat, and his leg was in a splint. The other person was Marcus. He had the guy's arm around his neck, helping him to walk.

Marcus saw the two of them together. He glared at Kelsey but motioned them over to him.

"Hey guys."

"How's he looking, brother?" Ren asked.

"His leg is broken. I set it with magic, then splinted it. Other than that, he's ok."

"Sorry about this, guys," the man apologized.

"It's alright, no harm done," Marcus said.

Marcus started walking the man to the ICU when someone called out to Ren. They stopped, and Ren looked in the direction it was coming from. He expected it to be one of his own or someone carrying an injured soldier. He did not expect to see the manager of the hotel they stayed at in Taormina running over to him.

Ren told Marcus and Kelsey to go on ahead of him. Kelsey took Ren's place and helped the man walk to the ICU with Marcus.

The hotel manager stopped when he reached Ren and put his hands on his knees, trying to catch his breath.

"Your Highness," he finally said. "I bring word from the others posted around the park."

"Go ahead," Ren told him. "Most of our injured have been cleared out and brought to the medical tent or the ICU. The very few that are left are being tended to now." Ren nodded, and the manager continued speaking. "There has been no indication of resistance from the humans and no sign of Verin or reinforcements."

"I had expected that," Ren admitted. "Truthfully, I'm not even sure Verin was behind this. He likely knows what Aligorth was up to, but I have no doubt Aligorth acted independently and out of his own self-interests. That's just the kind of man he was. There might not be any reinforcements at all."

The hotel manager nodded in understanding and continued speaking.

"Our sources confirmed with the other Heaven's Blades that every shade in the city has been destroyed."

"Every single one of them?" Ren asked, raising an eyebrow.

"Yes, Your Highness."

Well, that was a little unexpected. Ren had expected most of the shades to have been rifted, but not *every* single one of them. That meant that their job in this city was now over. They could move on to another place infested with shades and clear them out, too. And here he thought it would take years with all the shades they had in this city.

"Anything else?" Ren asked.

"For better or worse, yes. I and several others have contacts in our respective nation's government. We've already received word that they and governments worldwide are stirring in response to the exposure of our existence. We're hearing of a possible meeting with the president himself or his cabinet members." Ren nodded in confirmation.

"Once things are settled here, you are free to return home. No doubt your family is concerned for you."

"Then I shall head out as soon as I am able. I'll also reach out to my contacts in the Italian government and see if we can quell any moves they may attempt to make."

"I appreciate it."

The two of them shook hands before the hotel manager bid Ren a farewell and headed in a different direction.

Things are getting complicated, Ren thought. More weight just kept being added to the pile. He sighed, knowing there was still a lot to do.

Two

A Soldier's Fate

Ren's house was bustling. Word had spread that the president of the United States had sent an official request to Trinity through their contacts in the government to hold an immediate press conference. Though that warranted the number of people gathered, why they had to do it at Ren's house was a mystery to him. Not that it mattered; he had the space.

Kelsey had asked Ren if she could help, but he declined her offer, mentioning that there was no need. So she decided to keep Ellie company instead while Ren was busy, but that didn't stop her from watching him.

Right now, they were in his study. Ren was at his desk reading through some papers while Kelsey and Ellie sat on a couch off to the side. He sorted through the ones he had already looked over, setting them in a separate pile.

Glancing over at the stack of unread documents, he grabbed the topmost piece of paper, intrigued after its contents stood out to him. He was nearly finished with it when he suddenly stopped.

"Hey Kelsey, take a look at this."

Ren handed her the piece of paper. It turned out to be a memorandum for the press conference. Necessary preparations, dates, times, events, participants, and more.

"So, how are we going to handle this? Explaining the situation at the conference, I mean. Do you actually plan to tell the truth, or are you planning a way out of it?" Kelsey asked him. "We'll have to plan our trip, too."

"Odds are, most of our time will be spent in negotiations. We'll determine how long later. Besides, we still don't have a location settled on where it's being held. That's in the works as we speak, however."

"Do you want me to look for hotels? We may not know where the conference is going to be, but we can at least have a range of options before it's too late."

Ren was looking through more papers before setting the stack down. Then, he turned his focus onto Kelsey.

"Yeah, that would help, actually. But we can focus on that later. For now, let's go meet up with the others and see where they stand."

Ren stood up from his chair and walked around to the couch. Ellie was sitting at the end, sound asleep.

In her own way, the day had been just as long and endearing as it had for the rest of them. She may not have participated in the war, but Ellie had fought her own battle.

Ren picked her up, letting her head rest against his shoulder, and carried her into the living room with Kelsey. The remainder of their company was gathered around two coffee tables that had been put together to form a long table.

Kelsey made sure not to wake Ellie when Ren handed her over.

"You look like a father handing off his child," James Wilson said. He was the school principal of the high school Kelsey attended. And Ren, too, for a little while. He was also an incredibly gifted beastkin. His magic protected the school from any shades or Verin.

Ren rolled his eyes while Kelsey found an empty spot on the nearest couch and sat down.

"Did you guys make any progress?" he asked, sitting down next to Marcus.

"A little," Ren's father said. "Did you see anything that stood out in your set of documents?"

"No. It was mainly security and regulations stuff. There were some details on the state of the city and a few papers about the damage to the park. Nothing on the buildings yet, though."

"We're going to have to really figure out our funding for the damages. It's going to be a pretty penny."

"I know. I really don't want to use our palace's treasury either. Dipping into it will eat up a huge chunk of it. In the best case, our economy could stagnate. Worst case, it collapses."

"I've already sent a letter to my father," Marcus added. "We'll give what we can. It'll help, but in the end, the amount of money for reparations is going to be difficult."

"I would say let's sell off Algiroth and his sword, but we can't do that."

"Ren, what is wrong with you?" Kelsey asked, mortified.

"Not like that," he said back. "There are certain donors who would pay a lot of money to keep Algiroth's dead body contained so it can't be used by Verin or future terrorists. And the Demonic sword is worth a lot of money to the right people. There are specific groups of people that will pay to obtain one of them. And even more to destroy it."

"Oh, sorry, I didn't realize."

"It's alright. I'd be surprised if you did. If not partially concerned."

"What about the Church?" Marcus said. "They started this battle by bringing you here in chains. At the moment, they're severely weakened. We could force our way in at the worst and demand they help pay."

"Yeah, I like the idea of using the Church. I should get a hold of Arron," Ren agreed.

"Can you? It's not like you two have been in contact before. Nor me, for that matter."

"I'll find a way."

Ren heard Ellie wake up on the couch with Kelsey.

"Kelsey, I'm thirsty," she said quietly. "Can I have something to drink?"

"Of course. Here, stay with Ren. I'll be right back."

Ren and Kelsey got to their feet in unison. He picked Ellie up and carried her back over to his spot, rubbing her cheek with his index finger.

"So, any news on the conference?" someone asked.

"Nothing major," Ren's father said. "As to be expected. We've only received preliminary information. We're very little in the way of it right now."

"This blows," one of the Heaven's Blades gathered among them said.

"I did get a memorandum regarding the conference," Ren said. "Likely the same information you guys received. We'll come up with something to say; however, I have no intention of preaching to a bunch of useless humans who have no intent to pay attention or take us seriously. Those that do will only see this as another threat."

From behind him, someone cleared their throat. Ren looked behind him to see Kelsey staring.

"Oh, no offense, Kelsey. I mean everyone but you."

Kelsey handed Ellie a glass filled with apple juice and sat beside Ren since it was free. She found his hand atop his leg and slipped her arm around his, lacing their fingers. They were warm, which she loved.

"If that's the case, we need to decide what our plans are going forward. We still need to finalize the restoration plans, but honestly, we have more important matters to deal with," one of them spoke up. He was a vampire, and high-ranking. "We may have defeated Algiroth, but it will only do us so much good. Verin will probably replace him. And even if he doesn't, there are still three generals left. Not only that, but we still don't know where he is."

"The dude's been a ghost for centuries. Where the hell could he even be hiding?" Marcus wondered. "He could be anywhere in the human world or Nexus for all we know."

"Either way, we need to return to Nexus," Ren said. "It's time for us to head home. We've been gone for too long, and the answers we seek most likely aren't here in the human world. And we still need to find a way to get the stones off Kelsey's wrist. We can't do that here, but I'm sure we have information in the great library."

"Ren, that library is thousands of years old. How do you expect to find anything in it?" his father asked.

"I honestly have no idea. I haven't been in there since I was a little kid. I would need to see it for myself again before deciding what to do after that."

"Are we sure they'll even come off?" another monster asked.

"They have to. I refuse to let Kelsey deal with this anymore. She's done enough and shouldn't be involved in this war more than she has to."

"What if they don't come off?"

Ren didn't answer. It was clear that he was lost in thought.

"… I'll find a way," he finally said. "I don't know how, but I'll find a way."

"Don't I get a say in this?" Kelsey asked. They all looked at her. "Maybe I don't want to get rid of them. Maybe I want to be here; to help you. I haven't been able to do anything so far. But now I finally have a chance to help. I have a role to fill, and I can be of use. These stones brought me closer to all of you. I don't want to lose that."

"Kelsey, my dear, you will always be one of us," Ren's father said. "You've already done more than you believe. You accepted us and even aided us of your own free will. Most humans would not do that. So whether or not you have the stones, you will always be a part of our family, and you'll never lose us."

Kelsey looked utterly relieved to hear that. It was the validation she had been searching for. Proof that her time was worthwhile and that she hadn't been as useless as she had believed.

"Has anybody else thought that this happened for a reason?" Marcus asked. "The fact that the stones attached to Kelsey of all people. When we found the second stone, eleven powerful monsters and many members of the Church were gathered. Yet, out of all of them, the stones chose Kelsey, the only nonaffiliated human. Why? Perhaps … perhaps the stones chose Kelsey for a reason. Perhaps there is a purpose for her being able to wield the stones. Maybe that's why we can't remove them."

"I think that's a strong possibility," Ren's father agreed. "The stones are like a blessing. They will aid us with their power so long as Kelsey fights with us. Perhaps then, the stones will leave her of their own will when everything is over."

"Everything as in after we've defeated Verin and the Church. If that's the case—" Ren started to say.

"It's likely they won't come off no matter what we do," Marcus finished.

Ren released a heavy sigh. "No. That's not good enough."

"Ren," Kelsey started to say.

"I don't care if you use the stones, Kells." Kelsey looked at him in shock. He hadn't called her Kells since the fight with Agliroth. "But I refuse to let you wear them as they are. What happens if something happens to you and you have the stones on you? What if people try to capture you to get them? Who knows what they'll do to you, especially if they find out the stones won't come off. We need them off, or at least removable. If you want to continue using the stones afterward, that's fine. They did choose you, so I won't tell you not to use them. They probably won't let anyone else but you wield them anyway."

"The fact that you think so much for me means a lot to me, and I love you for it, but I should have a say in this, too. I agree that we should find a way to at least make them removable. But if we are able to get them off, know that I have no intention of leaving or no longer using them. I will fight with you, and you can't stop me."

Monster. The word swarmed in his head. Ren felt like he'd been sucker punched. His memory swallowed him whole, and he was back in the park after defeating Algiroth. Kelsey was staring at him, horrified. The word echoed in his head. *Monster ... monster.*

All the negative feelings in Ren resurfaced. Worse, though, was his inability to conceive the truth in them. Kelsey was acting no different than how she usually did. He got the impression their interpretation of the incident was different. Unless her actions since then have merely been that. A ploy to hide the crack formed between them.

Monster. That's right; he had to remember, Kelsey hated him. He was a monster. He'd almost gotten lost in her. He couldn't do that, not anymore. It was over between Kelsey and him. She had made that clear.

His expression grew serious again. The haze surrounding him had cleared. "Do what you want," he told her. She looked at him with a confused expression as he got to his feet. "I believe this meeting is over for today. We've got enough groundwork done. When we get more information on the press conference, we will send word. Help yourselves to any of the empty bedrooms."

Ren left Ellie with Kelsey and headed to his room. He reminded himself how lucky he was that he snapped back to reality beforehand. That was too close for comfort.

Inside, Nidar was lying on a large cushion, which acted as his bed most of the time. Ren walked over to a wardrobe, different and of a smaller size than the one storing his weapons. The interior was lined with bottles of varying liquors. He grabbed a glass and a bottle of whiskey, then plunked a large cube of ice into the glass from the freezer of his mini fridge. Raising the glass to his lips, he let the whisky pass smoothly down his throat.

He knew things were going to be hectic when he woke up, but he didn't care. Right now, there were too many things to worry about that he wanted to rid himself of, if only temporarily. And this was how he was going to start.

Three

Across Three-Hundred Years

Ren sat in his chair at the press conference. His father sat to his right. A wood table was laid out in front of them. Two seats to his father's right sat the president of the United States. With them were leaders from nations across the world, army generals, and cabinet members accompanying their respective nations' leaders. There was CIA everywhere. In fact, there was so much security it appeared that they dwarfed even the civilians gathered for the conference.

The tension in the room was so thick it could be cut with a knife. And yet, it wasn't coming from Ren or his father. It was formed from the many leaders, and the massive mob of reporters gathered.

Hundreds of reporters had gathered for this press conference, ranging from the biggest names to the smallest. Dozens of cameras filmed the conference, broadcasting it live to every available news outlet and station. Even the radio had it covered. The entire world was tuning into this. After all, revealing the existence of monsters was like meeting aliens. It was an altercation of the view of the world for humans on a global scale.

Those who weren't as able to adapt or understand the situation were extremely nervous. And no doubt they were plainly aware of what monsters were capable of. Their battle ability would decimate, especially with the use of magic.

Ren could overhear some of the conversations among the CIA and the security of other nations. Others he could lip read.

Behind and off to his side, Kelsey leaned against the wall next to a chair placed for her. She was terribly nervous, and having everyone take notice of her was making her uncomfortable. She hoped she wasn't sweating through her red dress. The straps were thin, and her heels were challenging to move in.

They had gotten notice of the finalization of the conference several days before. A hotel, transportation, and details of the conference had already been prepared for them. Ren had come up with something of a speech, as had his father, though he wasn't banking on it accomplishing anything. They were instructed to bring one person who was close to both sides, human and monster. That person would act as an ambassador and, therefore, an intermediary for any needed situation. Just like Kelsey in the beginning, these humans truly had no idea of the relevance the existence of monsters had on their society. Well, it would be good for them to learn the truths of their origins.

Kelsey was the obvious choice, given her relationships with everyone. Although he dared say she agreed readily, given she was still angry at him. She had been furious the morning after she found him drunk and asleep in his room. It had been two days since then, but she was still mad at him. Then again, he figured it was better than them being close again. He was hoping the distance between them had widened a little, actually. It would make things easier.

Standing next to Kelsey was Marcus, who was acting as security for Ren and his father. He was dressed in black breeches made of silk and a navy blue tunic with gold embroidery and trim. A wolf symbol that Ren recognized as his family crest, the emblem of his kingdom, was embroidered on his left side. The vest collar stuck up with its own design. A navy blue cape with silver trim and a golden underside was fitted over his shoulders. Two golden buttons on either side of his clavicles kept it secure through the golden chain fitted between them. He was dressed just like a prince of Nexus. Glorious was sheathed at his hip, visible for everyone to see. The blade radiated golden energy.

Ren and his father were dressed more humanely. Ren wore a black suit with a red dress shirt underneath and a black tie. His father wore a blue suit with a grey dress shirt and black tie.

The president of the United States cleared his throat and held up his hand. All the commotion quieted down, and he spoke.

"I would like to thank all of you for coming. You are free to ask any questions you would like, but know that any of us can refuse to comment on them. Please be mindful of the way you speak. Let us welcome Leo and Ren Nightwalker. They are the representatives of their people."

As soon as the president finished his introduction, he sat down. The room was flooded with questions and the flashing of pictures being taken.

"Mr. Nightwalker," one of the reporters spoke up.

"There are two Nightwalkers here, Miss," Ren's father said. "You may refer to me as Your Majesty and my son, Your Highness."

Ren and his father could tell their term of address confused not just the reporter who had addressed them but the other humans present as well.

"A question for you, Your Majesty. I'll be frank, and as the question everyone has been asking, what are you? There are still many who doubt your existence, myself included. You come out of nowhere and reveal yourselves, then expect us to merely believe in your existence, especially when you appear human as you do.

If so, where do you come from? Where have your people been hiding?"

Leo had anticipated nothing else but this immediately. Their perspective of the situation was just as they had expected it to be.

"My, that is a thorough question, isn't it? First off, I am a vampire." The fury of pictures intensified through the talking. "Also, you're entirely incorrect on all counts." There was another fury of pictures and muffled conversations that spread through the crowd.

"We were never hiding. We have the ability to take human form, such as I am doing now. By doing so, we simply make it easier to blend in with human society. So, if you still consider it as such, then I guess you could say we were hiding in plain sight. Nor do we expect you to simply accept us. We're not so callous as to believe such a thing. And we certainly did not come out of nowhere. After all, we've been amongst you since the beginning."

Leo's last statement drew a heavy silence over them. There was not a single whisper, not even a cough. No one broke the silence. That is, until another reporter spoke up.

"Your Majesty, what does that mean?" another reporter asked. "Could you please elaborate?"

"I'm talking about the very beginning. Since your species came into being," he answered. "This may come as a shock to you, but the monster race has been around far longer than humans. We were the first of evolved creations."

The looks on people's faces proved enough they had no idea what he was talking about.

"Charles Darwin's theory of evolution," Ren said. All eyes locked on him. "A human, and a smart one at that. He was correct. The human race came into being through the evolution of life forms. However, he got one thing wrong, and that is what you evolved from. The human race did not evolve from apes; you evolved from us."

Reporters looked at each other in shock. Ren's statement had the leaders of the other nations on high alert. Even the president of the United States leaned over in curiosity.

"The first humans," Ren continued, "were monsters that had no magic. They were of great size and strength with high mental pairing for their time, something akin to your imagination of bigfoot. Large creatures, around fifteen to twenty feet tall, with muscular bodies. Scales covered their backs and fur their front. Their skin was as hard as a rock and a deep grey color. They were known as humanculi. Kind of like homunculi given human form. In fact, their altering appearance is where the word homunculi comes from."

"Their only ability, akin to their strong bodies, came from their different color eyes. They were capable of seeing two different colors at the same time or going beyond it entirely. And they could alter the range of color they see in each eye at will. Do you understand what this means?"

After a long silence, the president of the United States spoke up. "They could see the full range of the color spectrum," he surmised.

"Worse," Ren said. "They could see the entire electromagnetic spectrum. These monsters developed themselves differently than other monsters since they were like no other. At the time, they were considered a failed species, being the only ones without magic. The scorn and rejection they received eventually turned into persecution. They finally left Nexus for another world entirely. One where they could prosper and live in peace. That became the human world, your world."

"Over time, our species did interact again, but by then, much time had passed, and the humanculi had evolved further into modern humans, losing their bodies, scale, and visual abilities. The humanculi eventually dropped part of their name, and the term "human" was born. Their race adopted the term as their own, which has persisted to this day."

"This is complete nonsense!" someone spoke up. "You expect us to believe this garbage? Paint whatever picture you want; no matter how you look at it, this is nothing but a massive joke taken way too far."

"You're free to believe what you will. That would actually make things easier on us if you didn't believe in what we're telling you."

"Let's say we believe you, and I'm not saying I do; if what you say really is true, why was this never known to us. How could such a thing be kept hidden?" the leader of another country asked.

"It wasn't kept hidden," Ren said. "It was simply never recorded in the first place. No one thought to document them, and your carbon dating cannot detect them since their structures degrade too quickly. After several hundred years, their bodies completely dissolve into the soil. By then, all traces of their existence had been erased before you had anything to look for."

"I'm sure this must come as a shock to you," Ren's father said. "There is much you don't know about your own existence, after all."

"Then how is it you know so much? Why do you know all of this, and we don't if it was never recorded?" one of the reporters asked. "Especially so at your age. You're what, eighteen, nineteen? Barely an adult. I'm not certain if you truly believe in all this or if you're just going along with it as you were told. Either way, you shouldn't even be here. A kid like you should be in school, learning the real truth and bettering himself. This is not a place for children."

Ren started chuckling. Eyes turned on him before he threw his head back and laughed hysterically. The reporters were confused at his outbreak.

"Not a place for children huh?" Ren asked."Perhaps, if I was one of you. But I am a vampire. I am the prince of my species and my father's only child. As such, I will inherit the throne in the future. You asked how we know the truth behind your existence. It's because my kind continues the legends and stories passed down for millennia. I have lived longer than you know. You stand there, throwing a tantrum like a child whose mother forced them to eat their vegetables at dinner. To me, you're the child here. So why don't you leave?"

The reporter was about to respond when Ren's father intervened.

"Ren, hold your tongue, please. I know you hate humans, but we can't afford the consequences of you ending up killing everyone over a conflict."

All eyes were suddenly on Ren.

"Very well, my apologies," Ren said.

The reporter was clearly dissatisfied. He had called Ren a child and been made a fool of because of it. On live television to boot. He'd just cast a permanent stain on his career.

"Um," one of the reporters raised their hand. It was a woman of middle age with brown hair tied into a ponytail. "Just, how old are you, if I may ask?" she wondered. "You certainly do look like a teenager."

"Three hundred and twenty-one," he said after a long pause.

The reporter dropped her microphone. "I'm sorry, did you say three hundred and twenty-one?"

"I did." He gave her a smile. Ren nodded. "In your world, I am registered as eighteen. However, as I said, that's not actually the case. I am much, much older."

"You're three hundred years old? Ha—" was the last thing that came out of her mouth before she nearly collapsed.

"I have lived a long time by human standards. By vampire standards, I am still quite young, however. Normally, we live almost forever."

"In that case, why reveal yourselves now?" another reporter asked. "After all this time, why expose the truth?"

"We didn't choose to reveal ourselves. We were tricked into it," Ren said. "By now, I'd bet all of you have heard of or seen videos of the battle that happened in Florida last week. That battle was not meant to occur in your world. We had hoped any conflict would be dealt with in our world. We had no intention of revealing ourselves and probably never would. However, we believe our enemy planned to reveal our existence from the beginning. It was a part of their plan, and they succeeded."

Ren quickly explained their war against the necromancer in their world and against the Radiant

Church, the most powerful religious organization in the human world. One that has existed for millennia and is made up of believers in religions from across the globe.

"Despite our best effort to keep things under wraps, the enemy was influential, and everything happened according to their plans," Leo added, taking over. "They started a battle in a public space by drawing us all in. No doubt they had planned to use the satellites to display the battle to your people from the beginning."

"You humans don't accept other species," Leo continued. "You have a hard enough time accepting your own. You reject anything you don't like or understand, pretending that it doesn't exist or you never knew about it. It's how you cope. If you knew of our existence, what would have happened? How would you have reacted? Even now, you're having difficulty accepting things. By the time we entered into your society, you had long since lost and forgotten your own origins. You believed you were this supreme race, and we saw your nature. By integrating ourselves into your society the way we did, we were able to live in peace and develop healthy relationships. If we hadn't, things would not have worked out as they did. We did it for the benefit of both our races."

"What are the intentions of the world governments now? Surely something must be done," a different reporter asked.

"Yes, of that, I can assure you," the United States President responded. We shall work together to decide what that will be."

"We will come to peaceful terms," Ren said. "You will find we mean no harm to you and will try and take our fight out of the human world. We only desire peace between us, despite your church. So, for now, we will work on coming to a peace agreement. However, I have only one thing to address to my people on this matter. Even if peace is obtained, as your prince, I implore you, do not reveal yourselves. No matter what, you must continue to remain as a human while in this world."

Ren's declaration threw the entire room into chaos. The massive uproar had been eloquently captured and put on repeat by the media. Attempting to quell the chaos, Marcus stepped forward and placed his hand on Glorious's handle. The golden energy around the blade bubbled off, immediately silencing the room.

"You want your people to remain as they were?" another country's leader spoke up.

"An unknown species has suddenly been revealed to the world, your world, where humans are the dominant species. How would you feel if a bunch of creatures you thought were myths and told in stories started walking around in their real forms? This is necessary to keep the peace. It's easier for all of us if we continue to remain as humans."

"You will find that so long as you don't press the issue of our existence or attempt conflict with us, we will not act. You will never even know we are here. We do try to maintain the peace as much as possible, you know. Unlike some of you humans, we make it a point to avoid war. That's why I speak to all the monsters watching this press conference. As your prince, I implore you to remain in your human forms. You are not to reveal your identity under any circumstances except for the most dire or to those who can truly be trusted."

"The best thing for all of us is to go about our business as we always have," Ren's father said. "That will ensure the peace. If you get to know us, you'll learn that we're no different from you."

"And yet you are at war with your own people and ours," one of the reporters said. Agreements started up between the people.

"We are at war, but not of our own volition," Ren's father said. "Your church hunts us. They want to wipe us out specifically because we are not human. They do not care for our actions or who we are. They only care to see us dead simply for being. So I would think of the actions of your own people before ours, good sir. And as for our own being an enemy, they wish to bring about the return of the Dark Ages. We fight to stop that."

"There was a time when humans and monsters lived together peacefully. I was alive to see it, so I can guarantee the truth behind my words. But that was a long time ago. Things have changed now. Right now, it's best not to rock the boat given that our existence has once again been revealed."

"The two who accompany you, they are monsters as well, I presume," the president of the United States asked.

"The man with the sword is yes," Ren said. "He and I are very close and have worked together many times. He is the prince of a different race of monsters. The girl, however, is human."

"She's human? Yet she's hanging around monsters."

"Like my father said. If you get to know us, you'll find that we're no different from you. She has connections to all of us. I will not go into detail regarding why, as it is her personal life, and I will not share it. However, she has been a great help to us many times."

The president cleared his throat, and all attention turned on him.

"Forgive me if I overstep, but I think it would benefit all of us to see your proper forms. I'm certain it will satisfy many people and convince those who refuse to believe in you. Seeing it in person makes it easier to know what one is actually dealing with."

Ren and his father exchanged expressionless glances. Their silent conversation lasted for only a few seconds before Leo gave a short nod to Ren.

"We could show you our forms, certainly," Ren's father said. "However, understand that because we are vampires, our true forms still resemble that of a human. Many other monsters have less of a human appearance."

The silence that passed through the room was as apparent of an understanding as it could get. Ren and Leo stood up and removed the clothes from their torso. The world watched as wings spread out from their back. Ren cast his gaze out among the crowd and bared his fangs.

"And that's pretty much it," Ren's father said.

The president nodded silently, but despite his attempts to keep a stoic face, his eyes showed how impressed he was.

"And you?" he asked Marcus.

"I'm a werewolf," Marcus said.

"Really? Now that I would like to see."

"Sorry, but I don't have a change of clothes, and this is one of my favorite tunics."

"You can use mine if you want. I brought spare clothes," Ren said to him. "They're in my bag in the back. But it's up to you."

Marcus was hesitant but finally nodded and walked out of sight. He appeared minutes later shirtless and barefoot, but in new pants. The anticipation was unbearable.

Standing next to Ren, Marcus started to grow larger. Light brown fur formed on his body. The pants he wore tore at his legs but stretched enough to stay on. His face elongated into a snout with razor-sharp teeth. A long, furry tail fell behind him.

He stood on his hind legs with his arms crossed. "Well, satisfied?" he asked.

"How come I've never seen you change clothes before when transforming?" Kelsey asked him. "The clothes I wear for work are magiced," he whispered back. "There's a spell cast on them to grow along with me. The clothes I had on before weren't like that. Normal clothes get destroyed unless they're very flexible."

"Thank you, Marcus. You can go change now," Ren's father said. Marcus nodded and walked out of sight again. When he returned, he was back in his human form, wearing his tunic.

Ren and his father put their wings away and their clothes back on.

"What exactly are your plans now?" one of the reporters asked.

"We are returning to our world. There are tasks that need to be taken care of over there," Ren's father said. "Of course, we'll keep representatives of our race here to help establish and maintain peace."

The press conference continued for hours before finally concluding. There were many other questions asked regarding the peace agreement, as well as their world and all the species of monsters that inhabit it.

In a closed room behind the conference hall, Ren, Marcus, Kelsey, and his father exchanged pleasantries with the president, promising to be in contact before parting ways. Afterward, they were driven back to their hotel for the night. It had been a long day, and Ren and his father were especially tired. Meanwhile, Kelsey was thankful just to be out of her heels.

"Kelsey, Let me see your feet, my dear," Ren's father said.

"Oh, um, sure." His request threw her off at first, but she realized what he was planning. He took her feet and started using healing magic on them.

"Thank you. That's much better. All of the pain is gone."

"You're welcome," Leo said back.

"Hey, just to be clear, we have to decide who's staying in what room," Ren said. "They gave us two rooms, but one is a double, and this one is a single. So, two of us are going to have to sleep together."

"Leo, you can have one of the beds in the double," Marcus said. Ren agreed.

"You sure? Alright. I'll be getting some sleep then." Leo left the room and headed for the other one.

"Kelsey, you're with me," Ren said. "Marcus can stay in the other room. My father is a bit of a heavy sleeper."

"And you're not?" Kelsey asked back, knowing full well Ren's sleeping habits.

"He's heavier. Besides, I'm exhausted."

Marcus didn't like the idea of Ren being alone with Kelsey right now. After she had called Ren a monster, he wasn't happy with her. And he knew Ren was trying to keep his distance from her as well. Not that Kelsey seemed to get the picture.

"Alright, if you say so. Have a good night, guys," Marcus said before leaving the room.

Ren collapsed on the bed. "Are you sure you don't mind sharing with me? I can always change rooms," Kelsey said.

"Of course not. I've gotten used to it by now. Come get some sleep." She nodded and climbed into bed next to him.

"Night."

"Night," he said back.

The day had indeed been long, and it didn't take long before Ren fell fast asleep.

Four

The Price of a Soul

Kelsey woke to the sound of their alarm going off. It was eight in the morning, far too early for her to be alert. She wanted to sleep in longer but knew she couldn't.

Today was Monday, but classes were still canceled. They were still in cleanup mode after the battle with Algiroth, so school was temporarily suspended for the time being. Of course, if it weren't, all she had to do was let their principal know, and he would have her covered.

She grabbed her phone from the nightstand and turned off the alarm. It was a quick glance at the ceiling before she felt something draped over her, followed by a light moan. Ren was lying with his arm around her. The feeling of secureness washed over her. Seeing his sleeping face made her heart skip a beat. He was so damn hot, too hot, actually.

Ren's eyes fluttered open. Oh, those eyes of his. They were unlike any other. With a deep cobalt blue, it was like staring into an ocean.

"Morning," Kelsey said.

"Morning," he said back.

He realized his arm was around her and quickly removed it. Damn him and his sleeping habits. He was too used to having her next to him.

"Can I use the bathroom first?" she asked. He nodded, and she got out of bed.

Ren sat up and rubbed his eyes. His eyelids felt heavy. Clearly, he hadn't slept off the exhaustion from yesterday. He heard the shower turn on and realized Kelsey would be in there for a bit. That earned him at least ten more minutes of sleep. Great, then he would take it.

He threw himself back down on the bed and closed his eyes. A resounding sense of ease and peacefulness washed over him. He felt so free.

"Ren … Ren, wake up." Ren opened his eyes.

Kelsey stood over him. She wore new clothes, but her hair was still wet. Had he fallen asleep? He must have been more tired than he thought. He had only slept for ten minutes, but it was such a good sleep that all the fatigue had drained out of him.

Ren felt his stomach churn. Time for breakfast, but first, a bath. He climbed out of bed, grabbed a set of clothes, and jumped in the tub, throwing in the necessary herbs to dilute its purity.

He let the heat of the water eat into his skin, warming him to his core. But he paid no attention to it. All he could think about was waking up to Kelsey. She looked so cute the way she looked at him.

He punched the wall. Damn it! His emotions were all jumbled up. Why, why couldn't he just get over her? After the fight with Algiroth, he was sure that Kelsey had made it very clear that there was nothing to them anymore. And yet, the way she looked at him, it was as if she still loved him. Was she just leading him on, trying to test him? Or was he the one in the wrong? Maybe he really was misunderstanding, as she had said.

It pissed him off. And despite everything, he was still hopelessly in love with her. There was no changing that. Yet, the very fact that he knew that only made it worse. It was because of that it was hard to distance himself from her. Every time he tried, she closed it. No, they were actually becoming closer. It was so damn frustrating.

Of course, another problem was Ren's father. The guy was either clueless or just trying to make Ren submit. Not only was he kind to Kelsey, but he was consistent in his actions of bringing them closer together. The latest bit with the hotel room only proved it. He chose the other room because he knew that Ren would end up with Kelsey.

Ren wasn't sure what his game was or if he even had one. But if he did, then he was certainly not making things easy. Surely, he would have intentions of bringing them closer, especially if he realized they were at odds right now. For all the times he was gone in the past, the guy was undoubtedly a great father. He cared for Ren just as much as his mother had, and Ren knew that plainly.

Not to mention, Marcus wasn't exactly hiding his dislike of Kelsey. He clearly was not happy with her; that was clear to everyone. And Ren knew precisely why, though many might not. No doubt his father would have put it together already.

Marcus and Ren had been friends since they were children. They've been at each other's sides for over three hundred years. A friendship like theirs was one that would last a lifetime. Being as close as they are, watching the girl you thought you could trust reject your best friend was enough to piss either of them off. And Kelsey calling Ren a monster was enough for Marcus to completely change his view of her.

He had thought Kelsey was different. Watching their relationship grow actually comforted Marcus in his own way. His disapproval of her was justified, and he knew Ren was trying to distance himself from her, which he supported wholeheartedly.

And lastly, there was Ellie. Though out of her control, she was probably the biggest hindrance to Ren's distance from Kelsey. After he and Marcus had rescued her from a succubus turned living shade, Ren took her in. Though not there when they rescued her, Kelsey was always around once she had settled in. Ellie thought of her as an older sister, the same way she thought of Ren as an older brother.

That was the biggest problem with distancing himself from Kelsey. Ellie liked her too much. He didn't want to imagine what she would be like once they had drifted apart permanently. It would be the cause of great distress in both their lives.

He had to come up with something. Perhaps the best thing was just to tell Ellie the truth and let her be upset. She'd get over it, hopefully, sooner rather than later. But he would do what he could for her in Kelsey's place.

Ren punched the wall in frustration again. Damn it! Why? Why did he think things would be different? He actually thought Kelsey was the one. What in the hell was he thinking? Kelsey was a human. There was only one way their relationship would have gone. She would have realized they were too different eventually, and they would part ways. Stupid! How could he think things would work out? Humans were all the same. In the end, he knew this would happen.

He was old enough now to know exactly how this was going to end. He should have stopped himself before things got out of hand. And now they were in their situation because of it.

A sudden knock on the bathroom door distracted him from his thoughts.

"Ren, are you alright?" Kelsey asked. He got out of the tub and ran his hand over his face, removing the water.

"I'm alright. I'll be out in a second," he responded.

Ren dried his body and threw on his pants. Simple blue jeans with a few tears in them.

He had to think about this. He had to find a solution to their problems. For now, Marcus was the best person to rely on. No one else would understand.

Kelsey was still drying her hair with a towel when Ren walked out of the bathroom.

"You sure you're alright?" she asked, turning her gaze on him. He nodded.

"Go ahead and use the blow dryer in the bathroom."

"Thanks."

She got up from the bed but only made it a few feet before she stopped dead. Something was floating behind Ren. A figure with golden hair and eyes. It had its eyes on her, a hand on Ren's shoulder.

"Ren, behind you!" she said in shock. He whirled around, but there was nothing there.

"What is it?" he asked, confused.

The figure stood behind Ren, quiet and undetected. It simply stared at her, then tilted its head out of curiosity, like a dog. Ren didn't seem to know at all it was there.

"Kelsey?" Ren asked.

"You can't see it," she said, now certain. But how was she going to explain it? "Never mind," she finished, and walked past him and into the bathroom.

What's up with her? Ren wondered. Yeah, something was definitely up. He was sure of it.

Kelsey emerged from the bathroom, brushing her hair. She set the brush down on her bag, which lay on a chair off to the side.

"Let's get going," she said.

Ren stared at her momentarily as she walked past him before following her. Whatever that thing was that Kelsey saw, it was gone when she came out of the bathroom. Not only that, but this was the second time she saw it, and both times, it was clinging to Ren. Clearly, the thing had an interest in him, as it only seemed to appear around him. But why was she seeing it now?

Kelsey really wished she could tell Ren about this. With him trying to avoid her, that didn't make things any easier. She could tell he was keeping his distance. He had made it blatantly obvious. More than anything, she had to talk to him and explain everything. Tell him that it was a misunderstanding.

Ren and Kelsey walked to the elevator, and he pressed the button. They waited in silence for it to come. Whatever that thing was around Ren, it was still gone. Though she had no idea when it would come back. Next time, she would have to do something.

"Are you alright?" Ren asked. Kelsey only stared at the wall before finally turning to face him.

"Sorry, did you say something?"

Ren raised an eyebrow at her. "I asked if you were alright," he repeated.

"Oh, yeah, I'm okay," she answered.

Liar. Something was wrong. She was more like him than he thought, keeping secrets, not wanting people to worry.

The elevator door opened, and they stepped inside. Ren hit the lobby button, and the door closed. It was just the two of them in there.

Kelsey felt the back of her hand brush against Ren's. He didn't react, at least, that she could see. She waited a few moments before gently grabbing his fingers and sliding her hand into his, feeling her cheeks burn.

Ren looked at her when Kelsey grabbed his hand, but seeing her face, he couldn't bring himself to take his hand away. No, he didn't want to. Instead, he gave in and increased his grip a little. He felt her fingers entwine with his.

Sly, very sly, he thought.

The elevator reached the lobby, and the doors opened. This hotel served breakfast to the guests, though they had no idea where. They decided to go to the front desk and ask.

"Excuse me," Ren said.

One of the women behind the desk jumped. She looked up at him, and her eyes widened. Then, the other woman mirrored her surprise.

"How can I help you?" she asked. Ren saw a bead of sweat fall down the side of her face.

"You can relax; I won't hurt you," he said, giving her a smile. "We were just wondering where the room for breakfast was being held."

"Oh, sure. It's down that hallway, second door to your left."

"Thanks," he and Kelsey said in unison.

The woman nodded back. "You're welcome."

Ren and Kelsey walked into the room. As soon as they entered, they could feel everyone's eyes on them. Well, that was to be expected. Ren was used to the treatment, so it didn't bother him all that much. Kelsey, however, was a different matter.

They found Ren's father seated at a table with a bagel, coffee, and his phone in front of him.

"Morning," Ren said.

His father looked up. "Morning," he said back. Then, he noticed them holding hands. "Did you sleep well?" he asked, grinning.

Ren raised an eyebrow at Kelsey, but she looked just as confused. His father chuckled when he saw their bewildered expressions.

"Marcus not down yet?" Ren asked.

"Over here."

They turned around and saw Marcus walking toward him, a piece of bacon in his hand. Bacon! Ren found himself staring.

"Ren?" Kelsey asked.

Marcus noticed them holding hands, but his expression didn't change, surprisingly. Kelsey was expecting some show of displeasure.

Ren was still staring at Marcus's bacon while almost everyone else had at least one eye on them. Their faces were pretty much everywhere now.

Ren's eyes move to the side. "You going to let that girl keep staring?" he asked Marcus.

"What girl?" Marcus asked back.

He looked over where Ren had previously been looking. An opportunity! Ren snatched the bacon out of Marcus's hand and shoved it in his mouth.

"Hey! My bacon!"

Marcus rolled up his sleeve, but Kelsey's laughter stopped them. Light chuckles came from around the room. Marcus grinned and shook his head. He put an arm around Ren's shoulder, and the three of them walked to the table to grab their food.

Ren carried his and Kelsey's food back to the table. She sat to his left and set their drinks down while Marcus sat to his right. They ate in silence for the most part before Kelsey finally broke it.

"I'm not taking no for an answer," she said.

They all looked over at her. She had her fork held out to Ren, a piece of food on it. She gave him a sly smile. Damn it! He leaned over and took a bite. Kelsey giggled, and he couldn't help but think it was the cutest thing ever. AGH! Damn her!

All four of them could feel the gazes on them from the people in the room. They held a mixture of emotions. After eating, they returned to their rooms to grab their things. None of them had more than a backpack each. Then, they met in the lobby and handed in their keys to the front desk before exiting the hotel.

"So, what now? Are we heading to the airport early?" Kelsey asked.

"No, not yet," Ren said back. "We have to make a stop first."

Five

Words Will Grant You Strength

Ren pulled out his phone and checked it's contents. Though their transportation was previously arranged, as this was personal to them and outside the press conference, they all unanimously agreed that their own wheels would be best. And so, Ren had booked the four of them a rental car.

The rental company was three miles from their current location. It was unfortunate, but they were going to have to walk.

"A little walking will do us some good," Marcus said. "I could use the fresh air."

He and Ren started walking, leaving Kelsey and Ren's father to follow behind them. It was a perfect day for a walk. Cool—not excessively, nor too hot, with a nice breeze.

Twenty minutes into the walk, the first kiss of rain pecked their cheeks. A refreshing feeling after so much sun and pleasant weather.

The first drop that hit Ren's skin left a plume of steam off his face and a tiny spark. It stung a little, but it was nothing he couldn't handle.

Ren threw a barrier up as soon as it started raining. He didn't have an umbrella or any crystalic lotion, so it would have to do. Being a vampire, water is one of his biggest weaknesses because of its purifying powers. He managed to get the barrier up before the rain really started coming down. It was large enough for all four of them., even if only he and his father needed it. Regardless, there was no reason for Marcus and Kelsey to get wet.

"You alright?" Marcus asked when the first spark erupted.

"Yeah, I'm fine. It was just the one drop."

"We should have checked the weather," Ren's father said. "A grave mistake on our part."

Ren kept focus straight ahead, but the others were looking around at the people who were staring at them transfixed. They walked with Ren's hand held above his head, the rain bouncing off an invisible force like a dome. The guy sure wasn't being secretive about using his magic, that was for sure.

Ren spotted a woman trying to cover herself and her son from the rain. They had no umbrella and would soon be soaked. They approached the woman, keeping within the barrier. When the rain stopped, she stood up and turned around.

"Where are you headed?" Ren asked her.

"We're headed to the mall," she said back. "This rain came out of nowhere."

"The mall is on our way. Why don't you two stick with us?"

"Would that be ok?"

"*Beshak.* It's no problem at all."

"Thank you so much."

The woman looked around, noticing how the rain never hit them. It bounced off and ran down around them.

"How are you doing this?" she asked.

"Magic," Ren answered.

"Magic? You mean like the fantasy kind of magic?"

"Yes, I suppose you could say that."

There was a long pause between them. "You guys aren't human, are you?" she finally asked. "You people are those monsters that were all over the internet. There was a massive press conference yesterday."

"All of us except the girl are monsters. She is human."

"Miss," Marcus said, getting her attention. "Allow me." He held his hand out, and heat enveloped the woman and her son. It took a few minutes, but when he finally lowered his hand, the woman and her son were dry.

"That's amazing."

"Actually, this is one of the simpler spells," he said.

"Why don't we get moving," Ren suggested. "It's better than just standing here. Besides, my strength is not infinite."

"Oh, I'm sorry," the woman said.

"No, it's quite alright. No cause for worry."

The six of them continued walking. The mall the woman and her son were heading to was indeed on their way. They dropped the woman and her son off at the front entrance to the mall she was headed to. She thanked them one last time before heading inside.

When they finally reached the car rental, they headed inside. Ren was helped by the person behind the front counter, informing them that they were only using it while they had time before their flight. However, as the rental company also had a location at the airport, they were allowed to drop it off there.

Ren gave his information and signed all the papers. Once everything was settled, the man handed him a set of keys, and they headed outside to the car. It was more of a luxury rental sedan, not that any of them were complaining.

Ren unlocked the doors, and his father got in the passenger side while Kelsey and Marcus got in the back.

"This is a nice car," Ren's father said, looking around it.

"No kidding," Ren said back. "Lucky us."

"So, where are we going?" Marcus asked. They were already into the drive when he finally asked. Even if he and Ren had been friends for three hundred years, it wasn't like he could actually read the guy's mind.

"To see Ken," Ren answered. "If anyone knows what's happening behind the scenes, it's him.

"Who's Ken?" Kelsey asked.

"That's a good question," Leo agreed.

"He's an info broker. Ken has his hands in everything. If there's something we need to know, he's bound to know it."

"This seems kind of shady," Kelsey said.

"I assure you it's nothing like what you're thinking," Ren assured her. "Ken makes an honest living as an author. The info broker thing is a side job he does to make cash and help people out."

Ren switched lanes as they drove. "You should be excited, Kelsey. In fact, you'll thank me later for this."

"What does that mean?" she asked, curious. Was he insinuating something?

"You'll see when we get there."

Ren pulled into the driveway of a two-story modern house. They had turned onto a private road about three minutes down. The house was made of timber with a grey stone front entrance and massive glass entry. A two-car garage was off to the side, connected to the house.

The four of them walked up to the door, and Ren rang the doorbell.

"Remember what I said in the car? You ready to thank me?" Ren asked, putting her on the spot. But Kelsey still had no idea what he was talking about. "Ken's actually written a few books you like. Now you get to meet him in person."

Kelsey was now certain that Ren had gone crazy.

"Books that I like? Ren, I've never read a book by an author named Ken."

"Yes, you have. Ken is just an abbreviated version. His full name is Kenton."

Kelsey's jaw dropped. "Kenton. As in, Kenton Smith?"

Ren only smiled at her before the front door opened to reveal a man in his mid-thirties. His brown hair was cropped short and styled up. A short brown beard covered his face. Kelsey recognized him instantly from his photo in his books.

"No freaking way. I'm about to meet Kenton," Kelsey said in disbelief.

"Ren?" He looked around at the four of them. "Marcus, too. And some new faces. Welcome, Your Majesty," he said, recognizing Leo. "Please, come on in."

Ken opened the door, and they followed him inside. He sat them down at a table before heading somewhere in the house. He returned a few minutes later carrying a book.

"Here," he said, handing it to Kelsey. He gave her a smile. "I overheard you guys talking. You're a fan of mine, right? That's a signed copy of my newest book."

"Wait, you're just giving this to me?"

"Of course, baby girl. Gotta keep the fans happy. Enjoy it."

"I will! Thank you so much. This is so cool." She beamed with excitement, causing him to laugh.

"Honey, is someone here?" A woman called.

"Yeah. A couple of old friends stopped by," Ken said back.

A woman came around a corner and stopped behind Ken, leaning against the back of his chair.

"Hi, Lucy," Ren and Marcus said.

"Oh, Ren, Marcus, it's been ages since you two have stopped by. Your Majesty, welcome. It's an honor to have you here. Wait just a moment; I'll grab you guys some refreshments."

"Thanks, Lucy," Ren and Marcus said back.

There was a moment of silence before someone spoke.

"The world is a storm, Ren," Ken said. "That little declaration you made sure hit home for many people."

"It was supposed to."

Ken sighed, then pulled out a cigarette and lit it. He breathed out a plume of smoke.

"It's crazy all over right now. No one knows what to do anymore."

"Because of the fact that we were revealed?" Marcus asked.

"Yes, and given Ren's little speech he gave. Our people are confused. We were suddenly exposed to the humans. Now that they know of our existence, many want to coexist; they just don't know how. The truth is no one knows if it's going to work. Many are still hesitant to believe that we can live among humans. Our people are convinced coexistence is no longer possible now that we've been exposed. Then Ren tells everyone to remain appearing and living as humans."

"Well, that should solve their problems then," Marcus said.

"Except that no one knows whether continuing to remain as humans is right anymore. Previously, many saw the benefit of staying as human in this world. We only remained so to blend in, but now there's no reason to. People are split between finally being able to live in our true forms or remaining in human form. The division is so widespread. And without knowing our enemy's movements, or the human's, it's difficult to deal with."

"Now that our kind has been exposed, there will no doubt be conflicts. There will be humans who seek to unveil us, to reveal who we are. Already, there are many who are opposed to coexistence. That animosity continues to spread. And now that they've been told to keep up their human appearance, humans will become even more suspicious of us."

"I've gotten word that violence has already started to break out, though I believe it was just a rumor. The concern is that it's going to keep happening. You saw how they reacted to you at that press conference."

Ren sighed. "Yeah, I know. I'm trying to figure out something."

"We need a way to please the human population," Kelsey said.

They all looked at her, and Ken blew out another plume of smoke.

"Yeah, that's exactly it. But doing that is easier said than done. You're a human, aren't you? Then you should know just how vindictive humans are. If they don't like something, they'll do everything they can to destroy it. And getting on good terms with all humans is next to impossible."

Kelsey sighed. "Yeah, I know."

"We'll figure something out," Ren's father said. "It's going to take a lot of time and planning, but I think we can work something out."

"You know it's not that simple," Marcus and Ren said simultaneously.

"There's no way the humans are just going to let us live in peace with them," Marcus said.

"And Ken's right. It's only a matter of time before violence breaks out," Ren added. "Assuming it hasn't already happened."

"Ren, I know you hate humans, but—" Leo started to say

"This isn't about my hatred for humans," Ren interrupted. "This is about protecting two species. We cannot afford to fight the entire human race and our own."

"That's why we'll be keeping our best negotiators here to look after the coexistence plan while we're in Nexus. The only real way to coexist is by doing exactly that. It's the same as dealing with a neighboring kingdom or land. Foster good relations through trade and interaction. It's just going to take a lot of time and planning. Hopefully, we can get the rest of the population on board."

"Are you sure leaving it to someone else is a good idea?" Kelsey asked.

"I agree," Marcus said. "It could be too much of a risk. Often negotiations don't go as well unless the head of both parties are involved."

"True, but the person I'm putting in charge is the secretary of defense. He's been a part of the government for a long time and has good relations with other government officials. And he'll also be sending us information constantly, letting us know what's going on.

So we will be well informed of the current affairs regarding our coexistence."

"That might not stop the humans from fighting back, from rioting or rebelling against the government," Ren said. "Frankly, it's impossible to find a solution that will satisfy everyone. And even if it were, we don't have that kind of time. I'm willing to bet the chaos has already descended. The retaliation has already started."

Lucy returned with six drinks and set them on the table for everyone, finding a seat next to her husband.

"I've received no word of any real conflict yet," Ken said. "Let's just hope it stays that way long enough for us to figure out a solution." He let out another plume of smoke. "That being said, solutions, fall-backs, are already in the works." He extinguished his cigarette in the ashtray in front of him.

"Word on the street is large factions of monsters are rising. They fear conflict with the humans despite all attempts to keep the peace. Instead, they seek a life away from the humans. Apparently, they plan to set up a special district built by monsters and for monsters only. There have been talks of it being inside human cities or in unpopulated areas where they can develop freely."

"That could pose a bigger problem," Leo said. "While it would stop any violence, there would be no peace between our species at all."

"What about our world?" Ren asked. "What's been going on?"

"About the same. Most feel that coexistence is practically impossible. Actually, another rumor I heard was that many of our kind back in Nexus wish to bring our people home and cut off from the humans entirely."

"That's even worse," Leo said. "Let alone minimal contact, we'd have no contact at all. We'd be forcing apart those who have made a life here. Separating friends and families. At this rate, our species will forever be divided. It seems our time limit is even smaller than we imagined."

"Any word on Verin or the Church?" Marcus asked.

"No, nothing. Verin hasn't made a single move since Algiroth's defeat," Ken noted. "Whatever he's up to, he's doing a damn good job of hiding it. There hasn't even been an increase in the number of shades lately. It's just quiet. As for the Radiant Church, they pretty much crawled into a hole after the battle in Florida you guys had. They suffered massive losses, not to mention humiliation. It's going to take a while for them to get back in shape, so I wouldn't expect them to make a move anytime soon."

"Well, at least that's good. One less thing we have to worry about."

Ren, Kelsey, Marcus, and Leo finished their drinks before gathering their things. Ren handed Ken an envelope. Inside was a stack of money.

"Your payment for the information." Ken nodded back.

"Just be careful from now on, Ren. You never know who is lurking around the corner."

"Thanks, Ken. Keep me updated. I need my own eyes and ears, too."

Ren opened the front door and headed for the rental car. The others were already inside, his father in the driver's seat. It was nearly time for their flight.

Leo reversed out of the driveway, then turned the car around and headed back down the private road.

Six

Any Time, Until the End of Time

Leo drove to the airport at a fashionable pace. Although, they would have reached the airport faster if they hadn't caught every red light along the way. Washington traffic, there was nothing else to say.

He pulled up to the parking garage and drove through in search of the rental company. Ren was the first to spot it. An entire section of the parking lot was designated for rental cars, with various rows associated with different rental companies.

Leo parked in a random spot near the front in one of the four rows designated for their rental company. He opened the trunk, and the four of them grabbed their luggage, which consisted of a single backpack each. Ren had the papers and receipt from the rental agency they got the car at for proof.

A pair of double doors stood attached to the building. A concrete walkway escaped from the doors, connecting the airport to the garage through four car lanes. The doors opened, prompting them to head inside. Off to the left was where the rental arrangments were dealt with. Each rental company had a sign with its own line section. Those that were in service were all occupied.

Ren's father handed him the keys to the rental car, and Ren got in line. There were two people in front of him, so he had to wait, leaving the others to stand patiently off to the side. When the person in front of him finished, Ren walked up to the desk. It was a man who appeared in his thirties. His dark skin and black hair complimented his black suit and red tie.

The man nearly had a heart attack when Ren approached him. Evidently, he recognized Ren and, therefore, had seen the press conference. His reaction drew the attention of others waiting in alternate lines and behind the service desks. But the man's expression, that's what really got him. Ren raised an eyebrow and suddenly burst out laughing.

"You should see your face," he said through his laughter.

Ren's laughter appeared to draw out the tension in the man's body because he slowly began to relax. No doubt, the curiosity of Ren's laughter had begun to replace his fear.

Ren handed him the keys to the rental car, along with the paperwork, once he had visibly calmed down.

"I'm just dropping off a rental car. The guy working at one of your locations in town said we could just drop it off here instead of having to bring it back."

The man grabbed the keys before checking the papers Ren had in his hand. Reading through them, he and Ren exchanged a brief dialogue in which Ren answered several questions. After verifying the return, the man recorded it on his computer. He handed Ren two pieces of paper and had him sign and initial them where instructed.

"Everything appears in order. You're all set. Thank you very much."

"Thank you. Have a nice day," Ren said back. He shouldered his back and returned to the remainder of his party.

Ren used his vampire powers to sense the man's blood flow. His heartbeat was steady, indicating that he was calm. Others, unfortunately, were not so calm. He sensed a collective pool of different emotions. Some were fearful, some intrigued, others were curious. Most were unsure of what to make about the situation, however. It appeared to be the only common trait between them. No doubt they were still trying to accept the existence of monsters.

"Let's find our gate," Ren said.

The four of them took an escalator up to the main floor. After the long wait of passing through security, they gathered together.

"Our gate number is G5," Marcus said. "As soon as we can find an arrival schedule, we can head there."

The Ronald Reagan Washington National Airport was not a small airport, so it took a while for them to locate their gate, but they eventually did so without complications.

Ren and the others quickly noticed the eyes of the many people staring at them. It made Kelsey far too uncomfortable. Risking a glance, she snuck a look at Ren to see how he was handling the stares. Unlike her, he walked stoically like usual, as if they didn't bother him at all. The guy had nerves of steel.

Kelsey slipped her hand into his, hoping it would calm her down. Usually, when she was uncomfortable or nervous, holding Ren's hand seemed to make it better. The very first day Ren brought Kelsey to Trinity, he held her hand as they walked inside, and all her nerves vanished. That was the day she had learned of the existence of monsters and was dragged into the world of magic and myth.

Even after being separated for three years and searching for the stones for over a month, it seemed that nothing had changed. She still felt the pull of his presence on her as strong as it did the day they had met.

Holding Ren's hand, all of her nerves disappeared.

"You never could handle being stared at," Ren said.

"Then and now. It still bugs me."

"And you always seem to hold my hand when it happens."

"What can I say, it puts me at ease. I don't know how it doesn't bother you."

"I've gotten used to it."

"I don't think I ever will."

"Ha. Says the girl who jumped into a war against monsters."

"Well, maybe if you could do things without me, I wouldn't have to."

His head snapped to her, but she was grinning wickedly. Ren's face turned red. Damn her! She laughed and increased the grip on his hand.

"It also seems like I'm the only one who can draw out your emotions," she said.

"I hate it," he said back.

"Don't worry, I'm sure you'll get used to it," she mocked.

Kelsey snickered, and Ren squeezed her hand, causing her to yelp. "Who's in trouble now?" he asked cunningly, giving her a smile.

Kelsey hadn't seen him smile like that since they fought Algiroth. She was glad to see him smile. Plus, he was super cute when he smiled.

Once Ren and the others reached their gate, they looked around for a place to sit. There was still another hour and a half before their plane arrived, but their gate was still swamped with travelers. It was going to be hard to find a place to sit.

"I've got to use the bathroom. I'll be right back," Kelsey said. She handed Ren her bag.

"Hurry up, or we'll leave you behind," he joked.

"Ha ha," she said sarcastically, and he started chuckling.

"Bro, how funny would it be if she came back and we were gone? Like boarded the plane and left, gone," Marcus asked. He and Ren started cracking up.

"You two have a problem," Leo said, but it only caused them to laugh harder.

Leo told them he was going to look around for a place to sit and headed off. Kelsey returned a few minutes later to find him missing.

"Where did Leo go?" she asked.

"To see if he could find a place for us to sit. We still have a while before the plane is supposed to arrive," Ren told her.

"Which means we're stuck standing here until he does," Marcus said with a sigh.

"You're a werewolf, dude; this is nothing for you."

"Says the guy who can fly and walk on walls."

"Yeah, I guess you've got a point there."

"Walking on walls," Kelsey said. "We haven't seen you do that since we were searching for the stones."

"Yeah, when we were climbing Mt. Whitney, if memory serves," Ren said.

Kelsey shuddered. "I don't even want to think about that."

"Speaking of Mt. Whitney, have you heard anything from you know who?" Marcus asked.

Ren shook his head. "I seldom do, though. He prefers his seclusion. That being said, I'm going to let him know I'll be returning to Nexus."

The man in question, taking the focal point of their conversation, was Ren's master. While his father had been the one to teach him of his heritage and duties as a future ruler, it was his master who taught him how to use and develop all of his vampire abilities. At nearly a millennium and a half, he was also currently one of the oldest living vampires.

Kelsey sat beside Ren when they boarded, putting her bag in the overhead compartment. They never said a word the entire flight back, only because there was nothing to discuss.

Several members from Trinity were waiting to pick them up from the airport when they returned to Florida. Namely, a number of Heaven's Blades and James Wilson.

"How did it go?" Razeial asked. Razeial was a Cyclopes and the rank six Heaven's Blade.

"It's tough to say," Leo said. "For now, we're working on coexistence plans."

"Let's talk at my place," Ren said. "We can discuss our departure for Nexus too."

Razeial nodded in agreement. "Then let's go."

They headed to the airport's parking garage. Ren followed Razeial to his pickup and climbed in the passenger seat. Then, they drove off in silence.

Ren opened the gates to his mansion with a button, and they drove through, past the endless Sakura Blossom trees that lined both sides of the road. His house was seated at the end of the road, which circled around a patch of grass containing a stone fountain with a tiger on top.

Parking out front, Ren unlocked the front door, allowing the others to follow him inside.

Seating themselves in the living room, the first thing they did was discuss their return to Nexus. There were dozens of portals around the human world, but they varied in distance and location, not just from each other but their connecting portals in Nexus.

As Ren explained to Kelsey, the portals all varied in size, an indication of the number of people that could be transported through them. The nearest portal, closest to the capital and able to carry them all, was located in a set of ancient ruins within Peru.

The ruins belonged to a civilization from Nexus in the past. Eventually, they died out, however.

Preparations would take several more weeks before they were ready to depart. They would take a flight to Peru early in the morning. Ren already knew the airport they needed to land at. From there, it was a four-hour ride to the ruins. Leo had an old acquaintance there who ran tours. He'd get in touch with them and have them pick them up.

Once they crossed over, they would head for the capital. It would be five days' ride by horse.

Then came the next issue, the stones. They needed to find a way to get them off Kelsey.

Ren's father set two books on the coffee table, filled with page markers. Rare books on ancient artifacts, taken from his personal collection. Each marker identified a possible solution to removing the stones.

They spent hours reading through and attempting to remove them. But in the end, the stones wouldn't budge no matter what they tried.

"So what now?" Razeial asked.

Ren sighed. "If we can't get them off, then there's little in the way of options. Kelsey will have to come with us to Nexus." She just looked at him without uttering a word. "The grand library underneath the palace has a vast amount of knowledge. I'm sure there's something there we can use to get them off. One of the books there will most likely lead us there."

"I think it might be our only real option," Marcus said. "We can't leave her here, and we don't have the knowledge to get the stones off."

"Leo, how long will you be gone?" James asked. "I have no idea. I don't expect us back for a long while, though."

"I see."

"Is it about our schooling?" Kelsey asked. James nodded.

"Ren's an adult and doesn't need to go, honestly. But you've been gone for a while now."

Kelsey wasn't sure what to say. He was right; she had missed a lot of school.

"That's why I was thinking of letting you guys graduate early. If you weren't able to attend anymore, that was my plan anyway."

"Can we do that?" Kelsey asked.

"I'll pull some strings, don't worry. Ren is, well, he's Ren." Kelsey started chuckling.

"What's that supposed to mean?" Ren asked.

"And you have enough credits already," James told Kelsey, ignoring Ren.

Kelsey nodded, grateful to him. "I can't thank you enough."

"Miss Rose, there's no need for you to thank me. You've gotten yourself mixed up in a war that was never yours, and you fight for us. It is I who can't thank you enough."

"I'll take you to your parents tomorrow and let them know the situation," Ren said to Kelsey. "I don't expect they'll be happy about it, but it has to be done."

"Ren," came a voice from the edge of the room.

Standing at the entryway to the kitchen was Ellie, with one hand on Nidar and the other balled up at her chest. Ren could tell everything she was feeling from the expression on her face.

"Are you leaving again?" she asked. "You're going somewhere far away, aren't you?" Then she started crying. "You're leaving me behind again."

Kelsey went to get up, but Ren was up first. He walked over to her and wrapped her in a hug. "I don't want you to go."

Ren held her tight in his arms, feeling her shaking.

"I'm not leaving you, Ellie. Not this time." She looked up at him. "You're coming with me. As long as I think we'll be gone for, I'm not leaving you here."

Nidar whined from his sitting position. Ren kept one arm around Ellie and extended his other out to Nidar.

"Don't worry, you're coming to bud." Nidar rubbed his face against Ren's, and Ren put his arm around the tiger's neck.

Ren let go of Ellie and Nidar and stood up. He addressed everyone in the room. "Come on, let's all get some sleep. We have a long day tomorrow."

Seven

The Coexistence Plan

Kelsey and Ellie sat in the passenger seat of Ren's Lamborghini as he drove to Kelsey's house. They needed to tell her parents about their departure for Nexus. Ellie had demanded to go with them to Kelsey's parents, so they brought her along.

Ren pulled into Kelsey's driveway and turned off the car. Kelsey opened her door and let Ellie out first before getting out herself. Ellie held her hand out to Ren, and he took it before walking to the front door.

Kelsey opened the door, and they walked inside. Both cars were in the garage, and the lights in the house were on, so she knew that her parents were home.

"Mom, Dad?" she called.

"Kelsey? Is that you?" her mom asked.

Her mother emerged from the kitchen and walked down the hallway to them. She wore an apron and had a spatula in her hand.

"Why didn't you tell us you were coming home?"

"It was a spur-of-the-moment thing."

Kelsey looked at Ren, and so did her mother.

"Hi, Ella," Ren said. He wasn't expecting a warm welcome. He figured they were terrified enough of him being a vampire. Then Ella wrapped him up in a hug.

"Ren. I'm so glad you're alright. Come sit down; dinner is almost ready."

"Thank you, but that wasn't my intention," he confessed.

"I know. But now that you're here, it's mine. You too, Kelsey, Ellie." Ren nodded, and they followed her into the kitchen.

"Where's Dad?" Kelsey asked.

"In his study working. Will you go tell him to come down for dinner?" her mother asked her.

"I'll go," Ren volunteered. "I'll let you two be alone for a bit." He walked off, passed the kitchen, and up the stairs to the second floor.

"Is everything ok?" Ella asked.

"There's a lot going."

"I know, I've been watching the news, and I saw the press conference."

"Also, there's something we have to tell you guys. That's actually the reason we're here. It's important."

Her mother looked worried. She knew something was going on. Things had been different since Ren had returned, and the two of them had gone on that first quest. With the existence of monsters, she was rarely home, always with Ren and others of his kind. She hadn't been going to school either. It worried her.

Ren turned left and walked down another hallway to a room at the end. A man sat at a desk in front of a computer. Ren knocked on the door with his back knuckles. Kelsey's dad turned around, surprised to see Ren standing there.

"Ren? What are you doing here? Is Kelsey with you?"

"Yeah, she's downstairs. Ella said to come down. Dinner is almost ready."

"Alright, I'll be down in a second." Ren nodded and headed back downstairs.

Kelsey was seated at the kitchen table, her mother over the stove. Ellie was in the living room, playing with Kelsey's younger sister.

"Ellie, come sit down. It's almost time for dinner," Ren told her.

"Okay." She walked over to the table, pulled out a chair, and sat down. Meanwhile, Kelsey's sister sat on her other side.

Ren was just about to sit down when Kelsey's father walked into the kitchen. He sat down to Ren's left, who sat next to Ellie. The table was quiet while Ella finished cooking. She sat everything on the table, family style.

"How's work?" Ella asked her husband.

Jacob released a heavy sigh. "It's … a challenge. We have to keep things together for as long as possible. We're doing the best we can for now, but."

"You've been working a lot lately, even on the weekends."

"Business not doing so well?" Ren asked.

"You could say that. It's becoming a challenge to keep the clinic running. And with the loss of the clinic comes the loss of my job. I'm going to have to start looking around." He placed a portion of their dinner on his dish.

"I see," Ren said. He thought to himself for a moment. "Your clinic treats health psychology, doesn't it?"

Jacob confirmed with a nod. "I'm still a psychiatrist. Our clinic focuses specifically on relationship development. We deal with other mental instability problems, too. People coming off an addiction, major recluses and anti-socials, those with hard pasts, the whole works. But relationship development is our bread and butter. Lately, things just aren't going well, however. No one has been coming to the clinic at all."

"Interesting," Ren said to himself.

"Ren, what are you thinking?" Kelsey asked. She knew that look on his face. Something was going through that head of his. And whatever was on his mind was meshing.

Ren pulled out his phone and dialed. It rang a few times before someone on the other line answered. They greeted Ren and introduced themself.

"This is Ren Allen Nightwalker, code three four six five seven, account number one one three five five six nine zero seven eight. Transfer two from my private funds to a Mr. Jacob Rose of Golden Rose Psychiatry. Then, introduce him to Andrew Moore and get them inducted into the coexistence plan."

"One second, please," the person on the other side of the line said. There were a few minutes of silence before the person on the other side of the line spoke again. "Accounting funds have been transferred, Mr. Nightwalker. Mr. Moore is currently in the office right now. Would you like me to patch you through to him?"

"I would, thank you."

"One moment while I put you through."

A long silence persisted while they waited for Andrew Moore to answer the phone.

"Hello? This is Andrew Moore. How can I help you?"

"Andrew, Ren Nightwalker."

"Oh, Ren! It's good to hear your voice, my friend. Is everything okay over there? How's the situation?"

"We're doing our best."

"We're in the same boat, then. I'm doing what I can to lend aid and help smooth things over."

"Thanks, Andrew, anything helps. In fact, the coexistence plan is the reason I'm calling. It just so happened that you were in the office."

"Do you have something?"

"A psychiatric clinic. Golden Rose Psychiatry."

"Hmm, I've never heard of them. What about them has you interested?"

"I'm on good terms with one of the owners. His daughter is also my girlfriend. They're aware of our situation."

"His daughter is your girlfriend? You mean the human who wields the stones?"

"Yes. That's her. Get them in touch with the secretary of defense, the one frontlining the coexistence plan. I've known them for a long time, and they aren't prejudiced, either. They'll be a big help in the plan, given that they actually have personal experience in all of this."

"Oh, sounds promising. Alright, I'll make some calls and get them acquainted. Good luck, Ren. Keep in touch."

"Thanks, Andrew." They hung up the phones.

"Um, Ren, what was that?" Kelsey asked.

"I'm getting you guys assimilated into the coexistence plan. Andrew Moore has been a friend of my father and me for years. He's also been assigned an active role in leading the development of the coexistence plan. Your father is a psychiatrist, and his clinic works to help improve relationships between people." Ren turned his attention to Kelsey's father. "Given your history and relationship with me, I'd like to stretch that further. I'm betting you can help improve relationships between different species, too. I want your clinic to be a major player in that and help the people of our races come to terms with each other."

Kelsey's father looked at him, surprised. "Ren, I don't know what to say."

Ren held up his hand. "Say nothing. It's beneficial to both of us. I need you as much as you need the business."

"What else?" Kelsey asked.

"You're going to have to be more specific, Kells," Ren said back.

"What else did you do? You said, 'transfer two'. Did you wire us money?"

"I did. I wired it to your father's clinic."

"Ren, you don't—" Ren stopped her by shaking his head.

"I didn't do it because I expected any gain from it. Jacob, Ella, I've known you for eighteen years. You two have been good to me, and you were friends with my mom. If you guys are hurting, I will gladly help you in any way I can. It's the least I can do."

"How much did you wire us?" Jacob asked. "Two, as in two thousand?"

"Two thousand! Ren, that's too much. You shouldn't have done that!" Ella responded frantically.

Ren suddenly chuckled. A rather unexpected reaction.

"Two thousand? How cheap do you think I am, Ella?"

"Oh no," Kelsey said. She had a bad feeling.

"I wired you two million." He gave her a smile.

Kelsey's father spat out his drink.

"Two million dollars! Ren, what the hell were you thinking? How could you just give us all that money!"

"Where did you even get all that money?" Ella asked.

"I'm an assassin, Ella. I make a lot of money. Two million is a small dent in my savings, and it's well worth it, I assure you."

Jacob and Hellen looked at each other. "You really make that much money?"

"My standard for kills is one million per request. The price increases from there depending on the job, but one million is the starting number."

Their jaws dropped, causing Ren to laugh. They looked at Kelsey, but she just shrugged.

"Anyway, as for why we're here, it involves Kelsey. But before that, I guess I should start at the beginning of everything. You need to know the truth."

Kelsey's parents sat there silently, waiting for him to proceed.

"First off, when I left for India three years ago, it was not just a simple relocation. The truth is eighteen years ago, I had my powers taken from me. There was an accident, and my mother fled here, seeking safety. However, she couldn't go alone, so I went with her. The cost to keep ourselves hidden from our enemies was my powers and memories. When both were taken from me, I regressed into an infant with some help from the magical department. And for the fifteen years that you knew my mother and me after that, I grew up completely human. The day my father returned and brought me to India, he relinquished my powers and memories back to me, and I resumed my role in Trinity. Rifting shades."

"After clearing out most of the shades in India, we relocated here, to Florida. We discovered that this city was a hotspot for shades. There were too many in one place. More than we had ever seen before. So we came here to rid them from the city. The problem was there were just too many of them."

"With the situation in place, as it was, we had determined without a doubt that our enemy was making his next move. Unfortunately, our hands were already full. We feared things would take a disastrous turn. That is, until we discovered the possible location of a map to two artifacts containing extraordinary power. The Sun and Moon Stones. Two stones so powerful, they could help us turn the tide in the war."

"The truth is, Kelsey wasn't in India with me for work like I told you. She was with me and my partner, Marcus Allagash. He was the werewolf you saw at the press conference, the one with gold eyes who stood next to Kelsey. The three of us journeyed across the country and Italy in order to find the stones."

"You went to Italy?" Kelsey's mother asked, shocked.

"Yes. The Moon Stone was here in America, along with the map. However, the Sun Stone was in Sicily."

"So you lied to us," her mother said to Kelsey, furious. "What in the world possessed you to suddenly run off like that? Never mind that you lied. You blew off work and school. You're in your senior year, Kelsey. Do you even want to graduate? Seriously, what was going through your head? Traveling not just around the country, but you even went overseas. With only the three of you. Do you have any idea how dangerous that was? And let's not forget, irresponsible. Ren, I understand. I understand why he had to go. But you, I don't. You had no part in it. Why were you brought into this?" her mother asked.

Man, was she furious. She and Kelsey's father both. But neither could blame them.

"I'm afraid that's my fault," Ren said. "I'm pretty famous in the monster world, as you know. I have many enemies amongst Verin and the Church. A living shade was after me, and my presence was attached to Kelsey since I had been around her. It attacked her in an attempt to use her as bait and lure me out. I saved her, but by then, she had already seen too much."

"I brought her to Trinity, originally intending to erase her memories. But she convinced me not to, and to bring her along, desiring to help us on our quest. You knew nothing of our existence, and I had no intention of involving you. So I used a little magic to manipulate your memory and convince you to let her go, on the impression that we were going to India for my job."

"I don't care how irresponsible you think it was. We were separated for three years. I finally got to see him again, only to learn the truth of his world and his quest. No matter what, I didn't want to be separated from him," Kelsey confessed. "I wanted to be a part of something great, a part of a new world."

Kelsey's father ran his hands down his face. Her mother, however, merely sat there, fuming.

"And did you find them? The stones, I mean," her father asked. Ren nodded, and Kelsey held up her left wrist to display the silver band and two stones embedded in it.

"They ended up attached to my wrist. We don't know why, but I can use their power," she said.

"The stones choose their wielder," Ren explained. "For some reason, they chose Kelsey."

"There's more to the story, isn't there?" Jacob asked. Ren nodded again. "My father and many others are headed back to our home, to Nexus. That includes me as well. With our existence exposed, we need to stabilize both worlds. However, we have to take the stones with us."

"… Okay," Jacob said after a long pause. "And what you're trying to tell us is?"

Kelsey held out her wrist. "The stones won't come off," she confessed. "We've spent days trying, looked through countless books, tried even more attempts to remove them, but they won't budge."

"And that's why we had to talk to you guys. With the stones attached to Kelsey, she will be in grave danger if left unprotected. There is a limit to how much power one can draw from the stones before it kills them. We simply cannot risk her or the stones. So, we are left with only one option. Kelsey must return with us to Nexus."

Kelsey's mother slammed her hands on the table.

"No! She's not going anywhere!"

"Mom, I have to. We have to find a way to remove the stones," Kelsey said back. "We can't do that here. I have to go with them."

"I'm in agreement with your mother, Kelsey," her father said. "You said you couldn't remove them. What makes going to Ren's world any different?"

"Knowledge," Ren answered. "We don't have enough of it in the human world. But Nexus is different. There is a high chance that if we search through ancient texts, we will find a way to remove the stones."

"Why can't you bring them here? Or give her a guard?" her mother asked.

Ren shook his head. "I wish we could, but we just don't have the manpower for that right now. Our enemy has made their move and is likely planning their next. We don't know when the Radiant Church will resurface. And we have to stabilize relations with the humans. Our hands are full. Currently, no one powerful enough to guard her is capable right now. I possess the key to accessing the latent power of the stones," he held up his wrist, revealing the blue and green bracelet, "but I have to head back to Nexus. As its prince, I must be there to help stabilize my country."

"Not a chance, Kelsey," her mother declared. It was likely that there was little they could do to change her mind right now. "You still have work and school. Or did you forget about that?"

"Neither is a problem," she said. "I technically work for Trinity now. I don't need my old job. And I've been allowed to graduate early."

"Who told you that?" her father asked.

"My school's principal. He's a monster and a supporter of Trinity. He covered for us when we went looking for the stones. He's already promised to help us this time, too."

"And how long do you plan on being gone for? Another month? Longer?"

"We don't know," she confessed.

"You don't know?"

"Finding the secret to the stones is very complicated," Ren spoke up. "There are hundreds of thousands of years of history in my kingdom's library. Countless artifacts and secrets the likes of which you can't imagine. And each level is more classified than the last. It's difficult to say how long it will take to search through it all. All I can tell you is to suspect it will take a while. Much longer than our search for the stones."

"Do you have to go?" Kelsey's mother asked her. But Kelsey only returned her question with a nod.

"I'm sure you have your doubts, but I assure you there's no need for concern," Ren told them. "Please trust me when I say that Kelsey will be well protected."

"Because your world is more peaceful than ours?" Kelsey's father asked.

"No. Because I will be with her. Once it's known she's connected to me, no one will dare attempt to harm her. Those who try will wish they hadn't. And I'm not just saying that because I'm confident in my own abilities. I say it because I'm confident in hers. Since Kelsey can use the stones, she is extremely powerful. In fact, she's probably almost as strong as I am now. Rest assured, knowing that she is more than capable of defending herself."

"And, for what it's worth, she shouldn't be fighting at all," Ren continued. "Our time in Nexus will be purely humdrum. We'll likely be glued to the castle the entire time. Everything will be taken care of for her by the servants, down to the most basic. Even her daily necessities will be provided. Which means Kelsey will literally be treated like a princess while she stays with us."

"Ren told me I can write you letters. He knows someone who will deliver them from Nexus to here and vice versa."

"We don't leave for another couple of weeks," Ren told her parents. "I'll give you the contact information of the person who will deliver the letters before we go. You can give them anything you have for us, and she will ensure they are delivered to us."

Ren looked at the time on his phone. "While we're here, you'll want to pack your clothes, Kelsey."

"Alright. Will you help me pack?" she asked. Ren nodded back.

They finished eating, and Ren walked to Kelsey's room. This was the last time she would see her room for a while. They were probably going to be gone a long time. A new adventure awaited them after all.

Eight

When the Flame Goes Out

Kelsey opened her drawers while Ren unzipped Kelsey's suitcase. This was the second time he was here helping her pack for a trip. Of course, this one was going to be a lot longer than last time.

Ren could tell Kelsey's parents had realized the distance between them. As if it wasn't obvious. They were too attentive for that. Ren had found it too much effort to try and avoid Kelsey like he had been trying. It was easier to just be normal. Sure, they were distant right now, but they were still technically dating. If, in time, their relationship came to an end, then so be it.

He grabbed a couple pairs of jeans from Kelsey's hands and placed them in the suitcase.

However, it was clear that Kelsey was trying to close that gap. She had caused their dispute, and now she was the one trying to repair it and return to normal. And what was Ren doing? Running away like a child. Running from her and from his problems. He focused on returning to Nexus and his duties, using them as a distraction. But he knew he couldn't do it forever.

Kelsey handed him three pairs of different colored shorts and then a skirt. He didn't even know she owned a skirt. Ren placed it atop her shorts, keeping it folded neatly. Next, she handed him three pairs of leggings, which he placed on top. He made sure everything was neat and took note of the room left. Luckily, it was a decent-sized suitcase, so she still had some room left.

Kelsey walked into her closet. All manner of clothes hung from hangers. She cleaned out the entire thing. Ren helped her take the hangers off and fold them, then place them in the suitcase. By the end, there was little room left.

With her closet empty, she moved on to her dresser and opened her bottom two drawers. Everything was folded neatly in columns. She grabbed everything and stuffed it into her suitcase.

"I'm all set. We should get going," she said. Ren nodded, and they headed down the stairs, closing the door to her room behind them.

Kelsey's parents were waiting for them at the bottom. Ren could tell from the looks on their faces that they were extremely nervous. Her mother especially looked like she was going to have a heart attack.

"It'll be alright, Mom," Kelsey said. But her mother didn't look at all convinced.

"Ren, please look out for Kelsey. As much as I don't want you to go, I know you will anyway. Since we can't be there, you need to be."

"I will," he said back.

Ren handed Kelsey's father a card. "This is the person I told you about who will deliver the letters."

Kelsey's father took the card and looked at it for a second. "Thank you, Ren." He shook Ren's hand, gripping it tightly. "Take care on the other side."

Ren held onto Kelsey's suitcase. Ellie was still playing with her sister in the living room.

"Ellie, come on munchkin', we've got to get going," he called. "I'll go put the luggage away," he said to Kelsey. "You'll have a few minutes. I suggest you say your goodbyes."

Ren took Ellie's hand once she showed up, and they exited the house. He wheeled the luggage up to his Lambo and put it in the trunk.

"Kelsey, is everything alright?" her mother asked.

"What do you mean?" she asked back.

"You know what I mean. Something is going on between you and Ren. He's keeping his distance from you. It's pretty easy to tell."

"Especially since he's never kept his distance from you," her father added.

Kelsey sighed and ran her fingers through her hair.

"I don't know what to do. I'm trying to keep us together, but I can't tell if it's working. At first, he avoided me completely. Now, half the time he acts completely normal."

Her parents just exchanged uneasy glances.

"What did happen?" her mother asked.

There was a long pause before Kelsey finally spoke. "It was after the battle in the park," she confessed. "Ren had just defeated that vampire he was fighting. I, I saw … something, though I don't know what it was. It looked like a person. But it seemed no one else could see it for some reason. Whatever it was, it looked right at me. I'm positive it could actually see me."

"And you're sure no one else can see it?" her father asked.

Kelsey confirmed with a nod. "Even Ren didn't seem to notice it was there. And that's one of the things that confuses me the most. Nothing gets past him, least of all something like that. The guy is a supernatural hotspot. His senses are off the charts."

Her parents could only agree with her statement.

"So?"

"I questioned it. If it was real, as I realized it was, surely I'd be able to interact with it. I thought perhaps if it could see me, it could communicate with me as well. But because it only appears around Ren, he was right there when I did. My first thought was that it was some kind of monster or the ability of a monster. But when I asked, Ren took it personally. I'm pretty sure he thinks I was talking to him."

"So, that's what happened. I'm sure someone like Ren, who relied on you like he did, would feel hurt by that," her mother said.

Despite her efforts to maintain her emotions, a small and quiet whine escaped her lips.

"I don't know what to do. I'm trying to tell him the truth and fix things, but it seems like every time I do, he pushes me away. And if I try harder to close that gap, he retreats even further."

"That's one of the things that makes falling in love so painful. But, you have to be the ones who work through it."

"Don't forget, Ren isn't a normal man," Kelsey's father spoke up. "Granted, he's three hundred years old, but in terms of love, he's as green as you are, Kelsey," her father said. "But, he is still a man. Consider this. Maybe words just won't cut it. You have to show him how you feel. Sometimes that's the only way."

"Just be honest with him," her mother said. "He will understand. I promise you everything will work itself out. It always does. Now, go and do whatever you have to do. You don't want to keep him waiting too long."

Kelsey looked at Ren through the front window. Ren was still leaning against the trunk of his car. "Alright, I'm leaving then. I'll see you before I leave." She embraced her parents and sister before walking out the door, closing it behind her.

"Come on, let's go," she said. She opened the passenger door and sat down with Ellie, never uttering another word.

Her parents had said something to her. Ren could tell, though he had no idea what it was. He couldn't read their lips behind the window, nor had he even tried to. Getting into the driver's seat, he pressed the break and pushed the ignition button. The car came alive, and he put it into reverse. Kelsey waved to her parents and sister as Ren reversed out of the driveway, then turned and drove off.

The drive to Ren's house was quiet. No one said a word. Ren looked over at Kelsey out of the corner of his eye and saw her staring out the window, jaw resting on her fist, elbow propped up against the door.

"You alright?" Ren finally asked.

"Hmm?" was the only sound she made.

"I asked if you were alright."

"Oh, yeah, I'm fine," she said, and returned to looking out the window.

"*Jhootha*," he said under his breath. Liar.

Kelsey's left hand rested on her quadriceps. Ren reached over without taking his eyes off the road and took her hand, switching his right hand on the wheel with his left. She never stole her eyes away from the window, only acknowledging that he was holding her hand.

Truth be told, she was too wrapped up in her own thoughts to care. She was only focusing on what her parents had told her. No matter what, no matter when, she had to tell Ren. She had to explain to him that she never called him a monster. And most of all, she needed to show him how much she still loved him.

Nine

Don't Let Go

Ren opened up his garage door as they pulled up to it. He drove inside, parking his Lambo next to his McClaren, then closed the garage door once he was parked.

Kelsey grabbed her luggage from Ren's trunk while he opened the door to the house.

Where's Nidar? he wondered. He was used to having the tiger meet him at the front door.

Curious, he searched the house. Ren found the tiger Nidar sleeping on the floor, curled up into a ball in the living room. His chest rose with every intake of breath. It was clear he was sleeping peacefully. Ren dared not wake him.

A sharp yawn escaped Ellie, who walked into the room, her eyes fluttering open and closed.

"Why don't you head off to bed, munchkin," he told her.

Ellie rubbed her eyes in response. "Okay. Night, Ren." She walked off to her room.

Ren felt a sudden sense of satisfaction knowing she had gotten used to living with him. Then again, he secretly wished she was a little younger so he could still baby her. She was ten years old, though, and growing up quickly. Hell, he was helping his father run their kingdom when he was her age. This was nothing, but Ellie wasn't like Ren; she was human.

Meanwhile, the first thing Kelsey noticed was Ren had disappeared. One second, he was there, and the next, he was gone.

She set her luggage down at the side of her bed, not bothering to open it. All her hygiene products were already at Ren's house, and they still had a couple of weeks before they would be leaving anyway.

Kelsey left her room to see where everyone went before she headed to bed. Ellie's room was first. Sure enough, she was already in bed sleeping. Nidar wasn't with her either. Now that she thought of it, she hadn't seen Nidar around the house yet, either. Where was that silly tiger?

Kelsey searched the house, but she couldn't find anyone. Every room was completely empty.

She finally tried the living room last and saw Ren sitting on the ground, leaning his back against the couch. Nidar lay next to him with his head on Ren's lap, eyes closed in sleep. Ren had one hand on Nidar's side, and the other gently scratched the top of the tiger's head.

Kelsey knew how close they were. Ren had basically raised Nidar as a kitten. They had been together for three years now. There was no way she was going to bother them right now. Not as they were.

She turned around and headed back to her room. Well, it wasn't really her room. It was one of the many spare rooms Ren had in his house. It just happened to be the one she always used, so it essentially became her own room.

Ren noticed Kelsey's presence appear while he was petting Nidar. He never took his eyes away because he didn't want to make any unintentional movements. He and Nidar hadn't lied down like this in what felt like ages. It was nice to be able to do the things they used to. They were finally getting more time together again, which Ren and Nidar both valued deeply.

Kelsey was only there for a few seconds, and then she was gone. She didn't even say goodnight. That wasn't like her. Ren was sure of it. Her parents had said something to her. Now, she was the one being distant.

He wondered if maybe they were finally at the end of the road. If both of them were avoiding each other, that would be the end of things. That meant Ren could focus on getting the stones off of her wrist and send her home. She would be out of Nexus, out of the war, and out of danger.

However, if Kelsey left, Ren knew he would most likely never see her again. But that was a price he was going to have to pay. Especially if it meant her safety. They would go their separate ways, and that would be the end of things.

An eternity without Kelsey. Ren had to admit, he wasn't for that. They had been through a lot together and grown closer through their challenges. Three years of separation sucked enough. If they ended their relationship, the separation would be forever this time.

Even though they were at odds right now, Ren could wholeheartedly admit he still loved her. That was something that would never change. A vampire can live their entire life off just one emotion. It was their desires and obsessions that drove them to live. For Ren, Kelsey was one of those obsessions. It's part of the reason he was torn so much. He wanted her to be free, but at the same time, he didn't want to let her go. After all, he was a monster. She had made that clear to him.

He let out a long and heavy sigh. No, he wasn't. Not to her. She had called him a monster, rejected him, and yet he just couldn't help feeling like he should trust her. Something felt wrong to him. Given the way she acted around him, why would she continue if she hated him? If he was such a monster, why stick around him and try to salvage their relationship? It didn't make sense.

He couldn't help but think there was a big misunderstanding between them. Actually, the more he thought about it, the more likely it seemed. He wanted to let her go, but he couldn't. Maybe … maybe he would try talking to her like she wanted. If they laid their feelings bare, it might just solve their issues and resolve the whole thing.

Well, who knew how things would turn out. He did love her, and he wanted to be with her despite everything. They just had to live through it. A lifetime without Kelsey wasn't a life he wanted. After all, forever was a long time.

Ten

A Secret Among Secrets

Ren opened his eyes slowly. A crack formed in the darkness of sleep before it was shattered by the light of day. He lay in his bed, the covers draped over him.

A heavy breath distracted him. Nidar lay beside him, the tiger's back pressed against his legs. The peacefulness of sleep still had its hold on him.

Ren scratched his sides gently before getting up. The time read just passed six-thirty. That left him a little over an hour to eat and get ready to head to the airport.

Two weeks had passed quickly, and today was the day they were scheduled to depart for Nexus.

Nidar opened his eyes and stretched before getting up. Ren rubbed the top of his head, and the tiger licked his face in response. Now fully awake, the two of them headed to the kitchen. Ren wasn't sure what, but he would whip them up something quickly.

When they walked into the kitchen, Kelsey and Ellie were already at the table eating. Ren looked at Nidar and raised an eyebrow, but the tiger just shook his head. He had no idea what was going on either.

"Morning," Ren said.

"Good Morning, Ren," Ellie said. He rubbed the top of her head, messing up her hair.

Kelsey just smiled and waved at Ren. He returned the gesture and gathered the necessary ingredients for a quick breakfast. One plate found its way to the table, where he would sit, and the other to the floor, where Nidar lay in wait patiently.

No one said a word to each other as they ate. They simply sat there in silence. It was super awkward, really.

"I'm going to shower and get ready," Kelsey said. She excused herself from the table and placed her dishes in the dishwasher before returning to her room.

"Ren, what's wrong?" Ellie asked. "Did something happen between you and Kelsey?"

"It's complicated munchkin'."

"Do you two not like each other anymore?"

"I'm not sure. It's more than that, and yet, it's not. There's a lot going on. We haven't really had the chance to talk. Like I said, it's complicated."

"I'm going to take a shower, too," Ellie said when she was done eating.

"Go on," Ren said. He took her dishes and placed them in the dishwasher with his own as Ellie returned to her room.

Nidar sat next to him and looked up at Ren, who only shrugged his shoulders.

"I don't know, bud." He placed a hand on Nidar's head. "I think I do need to talk to her. I just need to find the right time." Nidar growled lightly as if to tell him things would be okay.

Ren knelt down on one knee and placed both hands on either side of the tiger's neck. Fur cocooned his hand, enveloping them completely. Nidar put his front paws on Ren's lap and licked him. Ren scratched the side of his face before planting a lingering kiss on the tiger's forehead.

Returning to his room, Ren readied himself a bath, letting the water fill the tub while he dumped in a green liquid contained within a dark brown earthen jar. The green liquid mixed with the water in the tub, turning it the same color before it faded and returned to its original translucent state.

Herbs. That's what was contained in the jar, what he dumped in the tub. Because he was a vampire, without adding those herbs to dilute the purity of the water, it would destroy him. It's why he couldn't take showers, not without special precautions. Bathing was always his first choice.

The tub was made of polished tan and white sandstone. It sat higher above the floor on a raised platform.

When the water was at his desired height and temperature, Ren stepped into the tub and let the heat of the water release some of the tension in his body. His thoughts were focused solely on the trip at hand.

After a long soak, he emerged from the tub. No matter how things turned out, there was one thing that had become clear to Ren this past week. It was much easier to act normal around Kelsey than to try and avoid her. So, act normal, he would.

Drying himself off, he changed into his standard mission clothes, the ones he always wore at Trinity and when on jobs. Black pants, a tight-fitting shirt of blended white and light brown color, and a brown leather belt with a golden square buckle over his shirt at his waist.

Sitting on the edge of the bed, he slipped on his combat boots, pulling them over the bottom of his pants. He tied them off and stood up. He grabbed his pair of black leather fingerless gloves and put them on over his hands.

Finally, he grabbed his jacket hanging from the rack and slipped it over his shoulders. A deep mahogany leather with a high collar. The inside was lined with gray mountain hare fur with a peppering of hazel. A hood rested comfortably behind him, the back of the jacket stopping behind his knees and the front just below his waist.

Ren grabbed a large duffle bag and filled it with stuff to bring with him. Beyond some of the essentials, he also grabbed extra weaponry, including two boxes of bullets for his Berrettas and extra mags. Anything else he would need was already kept in the palace. Gabbing the strap, he hoisted it over his shoulder.

Inside his weapon wardrobe, he grabbed the silver case he always used to carry his weapons. At only slightly larger than a guitar case, it fit his bow, arrows, pistols, extra mags, and Shadow Hunter.

Ren exited his room and headed for his living room just in time to see Marcus and his father walk in.

"Hey, Ren," Marcus said. "Perfect timing."

"I was about to say the same thing," Ren said back.

"Ready to finally go back?" his father asked.

"I've been ready for a long time," Ren said. "We've been away for too long. It's about time we returned."

"You boys having fun?" Kelsey asked. She walked up to them, wheeling her suitcase. "Why am I the only one with a lot of luggage?"

"Because you've never been to Nexus before. Everything we need is already there. Besides, Ellie has a lot, too."

The saddened look on her face hit him harder than he would have expected. Ren put his arm around her, and she looked at him, a little surprised.

"I can't wait for you to see our world. I've wanted to show you for a long time."

"Well, you did promise to take me the next time you went," she said, leaning against him.

"Oh yeah, I did promise you that."

"Oh yeah? You forgot!"

"Uh oh, I'm in trouble!"

Kelsey released a heavy sigh. "What am I going to do with you."

"I can think of several things. All of which involve rope and a goat."

Kelsey and his father looked at him like he was an alien before he and Marcus burst out laughing.

"I don't want to know what's going through that head of yours," she said, disturbed.

"Ren!" Ellie ran up to him. She was dressed in a white dress with flowers along the side.

"Wow, look at you, munchkin'! You look like a princess." He picked her up, and she hugged him.

Only minutes later, there was a knock on the front door. Ren opened it, still holding Ellie. James Wilson was standing there with Jay.

"Morning, Ren," Jay and James said.

"Morning, guys. Come on in."

"Is everyone ready?" James asked, following him inside.

"We're all set," Ren's father said.

"Alright, then let's go. We're giving you a ride to the airport."

Ren set Ellie down, and she grabbed her suitcase. Like Kelsey, she had to bring one since she didn't have anything in Nexus either.

They headed out the front door, Ren taking up the rear and locking it behind him. He placed his keys in his pocket, then grabbed his bags and headed down the steps. Parked in front of his house was a gray minivan.

Marcus opened the side door, and they all piled in. Ren sat next to his father, Marcus next to Kelsey, with Ellie in the middle, leaving Nidar to take up the back. Marcus buckled Ellie in, making sure she was secure.

"Comfortable?" he asked.

"Yup," she said. "Thanks."

He rubbed the top of her head.

James and Jay finished loading the rest of their luggage in the back with Nidar, then hopped in the van. James got in the driver's seat while Jay rode shotgun.

At some point during the drive, Ren felt a tap on his shoulder. He turned around to see Kelsey leaning forward.

"Hey, I was just wondering, where exactly are we going?"

"Peru," he said. "All the other portals are far off. The ones that lead directly to the capital are on the other side of the world."

"So it's just a matter of time to get there," Kelsey said.

"Pretty much, yeah. And there's actually another reason," Ren said. "We want to check the other territories along the way. From the portal in Peru, it's five days to the capital on horseback. That should give us enough time for a rough check without requiring a full expedition. Verifying now will help us later."

"Seeing the results in person is easier than sending a representative and reading a report," Marcus said. "We do it in my kingdom, too. Sometimes me, my dad, or both of us will head out to surrounding towns and villages to check on them."

"What do you do after you see them?"

"The report on the affairs of our country will help determine that. Economy, trade, food, living quality, laws, and infrastructure are just some of the few. Even relations between sovereign nations are affected."

"It sounds like you guys are going to be really busy," Kelsey said.

"Yeah, we have a lot to do. It's a lot of work to run a kingdom," Ren said. "Most of which involves paperwork. It's almost all paperwork."

"If you're going to be that busy, when will we have time to get the stones off?"

"The one searching will be you. You will have free range anywhere you want in the library. I'll make sure of that."

Leo, Jay, and Marcus looked dead on at Ren. James shot several surprised glances at him through the rear-view mirror.

"Ren, are you serious?" Marcus asked.

"Yes."

"Ren, I'm not sure that's the best idea."

"It's fine. I've already made my decision."

Kelsey looked at them, unsure of what the problem was. She looked at Ellie next, but Ellie just shrugged at her.

"Um, is there a problem with me having 'free range'?" Kelsey asked, using Ren's choice of words.

"It's not you specifically, but yes," Ren's father said. "The library in our palace is one of the largest in the world. It has a vast collection of knowledge. In fact, there's so much knowledge, the library extends fifteen stories below the ground."

"Fifteen!" He nodded. "How am I supposed to find anything in all that?"

"Everything is categorized by name, year, and the level of secrecy."

"Kelsey, it's not the amount of knowledge that's the problem," Marcus said. "It's the type of knowledge itself. There are secrets buried in that library, the likes of which none of us could comprehend."

"The deeper the floors get, the more dangerous the knowledge becomes," Ren's father continued. "And, the lower floors contain information so secretive, they're layered with traps. Magic and man-made traps of all kinds, designed to protect their knowledge. And the deepest floor is the most dangerous. Even I am not aware of everything that's down there."

Kelsey looked at Ren nervously. She wanted his intake on the situation. How much did he know?

"Sorry, but I don't know anything," he said, as if he had been reading her thoughts. "I've never been to the last floor. Only the king is allowed there."

"How deep have you gone?"

"The thirteenth floor. The traps made it too difficult to descend any further."

"And you want to give me access to every floor?" Ren nodded.

"There are deactivations for each trap you encounter. Of course, we would give them to you."

"Then how come you only made it to the thirteenth floor?"

"Because even though the traps can be deactivated, the problem is some of them are so old that deactivating them doesn't work. The traps activate anyway or malfunction and don't go off at all. Once I reached the thirteenth floor, I got sick of deactivating them all and gave up."

"But you said only the king is allowed on the last level," Kelsey said. "So, how can you give me access?"

"With special permission, one can visit the final level, but they must journey there with the king in their presence. It almost never happens, though. I'm the prince and heir to the throne. I will give you permission in my father's stead, even if it means breaking traditions. However, if and when the time comes for you to head to the fifteenth floor, he and I will travel there with you."

"Now hold on, Ren," his father said. "What makes you think anyone will let that slide? The rules were put in place for a reason."

"I know, but sometimes, rules need to be broken. What's the point of being king if you can't make your own?"

"Hold on, hold on," Kelsey said, waving her hands at them to stop. "If this is so extensive, why go through all the effort? Why not just avoid the fifteenth floor in general? We can stick then the upper floors."

"Yes, that would be the best," Ren's father said. "There are secrets down there that are meant to be kept secret."

Marcus stared at Ren in silence. He knew him too well to be fooled by something like this. Ren knew something. He was sure of it.

"You have a theory, don't you?" he asked Ren.

Everyone looked from Marcus to Ren, who nodded silently.

"You plan on going down there. That's why you recommended it. That's the reason you're giving Kelsey access to all of them. You think the secret of the stones is located on the bottom floor."

"Exactly," Ren answered. "Up until now, the stones had been just a legend. I can't think of any other place to contain the secrets to control their power. They must be on the final floor."

Marcus narrowed his eyes at Ren. "That's not everything. You have another reason for going down there, don't you?"

Ren was quiet for a few moments before he finally answered. "I think the reason the fifteenth floor is so protected isn't just because of the secrets it holds that can't be learned. I think it's also because of the secrets that can be learned."

"What does that mean?" Jay asked.

They all looked at Ren, eager to hear his theory.

"I think the bottom floor might hold the answer to defeating Verin," he finally said.

Eleven

Gateway

Ren's theory left everyone speechless.

"You really think that?" Marcus asked.

Staring at him with faces of complete shock, the very notion that the library held the answer to their enemy had never even contemplated a possibility. But, then again, neither had they actually thought to consider it either.

"If not the answer, I believe it might have a clue, yeah. But before we know for certain that we have to go down there, we need to research the upper levels and find any information we can. All the way down to the fourteenth floor. Any and all information regarding the stones and on Verin or necromancers. If we can't find anything, then we head to the fifteenth floor. And that is Kelsey's job."

Ren looked over at her, setting those beautiful cobalt-blue eyes on her.

"You will be in charge of researching the stones and Verin. But, like I told you before, you won't be alone. I'll assign someone to help you. Maybe even two or three aids. It would take you decades to look through all that information alone. But with extra hands and knowing where to look on each floor, you can get your research done much faster."

"If the stones are as secretive as we think they are, and as much as Ren *says* they are, then you may end up skipping over the first couple of floors anyway, starting as late as the fifth floor. But it's hard to say," Marcus told her.

Fifteen floors. Decades worth of time required. What in the hell had Kelsey gotten herself into? No wonder they were going to be gone for so long. But there was nothing she could do about it. She would just have to go at it one day at a time.

James turned right and drove down the main road leading into the airport.

After several more minutes of driving, they finally pulled into the FBO parking lot and found a spot to park. Marcus opened the door, and they all funneled out, one at a time.

James opened the back of his minivan, and everyone grabbed their belongings after Nidar jumped out. Ren slung his bag over his shoulder, his weapon case in one hand and Ellie's suitcase in his other. James closed the back, and they headed to their plane.

A man belonging to security walked up to them. His dark skin contrasted with the light and dark blue of his uniform. His hair was braided along the length of his head.

They all stopped, and the man dropped to one knee in a bow.

"Your Majesty," he said to Ren's father. "Your Highnesses," he said to Ren and Marcus. "Welcome. Your private plane is already waiting for you. Follow me, I will aid you in boarding and securing your luggage."

"You have our thanks. Much appreciated," Leo said.

They all followed the man as he led them toward the plane. Suddenly, their names were called. A large group of people stood outside the FBO terminal. Kelsey's parents, along with Jessica, Lisa, and other members of Trinity, were waiting for them.

Jessica and Lisa ran up to Kelsey and hugged her simultaneously.

"What are you guys doing here?" Kelsey asked, surprised to see them. Their presence had her completely taken aback.

"We came to see you off," Jessica said. "All of you," she said, looking at Marcus and Ren. "You really are princes." Ren gazed at her briefly before nodding.

Jessica and Lisa looked at Ren and the older man beside him.

"Your Majesty," they said, giving a light curtsey.

Ren's father chuckled. "Please, just call me Leo," he said.

"Leo," Kelsey's father called.

When Leo saw Kelsey's father, Ren's father had a smile Ren had not seen in a long time; sadness

"Jacob," Leo said. They embraced. "It's been too long, my friend."

"Too long is right," Kelsey's father said back.

Leo looked from him to Kelsey's mother. "Thank you for taking care of Ren and Eris. I am forever in your debt."

Jacob put a hand on Leo's shoulder. "It was our pleasure to do so. Both of them mean very much to us. As do you. Eris will always be a part of us. Keep your chin up, old friend."

Jessica and Lisa silently grabbed Kelsey's attention. "Who's Eris?" Lisa asked.

Kelsey watched Leo and her father. Then her eyes turned to Ren. "Ren's mother," she finally said.

Jessica and Lisa followed Kelsey's gaze to Ren.

"Oh. I heard she passed away three years ago," Lisa said.

"She was murdered," Kelsey admitted after a long pause.

"Your Majesty," the security guard said. "Your plane is waiting. Please, this way."

"Time to go," Leo said.

"We'll keep in touch," Ren said to everyone. "Oh, and do try to get along with our kind. We don't bite." He smiled, revealing his vampire fangs.

"Ha-ha, Ren," Kelsey's father said sarcastically. "Very funny."

Ren chuckled. "Little bit," he said, holding his index finger and thumb close together. "See you all when we get back."

They boarded the plane and found a seat. Kelsey and Ellie put their suitcases in a storage compartment in the back, then sat on one of the couches while Ren, Marcus, and Leo greeted the pilots.

Ellie looked around at the plane, mouth ajar. Not only was it her first time on a private plane, it was her first time on an airplane in general.

"This is an airplane?"

Kelsey chuckled. "It sure is," she said. "This one is a private jet. It's owned and used specifically by Leo. Ren and Marcus use it for missions. Commercial airplanes are nothing like this. They're very cramped," she explained.

Ren sat down next to Kelsey, putting an arm on the top of the couch behind her. Marcus and his father sat on the other couch.

The pilot's voice came onto the loudspeaker and informed them of their take-off. The plane started moving, and they made their way onto the runway before finally shooting forward and rising into the air.

It was a six-hour flight from there to where they were landing in Peru. Once they reached cruising altitude, the rest of the flight was smooth and relaxing.

Ellie got up and wandered over to a window. She stuck her face to the glass to see out.

Kelsey looked at Ren's father. "Mr. Nightwalker."

Leo looked over at her. "What is it, my dear?"

"I was just wondering if you could tell me what Nexus is like? I don't really know anything about it. Only the brief bits Ren and Marcus have shared with me. I just want to know what to expect, is all."

Leo looked surprised at her asking him. He hadn't expected it. Still, he happily answered her question. "I would be delighted, Kelsey."

"Geographically, our world is very similar to yours. Oceans, rivers, plains, Mountains, forests, we have them all, just like here. However, unlike the human world, ours is less developed. Humans constantly expand and develop their infrastructure, unlike us. Ren and Marcus have already told you about our political standing and style. So you already know the basics. However, for the sake of your curiosity, I will delve deeper."

Leo was keen to identify all the aspects of their world without overloading Kelsey's brain. Just as Ren and Marcus had previously described to her, their world was essentially medieval, with some finer, unexpected Victorian aspects.

Nevertheless, some part of her still wasn't entirely convinced it was that similar. She expected the Nexus to be more—demonic. Maybe not evil, but at least dark, cloudy, lots of rain. That kind of thing. It looked like she would just have to see it for herself to really know.

Ellie finally tore her face away from the window and turned toward Ren.

"Ren, I'm thirsty. Do we have anything to drink?"

"Sure, what do you want?" he asked.

"Anything is fine."

Ren got up and walked toward the back of the plane. The jet was equipped with a small kitchen that they could use if they got hungry. He opened the mini refrigerator and grabbed a drink.

Marcus grabbed a remote and turned on two televisions mounted to the wall of the cockpit. He put on a movie for them to watch during the flight.

After hours of flying, the pilot's voice appeared over the speakers. "Everyone, we'll be descending in just a few minutes."

The plane landed, and the pilots emerged from the cockpit. They wished everyone safe travels before letting everyone off the plane.

A customs agent met them at their plane. Their monster energy indicated that they were of a weaker race at C-rank. However, as Ren's father had notified them beforehand, having a monster to meet them and not a human made the customs process even easier than it normally would have been.

Ren wasn't really worried about anything. The only thing he was concerned with was Ellie. He was glad her passport came in when it did. With how she came to stay with him, Ren had to have one made for her. There was no chance of him finding her old one, if she even had one at all.

Usually, they take months to complete, but he managed to get hers speed lined. It had her current picture and information. The only thing obviously different was her name. It now read Ellie Nightwalker. Ren thought it was fitting to change it.

Inside the FBO terminal, they spotted a man holding up a sign. It read Nightwalker in red. The man had brown hair cropped close to his head and a shaven face. He wore a blue button-down shirt and black dress pants and shoes. He was slightly overweight and shorter than a few of the people there.

"Alex!" Ren's father called.

"Leo!" Alex called back. They shook hands.

"It's good to see you," Leo said.

"And you. It's been too long. Many years so." His English was excellent. Almost perfect, in fact.

"Alex, this is my son, Ren." Ren greeted him and shook his hand. "And this is Marcus Allagash, Kelsey Rose, and Ellie Whinner."

"Nightwalker," Ren corrected. "It's Ellie Nightwalker." He grabbed her hand and smiled at her.

"I have heard a lot about you guys. You're quite famous, even here," Alex said.

"Alex will be bringing us to the portal," Leo explained.

"It's been a long time since you guys have returned to Nexus," Alex said. "I can get you to the portal, no problem."

Alex led them to a van that was parked outside. He opened the side door, and everyone piled in. Ren took the single bench seat at the back of the van. Marcus was about to sit next to him when Nidar hopped up next to him and lay down, putting his head on Ren's lap. All Marcus could do was chuckle and sit elsewhere.

Kelsey saw Ren sitting with Nidar and immediately knew her chances of sitting with him were gone. Instead, she sat a few rows up from him while Ellie sat beside her. Kelsey thought she was the cutest thing.

Once everyone was seated, Alex started the van, and they drove off. Kelsey, Ellie, and Marcus watched the scenery pass by as they drove through the city first before it transitioned into open land. Ellie watched from the window, noting every interesting thing she saw. Ren's father sat up front with Alex, engaged in a long conversation. No doubt, the two of them had plenty of catching up to do. Meanwhile, Ren gently stroked the top of Nidar's head with his hand, watching the steady rise and fall of his chest and listening to the sounds of his breathing and purring.

Over an hour into the drive, Kelsey looked back at Ren. He was leaning back, eyes closed, and his hand rested on a sleeping Nidar's head. She felt like she was never going to get to talk to him.

Her eyes fixed themselves on Ren's hand, watching his fingers move along the inside of Nidar's ear. She wished it were her that was receiving all of his attention. It felt like forever since he'd held her.

Kelsey lightly wrapped her arms around her waist, suddenly desperate for his embrace. She wanted nothing more than to get up and sit down next to him. To have him put his arm around her. To make her feel safe and set her heart aflutter. She sighed quietly and turned her head to look back out the window.

After almost two hours of driving, they turned down a side road. The pavement turned to dirt, and the van kicked up dust behind it as its tires spun along the ground.

They continued down the road for some time before coming to a stop. To their right lay a set of ruins. It sat atop a hill with giant Megaliths made of stone.

Everyone climbed out, relishing in the moment of being able to release built-up tension before looking around. Only, when they finally did, there was nothing. No people, no buildings, no sign of civilization at all.

Just a single set of ruins built out in the middle of nowhere.

The hill flattened out at the top. In the center, a circular base was built from the same stone as the Megaliths. Twenty-four of which circled around the base at an equal distance from each other. They stood thirty feet tall, and the horizontal stones on top all matched up end to end to form a connected circle.

Unlike the megaliths, however, the circular base was a different colored stone. What's more, the placement created a peculiar appearance. In fact, they almost seemed to form something. No, not almost; they did. It was a pattern. A smaller circle made from black stones formed only two feet from the inside edge of the Megaliths. Within the black-lined circle, seven lines of stones of the same color intersected each other. The resulting pattern created two sets of seven triangles with a heptagon in the middle.

Seven points, seven lines, seven triangles. A seven-pointed star. It was a heptagram.

At each of the seven internal vertices was a small circle. Using the circles, a second heptagram formed within the larger one. And in the center were two additional evenly spaced circles.

Strange symbols were inscribed all around the double heptagrams and circles. Kelsey realized she recognized those symbols. Which meant that Ren and the others certainly knew them as well.

Although she'd never seen these specific symbols, the style matched the same symbols they'd seen on the stone atop Mt. Etna in Italy. This was Lazarus, the common language of Nexus.

It was the damndest thing, but while most of them were unrecognizable, Kelsey was sure some of them were written in English. But it made no sense for that to be the case. What was going on? Something strange was happening.

Ren had been to this portal before, so he knew what to expect. Kelsey and Ellie, however, hadn't. They stared at the ruins in wonder.

"As I'm sure you've now guessed, these ruins are more than they seem," he said. "The internal design and placement of the megaliths are done very specifically. And the lettering inside the circles is Lazarus. This whole ruin is actually one giant magic circle. A teleportation circle used to transport us from this world to Nexus."

Kelsey and Ellie were amazed. They'd never seen anything like this before.

"It's about time you got here," someone said. The voice was sudden and unexpected.

Sitting on top of one of the megaliths was a man in his late forties. Only, he wasn't actually in his forties. His hair was mostly gray with streaks of black peeping through, and his gray beard was trimmed close to his chin.

Ren's face lit up when he saw the man. "Master!"

The old man dropped down from the megalith and swept Ren up in a hug.

"Ren, I feared I'd never get the chance to see you again."

Ren's master looked Ren over, checking out his appearance and aura. Then he smiled.

"You did it," he said. "I felt it the moment you awakened. Your monster energy came rushing through me. That's when I knew that you had finally fed and shed your incomplete state."

"I'm sorry to have concerned you, master. I'm alright now. Someone important told me that it was okay for me to accept what I am." Ren shot a quick glance at Kelsey, causing her cheeks to turn pink. It left him with a sly grin on his face, and his master nodded.

"Your Majesty," Ren's master greeted.

"Lord Vaylor," Ren's father greeted back. The two of them clasped forearms. "It's good to see you again, old friend. Truly. Thank you for coming."

"What brings you here?" Ren asked, curious. Though he had informed his master of his departure, his appearance was one he had not since expected. The vampire never left his sanctuary, after all.

"I have decided to return with you," the old vampire said. His remark surprised Ren even more than his arrival.

"When you told me that you were returning to Nexus, and with one of Verin's generals now defeated, I realized it was time for me to stop secluding myself as I had been. I will assist you in your research of the stones and in fighting this war. Besides, I miss having my apprentice at my side. So I made my way here to see you."

Ren's master looked at Kelsey's wrist and saw the bracelet with two glowing stones on it.

"So, you wear the stones, my dear. And it seems Ren wears the key. Interesting."

"Why is it interesting, Lord Vaylor?" she asked.

"I will explain everything while we head for the capital. We'll have plenty of time. Come, Ren, assist me in activating the portal."

"Yes, master."

Ren and his Master walked to the center of the magic circle. The two of them began chanting, and the magic circle began to glow white. Everyone stepped inside the circle as the light quickly enveloped them. Then, the light from the magic circle rose into the air, and they all began to disappear, starting from the feet. Their legs disappeared next, followed by their waist, then arms, and then neck. Kelsey closed her eyes as the magic finally reached her head and swallowed them whole.

Twelve

The World of Monsters

White blinded them. Even with their eyes closed, there wasn't a single shadow or color.

Slowly, the white began to fade, replaced with the gentle glow of sunlight. Dazzling rays poured down upon their faces, its heat gently kissing their skin.

"Kells, you can open your eyes. Open your eyes, *Rajkumari*," Ren said. His old habit of altering languages was returning it seemed. Or this was merely a temporary lapse.

Kelsey opened her eyes and gasped. The sky was breathtakingly blue, with no clouds in sight. The same sky as the human world's. With the brilliance of the sun raining down on them, it was as if the whole world was welcoming them.

"Hey, it's gorgeous out. We got lucky," Ren said. To which his father and Marcus nodded in agreement

They stood within another ruin, a mirror to the one in the human world. From the megaliths down to the magic circle, everything was identical.

Looking around, there was nothing but flatland in every direction. Green as far as the eye could see.

"Wow!" Ellie said excitedly. "So pretty."

Kelsey had to agree with her. It was beautiful here, nothing like she had imagined. In fact, Ren's father was right; it did practically look the same as her world.

When he saw the look on her face, there was no holding back Ren's laughter.

"What?" she asked.

"Nothing," he said through his laughter.

"Don't nothing me. What are you laughing about?" It was more of a demand than a question, but her obliviousness only added fuel to the fire.

Kelsey glared at Ren. She had a funny suspicion it was her he was laughing at.

"Well, we made it. But it's still five days' ride by horse," Leo said.

"Right, horse. About that," Kelsey said. "A couple of things. First, where are we supposed to get them? And second, what do we do if, for instance, some of us might not have that experience?"

"We can purchase horses at the nearest town. It's a half days walk there."

Leo reached into his bag and pulled out five black cloaks, handing one to each of them. They were soft on the inside, lined with fur, and tough on the outside, suitable for resistance to the elements. Each one also came with a hood.

The only exception was Ren's master, who was an unexpected addition. Luckily, the old vampire thought ahead and brought his own.

Kelsey watched Ren and the others throw the cloaks on over their shoulders. A thin rope hung from the front, which they tied at their chest, ensuring it was secure. Then, they pulled their hoods over their heads, concealing their faces.

Matching their movements, she put the cloak on, tied it, and pulled the hood over her face. Surprisingly, she found that not only were they large enough for comfort and undisturbed vision, but they still hid their faces completely.

Ren held his hand out and cast an incantation. A white light surrounded her before forming to the shape of her body and being absorbed into her.

"What was that?" she asked.

"A magic spell for speech. Now you'll be able to understand and speak Lazarus." Well, that was sensitive of him.

"Come on, Kells, it's a long walk," Ren said, chuckling.

She knew it! He had been laughing at her!

Kelsey noticed that he had started using her nickname again. Up until recently, he had been using her full name. Was this a sign that their relationship was improving again?

She watched Ren start walking, then turned her head to look at Marcus, but he just shrugged at her. Well, there was only one way to find out. She followed after him, hoping things were finally starting to look up.

Thirteen

A Connection That Crosses Worlds

The six of them walked the dirt road in silence, keeping their faces concealed beneath their hoods the entire time. Nidar followed quietly at Ren's left side.

Ren's father wanted to ensure that no one would recognize them should they be spotted along the way. No one knew he, Ren, and Marcus had returned to Nexus. It was of grave importance that no one knew they were there.

According to Leo, only a few close advisors, nobles, and servants within their palace knew. Thus, he stressed the importance of secrecy. If it were found that they were in Nexus before they were ready, they couldn't take note of situations and rumors as easily.

Kelsey wondered what the need was for her and Ellie to remain concealed then. No one would know them, so there was no need for them to stay hidden? She wondered if it was to maintain the same presence of mystery.

Ren eventually explained to her that it was because she and Ellie were human. Yes, no one in Nexus knew them, but one could easily tell they were human. As there were almost no humans in Nexus, it was exceptionally dangerous for them. If they got found out, they could be sold into slavery or, worse, even killed.

It was true that Nexus was relatively peaceful, but that notion didn't exactly extend to humans. Not so because they were different, but because their nature was well known, even without contact. Some monster races even feared them more than other monsters.

"That's why you must keep yourselves hidden," Ren said. "At least until we reach the capital. With those cloaks, no one will recognize that you're human. In the capital, you will declared official guests of the royal family and, therefore, Nexus as a whole. Once you are, no one can touch you without winning our, and my, wrath. That being said, I'm positive that once you and the citizens grow comfortable with each other, you'll have no problems."

"Regardless, you'll be safe in the capital at least," Ren continued. "Which means we can work without worry."

Kelsey nodded in agreement. He was right about that.

It took four hours of walking in silence before they came across their first impression of what was supposed to be civilization. There were three buildings in all, no doubt houses for whoever lived there.

The houses were made of wood. Their wooden shutters were kept open, leaving fresh air and the occasional breeze to wander through them. Behind the houses were three large farm fields. There was no telling what was being cultivated, but they were no small fields from the looks of them. Just how many people were living there?

Well, Kelsey had gotten her first look at the living style of the monsters in Nexus. Granted, this was probably the smallest and least developed before downright camping. Nevertheless, it was something she had been curious about. Now, she had a big city to look forward to.

As the sun began to dip below the horizon, the largest form of civilization they'd all seen yet appeared far in the distance. No small village. Instead, a smaller town.

The closer they got, the more features became distinguishable, especially the entrance. It was simple, consisting of two large wooden posts with a third laid across them overtop, and flanked by two guards. The guards wore only the simplest of protection, a few pieces of leather armor, and carried spears.

Ren and the others approached the entrance, and the guards crossed their spears, forcing them to stop. The first thing Kelsey noticed was they were very humanlike. In form only, alas. Their skin was paper white, and they had no faces.

"State your business," one of the guards said.

"We are headed to the capital," Ren said. "We simply wish to rest for the night and fetch some horses from the local stables. It has been quite a walk, as I'm sure you can imagine."

The guards stood there stoically. They weren't sure what to make of the situation. The most suspicious thing to them was Nidar, a creature they had never seen before, being from the human world.

"Who are you? What manner of creature is that?" the guard asked.

"We are merely a traveling group, nothing more. As I said, we are headed to the capital." Ren said again. "That animal is called a tiger. It comes from a far-off land. I found it many years ago and took it in when it was alone."

The guard looked them over once more. They were indeed a strange lot, but they didn't appear in search of trouble. Were they bandits or robbers, they wouldn't be traveling as they were. And none of the guards had heard any news of the sort.

Exchanging a quick glance at each other, the two guards released their spears, returning them to their sides.

"You have my appreciation for your understanding," Ren said. "I wish you and your families well in whatever future tidings you may have." The guards never said another word, only nodding back.

Ren and the others walked through the gate and into town. They stopped off to the side of the road. The dirt road beneath their feet was marked with use. Thin grooves had sunken in and morphed from the continuous use of horses and carriages.

"We should split up," Ren's master suggested. Half of us can look for an inn, while the other half can procure horses for tomorrow's journey."

"I agree," Ren's master said. "Ren, go with your father in search of our lodgings. You can take the girl with you too. Werewolf prince, Miss Rose, you two come with me to get the horses."

Ren took Ellie's hand, and then they and Ren's father went their separate ways.

At the first inn they saw, they stopped. It was two stories tall and made of wood with a stone front and base. The shutters on the windows were open, leaving a full view of the first-floor interior.

Leo opened the door, allowing Ren and Ellie to enter first. There were two tables for sitting and a front desk. A woman sat behind it, looking over a small stack of papers. When he asked for rooms, it turned out that the inn was completely full. With their first loss, they moved on to the next one, only to find it full as well.

Luck just was not on their side, it seemed, because their next two inns had no rooms either. One just had its last room purchased mere minutes ago, and the other, while it did have availability, did not have enough to accommodate them and their companions. Fortunately, the owner recommended them to another inn that could potentially accommodate them.

The inn they were recommended was located near the edge of town. It was three stories tall and had a stone façade. Its shutters were closed, so they couldn't see inside. Above the front door was a sign. Drunken Hostess.

Yeah, I can see this ending very badly, Ren thought.

Given its name and the mysterious atmosphere, he wasn't sure what to make of the place. Especially with Ellie there. But, there was always another side to everything, as he had learned through experience.

A bell rang when they opened the door. So far, none of the inns they had visited had a bell. It was common in establishments, but not all of them had one. To the left were stairs leading to the other floors. In front of the stair wall was the front desk. To the right was the dining area. There were at least a dozen tables, over half of which were occupied with two to four people.

No one was present at the front desk, so Ren rang the bell on top. A few moments later, a man came out from the back. In those few brief moments, the man took in everything he could. By their stature, two men, adults, and one child. And one strange creature of white and black. They were dressed in black and cloaked from head to toe, with their faces covered by their hoods. From their posture, he guessed that they were nobles. The question was, what were nobles doing in a place like this? Surely, there were more accommodating places. Trouble, a journey, maybe even an assignment from a high-ranking noble? It could be anything. Either way, there was a story there.

"How can I help you?" the man asked.

"We're looking for a single night's lodging. Would you happen to have two rooms available?" Ren asked.

The man looked them over. Finally, his eyes settled on Nidar. No doubt the tiger was strange to him.

"Is that a tiger?" he asked, surprising Ren and Leo.

"You know what he is?" Ren asked.

"I've been to the human world a few times. I've got family living over there."

This was it. This was the opportunity they were looking for to investigate the towns and villages.

Ren and his father exchanged glances beneath their hoods and silently nodded in unison.

"We have just returned from the human world and are heading home," Ren said.

"We have two rooms available right now," the man said. "Straight ahead, in the back. All the other ones are taken."

"We'll take them," Ren said. "We have acquaintances of ours on the way. We're going to need them both."

"How many?"

"Three."

"Two going to be enough?"

"We'll make it work."

"If you say so. Five Trenni silver." Ren grimaced beneath his hood.

Five Trenni silver. That was a lot of money for a cheap inn. But their rooms were located on the first floor. Rooms at the ground level, if an inn even had them at all, were typically used by the wealthy as they were always the best rooms. They were always the best rooms and, therefore, more expensive. The lower class took rooms on the higher levels, being cheaper the higher they went.

It was pretty rare for an inn, especially the further in the region one traveled, to have ground floor rooms. The value of coin out here was less than in the capital due to the rural nature. It made even constructing them difficult. They were as expensive to build as they were to stay in.

Ren wasn't keen on paying five Trenni silver since he didn't bring much money with him. Walking around with a bulging coin pouch was never a wise decision. One might as well paint a target on their back or wear it as decoration. But the chances of them finding another inn as perfect as this for information gathering were likely improbable. Not to mention, given their luck thus far and the consistent lack of availability, searching for other inns at this point would only be a detriment to them. It was better to just take what was in front of them.

Ren handed the man five silver coins and received two bronze keys in return.

"Take Ellie and Nidar to the rooms," he said, handing one to his father. "I'm going to find Marcus and the others."

"You want help?" his father asked.

"No. Ellie and Nidar need to rest, and I don't want them here alone. It's been a long day already. Where are the stables in this town?" Ren asked the guy behind the desk.

"There are two. One is south of here, on the other side of town. The other is a few minutes east of here."

Ren thanked the man, then adjusted his cloak and headed out the door. Two town stables was going to make this much more challenging. And it wasn't like he could just call them, either. It was better to stick close than wander aimlessly. He headed for the stables east of the inn, the ones closest.

The stable sat behind a single-story building. A dirt pathway on the right lead to them.

Ren headed inside to see if they were there. There was nothing but a front desk and a door behind it. A burly man manned the desk.

"Pardon me," Ren said. "I'm looking for my companions. Might three others all dressed like me have come here. They should have bought a small band of horses worth."

"They were here, yeah. Figured it best to wait for you if you came by. Said something about wanting to wait for their other companions. They're waiting out back."

"Thank you," Ren said.

The man nodded, and Ren walked to the stables out back. There were two in total, each one with room for eight horses.

Sitting on barrels of hay were Kelsey, Marcus, and his master, still hidden beneath their cloaks. Kelsey and Marcus sat next to each other, engaged in conversation. Ren caught a bit of it as he approached. Marcus was sharing tales of his horse-riding experiences.

"Ren and I had to catch the train, but it was moving too fast. Our horses couldn't keep up. But Ren said we 'absolutely' had to get on to the train. We had to brainstorm ways to get on board on the fly. So my dumb ass decided to jump straight off the horse to try and catch the train."

Kelsey burst out laughing, causing him to laugh too.

Marcus heard Ren approach before the others did. "Hey, there you are," he said. "Did you find an inn?"

"Yeah. It's about a ten-minute walk west from here. Not sure if it was luck or not that you guys chose this stable. The other is on the other side of town."

"We chose this one on purpose. When we were searching for the town stable and learned that there were two, we checked up on the inns nearby and found them all booked. The ones around here still have some availability. We figured this is where we'd end up."

"Good planning. Things turned out well for us, too. We found the perfect inn. The guy who checked us in has been to the human realm before."

"That's better for us. Did you get any info from him?"

"I didn't ask yet. I wanted you guys there first. Follow me; I'll lead the way."

The three of them followed Ren in silence. There were all manner of monsters walking around or riding horses. It was a strange experience for Kelsey and Ellie. They'd never seen so many monsters in their true forms. Least of all, going about their business as they pleased. It resembled very much their own world. Beyond the extent of appearances, they couldn't tell the difference.

Ren and the others reached the inn, and Ren opened the door first, hearing the familiar sound of the bell.

"Drunken Hostess?" Marcus asked, looking up at the sign.

"What? It was the first place with rooms to spare. Besides, it's not as bad as the name makes it sound," Ren said back.

They walked past the front desk toward the back of the inn. To the left was a small arched entryway connected to a hallway. There were six rooms total, three on each side. Theirs were the last two on the right side.

Ren knocked on the door before unlocking it. His father, Ellie, and Nidar were waiting inside.

The room was a decent size, with two beds and a fireplace. A stack of wood sat beside the fireplace. An animal rug lay in the middle of the floor with a wooden table and some chairs over it. A lantern sat on top of the table, and a second hung from one of the bed poles. The room had a single window on the back wall.

"Wow," Kelsey said.

To be honest, she wasn't sure what to expect. Staying at an inn, though similar in nature to a hotel, was vastly different in terms of living standards. But she had to admit, this wasn't bad.

"Damn, bro. First floor, huh?" Marcus noted.

"Not my idea. These were the last two rooms they had remaining. At least they can accommodate all of us."

"It's been a long day. Let's settle in a bit. We can get dinner afterward," Marcus said. Ren nodded in agreement.

Marcus, Ren's master, and his father abdicated the room to occupy the other. That left Kelsey, Ellie, Ren, and Nidar alone.

Ren sat down on one of the beds while Kelsey looked around the room. She noticed an adjoining room with a door. Inside was a single bathtub and a wash pan. She looked around for a few minutes before closing the door behind her.

Ellie sat on the second bed, petting Nidar. As for Ren, the second he closed his eyes, he was out like a light. When Kelsey finally emerged from the adjacent room, she sat beside him on the bed, propping his head up on her lap.

Marcus opened the door a little while later, only to see Kelsey playing with a sleeping Ren's hair.

"We're headed to dinner," he said. "Wake up sleeping beauty."

Kelsey chuckled and woke Ren up. His eyes opened to see Kelsey looking down on him, his head on her lap.

"Time to go eat," she said.

Fourteen

Words Best Spoken Cautiously

Ren yawned and sat up. He put his hand on his forehead before looking at Kelsey. She gave him a smile unlike any he had seen in a while.

Kelsey got to her feet, pulling Ren with her. He was still kind of out of it but quickly got ahold of his bearings.

Throwing on their cloaks, Kelsey took Ellie's hand before heading for the door, leaving Nidar to himself in the room. The rest of their party was already seated at a table. Each one contained four chairs, leaving the last one open. Rather than occupy it, Ren sat at a table instead immediately next to them. With three open chairs, Kelsey and Ellie joined him.

Ren did a quick scan of the dining area. Unlike when they first arrived, most of the tables were now occupied. There was no sign of the man behind the counter either. It appeared he was going to have to request him.

Kelsey observed all the different monsters around the room. Though they varied in race and appearance, she noticed two present that were greater in number than the others. The same race as the guards they met at the town gate and the other a hybrid of human and animal.

Like the ones at the town gate, the other members of their race wielded the same long limbs, pure white skin, and facelessness. As for the animal-human hybrids, they appeared mainly human but with animal parts or features.

Unlike the faceless monsters, Kelsey recognized the animal-human hybrid monsters. There were many stories about them back in the human world. She'd encountered some of them during the battle in Florida and some she knew personally.

"Beastkin," Ren said quietly. "And the other ones are nightcrawlers. They're common around these parts, farther from the capital. The beastkin, however, are generally well spread out. You'll see them often."

Seeing so many different races of monsters was fascinating. With the exception of the battle in Florida, she'd never seen them so exposed. And even then, not every monster fighting had taken their true form. Kelsey wondered what other races she'd encounter during her time here.

A woman approached both of their tables, dressed in an outfit far different from those worn by the inn's occupants. In her hand was a small pad of paper and a fountain pen. They guessed she was a waitress.

The woman stopped before them. Her brown hair was short-kept, curling at the base of her neck. And atop her head was a pair of small brown ears similar to a bear's with a small round tail behind her to match. She was a beastkin.

"I take it you are new around here. Welcome to the Drunken Hostess. What can I get for you, strangers?"

"The stew will be fine. With ale. We wish to retire for the night soon," Ren said back.

The waitress looked at the others, and they all nodded in agreement.

"Understood, I'll return shortly." The waitress bowed lightly before leaving with their order.

"Stew and ale?" Kelsey asked.

"They're common meals in this world," Ren said. "Better get used to them; there's going to be a lot. You're going to have to adapt until we get to the palace. Then you can eat or drink how you like."

The waitress returned with six large wooden mugs. Inside five was a golden liquid with a thick layer of foam on top. And in the sixth was a similar liquid, but of a much lighter color and with no foam. The lighter drink was placed in front of Ellie, and the other five were divided.

"Um, is that alcohol?" Kelsey asked.

"It is dear," the waitress said. "But it's meant for children. It's diluted. There's almost no alcohol in there at all."

"Perhaps a glass of water just in case would do," Ren said. "To help ease the lady's concerns."

"As you wish," the waitress said. She left to go get the water.

"You give alcohol to kids?" Kelsey asked Ren.

"Like I said, Kells, this is common, just like it was in your world at one point. Water and ale were the primary sources of drink. Wine if you were wealthy, and not as often, milk."

The waitress returned again with another wooden mug, this time filled with water.

"Thank you," Ellie said.

"You're welcome, dearie," the waitress responded, and then she was gone again.

"I'll be back," Ren said, getting to his feet.

"Where are you going?" Kelsey asked him.

"To find some information." He walked away without another word.

Only minutes later, their stew was delivered to their tables, along with two loaves of bread. The waitress set them down before each of them. That's when she finally noticed Ren's absence.

"Where did your companion go?" she asked.

"He'll be back momentarily," Marcus responded.

The woman put her hands on her hips but never said another word.

"Enjoy, darlings." She turned to leave again just as Ren returned with a man at his heels. The same man who had run the counter when they first arrived.

Ren retook his seat, and the man took the empty chair at his father's table. The first thing Kelsey noticed was that he looked like a human. No, he didn't just look it. He actually was in a human form.

"Quite the gathering. I take it this is the rest of your party?" the man asked.

Ren confirmed his suspicions with a nod before taking a drink from the mug of ale in front of him.

"Now," he said. "I asked you to our table because I have some questions for you."

"What kind of questions?"

"You have spent time in the human world, as you said earlier." The man nodded. "The truth is, we have just returned from the human world and are in need of information. I want to know the current state of things in this town."

"And why do you seek this knowledge if I might be so bold as to ask?"

Ren was quiet for a moment. "I wish I could tell you. However, there are too many eyes and ears here."

Several seconds of silence passed before the man got to his feet. He walked to the windows, their shutters still closed, and locked each of them. Then, he went for the door, his actions drawing the attention of the rest of the inn.

Once the inn was locked tight, the man retook his seat at their table.

"That takes care of the eyes and ears outside. As for those inside, most of them are regulars and good people. Our customers are known for being tight-lipped. They won't tell anyone anything about this conversation."

Ren exchanged glances with his father and Marcus, both of whom nodded in return. With everyone in agreement, the three of them pulled down their hoods, revealing their faces, and all conversation ceased instantly.

With the three of them exposed, Ren's master, Kelsey, and Ellie lowered their hoods as well.

The entire inn removed themselves from their seats and dropped to one knee, overtaken by surprise.

"Your Majesty, Your Highness, you have finally returned," the man said. "And Prince Allagash, Lord Vaylor, this humble old man greets you with much joy in his heart. It is truly an honor that you would choose our small humble inn to stay at. Welcome home."

"Forgive us for hiding our identities. We're trying to act in secrecy while we return to the palace, in hopes of learning the state of affairs of our world while we have been gone."

"I am honored to provide you with whatever knowledge I can. Perhaps it is a boon from the gods, but despite our remote station, word flows well around here. There's news of a rare import arriving in town soon. Word is it will fetch a hefty sum, but no one knows if it's true. While rumors always spread, our value of coin so far out has not gained in value. However, it has not degraded enough to affect our overall way of life here. Things tend to fluctuate within a certain margin based on the passing seasons, as is expected."

"Our exportation of wheat and milk has recently increased, and, to the benefit of the town, we have found use of those who are ill beneficial." Ren nodded, an indication for him to continue. "While the pay is little, rather than let them rot away in darkness, they are tasked with cleaning the streets and tending to mundane tasks in the form of official requests by the citizens. The lack of smell and increase in cleanliness is slow but improving."

"Labor in lieu of imprisonment. Very innovative. That's a good use of a little extra money towards the caretaking of the town and its people." The man nodded back in agreement.

"And as for the political situation?" Ren questioned.

"I'm afraid I cannot say much on that aspect, Your Highness. Forgive me for being unable to provide you with any real information. The duke in charge of our land, Duke Champaign, has not made any worthwhile changes. We had some problems with bandits a while back, but he took care of them. We did, however, get a new tax collector. The previous collector stepped down from his position due to his elderly age. A new one was recently appointed in his stead."

"Concern was high around here at the time," he continued. "With a new tax collector, there was no telling what kind of man they would be or how they would alter our flow of coin. Luckily, those concerns were unfounded. The new tax collector is a kind and generous man, just like his predecessor. No collection rate has been changed."

"I see. If he is as capable as you say he is, I doubt the alteration of taxes would too adversely affect the town's income. Still, I shall check the statements and situation when I reach the palace. We shall see if we can lower your taxes or not. A lower tax rate would spur the value of the coin here a little, allowing for greater access to your farms and fields. It would also help with your little cleaning project."

"Indeed, Your Highness. Thank you."

Their conversation continued for hours, alternating between Ren, Marcus, and Ren's father questioning the man and the occasional response from the other residents around them.

Ren finished his stew and ale and then got up from his seat. "We should get some sleep," he told the others.

"Oh, one last thing, Your Highnesses, Your Majesty."

"Go on, what is it?" Ren asked.

"I don't know how true they are, but I have heard rumors coming from the North. Word is preparations are in the making for the construction of a town."

"A whole town?" Leo asked.

"Yes, Your Majesty. Apparently, they stumbled across a bounty of hot springs while mining for ore."

"Hmm, interesting. I will look into it immediately once we return to the capital. If these rumors are true, then there are many questions that need answering. And many proceedings to attend. Building a whole town is not cheap, nor will it be quick. However, it could provide potentially exponential profits. Thank you for the information."

"And, again, if you could do us a favor and not mention our presence, that would be great," Ren requested.

"Of course, Your Highness. You have my word. I wish you all safe travels on your journey back."

"Much appreciated."

Ren surprised the man by holding out his hand. After getting his bearings, he happily shook it, following up with a handshake with Leo.

With the information fresh in their minds, they all returned to their rooms. There were interesting things happening while they were gone. They were going to be very busy for a long time.

Ren woke up with his arms around Kelsey. She was lying next to him, with her back pressed against his chest.

He sat up and rubbed his eyes. Ellie was lying next to Kelsey just like she had been with him.

On the other side of the room, Marcus was lying in the second bed. The werewolf in question rolled over before sitting up. He yawned and stretched before getting to his feet.

"What time is it?" he asked.

"Not sure. I just got up, too," Ren said back.

The two of them put on their boots and walked to the door. With their presence at the inn exposed, there was no need for them to conceal themselves.

"Good morning, Your Highnesses," someone greeted. It was a woman manning the front desk.

"Can I be of any assistance to you?"

"We'd like some water," Marcus said. "Might I inquire as to the location of your well?"

"The well is out back. Just head through that door right there." She pointed to a door at the back of the inn, twenty feet to their left.

"Thank you," Marcus responded.

They opened the door and stepped into the cool summer morning air. Clouds covered much of the midnight blue sky, though they didn't look like rain clouds. They expected a good day.

The well was circular and made of stone. A wood roof covered it on posts with a rope and crank attached to it. Marcus cranked the lever, lowering the bucket into the well. Once filled, he raised the bucket. When it reached the top, he grabbed it.

Ren grabbed another wooden bucket from inside the inn, and Marcus poured the water into it. This water wasn't for drinking. They would use it to wash their faces and wipe down the previous day's fatigue. Now with fresh water, the two of them headed inside.

While Marcus set the bucket down, Ren tossed some firewood into the fireplace and started a fire. It would take a little while for the room to warm up, but that didn't stop them from relaxing. Ren and Marcus sat next to each other, feeling the heat of the flames and enjoying each other's company.

When the sun rose above the horizon, they woke up the others.

"Kelsey," Ren called. "Kells. Wake up." Kelsey stirred then and opened her eyes. "Rise and shine." Kelsey sat up, and Ren woke Ellie next.

They used the collected water in the bucket to wash their faces. The cool water helped wake them up much quicker than without it.

Once everyone was ready, they gathered their gear and belongings and put on their cloaks.

Returning their keys to the rooms as they left, Ren and Marcus led the way to the stables. A stable boy was outside tending to the horses.

"Can I help you?" he asked.

"We're here to pick up our horses," Marcus told him. He handed the boy a piece of paper with a written description and signature on it.

"You are the group my father sold the lot of horses to. They are ready for you."

In the second stable, four horses were saddled and ready to ride. They were all around the same size and weight with matching brown coats.

"Only four? But there are six of you?" the boy asked.

"One of our companions will be riding our large feline friend here," Marcus said, indicating Nidar. "And the child will ride with one of us."

Ren climbed on Nidar and nodded from underneath his cloak as the others mounted a horse. Kelsey let Ellie ride with her.

"You know how to ride?" Marcus asked Kelsey.

"I used to take horseback riding lessons," she said.

Marcus nodded, pleased with her ability. "Well, alright then. Let's get going, shall we."

They rode onto the main street and toward the gate on the other side of the city. Two new guards were present this time. The guards let them through with little problems, and they were on their way.

Aside from Marcus, there was concern about Ren being unable to keep up. But when they looked to the side, Nidar was running alongside them with little effort. Thanks to Ren's magic and training, he wasn't just a regular tiger and was more than able to keep up with the horses.

"It's a hard days' ride to the village of Darrat," Ren said. "Then another hour to the next town. We should make it before the sun fully sets."

The six of them rode for hours in silence, only focusing on what was in front of them. They passed several towns and villages along the way, some of which they stopped at to gather information. Just like Ren had said, it was a full days' ride to Darrat, having stopped several times to let Nidar and the horses rest.

Darrat was much more rundown than any of them had expected, but they rode through without attracting any unwanted attention. Then, after almost another hour of riding, they finally came upon their first city.

Far out in the distance, standing as strong as a fortress and surrounding the entire city, was a giant stone wall.

Fifteen

Redswallow

The city wall looked even more incredible the closer they got to it. Its grand stature only empowered the city, and they weren't even close to it yet.

Ren's sudden laughter finally tore Kelsey and Ellie away from it. "You should see the look on your faces."

Nidar shifted beneath Ren. The tiger leaned forward to stretch and shook his body.

"You alright, bud?" Ren asked him. "Ready for the final stretch?"

Nidar looked up at him, and Ren saw the readiness in his eyes. He smiled with a light nod, understanding the tiger's feelings.

Ren spurred Nidar forward, and he shot toward the city. Trees passed by as they ran, the wind blowing at Ren's hair and throwing it behind him. He felt completely at peace in those moments.

It took ten minutes of fast riding to reach the city gates. Two guards flanked the sides, and three more stood around, securing the area. And along the top of the wall, three more guards watched in silence, as still as the wall they guarded, all dressed in blue and yellow armor with silver shoulder and forearm guards. Though they carried a variety of weapons, each one had a sword sheathed at their hip.

"There are so many guards," Kelsey said. "More than any other town we've been to."

"That's because this is a major city in our kingdom," Leo said. "A big city needs a lot of guards. Should something happen, the defense of the city and its people falls onto them."

"Plus, this city is under the authority of a marquis," Marcus said. "Marquis Redswallow."

"I've heard the marquis is a war hero, dating back to the last war with the kingdoms to the West," Ren's master said.

"That he is. He wiped out a whole battalion by himself and saved his assault forces in the process," Leo said.

"He also saved the ambassador from another kingdom during one of the battles," Ren said. "And his list of achievements doesn't stop there. To many, he's a hero and war veteran. However, some of the other nobles' opinions are not as grand. Jealousy and fear run deep in the hearts of the weak, unfortunately."

"I've been trying to make him a duke for a while now, but the process is slow," Leo said. "It requires approval from the archduke and the rest of the council."

"Perhaps we should pay him a visit," Marcus suggested. "It would do us a lot of good to find out what he knows."

"I agree," Leo said. "We'll pay a visit to his mansion once we've made it into the city."

Kelsey looked at Ren, noticing his change in condition. He was serious, his face paler. And she wasn't the only one to notice either. Marcus, however, was the only one to act, chuckling silently. Apparently, he knew something the others didn't. Ren's father was the second person to realize the reason, mouthing a silent *'oh.'*

There was no time to ask Ren what was wrong before they reached the gate. Then again, Kelsey figured it was something personal, so she would ask him later in private.

"Stop!" one of the guards said, approaching cautiously.

The first thing they noticed was that everyone hid their faces. The second thing they noticed was Nidar. Like many others, the tiger was a strange creature to them.

"Identification. What brings you to Vale?" the guard asked.

From atop Nidar, Ren looked at the guard. The guard managed a quick look at one of his cobalt blue eyes, the remainder still hidden beneath his cloak.

"We're traveling to the capital," Ren said. "While in Vale, we wish to meet with Marquis Redswallow."

"The marquis has little time for uninvited guests, least of all strangers such as yourselves. Commoners seeking time with the lord will be met by his aids. Identification," he repeated.

Ren had his identification. They all did, except for Kelsey and Ellie. The problem was, revealing them would reveal themselves and blow their cover. Ren would have to find a way around this without exposing them.

"I see you deny identifying yourselves. Strangers who refuse to cooperate must have something to hide. I think you're not who you claim you are." The guard drew his sword. "You can't fool me, hands of Verin."

The remaining guards around them and flanking the gates, and atop the wall, readied their weapons.

"Ren!" Kelsey screamed quietly.

Arrows were aimed at them from above. The guard nearly signaled to cut them down when Ren's chuckling stopped him.

"Do you find your death amusing?"

"Oh, no. I'm glad to see that things have been kept in line while we were gone."

"What nonsense are you talking about?"

Ren pulled his hood back just enough for the guard to see, revealing his face. The guard immediately dropped to the ground, placing his sword on the ground beside him.

"Your Highness, you've returned!" he said excitingly. "Forgive me, my lord. I dared to draw my words and my blade on you. I beg your forgiveness. Let your wrath be yielded upon my men. They merely followed my commands."

"Stand up," Ren told him. "On this occasion, I do not deem punishment necessary."

The guard looked up at him with benevolence. He couldn't actually believe he was being spared.

"You have done your job admirably, soldier. Your actions were not incorrect. However, as revealing my information, and therefore myself, puts me in a rather precarious situation, you understand my lack of cooperation."

"Yes, Your Highness. I understand completely."

"Good. You and your men all deserve a good rest and full stomachs tonight. I will see to it that you receive them."

"Your generosity knows no bounds, Your Highness."

Leo and Marcus pulled their hoods back as well. Like Ren, they exposed themselves just enough for the guard alone to see their faces.

"We want to meet with the marquis to discuss the status of his territory and abroad," Ren explained. "Perhaps news of events in the human world has already started to spread."

"Word has already has, Your Highness. It travels through the land slowly but surely."

Ren nodded to the guard and pulled his hood back over his head. "If you could be so kind as to do me a favor. No one knows we have returned yet, and I would appreciate it if it stayed that way. It makes information gathering easier."

"As you wish. I will make sure your identities remain unknown."

"Many thanks for your understanding."

"Of course, Your Highness. Please, enjoy your time here."

At the guard's signal, the other guards parted and let them pass.

Beyond the city gates, they stepped into a world that reminded Kelsey of home. Monsters of all kinds were walking everywhere. All shapes and sizes, all different colors and skins. There were more than she could count of all races, shapes, and sizes, with plenty more to be seen.

Leo led the way to the marquis's mansion. It was fixed to the far-right side of the city, within a secondary wall. The city wall sat directly behind it, with two gates linking the two at the back.

Made of stone and glass windows, it stood taller than any other building in town. Just looking at it, one could tell that it was undoubtedly a medieval mansion.

They walked up to the manor and were met with no ordinary group of guards. These were knights, and worked directly for the marquis. Ren and the other were stopped immediately at the entrance.

"We've come to see the marquis," Leo said.

"And just who are you? I've no knowledge of the marquis expecting any visitors. Do you have an appointment?"

Leo raised his hood just enough for the guard to see his face. "Do not bow," Leo told him. "It will draw too much attention."

"Your Majesty!" the knight said. He gave a light nod of his head.

"You are here in secret, then?"

"Yes. You can consider us unexpected visitors."

"Very well. I will bring you to Marquis Redswallow. He's in his study right now."

The knight led them into the manor, up to the third floor where the marquis's study resided. When they finally arrived, the knight stopped and knocked on the door, waiting patiently.

"Enter," came a deep voice from the other side.

The knight opened the door, and everyone stepped inside.

The marquis was at his desk looking over a stack of papers. Though his face was human, he had a mane of long, thick black hair on his head with black eyes to match and a shadow on his jaw. Two rounded animal ears stuck up on top. His arms were strong and muscular, and he was dressed in attire similar to what Marcus wore at the press conference back in the human world. Only the marquis's wasn't as fancy.

"Reynal, what is this?" the marquis asked, looking up from his papers.

"Forgive me, my lord, but it was necessary for me to bring these individuals to you."

"Oh, was it now?" He looked at the six of them. "Forgive me for being unable to greet you properly. I am a busy man with much to do. Who are you, and what can I do for you?"

"I think the question is, what can we do for you?" Leo asked back.

The marquis's eyes widened. "That voice!" Leo pulled down his hood. "Your Majesty!" The marquis dropped to one knee in front of his desk. "I am overjoyed at your presence."

He wasn't just strong; he was tall, too. The guy had to be near six and a half feet. It made Kesley feel like a dwarf in comparison.

Everyone else but Ren pulled their hoods down.

"Prince Allagash, it is good to see you again."

"And you as well, Marquis Redswallow."

"Please, everyone, sit down." He had servants grab chairs for them to sit in while his attention turned to Ren, who still had his hood up.

"And who might our hidden friend here be?" he asked. Ren said nothing back, only keeping quiet.

The marquis embraced Ren tightly, picking him right off his feet with their size difference. Ren's hood fell down with him when the marquis released him.

"Ah, Ren, it's good to see you again. So, what can I do for you guys?"

"We are headed to the capital," Leo said. "Along the way, we're gathering information. Domestic and abroad. It has been many decades, after all."

"Yes, I understand. I can't give you much insight into the affairs of foreign nations as much as I can ours, however. Only what I hear through rumors."

The marquis told them everything he could. Political and economic activities, plots by other nobles, trades, trends, and foreign affairs and influence as part of relations with neighboring kingdoms.

Ren and his father took in everything. Not a single piece of information was useless. And Jonah was someone they could trust, unlike some of the other nobles. They were confident that his information was credible. Information that was beneficial to Marcus as well.

As Ren's best friend and the heir to his own kingdom, Marcus needed to understand the internal affairs of Ren's kingdom. It was necessary to aid Ren when required and to keep the peace between their kingdoms. The werewolves and vampires have been allies for millennia, and he intended to keep it that way.

By the time the marquis had finished talking, the sun sat halfway above the horizon, casting the evening sky a dazzling orange, pink, and red.

"Thanks for the information, Jonah," Ren said, using the marquis's first name. Despite his earlier awkwardness, it was clear that the two of them were well acquainted and on favorable terms.

Ren looked out the window at the sunset. "We should get going," he said.

"What's the rush?" Jonah asked.

"We still have to find an inn to stay at," he confessed.

"No need. I'll have the servants prepare spare rooms for you. We have plenty. Besides, it's been a long time since I had company over whose presence I find pleasing."

Ren chuckled at his comment. "Then we'll take you up on your offer. Thank you."

"You're welcome. I will have the servants show you to your rooms, then bring you to dinner."

Sixteen

One Who Ends Life

S plash!

Water sprayed as hooves hit the ground. The uneven dirt road was buried in puddles from the previous night's rain. The mixture of water and mud flying behind them was proof of the speed they were riding.

It had been several days since the meeting with Marquis Redswallow. Ren and the others were currently riding through the kingdom, within the day's reach of the capital. Their long journey was finally coming to an end. And just in time, too. After three days of non-stop riding, the weariness of constant travel was starting to settle in.

Ren looked around at his surroundings. Everything was as familiar as the day he left. He knew the roads, knew the towns. Which meant he knew exactly where they were. Glancing up, his eyes found the sun, taking its position above his head. *Noon,* he thought. That was perfect.

"We're almost there, guys. Just another two hours until we reach the capital," Ren said.

"We're finally almost there?" Ellie asked.

"Yeah, we're almost there."

Two hours. He was only two hours from home. It invigorated him. He wished he could fly there as fast as his wings would carry him. But they were still keeping their identities hidden. Rumors of their return were floating around, but luckily, most just wrote them off as that—rumors.

"We should take a break," Marcus suggested. "Let's stop for a rest. After that, it's a straight shot to the capital."

Ren and the others agreed to take a break. They turned and rode off the dirt road into the brush. Ren dismounted Nidar and sat on the ground, feeling the grass beneath him. The tiger plopped down beside him, stretching himself out beneath the sun. It was shining directly on them, leaving the cloudless sky open to the full impact of its rays. It was another beautiful day.

Marcus sat down next to him just moments later, joining them at Ren's free side.

"We're almost there," Marcus said.

"Almost," Ren said back.

"I'm sure everyone will be glad to have us back," Marcus said. "It has been a long time."

"Can't say I'm not anxious or curious to see how things have developed," Ren said back.

"I wouldn't be too worried. After all, you put Randolph in charge of the kingdom while you were gone. Besides, Neil is at his side. Your personal aid is truly one of a kind."

"I have the utmost faith in his skills. In both of them."

"Ren, can I sit with you?" Ellie interrupted.

"Sure, munchkin'." She sat down in his lap, leaning her head against him.

"So, what do we do about Verin?" Marcus asked.

"I don't know," Ren said back. "With Kelsey looking into the stones, that might provide us with a little insight. At least, I hope."

"You mean the fifteenth floor of the library."

"Yeah. And with us having to do our jobs, the mountains of paperwork will take up most of our time."

"So that leaves us with what? Should we rely on an outside source?"

"I'm not so sure that's a good idea. Aside from your kingdom, I don't necessarily trust that whoever we pick doesn't work for Verin himself. And, of course, that applies within my kingdom, too. That's why I'm going to call all the nobles together and have a full assembly to address the matter."

"So we lure them out. Then, we can figure out to whom to entrust the job. Have you thought about using someone within the court in the palace?"

"It's crossed my mind, but I haven't made a definitive choice yet. Though I do have my picks on hand. There are more than a few capable people for the job, but this is about being more than just capable."

Marcus leaned in close and whispered to him. "What about your cousin?"

Ren looked at him like they were both thinking the same thing. "I already have. He's top of my list."

"As close as you two are, and given as much authority as he has, not to mention his list of contacts, he might be the best option for you to use. And I'm sure he'd do it, too."

"Probably. Verin's forces did kill his uncle. And they were pretty close. As close as I am with my father."

"Consider it. If we do decide to ask him, I'll be there with you. This is a big deal for all of us. With both of us there, it might spur the importance of the situation," Marcus said. "I'm sure he's already heard of everything that happened in the human world. He knows what's at stake and how important it is to find Verin, especially now."

Ren nodded. "We'll see what he says." Marcus returned the gesture.

"We should get going," Ren's father said.

Ren almost got up when he noticed Ellie wasn't moving. Her eyes were closed as she leaned against him. She was fast asleep.

"Do you think you can carry two, bud?" he asked Nidar. The tiger made no movement, only staring at him. Finally, he looked from Ren to Ellie, then ahead of them toward the direction they had been traveling. Returning his gaze to Ren again, he nodded and got to all fours.

Ren placed Ellie on Nidar's back and climbed on behind her.

When everyone was mounted up and ready, Ren ushered Nidar forward, and they returned to the road, continuing on as they had been toward the capital.

Nidar kept a fast pace, but not too fast. He made sure not to make any quick or excessive movements so as to not wake Ellie.

Kelsey chuckled when she saw Ren and Ellie riding Nidar. She was still fast asleep, and Ren had one hand around her to support her. Once again, Kelsey was amazed at how smart and capable the tiger was. He was stronger and more intelligent than any other tiger she'd seen, either in person or otherwise. It likely had to do with how Ren raised him, and some magic, too.

When Kelsey laughed, Ren knew it was directed at him. He smirked, then rolled his eyes and shook his head.

Splash! They rode through another puddle. The evidence of rain slowly disappeared the closer they got to the capital. Now, there were far and few signs of it. They rode down the dirt road, which left them exposed to the world. Green spread as far as they could see in all directions. They were surrounded by an ocean of green grass. The only break was the dirt road they rode on.

A cool and refreshing breeze blew across the grassland, enveloping them in a gush of fresh air. Ren breathed in through his nose, stretching his arms out to the side, and took in a big lungful of air.

Ren looked at the sky again, then at the surroundings, noting their location.

"We're getting close," he said to the others. "Only another forty-five minutes or so. Give or take five, maybe ten minutes."

Forty-five minutes was both a good and a terrible sound. They were almost to the capital; the minutes were counting down. But they still had a whole forty-five minutes to go. Another forty-five minutes on horseback after days of riding. Or, in Ren's case, tigerback. Hopefully, it would go quickly.

The slight gathering of clouds in the bright blue sky seemed like something out of a movie. White fluffy spots of different shapes and sizes floating blissfully through the sky.

They rode for another couple of minutes before Ren pulled Nidar to a stop.

"What's wrong? Why are we stopping?" the others asked.

"Do you smell that?" Ren asked. He dismounted, careful to ensure that Ellie didn't fall off. Marcus and Ren's master dismounted and followed him.

Ren walked into the grass before he came to a stop. They were out of earshot from the others at that distance.

"What's up?" Marcus asked, walking up to him.

"That's what's up," Ren said back. They stopped dead in their tracks.

Lying on the ground was a girl, turned entirely to stone. She was human-sized with butterfly wings on her back. Her hair was sprawled out beneath her, and her eyes were still open.

"An Irshi," Marcus said.

"It was almost too faint for me to notice, but I smelled blood."

Marcus wasn't surprised Ren had noticed something like this. His senses and ability to detect blood have always been incredibly high, even before awakening.

Ren's master knelt down and examined her. Her skin, though it was hard to tell, had been severely burned. The texture of the skin just barely reflected through the stone, so he could tell. There was a pool of dried blood beneath her body. And on her neck were two large holes that looked like fang bites. Something had bitten her, something big. This was no accident. Nor was it swift. Whatever had attacked her hadn't killed her right away.

"What could have done this?" Marcus wondered.

"Fang bites, petrified, and terribly burned. And based on her position, I'd say she was induced with paralysis," Ren said. "There's only one kind of creature I can think of that could do something like this. A chimera."

Marcus swallowed. "What in the hell would a chimera be doing all the way out here?"

"I don't know. And I don't want to find out."

"Then I suggest we get going in case it returns and we do," Ren's master said. They nodded and headed back to the others.

"Come on, we're almost there," Ren said, not giving them time to ask any questions. Urging Nidar forward with great haste, they raced toward the capital.

When a blood-curdling roar appeared out of nowhere, Nidar skidded to a stop, the others nearly losing control of the horses.

The Sudden gathering of magic took them by surprise. Just as well since they couldn't see the caster.

"Move!" Ren yelled.

They all scattered as a sphere of flames struck the ground. Ren turned Nidar around just in time to see a beast of an amalgamate of parts land. It had the body of a giant lion with a goat head on its back, large webbed wings, and the tail of a snake. A chimera. Ren knew instantly that this was the chimera responsible for the death of that Irshi. And on its back sat a man with long brown hair, bangs pushed to the side of his face and fell to his jawline. A mask covered the right side of his face, giving a view of one black eye and a scar across his cheek.

He was dressed in a black and red military uniform with armored boots, brandishing three blades of different sizes in the back. A military hat with a golden ranking symbol on the front sat atop his head and a red cape atop his shoulders.

Dozens of shades gathered around them, their presence gone unnoticed until then. Their numbers circled them, containing them to their spot. They were surrounded.

Seventeen

Island of Vesta

The identity of the man atop the chimera was perhaps less important than how he managed to tame the beast. Chimeras were artificially created creatures using black magic. They should be uncontrollable, and yet, they were witnessing anything but.

"Finding you was a lot easier than I thought it would be," the man said. "Once I learned of your arrival and your heading, all I needed was to throw a bit of bait in your path, and you'd flock right to it. You're very predictable, you know. But that does make it exciting in its own way, I suppose."

The recognition that this stranger knew them and their movements was suddenly more important and far more concerning than how he managed to take the chimera.

From atop the chimera, the man gave a light bow. "The pleasure is all mine, Prince Nightwalker. I am Wei Shu."

"How do you know who I am? More so, how did you know where I was going?"

"Simple, where else would you have gone upon your return? Word gets around. We have our supporters, just as you do, you know."

We? That was something for Ren to take note of. So he didn't work alone, and by guess, he wasn't in charge either. Either way, he was clearly an enemy.

Ren watched from above as Wei slipped on a pair of golden gauntlets and then punched his knuckles together.

"The others disagree with me, but I know what you'll be capable of if left alone. You've become a problem that needs to be dealt with, and if they refuse to act before it's too late, I shall instead. So let's get started, shall we?"

The chimera flew at them, and the shades all charged. Ren drew his pistols and fired, but the chimera flew into the air, avoiding the bullets.

He continued to fire. He dropped his last empty clips and holstered his guns.

"Damn it! Quick bastard."

Ren drew Shadow Hunter, spinning it around in his hand. His wings shot out from his back, and he launched himself at Wei Shu. Ren crashed into him and tackled him clean off the chimera.

Nidar leaped into the air and sank his teeth into the beast's wing. His claws ripped its hide to shreds, causing it to roar in pain. The chimera spun around, bathing the area in flames from the goat head on its back. Nidar jumped off the beast, avoiding the snake tail snapping at him.

Rising to his hind legs, the tiger's claws found the lion head's right eye. It roared in pain and backed off before the goat head unleashed a barrage of magic. Alas, Nidar was far too quick for it to catch.

Marcus and Kelsey unleashed the full fury of the stones and ice daggers on the shades, cutting down half of them with great speed. Ren's master and his father worked together to quickly rift the other half.

Wei Shu crashed into the ground when Ren spread his wings, coming to a stop, and released him. The impact did little to jar him, however, as the guy got to his feet immediately.

Shadow Hunter's blade stopped dead against Wei' Shu's gauntlets. That's how Ren knew they were no normal weapon. Even with ki flowing through them, each impact canceled the other's out. Ren swung Shadow Hunter, and Wei Shu raised his hand, the blade sliding off the back.

Quicker than he could react, Ren was struck in the stomach. Wei Shu's ki flowed through him, and Ren was sent flying, tumbling across the ground. He got to his feet, holding his injured stomach.

This guy was no joke. Ren could tell even in their short exchange of blows. Whoever he was, he was a threat, and right now, they didn't need another one of those. There were other consequences at stake. Engaging in combat here only put them at a disadvantage. They needed to regroup and get out of there fast. Their only chance was to create a distraction. But what kind?

"Your speed is impressive, as is your skill with a blade. I understand how you have risen to the status that you have. Unfortunately, it seems this little introduction has reached its conclusion."

Wei Shu looked to the side when the last of the shades had been rifted. His momentary distraction was enough for Ren to use for his gain.

Burying the tip of Shadow Hunter's blade into the ground, Ren gathered his magic into the sword, feeling his partner lending him his own strength. The magic grew quickly, radiating off the sword in a golden glow.

"Everyone, close your eyes!" Ren yelled.

Marcus and the others immediately shut their eyes when they saw the magic gathering around Shadow Hunter. Wei Shu looked back at Ren as a blinding gold light appeared and ripped through the area. The general threw his hands up but failed to shield himself from the rays, blinding him temporarily. He dropped to his knees and the chimera reared back before running off, blinded by the golden light as well.

Ren grabbed hold of Nidar and hopped into the tiger's back. They shot forward as fast as he could run. Only when the general and chimera were long out of sight did they finally slow down, giving time for the others to catch up to them.

"What was that?" Marcus asked, just as taken aback as the rest of them.

"That was one of Verin's generals," Ren answered, rendering them a loss for words. "And we need to get out of here before he recovers and comes back."

They started moving again, riding non-stop until the capital came into view. Kelsey almost fell off her horse. Her jaw dropped wide open.

In the distance, a mountain range spread out along the horizon. And above, floating high into the sky, was a giant floating island.

Eighteen

Homecoming

"Oh. My. God!" Kelsey said in shock. Her brain was doing backflips in her head.

Wow, wow, just wow. She was speechless. *A floating island!*

Ren nudged Ellie, who was still sleeping. "Ellie, we're almost there, munchkin'."

Ellie opened her eyes halfway and yawned. "We are?" she asked, still partially asleep.

"Look over there." Ren pointed to the floating island in the sky.

Ellie's half-open eyes suddenly opened as wide as they could go. "WOW! What is that? It's flying!"

"That's my home," he said. "Welcome to Vesta."

"Ren, your home is amazing! It flies! Just like an airplane!"

Ren chuckled. "It doesn't actually fly munchkin'; it just floats."

"Five whole days, and we finally made it," Kelsey said.

"Technically, we haven't made it yet," Ren said. "We still have to get to the island."

"Yeah, about that," Kelsey said. "How do we get up there?"

"With that," Ren said. He pointed ahead of them.

It wasn't more than a fifteen-minute ride to a town in front of them. But it wasn't the town Ren was pointing to; it was the flying ship heading up to the island.

"A flying ship. I guess I shouldn't be surprised about that."

"It's even more impressive in person," Marcus said. He touched his heel into his horse's side, and it started running.

"Ready?" Ren asked Ellie. "We're going to go fast."

Ellie grabbed Nidar's fur on the back of his head. "Let's go," she said.

"Come on, bud. Let's catch up," Ren told Nidar. Nidar roared and took off running.

Ren and Ellie had to hold on with all their strength to keep from falling off, but with Nida's speed, they caught up very quickly.

They reached the edge of the town and stopped. Appearances could certainly be deceiving. The town itself was still relatively small, but what they had seen from a distance was only a small portion.

At first, it appeared rundown, but a closer inspection revealed an unexpected beauty. Built into the face of a cliff, the rest of it descended down a large slope. The roads were made of large stone slabs, the buildings of earthen materials. Lights secured to the faces of the buildings and lanterns that hung from street lamps cast an orange glow along the buildings and streets.

"This town serves as a port town and main transport to Vesta," Leo said. "The cliffs and rocky terrain make it a suitable place for building high and docking flying ships. You won't find another town or city like it in these lands. Follow me; the docks are this way."

Leo turned and rode down a pathway leading down the cliffside. They had to be slow and careful, lest their horses lose their footing and they all take a long and painful tumble.

He led them all to the edge of the town, where a giant wooden tree stood fifty feet off the ground on a platform. No, it wasn't a tree; it just looked like one. The entire construction was the docks. The trunk was hollow, with five sets of stairs that ascended to the upper levels. The main branches led to the individual docks on both sides.

"Wait here, and don't remove your cloaks," Leo said. He dismounted and disappeared into a crowd of people. Minutes later, he returned with slips of paper for each of them.

"The next ship to Vesta doesn't arrive for another hour, so get comfortable. Here," he said, handing the passes to everyone. "Don't lose them."

Ren found a small open area to rest while they waited. He helped Ellie down from Nidar's back before plopping down on the ground and crossing his arms beneath the back of his head. Nidar curled up next to him while Ellie just sat next to them quietly.

Marcus spotted Ren first, taking the next open spot and copying his eased demeanor. Kelsey found them next, sitting beside Ellie and watching the scenery. She focused on what was in front of her until her eyes started darting back and forth toward Ren. Soon, she couldn't take her eyes off of him.

They were lying there in silence when the first sound of wind hit Marcus's ears. A large object was heading toward them and closing in. "Ship's here," he said. "Let's get moving."

He and Ren were on their feet, forcing the others to follow them. At the base of the tree dock, a loud voice boomed over the area, calling for all those headed to Vesta. Ren and the others joined with a crowd of people and began their ascent up the tree, taking it all the way to the top branches. Thank the gods none of them were afraid of heights; otherwise, they would have died from shock.

Minutes later, a ship came into view. It was hard to make out any details until it got closer. By all rights, it resembled a nineteenth-century flagship. Only this one had large sails on the side spread out like wings and a small pair toward the back.

"That's our ride," Ren said. "Get ready."

The ship flew in, slowing to a complete stop next to a wooden dock that made of one of the tree's branches. Dozens of ropes were thrown over the side to men on the dock below, who tied them around posts, securing the ship in place. Once secure, a wooden ramp was laid out.

Before the group boarding the ship could do so, another group already on the ship had to disembark. Only when the previous passengers were all off the ship was the group Ren and the other were a part of allowed to board.

Ren stepped onto the ramp and headed up to the ship. The feeling of being on that ramp, or moreover, of stepping onto that ship, was something he had long since forgotten. Still, it was something he appreciated. He had taken these ships many times, after all. This was nothing new to him, but it had been so long; it was like when he reunited with Kelsey back in the human world.

"Why don't you sit down," he suggested to Kelsey. "It takes an hour to get to the capital. You should get comfortable." Oh great, more waiting.

Kelsey took a seat, and Ren sat down next to her.

"Ren!" Ellie ran up to him. He held out his arms and caught her as she plopped herself into his lap. "Where are we going now?" she asked excitedly. "Are we going to the floating island?"

"Yup. This ship will take us there. So we'll have to wait just a little bit longer."

Ren was playing with Ellie when his master sat down next to him.

"So, any plans on telling this old man exactly what you'll be up to, Ren? I've been wondering what your intentions are for when we get to the palace," he whispered.

"I plan on taking an R and R day."

"No, I mean after that. What kind of plan do you have? You brought Kelsey here because of the stones. And? You've not told me anything else this whole trip." Ren nodded.

"I apologize for that, Master. I plan on having her look through the ancient library. If we don't find anything, we'll head to the fifteenth floor."

Ren's master gave him a surprised look, the same that everyone apparently carried when they learned of his plans.

"I see. So that's your plan. I fear the depths of that abyss may be the only truth in this quest of yours. However, that chimera and that man who controls it has me concerned."

"Me too. Would you mind investigating that for me? See if you can find out who they are."

"I'll look into it, as was already my intention. We cannot allow such a creature to continue thriving in these lands."

Ren continued his discussion with his master when he found Marcus and Kelsey had started one of their own. Marcus was still a little drawn back, but he was mostly normal around her again.

When the ship finally docked at the island, they all got to their feet. The ship was tied off before the ramp was lowered, and they all descended it. Their dock was just one of many, all lined up. Not far from the docks sat a few buildings with a small creek behind them. A bridge connected both sides of the creek, and from there, it was a few minutes' walk down the dirt road that led directly into the capital city.

"There are no walls," Kelsey stated.

"Nope," Ren said. "We don't need them. The purpose of a wall surrounding a city or town is not only to provide protection and security but also to instill a sense of the laws that are in play and are to be followed. They also act as a barrier for tolls, therefore providing a count of all the people that come and go and ensuring the flow of commerce. We've no need for something like that at the capital."

"Why? Are the people that live or travel here that well mannered?"

"No. It's because it's on a giant floating island, that's why." He gave her a sly look.

"Oh, yeah, that makes sense."

"The only way to get to and from the island is by taking these ships. That is, unless you can fly. But the wind pressure would knock you clean out of the sky before you could reach it."

"Why don't the ships then?" she asked.

"Magic," was his only response. Well, she couldn't really argue with that.

One at a time, the horses and animals that were kept below deck were released. Once everyone had their horses, Ren climbed on Nidar, and they headed for the capital.

There were a dozen guards posted outside the front of the city. Kelsey couldn't tell what kind of monsters they were since they were primarily human but had a set of curled horns on their heads and tails behind them.

"Demonic beastkin," Ren said, as if he were reading her thoughts. "Basically, they're demons."

"Demons. Is that bad?"

"No different than other monsters. Demons are one of the friendlier races."

They've all been pretty friendly so far, she thought.

The guards conducted a quick inspection on all those entering the city.

"Stop there," one of them said to Ren and his party. "Identification, please. What brings you to the capital today?"

"We're returning home from many years abroad," Ren said.

Now was the time to reveal themselves. There was no need for them to hide any longer. Ren and his father lowered their hoods, and the guards nearly dropped their weapons.

"Your Highness! Your Majesty!" they said excitingly. "You've returned! What a glorious day for Nexus. Please proceed. The citizens will be overjoyed at your return. Quickly, inform the citizens. They'll all want to hear the great news." One of the guards grabbed a horse and rode off through the gates, shouting of their return at full speed.

"It's going to be a swarm," Marcus said, lowering his hood.

"I was thinking the same thing," Leo said. "That's why, Ren, switch places with Kelsey. As a precaution, let her ride Nidar."

Ren's father was correct in his thinking. The ride to the palace wasn't long, but no doubt the citizens would swarm them like Marcus had said. Having Kelsey and Ellie guarded on all sides was a good idea. It practically ensured their protection and the protection of the stones.

In agreement with his father, Ren nodded and dismounted from Nidar without a word. Kelsey took his place behind Ellie, holding onto Nidar's fur.

Ren knelt down to Nidar's level. "I'm leaving them to you, bud. If something happens, you know what to do.

Take them, and we'll regroup later." Nidar growled in a clear understanding. Then, they all watched as Ren put his foot in the mount of the saddle and swung his leg up and over. He sat on the horse proudly, putting his other foot in the other mount.

Ren and Marcus ushered their horses forward and took the front, leaving Leo and Ren's master to take the rear.

"Welcome home," the guards said and moved to the side, allowing them to pass.

The main road was made of cobblestones. The buildings were made of wood and stone with wooden shutters. The roofs varied from wood to stone to clay tiles. Chimneys stuck out from each one, many with smoke coming out. They lined the streets like a wall on both sides, pushing them forward.

Monsters started rushing out of the buildings and into the street. They filled in both sides, becoming more and more compact. Some looked out through windows and balconies, others sat on top of stacked boxes to get a look.

With the exception of Kelsey, Ren and the others waved as they rode, the citizens shouting and cheering with joy. Out of embarrassment, she lowered herself, trying to hide her face. There were so many people watching. But Ren and the others were following customs. As royals, their actions of gracing the civilians were expected. It set a good look for the royal family and the kingdom, instilling a sense of greatness and that the ruling class still looked after those they ruled over.

Though there were many who disagreed with them, Ren and his father were of the opinion that a ruler's duty was always to his people, as they were what made the kingdom in the first place. As such, it was important to demonstrate themselves as powerful and righteous, but also that they acknowledged the citizens and were working for them.

The parade through the streets continued until they reached the palace.

"Oh wow. *That's* your palace?" Kelsey asked, shocked.

A giant tower made of white and blue stone stood hundreds of feet tall. Two smaller towers of the same material that were less than half of the height sat behind it. Attached to the front of the largest tower was a three-story wing that curved toward the front. Another three-story wing continued behind the larger tower. Then, there was the bridge made of white and tan stone. It connected the tower to another part of the palace only two stories high with a series of towers.

Kelsey couldn't see anything beyond that, but she was certain that the structure continued on. Surely, there was much more of the palace than what she saw.

In front of the palace was a cobblestone road that encircled a massive garden within a monumental front courtyard containing several fountains, benches, trees, grassy areas, and resting spaces.

Ren smiled. "Yup, that's it," he said, answering Kelsey's question. "We're home."

Nineteen

Black Dragon Divertimento

Riding up to the front gates of the palace, the guards standing in front of the gates greeted them with much enthusiasm and opened the gates.

The massive golden gates swung inward without making a sound, and they rode through, continuing onto the cobblestone street around the courtyard. Then, the guards closed the gates behind them.

"It really has been a long time," Marcus said. "I wondered when I would ever get to see this place again."

Ren had a distant memory of everyone gathered over at his house back in the human world. He found it comforted him more than being back here at the palace.

"Yeah, but being back in the human world wasn't so bad," he said.

It took him a minute, but Marcus realized what he was talking about. "I guess you're right."

A hoard of gleeful servants rushed out of the palace to meet them at the entrance. Ren was the first to dismount, feeling whole again the moment his feet hit the ground.

"Your Majesty, Your Highness, welcome back. I shall lead your horse to the stables should you desire," one of the servants said.

"Please do, thank you," Ren said.

The servant took the reins and led all four horses out of view to the stables behind the palace. The remainder of the servants formed a line on either side for them to walk through. They greeted in unison, a welcome that Ren and the others had grown used to going without after so many years in the human realm.

Ren felt Nidar brush up against him as they walked, the tiger's tail flicking back and forth against his leg. It was a tactic Ren had long since taught him as a sign of tameness, proving that he was well-behaved.

The massive double doors of the palace were made of a deep red wood with gold inscriptions and fitted with glass at the top. The main foyer was wide open with a three-story vaulted ceiling and polished white sandstone floors. Three large beautiful chandeliers made of gold and glass hung from the vaulted ceiling. A balcony lined each side that turned into the second floor. A set of grand marble stairs sat proudly in the back, widening at the top before splitting in opposite directions and connecting to one of the balconies. Its golden handrails mixed elegantly with the color of the marble and sandstone. Polished sandstone pillars of beige and cream lined both sides of the room beneath the balconies.

Both off the balcony above and off the first floor below, a corridor on each side led to each end of the large wing. And at the back of the room, located on each balcony just off where it met the grand staircase, a second set of stairs rose to the third floor.

Standing in the majesty of Ren's and his father's palace, Kelsey felt poorer than she ever had. She knew Ren and his father were wealthy, of course, being royalty, but she had no idea they were this wealthy. The building might as well have been made out of money. It made her extremely self-conscious.

Up above, a second line of servants stood on the balconies to greet them. Truth be told, even Ren felt it was a little much. It had been a while since he had been greeted like this. He didn't have servants back home, after all. They had all grown used to doing everything themselves. If it made even him uncomfortable, no doubt it also affected the others. Nevertheless, he did nod in approval. Everything was coming back to him. All the sights, all the sounds, all the smells. It was good to be home.

"Well now, what's this we have here?" came a voice. "A long-lost bird has finally returned, it seems."

They all looked to see a young man walking down the grand staircase. He appeared close in age to Ren and the others, appearance-wise anyway. His black hair was chaotic, combed over and left to fall on his right side, but combed away and tucked back on his left. The rest was left to stand on its own as it felt free to. Streaks of red ran through his bangs and along the left side of his head.

The man was dressed in a black and red vest with gold thread for trim, the collar high and stiff. Three sets of gold buttons knotted with matching string over his chest kept it closed. Beneath the vest rested a pair of black pants, each leg containing a single golden stripe in the front and back. A pair of black boots encased his feet.

Kelsey's eyes were drawn to the red sash tied into a bow over his left hip, the long ends left to flow freely as he walked. The man's hand slid gently over the railing of the grand staircase, revealing a long red wristband trimmed in gold at both ends. His other hand rested behind his back, concealing the identical wristband that it carried.

The man stared at them with bronze eyes only slightly darker than Marcus's gold ones. Kelsey noticed how much he looked like Ren. In fact, the resemblances were as clear as day. She made a mental note of it. Perhaps she'd learn more another time.

Ren beamed with delight as the man walked up to them. It was a smile Kelsey had never seen on him before.

"That's Ren's cousin," Marcus whispered into Kelsey's ear. "He is the other half of the power struggle."

"Power struggle?" she whispered back.

Marcus nodded. "Most of the nobles and citizens support Ren as the heir to the throne, but not all of them. There is another faction that desires Ren's cousin to take the throne. His cousin's mother is Ren's mother's sister by blood, so he technically has a chance."

"What! Isn't that bad? What's going to happen?"

Ren smiled at his cousin. "Cole! It's been too long, Cousin." Cole chuckled, and they embraced each other like brothers.

"It's good to see you again, Ren. I hope things have been well for you while you were in the human world."

"As well as they could be Cousin, as well as they could be. I'm sure you've heard the news of the recent battle." Cole nodded.

Kelsey pulled on Ren's sleeve. "Um, Ren," she said quietly. "I thought you guys were on bad terms!"

"What are you talking about?" he asked, raising an eyebrow.

"Marcus told me you two are competing over the throne."

Ren and Cole looked at Marcus. "I never got to finish explaining," he confessed.

Ren's cousin released a heavy sigh. "I'm afraid it's true," he confessed. They all looked at him. "I will seize the throne with my own hands. I'm the bad guy, after all. Muhuhahahaha." He wiggled his fingers at her like he was casting some weird voodoo magic.

Ren and the guys burst out laughing.

"The truth is," Cole said, "it's my mother who wants me to succeed the throne. Most support Ren, myself included."

"You're on Ren's side?" she asked, surprised.

Cole nodded in confirmation. "I have no intention of being king. It's not for me. I've never been one to sit behind a desk all day buried in paperwork. But my mother wants what's best for me, and as royalty, I have the right to claim my seat. She bears no ill will toward Ren, but I'm still her son. The only ones who support me are those who were loyal to my father, and now my mother."

"I've already expressed to her my stance on things," Ren said. "If you ever do decide to make your claim, I will acknowledge it. Though I will not so readily give up on it."

"I have no intention of starting a bloodbath with you, Ren. You know that," Cole responded. "Let her have her aspirations. They are not mine, and I will follow what I desire."

"Then what do you want?" Kelsey asked curiously.

"I want to be one of Ren's vassals. Or, more specifically, I wish to be his personal aid when he becomes king."

"I can't say I know what all of this is like. It's so foreign to me. I'm just glad we don't have to fight each other. One more enemy is something we don't need. There's enough going on right now."

"You're an interesting girl," Cole said. "What's your name?"

"I'm Kelsey."

"Kelsey. It's a pleasure to meet you. This lot bringing a guest is rare. What brings you to travel with them?"

"It's complicated," Ren answered for her. "She's not from here."

"I see," Cole said, clearly confused.

"I mean, she's not from Nexus. She's from the human world. Just for now, this stays between us, okay." Cole nodded, though curious. "Kelsey isn't a monster; she's human."

Cole's eyes widened with disbelief. "And you brought her here, why? Don't get me wrong, I see no problem with it, but you hate humans. Not to mention she'd have to been introduced into our world. This whole thing seems a little far-fetched, Cousin. Even for you, it's hard to wrap my head around. You must trust her a lot."

"Like I said, it's complicated. Let's talk at dinner. For now, it'll do us some good to rest."

"Sure, I understand. I bet you rode through the kingdom. Get some sleep; we'll talk at dinner." Cole placed a hand on his shoulder and walked off.

One of the servants, a butler, approached Ren and the others after Cole left. "Your Highness, I will take the liberty of showing the two ladies and Lord Caster to their rooms."

"Please do. The little one can stay with me, though," he said, taking Ellie's hand.

"Certainly. Well then, please follow me, and I will show you the way." He headed for the stairs with Kelsey and Ren's master following him.

"Shall we go as well?" Ren asked. Marcus and his father nodded and headed to their rooms. It was no surprise that Marcus had his own.

The third floor was a series of rooms with a soft carpet floor. All of the doors were made from white wood. The butler stopped in front of one of them.

"This will be your room, miss," the butler said to Kelsey. "Your luggage is already inside waiting."

"Thank you," Kelsey said. "See you at dinner." She walked into the room and closed the door behind her.

The butler moved to another room down the hall. "Lord Caster, you may stay in this room. We will send someone to escort you and the miss to the dining hall for dinner. Your Majesty and Highnesses, do you require me to escort you, or will that be all for now?"

"No, that will be all for now, thank you, Donavan," Ren's father said.

"Certainly, your Majesty. Dinner will convene in a few hours. Perhaps you would get some rest in the meantime."

"That sounds like a pleasant idea." The butler bowed back before walking back the way they had come.

"Come on, Ellie, this way," Ren said. He led her to another room and opened the door, setting his bag down on a chair and Ellie's suitcase in front of it.

"Wow, your room is so big, Ren."

"Well, being royalty has its perks," he said back.

Ren's room was a blend of white and cream with white barrel-vaulted ceilings. Gold trim and ornament decorated the walls and white wainscotting.

They entered into a long and narrow node. At the end was a large window spanning ten feet high and five feet wide with brown curtains tied to the side. Directly to the left, passing through an opening almost the length of the node, the room opened up to a massive canopy bed large enough for four people. Several chairs and end tables filled the space. North of the bed, two windows of the same size as the one in the node straddled a pair of double doors leading to a large balcony. Another chair and end table filled the corner.

South of the bed, an arched doorway led into a small space with two doors. One led directly into a giant bathroom. The one to the right led to Ren's closet, one large enough to be considered its own full room. Opposite the bed was a fireplace. Atop the mantel sat a clock, a series of pictures, and two golden candle holders on the ends. Mounted on the wall directly above the fireplace was a mirror, its edges crafted from gold.

In between the bed and fireplace, what would be the center of the room, was a small white table of the same wood as the door. A white leather couch rested on one side, facing the back wall. Two more of the chairs sat opposite it.

Like the left side, the right side of the node also opened up into a large room. This room only contained furniture meant for seating. There were several couches, chairs, and tables. Beyond them, directly ahead, was another door.

"Ren, what's behind that door?" Ellie asked.

"My study," he said. "The room before it is a common space. Something akin to a living room but more private, yet less so than my study. Come on." He led her to the room and opened the door, letting her walk in first.

Ren's study was colored the exact same as his bedroom. To the left were two more windows, again of similar size to the ones in his room and the node. Another door led outside to the balcony, connecting the two sides to each other. In front of the door and windows was a large wooden desk filled with accessories. A chair with padding made of cream leather sat behind it.

Ahead of them, in the center of the room, a second fireplace rested in the wall. Two leather couches sat opposite each other in front of the fireplace, with a table in between. Large portraits and paintings covered the wall. And to the right, at the other end of the study, a single door connected to the main corridor.

"Let's put your clothes in the closet first. We can head into town in a few days and find you things from this world. That way, you'll blend in and won't stand out."

Ellie agreed, and they returned to the bedroom, closing the door to the study behind them. Ren opened the door to his closet and walked inside. It was filled with clothes, shoes, and other accessories.

Typically, a servant would have been the one to do this, but Ren cared little for that at the moment, thinking only to do it himself. He moved a gathering of his own items to clear a space for Ellie's. She was definitely going to need different clothing and footwear. Though he believed her too young to wear heels, etiquette training for royals usually started very early in their childhood. Ren started his when he was five. It was something to consider. Aside from that, he'd pick her up accessories to wear, like hats and jewelry. Perhaps a pretty necklace. Well, he'd have to see what was being sold.

Ren looked at the grandfather clock in his room once they finished. There were still several hours until dinner. It was perfect for resting after all their travels. He let Ellie lie down in bed while he found the nearest couch and plopped down. It was a short-lived rest but worthwhile nonetheless.

The time on his clock indicated that it was late enough for them to start heading for dinner. Since Ren knew the palace like the back of his hand, he had no need for a servant to fetch them.

"Come on, let's head to dinner. Stay with me so you don't get lost," he said to Ellie.

They exited the room and headed down the hall to the stairs. Ellie walked next to him, keeping close. She knew he was right about her getting lost. The place was massive, and she'd only seen a small portion.

A knock on Kelsey's door woke her up. It was evening now, seeing how low the sun sat over the horizon. She figured it must have been one of the servants there to gather her for dinner.

The door opened, and Ellie walked over to her. "Kelsey, come on, we're going to eat." Kelsey climbed out of bed and followed her to the door.

"Ellie, wait. We need someone to show us the way." "We do. Ren's leading us."

Ren was leaning against the wall outside with his arms crossed. Kelsey knew instantly that Ellie had dragged him here. Then she noticed the golden necklace around his neck, one she had never seen him wear before. In fact, she'd never known Ren to wear much jewelry at all.

"Hey," he said. "Come on, follow me. I'll show you to the dining hall."

They made their way down the stairs to the bottom floor. Kelsey never looked at Ren, but she reached over and grabbed his hand. Her touch surprised him, and he tried to pull away when his instincts took over, but she only increased her grip, refusing to let him go.

Twenty

Don't Look Back

The table in the dining room was the largest one Kelsey had ever seen. The dark brown wood was so rich it was almost black. It had to sit twenty people at least, for what purpose she'd never know.

Overhead, large chandeliers hung from the ceiling. On the table, three three-arm candle holders and two five-arm holders lined the middle. Flames atop the candles burned patiently, standing still as they breathed.

Everyone else was already sitting when Ren, Kelsey, and Ellie arrived. Ren's father sat at the end of the table, farthest from the door. Cole sat directly to his left, followed by Marcus and then Ren's master, leaving the right side of the table completely open.

Ren pulled his hand away when he noticed everyone staring, much to Kelsey's dismay. Then he remembered there was no need to be so reserved. They still had much to talk about, but he and Kelsey were at least acting normal around each other again.

He sat next to his father, letting Ellie take the seat to his right, then Kelsey next to her. They all waited for the food to be served before delving into the important topic. Instead, they filled themselves with small conversations.

Their dinner was wheeled out several minutes later on metal carts. There were six in total, each containing three plates with metal domes over them. The servants placed the plates on the table before removing the dome. The food steamed and filled the room with enticing smells.

Kelsey had expected one main course and a side for their dinner. What she got was anything but. There was duck, boar, fresh vegetables, freshly baked bread, fish, and other side dishes. The servants refilled their empty glasses with wine. All except for Ellie, who got freshly squeezed lemonade.

It was just like Ren had explained on their trip through the kingdom. Now that they were at the palace, they had access to a variety of things that most places did not. In this case, lemon trees grew in the palace's botanical garden, so it was easy to make.

Before Kelsey and Ellie could start eating, Ren held his hand out in front of them.

"Don't eat yet," he said. Though confused, they complied, never taking a bite.

It was Ren's father who took the first bite as the servants placed the first dish in front of him. It contained but a small sliver of meat and nothing more. They watched him silently as he bit into the meet, then the fish, and the bread, and finally the other dishes as each was placed before him one after the other. Finally, he gave a nod, and Marcus, Cole, and Ren's master began to eat.

"What just happened?" Kelsey asked.

"It's a customary tradition in the royal family," Ren responded. "When there are guests, the head of the table will taste all of the food first. It's precautionary should the food or drink be poisoned."

Kelsey's face turned as white as paper. "Poisoned!" Ren nodded back.

"Though the practice does not usually extend outside of the royal family, it wouldn't bode very well should one of our guests be poisoned," Leo explained to her. "Politically, it puts us at a terrible disadvantage. The royal family's reputation would plummet, allowing for any political agendas aimed against us to occur much more easily. A position made even worse should said guest or guests die as a result."

"Would someone really try to poison our food?" Kelsey asked him, suddenly terrified.

"I doubt it. I see no reason, if not for a personal grudge, but everyone who works in the palace has a clean background. Besides, all of the food is tasted for poison by a taste tester before it's served anyway. It's merely a secondary precaution. One can never be too careful. We shouldn't have anything to worry about."

She had to admit he was right about that one. You could never be too cautious. But even still, the thought of someone poisoning her food or drink kind of terrified her.

"Have you ever had to taste first before?" Kelsey asked Ren.

"Yes, plenty of times," he answered. "But only when I have guests. Were it just Marcus, my father, or Cole, we wouldn't bother. I've built up an immunity to a rather vast variety of poisons. We both have," he said, indicating Marcus. "I wouldn't worry about it."

"Just enjoy the food," Marcus said. "He's right when he says you have nothing to worry about."

Kelsey gave one last look at Ren, who offered her a reassuring nod. Though she was still filled with anxiety, she took their word for it and started eating.

Partway through their meal, the doors opened, and one of the butlers entered, approaching Ren. The butler whispered something into his ear, and Ren nodded back. With a bow, the butler exited the room. Only moments later, the doors opened again, and Nidar was ushered in next to one of the maids.

"Ah, Nidar, there you are," Ren said. "I was wondering where you went, buddy." Nidar sat down next to him, and Ren ruffled the fur on the side of his neck.

The maid who entered with Nidar cleared her throat. She appeared only a few years older than Kelsey.

"Re—" she began to say before correcting herself. "Your Highness, welcome back. I'm glad to see you've safely returned after your long stay abroad. Is there anything I can be of assistance with?"

Ren looked at the woman before his eyes widened. "Lisa?" he asked, shocked.

The maid smiled at him, her cheeks stained pink. "It has been a long time, Your Highness," she said.

Even at a glance, Lisa appeared beautiful. She fingered the ends of her fluffy hair, which was cut to her neckline, her bangs curved left over her eyes. But the color was unlike any Kelsey or Ellie had ever seen before. It was silver, not dyed. And Ren obviously got on well with her.

"Re—, Your Highness, if it's alright with you, might you be willing to share some tea with me later?" she asked, blushing.

Ren gave her that ice-melting smile that could stop any girl's heart. "Sure, I'd like that."

"Then, if you'll excuse me, I'll return to my duties. Your Majesty, Your Highnesses," she said to Leo, Cole, and Marcus.

Lisa turned and headed for the door, closing it behind her, but not before glancing at Ren one last time. Suddenly, intense irritation burned through Kelsey. She jabbed it into her food, wanting to jab it somewhere else, but kept it to herself.

"Well, Ren, that was interesting," Leo said. "Do I sense a blossoming story for your old man?"

Ren returned his father's comment with an annoyed look, making him chuckle. Distracting himself from his father's antics, he took an extra plate from a servant and piled food on it before placing it on the ground in front of Nidar. The tiger eagerly ate away at it while Ren just sat there, petting him. Nidar moved his head around in Ren's hand while he ate, enjoying the affection he was receiving.

"When you first brought him home, I was completely shocked," Leo said. "Never in my wildest dreams would I have imagined you two would become this close."

Ren never returned a response, only focusing on giving Nidar all of his attention. Meanwhile, Marcus called one of the servants over to him.

"How can I be of service, Prince Allagash?" they asked.

"Can I get a current report on the affairs of my kingdom? Anything will do. As recent as you can, please. I want to look things over while I'm free."

"I will see what I can do. Your Majesty, may I have permission to search through the capital records for the Wolfbane Kingdom?"

"Yes, go ahead. Give him anything you can."

The servant bowed to them. "I shall get on that immediately."

Cole cleared his throat once the servant was gone, drawing all the attention to him. "So, Ren, why don't we get to the main subject."

"Right, what do you want to know?"

"Everything. You've been gone a long time. Now, on your return, you bring with you not only an animal from the human world but two humans as well."

Ren nodded at his request. But to tell everything, he would need to start at the beginning, the very beginning. And so he started with how he was turned human and met Kelsey. After his mother died and he left for India, he returned to Trinity, where powers and memories were restored.

Cole's expression sank at the word of Ren's mother. The whole kingdom, no all of Nexus, had learned of her passing after it happened. It left a canyon of sadness gouged through them all for many years. For some, it still persisted.

After clearing the shades from India, they returned to the States, and Ren was reunited with Kesley, though at a price. That was when they got word from James Wilson, claiming that he had found the location of the map of the Sun and Moon Stone.

"Though I understand your reasons, are you so sure your decision was wise, Cousin?" Cole asked. "Introducing a normal human to our kind."

"At first, I never intended to bring her into our world at all. I was fully prepared to cut ties. But she convinced me to let her be a part of our world. And despite everything, after we found the map and started searching for the stones, she did prove herself capable."

Cole sighed, shaking his head. "That may be the case; however, I still think you made the wrong decision. You should have left her behind. No offense to her, but a human can't keep up. Our kinds are just too different. And besides, think about our current position. What could befall her now that she's involved with us? Is that the reason you brought her here?"

"Partially," Ren answered. "I understand your concerns, Cousin, but they are unfounded. Trust me when I say you underestimate her far too much. Especially now."

"Now?"

Ren nodded back. "I told you we searched for the stones." This time, it was Cole's turn to nod. "I never told you that we found them." Cole's eyes widened.

"You actually found the Sun and Moon Stone?"

"We did. And that's the reason why we brought Kelsey here."

"You asked what could befall me for becoming a part of your world." Kelsey raised her hand and jangled the bracelet with the stones on it. "I'd say things have been going pretty well," she said.

Cole caught sight of the red and purple stones embedded into the silver bracelet. "You don't mean, are those?"

"Yup. The stones," she said.

"We still don't know why, but the stones chose Kelsey," Ren explained. "She wields them now. And with the stones on our side, we've made the biggest impact in this war against Verin yet. In that battle in the human world, we defeated one of his generals."

"Really?" Cole asked, surprised. "That vampire?" Ren nodded.

Many had heard of the battle in the human world, but not many knew that the enemy was one of the generals.

"Actually, that's one of the things I wanted to discuss with you," Ren continued. "Though he was a general, he was only fourth-ranked, the weakest of them all. It's what comes next that you need to know. The vampire who served as Verin's fourth general was Algiroth."

Cole's face contorted in anger, his fists turning white.

"It turned out humans never murdered my mother; Algiroth did. And I'm fairly certain he was the one who killed your uncle. Or he at least had a hand in his death."

From his expression and how tightly he clenched his fists, it was clear just how angry Cole was at the moment. Algiroth was more than just a traitor. He had a hand in many great sources of sorrow.

"Did you make him suffer?"

"Perhaps, though, I wish I could have done more. I certainly wounded his pride. Against his weapon, however, there was no opportunity to really do so. It took everything I had to defeat him."

"Just what kind of weapon was it for you to struggle so much against?"

"A demonic sword. And unfortunately, he ended up fusing with it completely." Cole's jaw dropped. "I only managed to defeat him after Shadow Hunter let me release. After the battle, and with the situation of the stones, we had to return, and with little options but to bring Kelsey with us. They may have chosen her, but unfortunately, they also refuse to leave her. We're unable to remove them from her wrist."

"You can't remove them at all?"

Ren shook his head. "And we tried everything we could. That's why we came back here; to find a way to remove the stones and work on peace treaties and coexistence with the humans."

"I see. I understand everything," Cole said. He tapped his fingers on the table, using his other hand to support the weight of his face. "And the kid? How does she fit into all of this?"

"Marcus and I saved her from a succubus turned living shade."

"A succubus! And she was a living shade?" Ren nodded, and Marcus nodded when Cole looked at him for confirmation.

"The succubus killed Ellie's parents, and she had no other family who would take her in. I couldn't leave her, so I decided to look after her instead."

Cole looked at Ellie. "I'm sorry to hear that. That must have been hard for you."

"It's okay. I was scared and lonely at first, but now I've got Ren. And I've got Kelsey, and Marcus, and Nidar, and Leo too."

"Is that so? Well, then, I'm glad that things worked out. Is Ren taking good care of you?"

"Yes. Ren's a great big brother."

Ren placed a hand on her head. "Thanks, munchkin'."

The side of Cole's mouth twitched up. "You've changed in the time you've been gone, Ren. You'll be a great ruler when it's your time."

Ren looked at him, a little shocked. "Thanks, Cousin. That means a lot."

The servant who was searching for documents on Marcus's kingdom returned with a small stack of papers and handed them to Marcus.

"Prince Allagash, this is all I could dig up for you. It dates back as far as ten years ago and as early as a few months ago."

"That's perfect, thank you."

"Also, this arrived moments ago. It's addressed to you." He handed him an unopened letter.

Marcus opened the envelope and read its contents. It was a letter addressed to him from his dad. Once news of their arrival reached him, he immediately headed out and was already on his way. He expected to arrive within the morrow', the day after at the latest.

"I see," Marcus said after reading the letter. "It appears my father is headed here. I'll wait here for him to arrive. No doubt he has business with you, too, Leo. Then we'll no doubt depart together. Cool with you guys if I crash here?"

"Always Marcus," Leo said. "You never need to ask when and if you want to stay."

"Thanks, Leo."

"Well then, I think we should rest up for the rest of the night," Leo said. "We can get back to work tomorrow. For now, let's settle in and relax."

Everyone was in agreement. They were all exhausted from the trip. The little bit of sleep before dinner helped, but now that it was getting later, the fatigue was catching back up with them.

"Your Majesty, Your Highness, I shall have Everett prepare all the paperwork for you. It will be delivered when you are ready upon your request."

"Yes, thank you," Leo said. "And tell Everett to come to my study later. It has been a while. I wish to catch up with him."

"Understood. I will inform him you wish to see him."

"Alright, come on guys, let's get some rest. I will see everyone tomorrow morning for breakfast," Leo said.

Everyone bid their last farewells before splitting up and returning to their rooms for the night.

Twenty-one

Scorched Earth

Ren woke up as curtains were drawn apart. Sunlight pierced the room. The servants arrived just after the sun had risen above the horizon, as they did every morning, to prepare his wake-up and get him ready for the day.

"Rise and shine, Ren." Ren was lying on his side with his arm resting on Nidar, who slept beside him. On his other side, Ellie was still curled up in the covers.

Ren opened his eyes to see Cole standing above him. Cole smiled and pulled the covers off.

"Your Highness, it would do well for you to get up. Breakfast will convene shortly, and you have work to do today," one of the servants said.

Ren recognized that voice anywhere, for its owner was no ordinary servant. Dressed in fine clothing fit for a noble, their long black hair was styled finely with their bangs out of their face and the remainder tied into a ponytail. Their blue eyes sat behind a pair of black-framed spectacles.

Much like Ren and Cole, the servant appeared by all rights human. But as a vampire, one would expect such a thing.

"Neil, long time no see," Ren said. Neil was Ren's personal aid, a servant who worked directly for them, with a status far above the other servants. Near every noble had their own aid, especially the high-ranking ones. It was the same position Cole desired, as he told Kelsey yesterday.

"Your Highness, breakfast will soon be served. Once you have eaten, I will have all the paperwork you requested delivered to your study."

"Very good. When is King Allagash getting here?"

"He should arrive any time after mid-day. I have already taken meeting him into your schedule."

"Thank you, Neil."

Neil smiled and sat down next to Ren on the edge of the bed. A manner most wildly inappropriate for someone serving a royal. Normally, a heavy punishment would be brought forth. However, it was a good thing Ren didn't care a whiff, as he and Neil were exceptionally close.

"I'm just glad to see you've returned after so long. Alive and … whole. It was something I feared I'd never get to see. I'm glad our race is so long-lived. Though things remained steady and prosperous under Archduke Randolf, as expected, I always prefer serving you."

Ren had to admit, he was touched by his friend's words. Sometimes, he believed Niel was too good for him.

"And as I expected, no one else compares to you when it comes to this. I'm truly glad I have you as my personal aid."

Neil nodded back, pleased. "Now, let's head to breakfast, shall we?"

Cole handed a set of clothes to the servants, who proceeded to dress Ren. While Ren was getting changed, Cole woke up Ellie and Nidar. More servants came into the room and dressed Ellie for the day.

Because it was Cole's desire to be Ren's personal aid, he often accompanied Neil so as to learn the practice from him and prepare him for the day he took over. When that happens, Ren would have to find a suitable position for Neil, should he desire it.

Once Ren and Ellie were dressed, they, along with Nidar, Cole, and Neil, headed for the dining hall. Neil opened the door, allowing Ren and Ellie to enter first. No surprise, Ren's father was already sitting down when they arrived. The guy had a cup of coffee in one hand and a piece of paper in the other.

Kelsey was the last to arrive, though not unexpected. Admittedly, Ren was curious to see how long it would take, given how much the maids wanted to doll her up.

He took the spot next to his father and Cole the other. Ellie sat to Ren's right once more, just as she had the night before.

A maid approached them, placing drinks before each of them.

"Good Morning, Your Highness. Might I ask what the little one will have this morning?"

"Any juice or milk will do fine," Ren answered.

The maid bowed to him and walked out of sight.

Ren and his father discussed their handling of their workload. Who would handle what documents and the political state of affairs. Leo mentioned the need to hold an assembly among the nobles. Doing so solidified their return and reclaim of authority while weeding out their enemies working in the shadows or behind their backs.

Breakfast was placed in front of them not long after. Leo finished first, excusing himself from the table. Ren finished next, following his father's example and excusing himself. Nidar got up from where he was lying and followed him out of the room. They took the stairs to the third story and headed to Ren's study.

He opened the door and stepped into the room. Ren's desk sat directly ahead of him on the opposite side of the room. The curtains were drawn open, letting sunlight shine in. The doors connected to his bedroom and the balcony remained closed.

Ren sat in his chair. A stack of papers already lay on his desk, a pen, and an extra bottle of ink at the ready. He watched as Nidar hopped up on one of the couches facing the door and lay down. Ren could tell Nidar picked that spot purposefully. It was clear his feline friend intended to act as a guard, choosing a place where he could watch both main entrances to the room and be aware of any movement. Ren appreciated that greatly. It was one of the things that made them so close. They protected each other.

Ren grabbed the stack of papers and began sorting through them, separating them based on contents. Then, he got to work.

An hour later, there was a knock on his door.

"Enter," he said. The door opened, and Neil came in carrying a large stack of papers.

"Your Highness, these are rural documents regarding the agricultural development of many of the villages to the West. There appears to be a food shortage."

Ren stopped writing when Neil said that. "A food shortage?" Neil confirmed with a nod.

"I'm not sure what the cause is, but if it continues, it could have lasting effects throughout the kingdom. Those farms are a major source of our food."

"I know. I'll take a look." Neil bowed and left the room.

Ren finished filling out the documents that he had been previously working on, setting the stack to the side. It was primarily rural agreements and finances. One of the more normal forms of daily paperwork. It was a pain, but it had to be done.

With that stack finally finished, he moved on to the more concerning stack. The food shortage that Neil had told him about. If left unmanaged, it would have severe repercussions. People would starve, assuming they weren't already. Ren could only hope that it had not yet gotten too severe, or better yet, that the shortage was in the very early stages, and they had caught it immediately.

He started reading through the documents, reviewing testimonials, traded goods and their quantities, imports and exports, identifying resources, and determining the economic implications behind their resources. Given their current financial standing and their current food supply, he had to take into account all the able bodies capable of work, payment for their work, repair, and the current value of trade within the kingdom, not just in terms of money, but in terms of product as well. And that was just the start, really. If necessary, they might even require a request for aid from neighboring kingdoms, and that was an animal in its own right.

But before anything else, he had to figure out what the cause of the food shortage was. Without identifying the cause, he could not determine a solution. Which meant, he would need to dispatch a party to the region to identify the problem. If they could do that, he could start making progress on fixing the problem.

Ren pulled a string on the wall behind him. The sting was connected to a bell, a form of communication for calling servants. Only minutes later, Neil walked into the room.

"Your Highness, do you need something?"

"Can you send Cole in here?" Ren asked. "And by all means, feel free to stay when you do."

"Right away."

Neil left the room to look for Cole, leaving Ren and Nidar alone to his work.

Another knock on Ren's door came ten minutes later.

"Come in," he said. The door opened, and Cole and Neil walked into the room.

"Hey, Ren, you wanted to see me?" Cole asked.

"Yeah. Take a look at this." Ren handed him one of the papers he had finished working on. Cole read over it before setting it back down from where Ren had picked it up.

"A food shortage huh? That doesn't sound good. What do we know so far?"

"Not much, unfortunately. At the moment, all I was able to determine was a high deduction in exportation and production. That's where you come in."

"I'm listening."

"I want you to head out there and take a look. See if you can discover what's happening, and report back to me. I can't do anything without knowing what the cause is, and unfortunately, I can't go there myself right now. I have too much work to do after just getting back."

"So you want me to go instead. Alright, I'll head out there the day after tomorrow to take a look. I'll need a little time to prepare for the journey and gather a few additional hands. The more eyes and ears, the better."

"Thank you."

"I'll send a messenger bird once I find out the problem and return to the palace. We can determine a solution when I return."

"That's fine. But once you get back, I'll have another job for you."

"Ah, working me like a slave, huh?"

Ren laughed at his comment. "Not quite. I want you to help Kelsey."

Cole wasn't sure what he wanted him to help her with. Was she even doing anything while being here?

"What would I be doing to assist her?" he asked.

"Research. She's going floor by floor in the library looking for any information on the stones. I want you to give her a hand. And while you're at it, find anything you can on Verin."

"On Verin, huh?" Ren nodded.

"Marcus and I want your help in finding him. We don't know where he is, what he's planning, or when he'll attack next. You have a lot of contacts. If you can help us find out information, it will help us find him and end this war."

Cole looked amused at Ren's assignment for him. "Alright, I'll do whatever I can."

"Thanks again, Cole."

"You're welcome." He scratched Nidar under his chin when there was another knock on the door. Nidar stood up, his tail wagging behind him.

"Come in," Ren said.

Marcus opened the door and walked in. "Hey, Ren."

"What's up, bro?"

"My dad just got here."

Ren looked out the windows behind him. The sun was already starting to set, staining the sky orange and pink. "Well then, looks like it's time for a break."

He got up, and the five of them walked out of the room. They headed to the first floor, turning left at the bottom of the stairs and down the hallway. Marcus opened the door to a room, and they all filed inside. The room was a lounge room specifically meant for relaxing or meetings. Directly ahead of them, a fire blazed in the fireplace, bathing the room in warmth. Windows sat on either side, the curtains tied open to reveal the sunset.

Ren nodded with approval. Yup, now this was peaceful.

Ren's and Marcus's father were already inside. They sat opposite each other, a pot of tea between them while they were mid-conversation.

It had been almost fifty years since Ren had last seen Marcus's father. He had the same light brown hair and golden eyes that Marcus did. However, despite their similarities, Marcus took most of his appearance from his mother.

His father had a well-trimmed beard and a goatee with the beginnings of silver. He had the physique of a seasoned warrior, with a large chest and arms coated in the same light brown hair and the scars to prove it.

Dressed in silver, the symbol of his kingdom was embroidered beautifully over his heart. The sleeves gripped around the top of his biceps. Black pants and armored boots to match adorned his lower half. Resting next to him over the back of the couch was a black cloak fit for a noble, his kingdom's crest embroidered in the center, large and bold for all to see.

"Now there's a sight for sore eyes," Marcus's father said, looking at Ren.

Ren only shrugged back before firing back a comment. "I guess it's true when they say werewolves are the hairiest monster race."

Marcus's father rubbed his bearded chin, a little unpleased and worried at the same time. Looks like Ren won that one.

Ren started chuckling and Marcus's father got up to embrace him.

"It's good to see you again, King Allagash."

"It's good to see you, Ren. You've certainly grown since I last saw you, and not just physically." He was quiet for a moment. "I'm sorry about your mother. Eris was a wonderful woman and a great mother. She'd be proud of you."

"Thank you," Ren said back, giving him a sad smile.

"Dad," Marcus said in greeting. The smile on his face proved he was overjoyed at their reunion.

"Marcus, my son." Marcus embraced his father. "It's good to see you well. I've been keeping tabs on you. I have heard of your accomplishments while you were in the human world. You make me and our kingdom proud. Keep it up."

Marcus bowed his head. "Yes, Sir."

Marcus's relationship with his father was different than Ren's relationship with his father. Marcus's father was much more stern. However, despite that hardness, it didn't take much for one to see that he cared for Marcus very much.

"How's Mom doing?" Marcus asked.

"I'm afraid she caught a slight sickness. Thankfully, she should be getting over it any day now. And who might this be?" he asked, changing his focus to Nidar. The tiger sat and held his paw up for Marcus's father to grab.

"This is Nidar," Ren said. "He's an animal from the human world called a tiger. Specifically, he's an Indian white tiger. I found him as a cub and took him in. We've been together ever since."

"More like they're stuck together like glue," Marcus said. Nidar licked Marcus's hand before moving to sit next to Ren. "See?"

"What an interesting animal. I see a resemblance to some of the other monster species, especially the beastkin."

"He's basically a very large cat. They're top predators, but I've trained him very well."

"Yes, that much is certain. He would make a fine mount in a battle."

"As a matter of fact, he is. I rode him into battle back in the human world."

"Yes, I had heard about that battle. Unfortunately, I've yet to receive the entire story."

"Then allow us."

Ren, Marcus, and Leo relayed the details of the battle in Florida. To completely bring him up to speed on the situation, they also included their quest for the stones. In turn, Marcus's father shared news regarding Nexus with them. To their benefit, the information he provided was very thorough and had not been made known to any of them yet, given so early in their return. And much of it was information that the common folk would find hard to come by.

It was night by the time they finally finished talking, and the servants had come to refill their tea several times.

"I see," Marcus's father said. "Truthfully, I was not aware of the general's identity. It's unfortunate to know about Algiroth, but that's one general down."

"We haven't learned anything else since, as neither Verin nor the Church has made a move. However, Cole agreed to start searching for Verin, so we'll leave it up to him to find him," Ren said.

"And the girl with the stones?"

"She's somewhere around here."

"Keep her close. It'll do her good to research them; just make sure she's safe. We can't lose those stones. They are, perhaps, our greatest asset." Ren nodded in agreement. The stones were much too precious.

"Then I shall retire for the night. It was a long ride. But before I do, I think I will go see Lord Caster. It will be good to see an old acquaintance."

Ren informed him where his master's room was located. Marcus and his dad agreed to leave the following morning. They needed to return to their kingdom, and Marcus wanted to see his mother.

Marcus's father exited the room, leaving the rest of them alone. It was a good time for Ren to tell his father about the food shortage and that he was sending Cole to investigate. He would send him the paperwork to look over once he was finished going through it.

Leo was just as surprised as Ren first was; however, he was without worry, knowing that Ren was already handling it.

With nothing left to discuss and the sun nearly set, they returned to their rooms. There was still work to be done, after all.

Ren sat down in his chair at his desk. He, Nidar, and Neil were the only ones in the room now, and Neil started a fire in the fireplace. It didn't take long before the fire was blazing, and the study was warm.

Ren caught Neil by surprise when he asked to have most of the paperwork brought to him instead of his father. Neil objected at first, aware of the sheer volume of work that had to be done and the workload required, but Ren wanted to lessen the load on his father. In the end, Neil caved, nodding back. He bid Ren a good night and left the room, leaving Ren to finish his work alone with Nidar.

Twenty-two

The Crystal Garden

Ren set his pen down and stretched. After working non-stop all day, he needed a break. He even worked through lunch, and so far, he'd only gotten through half of his work. There were over a dozen stacks of papers. They completely covered his desk and a spot on the floor in front. Everything was organized, so it was easily identifiable. The stacks on his left he had already completed, while all the stacks on his right remained unfinished.

Taking most of his father's work was indeed a great burden. There was so much more than he expected there to be. Normally, they shared the paperwork equally, but Ren wanted to let his father rest and take the workload off of him. Alas, Ren had asked for it, so he couldn't back out now.

No doubt his father had recognized Ren's ploy by now, having probably barely any work. Such was the life of a prince, but what was he to do. That was the job description. It didn't matter what it was; nearly everything that happened in his kingdom passed by him, and sometimes the surrounding kingdoms.

Ren had the fire going. The only noise was the crackling of the flames. Nidar had gone off somewhere, leaving Ren to only himself. It was nice being alone for a change, not that having Nidar there made a difference. He was quiet the whole time anyway, leaving Ren to complete his work peacefully.

The only time the tiger ever moved was when someone approached the door, or he decided both of them needed a break. On top of that, Marcus and his father had left yesterday morning and Cole this afternoon to inspect the food shortage in the Western villages. And with Kelsey in the library researching, he didn't bother.

Despite their initial belief of starting on the first floor, the head librarian had her and a few of the servants begin on the sixth floor, where she was for now. He had no idea where Ellie was, and he hardly ever bothered his father while they were working. As for Neil, the guy wasn't much of a 'having fun' kind of guy. It broke his character, which was all professional.

Rising to his feet, Ren put out the fire before retreating to his bedroom. He needed a break.

Rummaging through his dresser he found his phone and headphones that he had brought with him from the human world. They were useless in this world, for the most part. However, on rare occasions, Ren would use it to listen to music. And he knew the perfect place to relax and do just that.

Heading to the first floor, he turned right at the bottom of the stairs and down a corridor. Taking it all the way to the end, followed by several more turns and corridors, he entered into another section of the palace entirely. The area opened into a large courtyard surrounded by columns on all sides. The courtyard itself was filled with grass, trees, flowers, benches, and the occasional fountain. Cobblestone walkways connected it all together. A colonnade surrounded the courtyard at the edges on all four sides.

Ren's father loved this courtyard. It was, on most occasions, the location where he and Ren's mother would share lunch and tea. That is, when she was alive. However, it appeared that despite the courtyard no longer braced with his mother's presence, it was, instead, braced with another's.

Over by one of the fountains, Ellie was playing with Nidar. Two maids accompanied them, merely watching over silently, one of which was

Lisa saw Ren first. He was walking through the corridor that braced the left side of the courtyard when she ran over to him.

"Ren, I mean, Your Highness." She bowed.

"Lisa, for all the time I've known you, and as well as we get on, I think you can call me Ren. Especially when it's just the two of us. Consider it an order."

She kept her head lowered, but a joyful smile escaped her lips. "I understand. Would you like to join us for some tea by the fountain?"

"No, thank you. I'm headed to the Crystal Garden to relax."

Lisa never responded; however, he could see that she was disheartened at his refusal. Perhaps this was the right moment to raise a question that he had been contemplating asking her.

"Hey, Lisa, how would you like to be a personal maid?" he asked.

"Me, a personal maid?" Lisa didn't bother trying to hide her surprise.

For a maid, and a commoner one such as her, being a personal maid was a great honor. It signified that they were worthy of working directly for their lord in recognition of their skills and loyalty. The only position higher was a head servant. However, that only raised another question.

"It would be an honor, but to who?"

"To Kelsey, the human girl who arrived with us. It will do her well to have her own personal maid. Mind you, this is a compliment, but given your youthfulness, I think it would help her relax and adjust to life here better. In fact, it could be good for both of you."

Lisa bowed low, much lower than usual. It was a clear sign of her appreciation.

"I will gladly accept this position."

Ren returned her enthusiasm with a nod. "If you have any questions or problems with the head maid, come see me."

With a wave of his hand, he walked past her, continuing on toward the back of the palace. A set of stone stairs led to a third story. Taking them up, Ren stopped before an iron door. On the other side was the most beautiful botanical garden one could ever witness. It was impossibly massive and sat on the roof of the back end of the palace.

This garden was Ren's favorite place in the palace. It always put him at ease, especially since, except for the groundskeepers, no one ever ventured there. Here, in this place, he felt at one with nature. He could relax in peace.

Even after over fifty years, Ren still remembered the layout. Near the center of the garden, a little off the path, was a six-foot boulder. The top was flat and worn, perfect for sitting on and relaxing. It was his favorite spot in the garden. Climbing to the top, Ren put his earphones in and laid on his back, letting the music sweep him away.

✝

Kelsey was tired of looking through books, so she set everything she was reading aside in a neat pile and left the library. The head librarian had her begin her search on the sixth floor, not the first as she initially believed. As much of a blessing as it was, it was also terrible. Now, she had to climb six flights of stairs, and more the further she delved into the depths of the library.

The library was located on the East side of the palace, the total opposite side their rooms were on, and was more toward the back. She had to walk all the way up to the front of the palace and cross the bridge to get to the other side. It was killer, especially as exhausted as she was.

Kelsey reached the palace's massive courtyard in the center. It was surrounded at the edges by a colonnade on all sides. As she walked by, she saw Leo, Ellie, Nidar, and two maids. When they saw her walking, Leo called her over. She stepped onto one of the cobblestone paths and walked over to them.

"Kelsey, I was looking for you," Leo said. "Have you seen Ren?"

"No, I've been in the library all day."

"He's in the Crystal Garden," Lisa said.

"Ah, perfect. I need to speak with him. Ren seems to have taken on all of our work by himself, leaving me with little to do, so I'm taking some of it off his hands. Would you mind going to grab him, Kelsey?"

Oh great, as if she wasn't tired enough. But she couldn't exactly refuse, now could she. Besides, it gave her the chance to see Ren. She was always up for that.

"Sure thing. Where's this garden?"

"I'll have one of the maids escort you this time. However, Ren tends to spend a lot of his free time there when he needs to relax. It's his favorite spot. You may find yourself there often. Just in case you do, cross over to the other side of the courtyard and head toward the back of the palace. You'll see a set of stone steps. Take them to the top. They should lead you to an iron door. It's the door to enter the garden. "

"Alright, I'll go get him," she said.

"Thank you," Leo said. "I'll wait here for you."

"Miss Kelsey," Lisa said. "Before you go, Ren has asked me to be your personal maid. So I will be taking care of you from now on."

Kelsey didn't fail to notice Lisa's lack of formality. She just called him by his first name outright. "Really? He told you to do that?"

"Yes. He thought it would benefit us both, believing we would get along well."

"Well, alright then. I guess I'll be relying on you from now on."

"I'll do my best to serve you."

The second maid that was with them led Kelsey to the botanical garden, just as she was instructed. Kelsey crossed the courtyard and headed to the back of the palace. She saw the stone steps just as they had told her about. They were tucked away behind a wall, the opening disappearing from view completely unless you were directly in front of it.

Kelsey had expected the maid to follow, but she didn't; instead, she waited patiently at the bottom. Heading up the stairs, Kelsey opened the iron door and stepped into the garden. It was beautiful. Her jaw went slack when she saw it.

The garden was absolutely massive. Kelsey wondered how she was going to find Ren among it all. He could be anywhere. Her only option was to first follow the paths. Hopefully, they would lead the way.

Only one path lay before her, the one she currently stood on. It led forward, so she followed. There were no signs, no directions, just plants and the cobblestone path beneath her feet. She had no idea where she was or where she was going. Minutes felt like hours. That's when she saw it. A person. They were translucent and radiated gold. It was that spirit. The same one she kept seeing around Ren.

If the spirit was there, that meant only one thing, so was Ren. So she followed it. Whether it disappeared or she lost sight of it, she didn't know, but soon the spirit was gone, leaving her to herself again.

She finally found Ren lying on top of a boulder. He had headphones in his ears, his phone in his hand. It was comforting to know that she wasn't the only one to bring her phone despite its uselessness. Ren, Marcus, and even Ren's father, they'd all brought their phones with them. At this point, it was more habit.

Ren noticed Kelsey approach and took his headphones out.

"Hey, what's up?" he asked.

"Your father is looking for you. He's in the courtyard."

"Alright, thanks."

Ren jumped down from the boulder and started walking, pocketing his phone and headphones. Kelsey followed behind him from a distance. It was clear Ren was here for a reason and needed his space. In light of that, she decided to maintain that distance instead of walking beside him.

Suddenly, a transparent figure appeared next to Ren. It was back. She was seeing it again. The truth was it freaked her out, especially since Ren didn't seem to realize it was there.

The figure was a little taller than Ren, just like last time, with long golden hair down to the base of his back. It wore beautiful golden robes and was barefoot. Then, it turned around, and she caught a look at its beautiful face. It was definitely male, with golden eyes, just like Marcus. Kelsey didn't know if the figure knew she was there since it didn't make any reaction. It merely turned back around before finally disappearing one more time.

Twenty-three

The Midnight Ball

Ren and Kelsey sat in his father's office. He had summoned them for a meeting, though they had no idea why. Ren wondered if something had happened. Was it something to do with the crop failure and food shortage, or was it something else? Had he heard from Cole?

It had already been a week since Cole departed on the mission Ren had sent him on. He arrived in the Western towns two days after he departed. Only yesterday did they get his first report. There was a drought. The very notion came as a complete surprise to Ren and his father.

The Western Regions had the best soil for growing crops. It also rained frequently. They weren't known for receiving droughts. Even as old as he was, Ren had never known the region to experience such a thing.

From Cole's reports, the testimonies of several different villages matched; it hadn't rained in months. In that case, it makes sense that there would be a drought.

Why the lack of rain was the question plaguing Ren's mind. Nevertheless, he was sure glad he sent Cole to investigate. With that new information, Ren had already begun to contemplate a solution.

"I'm sure you two are curious as to why I called you here," Ren's father said.

"A little, yeah," Ren said. "Is it about the drought? Did Cole find anything else?"

"No, it's not about that, unfortunately."

Ren sighed. "Damn. I was hoping for more information before I put my new development plan into action."

"Well, given how long it's going to take to get the funds and the council on board, not to mention the labor, materials, and transportation, it'll be quite a while before the development even begins."

"Oh, don't worry, I'll get everyone on board; you can be sure of that. And as for the money, we'll find it."

"Find it. Don't be a fool, Ren. I don't need you edging on the other nobles or those in the council more than necessary with questionable antics. All we need is to give them leverage to use against us."

"I'm aware of that. I know what our current funds are, along with how much we have in the treasury. I'm already drafting a budget. I'll get it approved by the council as soon as they agree to my plan and find the best prices I can, ideally without demanding too much of the kingdom's tax income.

"Alright, I'll leave it to you then." Ren nodded back in appreciation. "Now, as for why I've summoned you here. Ren, I want you to check in on the citizens."

"Check in?" he asked.

"Yes. You know how popular you are. Go out into the town and immerse yourself in the flow of the capital. We have to make sure we maintain the people's graces. Given your popularity among the citizens, it will be a good way for both to interact. Satisfy them with our presence and assure them we are looking over them. As we've always done, it's best to present ourselves as much as we can, even if it's from a distance."

"Besides, it's also a chance for us to gain information," his father continued. "News directly from the citizens themselves is of its own value. Their take and feelings towards matters is something to account for in our decisions as this kingdom's rulers."

"Yes, Father, I'm well aware of that," Ren said back. His father was treating him like a rookie, like he had when Ren was just a boy, learning to be a prince. It irritated him, especially since he knew why he was doing it; because Kelsey was there.

"Actually, this is good timing, too," Ren told him.

"For what?"

"I was thinking about throwing a ball within the palace."

His father raised an eyebrow at him. "What kind of ball?"

"An open one. No status restrictions, no species restrictions. One all the citizens can attend, from noble birth to lowest. We haven't held an event the citizens can attend in half a century, nor have the citizens stepped foot into the palace. I'd say we're overdue. Interaction, remember? The nobles and commoners need time to share between them. Besides, it would do everyone some good to attend a party and enjoy the night without worries."

Ren's father considered Ren's idea. "A ball could be a good idea. Where are you planning to host it?"

"In the main hall, of course. I'll send out the invitations to everyone. Going into town is convenient since I had intended to go soon to start the preparations."

The main hall was the castle's formal gathering place and where all the palace's special events were held.

"And just where are we getting the money to fund this? Do you plan on using the treasury?"

Ren shook his head. "I have no intention of using the treasury or the income from taxes. I'll be using my own private funds to fund the ball."

Ren's father sighed. "Very well, do as you will. You have my permission."

"Um, then, why did you call me here?" Kelsey asked, feeling like she had been forgotten.

"I was just about to get to you, Kelsey. I want you to accompany Ren while he goes into town."

Ren had a discouraged, if not unwilling, look. "Why?" he asked.

"Because it'll do her some good to get out of the palace. She should get to know the town and the people. It will help her in the future to have good connections and relationships."

"So she has to come with me?"

"You're already going; just take her along. We can save requiring a guard to go with her."

He had a fair point, and Ren couldn't argue it. However, things were still a little awkward with Kelsey. They weren't completely at odds anymore, and Ren didn't bother trying to keep his distance so much anymore. It was more troublesome to try than just be himself. And the lack of communication between them lately hasn't helped much either. He and Kelsey spent most of their time working. Because of that, they had barely seen each other at all in the last few days, let alone talked.

"If you don't want to, I'll go by myself another time," Kelsey said.

Ren realized she was talking to him. He set his gaze on her, watching her flinch. She was expecting him to reject the idea. She knew he didn't have any intention of accompanying her, not unless it were a direct order from his father. So when Ren smiled at her, it surprised her. She quickly looked elsewhere, shielding her face from him so he didn't see the creeping red stain on her cheeks.

"No, it's fine. This is a good opportunity."

"For what?"

"To get you some clothes and items from this realm. I'll take you to the market," he explained.

"Oh no, I'm fine. You don't have to do that, Ren."

"Too bad because I'm doing it. Come on, let's go."

Ren headed for the door. "See you later, Dad."

"Have fun," his father said back.

Ren exited the room, leaving Kelsey to scramble to her feet. "By Dad, we'll be back," she said to Leo, and hurried out the door after Ren.

Kelsey's sudden use of the word dad surprised him, but it made him happy to hear her call him that. A little too happy, actually.

Dad, huh? he thought. He chuckled to himself. *You found a good one, Ren. Don't let her go.*

Ren and Kelsey left the palace through the front entrance. He called for a carriage to head into town, and soon, a horse-drawn carriage stopped before them in front of the palace entrance. Ren opened the door and helped Kelsey inside, taking her hand and guiding her up. Then, he climbed in and closed the door.

The carriage's interior was of the finest quality craftsmanship. The leather seats were soft and cushioned. Windows were built into the door, and on the wall opposite it, the curtains covering them tied open, exposing them to the view outside.

Kelsey felt the moment the carriage lurched forward. There was no shaking, no creaking, nor any exposure from the outside elements seeping in. The giant gates to the palace opened when they approached, and they rode through.

At Ren's command, the carriage stopped in the middle of the city. He opened the door and stepped out, extending his hand to Kelsey. She took it, and he helped her down. Ren ordered the coachman to leave them and return later. It was clear the coachman was uncomfortable leaving them, especially without any guards, but he complied with Ren's command. Soon, the coach was out of sight.

Ren took Kelsey's hand and led her through the town. The growing number of eyes on them began to make Kelsey uncomfortable the further into town they walked. She was expecting them to get swarmed, but to her surprise, they weren't. In fact, it was the complete opposite. Ren stood out like a sore thumb, waving consistently as he passed by people greeting him.

She'd seen it before when they first arrived in the capital, but up close like this, Kelsey was beginning to understand why Ren's father said he was popular among the people.

"Come on, we're heading to the town square," Ren said. "It's in the center of this town, near the cathedral."

Kelsey followed silently at his side while he led the way to the town square. She knew the moment they'd arrived, without him even having to say anything. The cobblestone roads branched out in all different directions, starting from the center, a massive circular patch of green space. Red brick separated the grass from the cobblestone roads. In the center was a giant white fountain surrounded by four benches, all of which were occupied.

Narrow paths cut through the center of the square, a couple of trees scattered about to provide shade. Kelsey caught sight of children playing and splashing about in what she recognized as water. She realized they were playing in a pool. One that wouldn't rise past her ankles should she enter.

Buildings lined both sides of the streets, most of them two stories tall. Each one was different and occupied by various professions.

Doors were propped open. The smell of food hit Kelsey like a truck. The few buildings she saw with lines out the door were likely exactly what she was smelling. Past the long lines, the streets were packed. Monsters roamed about everywhere freely. The buildings were filled with people. The ones she guessed were restaurants even had outdoor seating.

'*Wow,*' she mouthed when she saw the square.

Ren chuckled when he saw her face and slack jaw. "Come on," he said, and started walking.

"Oh, Your Highness!" came a voice.

A lady working at one of the shops had called out to him. She appeared in her late forties and looked completely human. She was slightly overweight but had a bright smile that shone like the sun.

"Your Highness!" another said.

"Prince Ren!"

"Good afternoon, Your Highness!"

"Good afternoon, everyone," Ren said with a smile.

There it was again. That smile of his that could melt ice.

Kelsey followed Ren as he approached the lady who had first called out to him.

"Miracle, it's been a long time," Ren said.

"Indeed. About fifty years now. How was the human realm, Your Highness?"

"Ha, don't get me started," he responded, forcing a laugh out of the woman.

The woman looked behind him to Kelsey. "And who is this?" she asked.

"I'm Kelsey, it's nice to meet you."

"My, what a pretty girl." The woman elbowed Ren playfully. "I see what's going on here," the woman said. She gave Ren a sly grin, and he slapped his forehead with the palm of his hand.

Kelsey chuckled, watching him. It was a very Ren-like response.

"Ren and I are old friends," she told the woman. "We've known each other since I was a little girl, so we're what you would call childhood friends."

"Oh, how nice. Since you were children, huh. As long as His Highness has been traveling to the market, I've never seen him do it with a female companion, least of all one as pretty as you."

Kelsey blushed, clearly caught in the woman's clutches. Ren merely rolled his eyes. Miracle and her antics.

"This is actually my first time here," Kelsey said.

"To the central district?" the woman asked.

Kelsey shook her head. "To the capital. To Nexus, actually."

The woman just gave Kelsey and Ren a lopsided look, clearly confused.

"Oh, I'm not a monster. I'm human," she confessed.

The old woman dropped what she had in her hand and looked at Ren in surprise.

"What?" he asked, raising his shoulders. She just continued to look at him. "It's a long story."

"You sound like Cole," Kelsey said, laughing.

"So, what brings you out today, Your Highness?" the woman asked, finally overcoming her surprise.

"A couple of reasons. While I'm out to assess the capital, the palace will be hosting a ball in a few days.

This is as good a time as any to cross interactions off my list. And, my father requested I show Kelsey around the capital."

"A ball, that sounds lovely."

"It's open to everyone, regardless of status. So please, do attend if you have the time."

"You're throwing us a ball? How thoughtful you are. But, Your Highness, how will you be orchestrating it? Especially so soon after your return."

"Don't worry, everything is coming out of my pocket, and I'll make sure it's a perfect night."

"I see you haven't changed in these fifty years. But that's why we all like you."

"Is this a normal thing?" Kelsey asked.

"No, not often," the woman said. "But it's well known that whenever Ren throws a ball for us commoners, he always pays out of his own pocket. It's his way of supporting the kingdom and us."

Ren scratched the side of his face. His own way of concealing any embarrassment.

"Cole told me he tried to do the same thing," Kelsey said. "But he was never able to officially host it. You two really are cousins."

"Yes, Prince Cole follows after His Highness quite nicely. One can see the bond that they share."

"You seem to know a little about him," Ren noticed.

"A little, yeah. He visited me in the library before leaving on his expedition. He's got so many fascinating stories. And he makes me laugh."

A sudden irritation overcame Ren. "Is that so? How nice for you."

"I wonder if he'll be back in time for the ball? I hope he is."

One of Ren's eyes suddenly twitched. It went unnoticed by Kelsey or the woman working at the shop. "I'm sure he will be," he said, holding in his annoyance.

Only when the next group of customers arrived did Ren and Kelsey finally move on. Now free with Kelsey all to himself, Ren's annoyance vanished as quickly as it appeared.

Kelsey stopped in her tracks when the smell of freshly baked goods hit her nose. The smell was divine. Ren was quick on the uptake and opened the door for her. They walked inside, and Ren waited patiently while Kelsey looked around. She spotted a loaf of bread behind one of the counters.

"Oh, Cole told me this was his favorite bread! I wish he was here; I would get him some."

Annoyance suddenly reared its ugly head at Ren again. "He should be back in a few days," he said.

"Yeah, but by then, it won't be any good. He likes it fresh. I'll just come back once he's returned."

Ren squeezed his fists tightly, his knuckles turning white. But he kept a mask on. "How thoughtful of you," he said, gritting his teeth.

Kelsey looked around again until she found some sweets. A cake that looked adorable, and some cookies with white swirls and chocolate in the center. They also had strawberry jam crusted over the top like a thick glaze.

"These look delicious. Oh, I should get some for Marcus, too. He would love these."

What the hell is with her? Ren wondered. Well, she was right; Marcus would love them.

Kelsey bought a few pieces of cake and two dozen cookies for her and Marcus.

Ren was grateful when they finally left the bakery. Not that the store itself was bad, but listening to Kelsey focus all of her attention on other people was seriously getting to him. Even after they left the bakery, his irritation never faded. It persisted the entire time they wandered, and he still had to take her around for new clothing and anything else she might need.

As irritated as he was, the thought of walking around and shopping, even for Kelsey, no longer appealed to him. Ren wanted to get back and work as soon as possible. Being with Kelsey was starting to become more than he could handle. This was going to be a long day and a very difficult battle.

Twenty-four

Dance In the Vampire Palace

Ren and Marcus readied themselves for the ball. They stood in Ren's room, using a large mirror to put on the finishing touches and ensure their attire was perfect.

All of the servants and most of the guests had already arrived for the ball, leaving the two of themselves to each other's company.

Marcus threw a cape fit for a royal over his shoulders, finishing up his outfit. Dressed in silver and white, the polished buttons and clasps reflected any light that hit them off. His white pants matched his vest and jacket. White shoes adorned his feet, blending in perfectly with the white of his pants. A silver chain attached his white cape at each shoulder, the chain hanging low over his chest.

"Fancy," Ren said, indicating his choice of colors. Silver was always Marcus's preferred color for formal attire. It made him appear noble, draped in the light of the moon. It was a color fit for a werewolf.

"Thanks. I can't believe we're already having a ball," Marcus said.

"Yeah, I'm starting to regret this decision. I just want to get back to work," Ren responded.

"You're a workaholic."

"I can't help it, alright," Ren said back.

Ren was dressed in the complete opposite color spectrum. His pants, vest, and jacket were all dark blue. They were too light to be navy but too dark to be royal. And the colors contrasted perfectly with his deep cobalt blue eyes and bleach-blond hair. Hair that had grown significantly in length. It now hung low all over, the back parted over his shoulders to his collarbones, and his bangs parted in three, the middle left to drape over his nose. It made him look regal in his own way, bringing out the depth of his beauty even further.

A silver tie fell at his chest over a gray shirt. Black gloves fit over his hands with a pair of matching shoes over his feet, and a black noble's cape was tied over his left shoulder to finish his outfit off. A silver plate secured it to his shoulder, with a matching set of three silver chains connecting it to his breast.

"I think it's time to go," Ren said. Marcus agreed, now ready himself, and the two of them exited the room for the ballroom. As it always did, the main hall served every ball the palace held.

Ren closed the door behind them and they headed for the grand staircase, taking them down to the second floor. Eventually, they reached the long bridge connecting the main and East portions of the palace. Down one of the hallways, an open door led to a massive room, the ballroom. Another grand staircase descended from a balcony to the main floor below, where the ball's attendees were already gathered and mingling.

A servant stood at the door to greet them. His job was to announce the guests, especially those of high class, like Ren and Marcus.

"Your Highnesses," he greeted, bowing to them.

"Good evening," Ren said.

"We're glad you could finally make it."

"Sorry for the wait; it took us a little while," Marcus said.

"Please, allow me to introduce you," the servant requested. Ren and Marcus nodded in agreement.

Looking out from the balcony, Ren could see everyone. He noticed the many nobles and commoners gathered. As he'd hoped, everyone appeared well-mannered and polite to those of different classes.

Ren spotted his father with a few retainers already gathered below. They were surrounded by a group of nobles. And then he saw her. She was dressed in a black and red dress that made her copper hair shine in a way it never had. The dress hugged tight to her waist and flared around her hips, showing off all of her curves. Black gloves attached to sleeves made of lace raced up her arm. The cuffs of the sleeves were impossibly long, dropping to her knees.

Kelsey's hair had been styled, tied into a large, thick braid that fell over her shoulder. A second thin braid circled the back of her head before turning into a small ponytail.

Ren felt his heart suddenly race. The world around him fell away, and all he saw was the beautiful girl below him. She was absolutely stunning.

The servant cleared his throat, drawing Ren back to the world around him. Both the servant and Marcus held their gazes on him, entirely aware of who he had been staring at.

"She is certainly beautiful. Perhaps it would do well to approach her rather than remain content to stare at her from afar."

Ren suddenly felt defenseless, exposed. He was wearing his emotions on his sleeves, despite himself and all his training. But when it came to Kelsey, he just couldn't control himself.

The servant approached the balcony, casting out a booming voice. "Presenting His Royal Highness, Prince Marcus Allagash!"

Marcus walked into view and began his descent down the steps. He had most eyes on him, the shallow gathering of small conversations remaining. In his white and silver attire, the guy looked like the moon incarnate. He was every bit the prince he was supposed to be.

"And finally, presenting His Royal Highness, Prince Ren Nightwalker." Ren walked into view, and just like that, all the attention was on him. Conversations halted, and eyes settled, every person in the room taking in the majesty that was their crown prince. In his blue suit, Ren was a feast for the eyes. And he had the quiet gawking from every female in the room, each of whom hid their desire to have a piece of him behind stone faces or fans.

As soon as she saw him, Kelsey's heart did summersaults in her chest. She felt her stomach drop and her cheeks burn. Ren sent her every desire into overdrive. She'd never seen him so in his element, so much the prince he was.

Marcus stopped to wait for Ren, and they descended the steps together. Despite her best efforts, Kelsey couldn't take her eyes off Ren. She really hoped no one would notice her blush, but surrounded in heat and wine, perhaps she could play it off if she needed to.

The servant followed Ren and Marcus down the steps, and Ren turned to him at the bottom.

"Thank you for waiting to introduce everyone. Take a break and enjoy the ball; that's an order."

The servant failed to conceal his smile. "As you command, Your Highness."

Ren and Marcus were immediately swarmed with people when they reached the bottom of the stairs.

Admittedly, Ren was rather distracted. He completely blocked out the people around him, leaving Marcus to confront them alone.

Ren looked around, searching for the girl that made his heart skip a beat. He found her on the dance floor, arms wrapped around the neck of a familiar face. Cole had his arms around her hips as they danced, and Ren suddenly wanted to tear him apart. His effort to approach them failed when Kelsey took his hand and led him elsewhere on the dance floor. Well then, apparently, that was going to be an all-night thing.

One daring and lucky girl approached Ren from within the crowd, finally distracting him from Kelsey and Cole. She was dressed in a blue gown that matched her light-blue eyes, the dress embroidered with silver flakes, causing it to twinkle like a sea of stars. Her blond hair was tied into twin drills.

"Um, Prince Nightwalker." Ren could tell she was nervous. "Well, could I, or, that is to say, would you do me the honor … of dancing with me tonight?"

From the commotion of accompanying women, it was clear that the rest who had failed to make the first move were dissatisfied. Each had wanted their own piece of Ren, and now he'd been stolen from them. It was a good thing the ball was long.

Marcus put a hand on Ren's shoulder. "Think you can handle this?"

Ren chuckled and held his hand out to the woman, giving her that ice-melting smile and nearly causing her heart to explode. "I would love to dance with you." The woman took his hand, and he led her to the center of the room.

Ren's and the woman's dancing quickly gathered the attention of those who weren't already dancing.

Standing off to the side of the room after finally finishing their dance, Kelsey watched Ren with captivated eyes. The guy was graceful, brilliant, and fluid, like water. The way he moved was cleaner and more precise than she had ever seen. His dancing skills were on a completely different level. It was like there was nothing he couldn't do. He was unmatched in everything. And the girl, she was actually keeping up with him. The way they danced, it was like they had rehearsed it. All of her, from her dress to her hair to her makeup, was beautiful. It was like they were made for each other.

A twitch of pain suddenly passed through Kelsey's chest. Watching them, watching Ren's hands placed delicately on her, Kelsey found herself clenching her fists. She didn't want to see him dance with other women. Especially not when it felt like he'd be taken from her at any second, whisked away to some new life without her.

"If you want to dance with him, all you need to do is ask," Cole said, appearing next to her.

He watched her while she watched Ren and the woman dance, never taking her eyes off of him.

"I know," she finally said, "but there are so many people here, and I don't know if I'll get the time or the chance."

"You have to make that chance. If you don't, he'll be surrounded by other women the entire night. Trust me, Kelsey, every girl in here wants a piece of him."

The music came to a stop, signaling the end of the dance, and Ren felt someone pull on his jacket. He looked down and saw Ellie standing there. She was dressed in a ruby red dress and black shoes. Ren.

"How come only she gets to dance with you. It's not fair. I want to dance with you, too, Ren!" Ellie said. Ren chuckled and looked at the woman. She was smiling and nodded back, understanding the situation.

'Thank you,' Ren mouthed to the woman. In response, she gave him a light curtsey before rejoining the crowd.

The music began to kick up again, and Ren focused on Ellie. "Ready munchkin'?" he asked. She nodded, and he raised her up, setting her down on the top of his feet. Their difference in height was too vast to dance together normally. Besides, Ren rather liked this method. It was a form of closeness in its own right.

"Thanks, Ren," he heard Ellie say.

"For what, kiddo?"

"For bringing me here. For not leaving me alone by myself. And for throwing this party."

Ren spun around with Ellie on his feet before responding.

"Of course, Ellie. We're family now. That means we're in this together." Ren suddenly stopped dancing, and Ellie stepped off of his shoes while he knelt down to her level. "Even on my quests and missions, you'll know where I'm headed and that you're always on my mind. I'm not going anywhere on you. It's you and me from now on, okay?"

"You're forgetting someone, though," she said.

Ren had the ready suspicion he knew who the target of her words was, Kelsey.

"And who's that?" he asked anyway.

"Nidar!"

Alright, that one threw him off guard. Ren burst into laughter. "Yes, you're right about that. Our furry feline companion is always with us, too. How could I forget."

Ren hugged Ellie tight, feeling her wrap her small arms around him back.

"Come on, the dance isn't over yet," he said.

Ellie beamed as she stepped back on his feet, and Ren continued to lead her in their dance.

"What about me? Do I count in that?" someone asked.

Marcus approached the two of them, and Ellie turned to him. Her surprised face caused Ren to chuckle.

"Of course you do, Marcus," Ellie said. "You helped Ren save me, after all."

The music faded off before starting again in another tune. Marcus reached his hand out in response, extended to Ellie.

"I believe it's time to change partners. May have this dance, Princess?"

"You may," Ellie said, taking his hand.

Ren chuckled and let Marcus take his turn dancing with Ellie.

"Finally alone, huh?"

Ren turned as Kelsey walked up next to him. For the first time, he noticed the red high-heeled shoes on her feet. Each one had a strap on the front.

"Hey," she said.

"Hey," he said back. And then he was staring again. "Wow."

"Wow yourself," she said back, gently pushing his bangs aside. "Do you want to dance?"

"I'd love to," he said before he'd even realized what he'd said.

Kelsey wrapped one arm around his neck, the other gently held in his hand. He placed his free hand on her hip, and they were dancing.

The two of them danced together for a while, longer than their other dances or partners, before Kelsey switched to Marcus and Ren walked off. He grabbed a glass of Champaign from one of the servers and found a spot to the side and out of sight to watch the ball alone.

"Taking a break, I see." Ren's father walked up to him.

"Yeah, I needed a breather." Ren took a sip of his Champaign as a few other people made their way over to them. One was Marcus's father, the other a marquise, and last but not least, the archduke himself.

"Archduke Randolf," Ren greeted.

"Your Highness, welcome back."

"Thank you. And thank you for looking after things while we were away."

"Of course. You were needed in the human world with Verin's growing influence. I'm just glad to see that you all have returned safely. Annabel and Queen Allagash were worried sick, wondering what you and Prince Marcus were up to."

Ren chuckled. "Sounds about right."

They all engaged in conversation for a while before eventually parting ways. By now, the ball was beginning to end, and people were trickling out that later it got. Nor were they alone in their sentiments. Ren also felt fatigued from the day catching up with him and bid himself a good night. He looked for Kelsey to tell her he was leaving the ball, only to find her dancing with Cole again. Based on the smile she had on her face and how engaged in the conversation they were, he decided it was best to leave without telling her.

Ren noticed quickly that Kelsey had been getting on with Cole a lot lately. She had said she enjoyed his company. Perhaps this was what they needed to widen the gap. Perhaps Cole could be the thing that finally broke them apart. But did he really want that? Honestly, he wasn't sure anymore.

Ren considered it a possibility of his cousin's entrance into their relationship. It would sure make things easier if there were someone else for them to fall back on. But one thing was certain: his relationship with Kelsey was sinking fast, and they were almost at the bottom.

Twenty-five

The Proposal

R en signed another document. The stack of papers on his desk felt never-ending.

He grabbed another piece of paper and read it over before signing it, repeating the process over and over again.

It had already been three days since the ball, and Ren had locked himself in his office the entire time. He hadn't talked to anyone or bothered to leave, spending what made up all of his time in there.

Perhaps he had been pushing himself, but he had little choice. He left his work for practically two days while he prepared for the ball. It was a given that it would all pile up.

By keeping himself locked away, he could focus on his work freely and not be bothered by distractions. If he was being honest, it wasn't so much about getting the work done, not that that wasn't a big part of it, but more about maintaining that distance between Kelsey and him.

Ren read through a stack of papers and separated them from the rest. This stack was much more engaging at the moment, drastically needing his attention. It contained all of the documents required for his proposed solution to the drought in the West.

With the lack of rain causing the drought, he had proposed a contingent source of water supply to feed the fields. After some research on the agricultural impact of land and a quick study of the geography using existing maps, he determined the best course of action to take. That's where the contingent water source came into being.

The Western Region had three massive lakes. By tapping into those lakes with controlled aqueducts, they could easily supply the required water necessary to sustain the land and crops.

Looking at the documents, his proposal was being finalized, which meant it needed his signature of approval from the council before it could proceed any further.

Before signing, Ren did a quick check on the numbers to make sure everything was in order. He reviewed the time it would take to construct the aqueducts, including the digging, formwork, the actual construction of the aqueducts, the work for the water gates to control access, and filling the aqueducts. After that, he reviewed the budget and verified the price of materials and labor for the project before moving on to the schedule.

More so than the budget, the schedule was the real hard line they couldn't cross. Ren had to ensure that it didn't run too far over. The longer it took, the more effective the drought became. The losses were a lot heavier than the cost of building the aqueducts should they get behind schedule, or, in the worst case, fail completely.

Ren finished scanning the documents, verifying that everything was in order. He signed the documents and set that stack aside so that it wasn't misplaced.

"Alright, that's finally done with for the moment. What's next? he wondered.

⸸

Kelsey was in her usual spot, the library. To say it was grand was an understatement. It was incredible, to say the least. There were so many books, too many, actually. The amount of knowledge the place contained was unparalleled. It put the libraries in the human world to shame.

After several weeks, she was already on the seventh floor. Yet, even after all that time and already progressing floors, she had found nothing on the stones. All this knowledge, all this history, and there was just nothing.

Kelsey had a strong suspicion that Ren was right. The information they sought would only be found on the fifteenth floor, the lowest and most dangerous part of the library. But if she was being completely honest, a small part of her thought that perhaps they would never find the information they wanted because it wasn't even there.

The thought of having to carry the stones forever, never able to take them off, she couldn't say she hated the idea. Having the stones gave her power and kept her close to Ren and the others. Besides, it wasn't like having them was a bother, either. They didn't get in her way. Half the time, she forgot they were even there.

A sigh escaped from Kelsey's lips.

"Can't find anything?" Cole asked.

Ren's cousin sat across from her with a book in his hand. Ren had asked him to help Kelsey search for the stones and assist with finding Verin. However, just like she, Cole had yet to find any information on the stones or Verin. Regardless of their findings, however, she was grateful for the help. She needed all that she could get of it. There was too much information for her to go through alone, even with the few servants helping her.

Kelsey shook her head in response to his question. "No matter how much I search, I can't find anything,"

"Me neither. I think this floor is another bust."

"And we still have eight floors to go."

"Well, technically, we have five. Once we get to the twelfth floor, the traps start to occur. Nevertheless, I think it's time to move on. We can finish up this floor tonight and head to the eighth floor tomorrow."

Kelsey rubbed her nose between her eyes. "I think I'm going to take a nap. I'm getting tired. I'll be back later."

"Alright, go rest. I'll be here."

Kelsey got up to leave when she heard her name. It was faint and came from across the room.

"Kelsey," it appeared again, this time noticeably louder. That's when they noticed Ren's father approaching. He appeared rather disheveled despite his polished appearance. But his eyes gave his inner turmoil away.

"Uncle, what are you doing here?" Cole asked. They were both rather surprised to see him.

"Kelsey, I need your assistance,"

"With what?" she asked back.

"It's Ren. He's been locked in his room for three days now," he confessed. "He won't eat, he's barely slept, and he refuses to see anyone. I'm worried."

Three days? That was certainly something to worry about. No wonder the guy looked so concerned.

"Then why don't you talk to him?"

Leo sighed and ran a hand through his hair. Yup, he and Ren were definitely father and son.

"I tried; he refused to see me, too. It's always the same excuse, that he's busy."

"Why would he do something like that?"

"I'm afraid he's trying to place all the responsibility on himself. He's always been like this, but ever since we came back from the human realm, it's gotten worse. And he hasn't left his room since the ball. Kelsey, did something happen?"

"What do you mean?"

"I don't know. I was just wondering if you had heard anything or perhaps knew what was going on with him."

"Sorry, I have no idea. To be honest, we haven't seen each other much. I spend most of my time here. This is the first I've heard of this."

Leo released a heavy and frustrated sigh. "I see."

Kelsey could tell he was worried. And, knowing his situation, it worried her too. If Ren wasn't eating or sleeping, something had to be wrong.

"I'll go see what's wrong. Maybe I can get him to eat and take a break."

"Thank you. I want to go myself, but he won't see me, and I don't want to push him."

"I understand. Let me go see what's wrong with our prince." She smiled and walked to the stairs, taking them to the top floor. After leaving the library, she headed for Ren's room.

No food, no sleep, locking himself in his room for three days; something wasn't right with him. Ren had always been reckless, but this was too much, even for him. It looked like it was up to her to knock some sense into him. She'd force-feed him if she had to.

Kelsey saw a maid standing outside Ren's door with a tray in her hands. It carried what she presumed was Ren's lunch on it. Kelsey recognized the maid instantly since it was her personal maid.

"Lisa."

"Kelsey?"

"Are you trying to give that to Ren?"

"Yes, but he won't let me in. He said he's too busy. I had thought he would at least see me. He hasn't eaten or slept in three days. I'm worried."

"I know, Leo sent me here to see if I could help him."

"I see. Then maybe it's a good thing you're here. Why don't you try and give this to him?"

"Don't worry, I'll make him eat."

Kelsey grabbed the tray from Lisa and opened the door. Ren looked up as soon as he heard the door open. He saw Kelsey holding a tray of food and a nervous-looking Lisa attempting to stop her.

"Um, Kelsey, I don't think that's such a—"

"It's fine," Kelsey said, cutting her off. "We'll call if we need you."

Kelsey closed the door behind her.

Nidar poked his head up when she came in.

"Kelsey, what are you doing here? I've made it clear I don't want to be disturbed," Ren said.

Kelsey walked over to him, set the tray down on a chair, took the stack of papers he was working on from him, and set them on the ground. Then, she grabbed the tray and placed it in front of him.

"What do you think you're," he started to say.

"Eat, now!" she interrupted.

Ren held her gaze for only a few seconds before responding. "I'm not hungry. You're interrupting me; now leave."

Kelsey didn't even budge. "Eat."

"No."

"Ren Allen Nightwalker, you eat this food or so help me—"

"So help you what, Kelsey? So help you what?"

Ren got up from his chair, and Nidar jumped down from the couch he was lying on.

"Eat, now. Or I'll force you to eat it."

"I'd like to see you try." Ren's tone was ice-cold, but Kelsey didn't even flinch, let alone back off.

Nidar walked up to them and bit the end of Ren's sleeve, tugging on it. Ren turned his attention to the tiger, and Kelsey rose to the tips of her toes, planting a soft kiss on his cheek. Ren looked at her in surprise.

"Eat … please," she said in a worried tone.

Ren sighed and ran a hand through his hair. "I'm sorry. I'm just a little stressed out."

Kelsey placed her hand on this side of his face. "It's alright. I'm sorry I haven't been around to help you more. We haven't seen each other much either. We should start spending more time together again." He nodded, and she led him over to the couch.

Ren sat down, and Kelsey grabbed the tray of food, placing it on his lap. She sat next to him, tucking her legs in to the side. "Thanks," he said before taking a bite.

Kelsey watched him eat, a feeling of relief washing over her. Now, she just needed to get him to take a nap.

When Ren finished eating, he set the tray down and returned to his desk. "Thanks." He grabbed the set of documents Kelsey had taken away from them and started reading them again.

After a long silence, Ren looked up, away from them. "Is there something else?" he asked when she didn't leave. Kelsey just stood there, watching him, her hands behind her back.

"Oh, no, not really." She fidgeted, and he sighed.

"What's wrong, Kelsey?" he asked, getting irritated.

"I, I guess, I was just wondering what you were doing."

Ren sighed and motioned her over with his head. She walked over to him, and he eased her into his lap.

"I'm reviewing an income tax report on the holdings and charity some of the orphanages have received and comparing it to this funding report."

"You give them money?" He nodded.

"Plenty of people donate to the Church, and the Church takes a chunk of that to support their orphanages and branches. However, a portion of the taxes is granted annually to those run directly by the Church in the form of a grant. The funding report we receive every year grants us the necessary information to provide that funding.

Ren handed Kelsey the document, and she looked it over. He explained everything that the document stated, including how to determine what funding and calculations to provide it. He also explained the income report to her and answered any questions she had.

Rather surprisingly, Ren found that Kelsey wasn't just engaged but was actually quite good at it. It was both good for her and interesting for him. He never thought he'd be teaching her economics and politics.

Somewhere in the time Kelsey was reviewing the documents, Ren's head started to dip. Kelsey saw him move out of the corner of her eye and found him half asleep. She smiled. Finally, no more grinding away endlessly.

Kelsey pushed his bangs out of the way and kissed him on the forehead. Then she moved him to the couch, laying his head on her lap. Seeing his sleeping face gave her butterflies.

Sleep well ... my handsome prince, she thought.

When Ren woke, he saw Kelsey above him. He realized his head was on her lap. Kelsey gently played with his hair with one hand while the other held the book she was reading. She chuckled lightly after reading something.

"What's so interesting?" he asked.

Kelsey looked away from her book, directing her attention to him. "Oh, you're awake."

Ren sat up. "How long was I asleep?"

"About three hours." She closed the book and set it aside, grabbing a cup of Champaign-colored liquid with a saucer underneath. The liquid was hot, steam rising into the air. "Here, drink this, it's tea. It'll help you get your energy back."

"Thanks," he said, taking the cup. "Where did you get this?"

"One of the maids brought it. You should have seen the look on her face when she saw you sleeping." Kelsey giggled. "She was so shocked she actually called others over to make sure she wasn't hallucinating." Ren rolled his eyes, making Kelsey laugh.

Ren finished the tea and handed the cup to Kelsey. She put it on the tray his food had been on.

"Now we just need to get you to bathe," she said. "While you do that, I'll take this to the kitchen. See you at dinner, yeah?"

"Yeah, okay."

She grabbed the tray and left the room. He guessed she was right. A bath wouldn't hurt.

Ren got to his feet and walked to the bathroom connected to his room.

When Ren emerged from the bathroom, he felt five times better, and hungry again. He sat down at his desk and sorted through all of the papers, but he didn't get far before there was a knock on his door.

Nidar's head popped up, and he started growling. Whoever was behind the door was someone the tiger didn't recognize.

"Enter." The door opened, and a man entered the room. Ren knew this man; Vincent Sway, a member of the council. But what was he doing here? Ren immediately grew cautious.

"Your Highness," the man said.

"Councilman Sway. To what do I owe the pleasure of your sudden and unannounced visit?" Ren's subject of word choice didn't go unnoticed by the councilman.

"Forgive me, Your Highness. This is a rather urgent situation, and one I don't wish for others to overhear at the moment. Hence, my secrecy at coming unannounced. I've come here regarding a matter concerning our kingdom and the Kingdom of Dridia."

Dridia? That was a neighboring kingdom bordering the mountains. They were famous for their mines containing gold and precious gems.

"To be honest, I do not wish to burden you with this. However, there is no one else to turn to," the councilman said after a long pause. "We have received a notice from the King of Dridia, and its contents are rather undesirable. Dridia wishes to further our trade and its own territory. For this, they have promised more precious materials and the hand of their first princess."

"The hand of their first princess. You're talking about a—"

"Yes," the councilman interrupted. "But that is not the main issue. I'm afraid the King of Dridia has included a secondary clause. If we do not accept the terms of the union, Dridia has threatened to cease all trade with our kingdom entirely."

Ren's eyes widened. He couldn't believe what he was hearing.

"The king cannot know of this, nor do I want him to. If he found out, His Majesty would do everything to stop this from happening."

Ren knew exactly what he was talking about. "You're right about that," he admitted.

"And so I have come to you. As the next person in line for the throne, it's only fitting to have a princess at your side when you ascend." The councilman lowered his head, surprising Ren. "Your Highness, you are the only one I can ask this of. We cannot lose Dridia, or its mines. Please, I beseech you, for the benefit of the kingdom, accept this union. Agree to this marriage proposal with Dridia's princess."

Twenty-six

What I Failed Say

"You want me to marry the princess of the Dridia Kingdom?" Ren asked. All he could do was stare at the councilman.

"If you agree to the arranged marriage, the proposal will fall through, and we'll have no worry over the exchange of resources. Doing this would secure the future of our kingdom," the councilman said back. "Lord Cole has no qualifications given his abdication. And your father, His Majesty … well, that's another problem entirely. After your mother's death, I don't dare force him into another relationship. That would be cruel, even for me. That's why I've come to you."

Ren gripped his fists tightly. He wanted to smash the very desk he sat at to splinters. Damn the King of Dridia and his ploy. Roughly ninety percent, close to all of the jewelry and artifacts that his kingdom used and distributed, were made from jewels sourced out of Dridia. Their loss would devastate them financially.

"Please, Your Highness, agree to the arrangement. For your father, for your kingdom, for your people."

Ren wasn't sure what to do. This was a decision he hadn't expected to be making yet. He expected to have to marry for political reasons one day, but not this soon. Then again, he was over three hundred years old, so maybe this was good timing. Still, a decision like this couldn't just be made like that.

"Give me some time to think about it," Ren said. "A few days at most. I need time to consider everything. When I have reached my decision, I will summon you here."

"As you wish, Your Highness. But I recommend not taking too long. The longer we wait, the quicker our chance fades away."

The councilman bowed and left the room, leaving Ren and Nidar alone. Ren sighed and leaned back in his chair. A marriage proposal, an arranged marriage. He really didn't want to, but he recognized that he would have little choice in the matter. If Dridia's threat was as great as Councilman Sway had indicated, the damage caused by his refusal could be irreversible.

So much money flowed through jewels and gold it could cripple them. Not to mention the loyalties and privileges of the nobles who purchased them. He couldn't risk it. Nor did he have a plan to fight back yet.

The king's proposal and warning had thrown him off guard. They'd all been taken by surprise.

Admitting it made him want to vomit, but he'd recognized for decades already that the good of the kingdom would always come before his own desires. What he wanted didn't matter. It was all for the sake of the kingdom. That was one of the prices he had to pay for being the heir to a nation and a noble.

Ren went back to work, going through the mounds of papers as fast as he could. He worked non-stop for hours until he finally finished.

He needed fresh air, especially after the morning he'd had.

Opening the door behind him, Ren stepped out onto the balcony. There were several chairs, a porch swing with a canopy, and a glass table. He took the swing, sinking into the soft cushions. Nidar jumped up, lying next to him. Ren sat there in silence, letting the bench swing back and forth.

It was peaceful. With the exception of Nidar's breathing, there were no sounds. And most importantly, it helped to clear his head, even if only momentarily.

"I figured I'd find you out here," said a voice. Ren looked to see Marcus walk onto the balcony. He took a seat next to Ren, who scooted over for him. "You weren't in your room or study, so I thought you might be out here."

"I've missed this," Ren confessed. "I haven't been out here in a long time. I almost forgot how amazing it was. Everything's so … calm. I could spend an eternity here."

"Especially since you've been working non-stop. I heard you were shut in here for three days."

"Yeah. I just had too much work to do."

"I saw it coming in. I'm glad it wasn't me doing it." Ren chuckled lightly.

"You alright? You look distracted. Do you have something on your mind?" Marcus asked him.

"You could say that." Marcus just looked at him, his way of telling Ren to continue explaining. "A member of the council came in a little while ago."

"A councilman? What did they want?"

"Promise to keep this a secret? This can't leave this balcony. No one can know … yet."

"I promise."

Ren stared off into space before answering. "The King of Dridia has pulled one over on us. He wants an increase in trade for his daughter's hand in return. The problem is, he's threatened to cease trade entirely if we don't accept."

Marcus's eyes suddenly widened with shock.

"No one other than me, a few other council members, and now you know about this. Not even my father knows."

"Your father doesn't know?"

Ren shook his head. "They didn't want to tell him, not that I blame them. If he knew, he'd destroy the whole thing in an instant."

"So they came to you."

"Who else to dump this on than their prince, the heir to the throne? Especially given that I have yet to even select a queen candidate, let alone get engaged. Well, I was expecting something like this sooner or later."

"Being in the human world for so long helped delay it, no doubt. Did you accept?" Marcus asked, curious.

"Not yet. I told him I needed time to think about it."

"I see. And? You can't seriously be considering it."

"What else am I to do? Dridia has us by the tail. You know what would happen if we refused and he made good on his word. I can't risk that. The kingdom will always come before me. That's the reality of it."

"What about Kelsey and Ellie?"

"Honestly, I'm not sure what to do about Ellie. As for Kelsey, I'll get the stones off of her as soon as I can and send her on her way."

"You mean back to the human realm?" Ren nodded. "You realize you'll never see her again, right?"

"I know."

"Ren, come on, man."

"Don't Marcus. You know this is how things work."

"That doesn't mean it's right, bro. I know you still love her."

Ren confirmed his words with a nod. "I know, but sacrifices have to be made. If I could choose Kelsey, I would. Unfortunately, the cards have been drawn, and the hand has been dealt. Besides, I haven't completely decided yet. I'm going to weigh the options and see how beneficial this marriage would actually be for the kingdom. If I can find a way out of this, you can be sure I'll take it."

Marcus sighed and ran his hand through his hair. "Well, it's up to you to decide. Whatever you decide to do will be for a reason. Just don't regret it."

"It won't matter even if I did."

"I guess so."

A knock on Ren's door came from inside. He and Marcus got to their feet, ready to answer, when the door opened, and Cole walked into the room.

"Hey, Cole," Ren said.

"Hey, Ren. You have a visitor." Ren could tell from his expression that he was not happy.

"I do?"

Cole nodded. "I don't like this. The others may not know why she's here, but I can guarantee I do."

"What do you mean? Who is it?"

"The first princess of Dridia," Cole said after a long pause.

"She's here?" Marcus asked. He and Ren were equally surprised.

"She just arrived, claiming she wanted you in person before your arrangement."

"I didn't expect her to arrive so soon. I only just got the news today."

"I don't agree with this. Especially not when there are certain people here who have a clear interest in you."

"Disagree all you want; it's not up to you. It's up to me to decide in the end. You haven't heard of the consequences of rejecting the proposal. If you had, you'd understand where I'm coming from. Besides, I haven't decided yet. Take me to her."

"Follow me."

They walked to the courtyard in the center of the palace. Ren saw a woman he didn't recognize. She wore a dress of white and pink, and wore a large hat over her head. He could only assume that was the princess who had come to see him. And she wasn't alone. With her were several servants and one other person. Kelsey sat beside a tree with a book from the library spread out in her hands.

The woman in the dress turned in their direction when they got close. Now face to face, Ren and Marcus were stopped in their tracks, looking at the woman with wide eyes. The princess of the Dridia Kingdom, the woman Ren might soon marry, was Juliana Haynes, one of their own and a member of Trinity."

"Julie?" Ren and Marcus said at the same time.

"Ren, Marcus!" Julie ran over to them and threw her arms around them, taking them all to the ground. Ren and Marcus were still in shock, but they were glad to see her.

"I'm so glad to see you guys."

"We're glad to see you too," Ren said. "We didn't know you were back in Nexus."

"I arrived a few weeks ago, not long after your press conference, Ren."

"Have you been in contact with anyone else from Trinity?"

"Most of them. Only a few came back here like me. The rest are still in the human world working."

"What are you doing here?" Marcus asked her.

Julie looked at Ren. "The marriage proposal," she whispered into his ear, and thanks to Marcus's insane hearing, he heard it too.

"Wait, you mean?" Ren started to ask.

She nodded. "I was surprised when my father first told me about the proposal. But when I learned it was to the heir of the Nightwalker Kingdom, I had to come surprise you."

"Who knows the reason you're here?" Marcus asked.

"Only you two. I haven't told anyone else the real reason I'm here. I'm keeping it a secret for now."

"So are we."

"You mean no one knows? What about your father?" Ren shook his head, surprising her.

"Let's just say your father has made things difficult."

"I know, I heard. I'm sorry. Mother and I are figuring it out now. We'll think of something to stop my father's plan, don't worry."

Marcus helped Julie to her feet.

"Ren, show me around your palace," Julie said.

"Sure. A little fresh air will do me good. I just finished all my work, so I need to get out of my study."

"Awesome! I've never been to the royal palace, only read about it."

Julie grabbed Ren's hand, which Kelsey easily took notice of, and she didn't like it. She knew they were old friends and co-workers, but that did not distill her burning emotions. Just the fact that Ren was holding hands with her royally pissed Kelsey off. She couldn't stand seeing him get close to other girls. It just drove her insane. Besides, Kelsey suspected that Julie still held a candle for Ren. If that were still the case, things were going to get even more complicated, and she didn't need that. It was already complex enough as it was.

"You coming?" Ren asked Marcus. The werewolf merely held his gaze, his thoughts unrecognizable.

"I'm good. I think I'll hang back here."

Ren nodded and was suddenly yanked to the side.

"Ren, come on!" Julie said, pulling him along with her.

"Okay, okay, I'm coming."

Ren smiled at her, and Kelsey's irritation doubled instantly. She slammed her book shut, and the two of them disappeared out of sight.

Ren took Julie around the palace as promised. He watched her spin around in circles, taking everything curiously, just as she did everything else new to her.

"I see you haven't changed."

"Oh, and you have?" she asked back, taking his hand again. "Well, shall we continue?"

"Ren!" someone called. Ren turned around, and Ellie tackled him with a hug.

When Ellie noticed Julie holding Ren's hand, she immediately threw herself between them and wrapped herself around Ren's arm, breaking them apart.

"Ren, who is this?"

"So you're Ellie. Ren's told me so much about you back in the human world. I'm Juliana. You can call me Julie," she introduced.

"Ellie, Julie is an old friend of mine," Ren added. "We work together at Trinity. She's also a princess."

"Why is she here?" Ellie asked.

"She's here to see me. Our kingdoms are working on something together." Well, technically, it wasn't a lie, but it certainly wasn't the whole truth. Not that Ellie needed to know that.

Ellie stared at Julie silently. "When is she leaving?"

"Ellie, don't be rude!" Ren said, raising his voice.

"No! Ren, what about Kelsey?"

"What about Kelsey?" he asked back.

Ellie stared at him with a blank expression. "Ren … you're an idiot."

"What?" he asked, shocked.

Julie suddenly burst into laughter.

"Hey, what the hell is that supposed to mean?" Ellie never answered him, while Julie just kept laughing. "Hey!" he said again.

Ellie held her hand out. "I'm coming with you."

Ren took her hand. "I'm showing Julie around the palace."

"Fine."

Ren finished showing Julie around the palace with Ellie. They were returning to the foyer when they passed by one of the rooms and saw Marcus and Cole inside. They sat facing each other, a chessboard seated between them.

"Ha, checkmate!" Marcus said.

"God damn it!" Cole said back.

"You're never going to win, you know," Ren said.

Marcus and Cole looked to see him standing in the doorway with Ellie and Julie. Cole realized that Ren had been addressing him.

"We'll see about that. Momma didn't raise no quitters, Ren," Cole said back.

"But she did raise failures," Ren shot back.

"Oh, screw you!"

Marcus chuckled in amusement. "Hey, Ellie, want to play?" he asked.

"Sure!" She ran over to them and grabbed a third seat, sitting next to Marcus.

With Ellie gone, Ren and Julie left the three of them alone. They were nearing the main foyer when a sudden burst of pain blew through Ren's body. Had Julie not caught him, he would have collapsed.

"Ren, what happened?"

Ren's vision focused, blocking everything else out. He saw the blood running through her, heard the beating of her heart. The smell of iron hit him like a truck, and his fangs shot out to their full size.

"It's my urgest," he said. "They just came out of nowhere."

Julie knew what was happening to Ren before he even said anything. She'd seen his symptoms plenty of times before.

"You may have fed before, but your body still isn't used to taking in blood naturally. Until it acclimates, you'll keep having attacks. They won't be as frequent as before, but they'll be much stronger. You should feed more often."

"I don't like drinking blood, especially without permission."

"Well, regardless, right now, blood is what you need. Come on, let's go find Kelsey."

Julie pulled him along with great haste. Kelsey could be anywhere, and Ren's palace was too damn big, especially at the worst times. His urges hit again before they could find her.

"Kelsey!" Julie yelled. "Kelsey!" But it was no use.

Julie knew how Ren felt about it, and she had a suspicion she knew how Kelsey felt about it, too, but right now wasn't the time to worry about that.

"Screw it, drink," Julie said. She pulled her dress down, revealing the side of her neck. "Don't think about it, just take it. You're going to get worse if you keep holding back."

Ren realized she was right. He would have preferred feeding from Kelsey, but they couldn't find her. He was short on options, and Julie was giving him one. It would be best for him to take it.

Kelsey walked with a tray in her hand and a piece of cake on top of it. She took some to share with Ren, completely intending to use it as an excuse to spend some alone time with him.

She walked with a smile on her face and a spring in her step. Getting to spend an afternoon with Ren and eating cake made her giddy. Everything was already planned out. First, they would eat the cake, then she'd close the distance between them, getting as close as possible. Ren would put his arm around her, then they would lean in, and she would finally get the idiot to kiss her. Yup, this was going to go perfectly.

Kelsey rounded a corner and stopped. Ren was slumped over in Julie's arms. The poor girl was barely managing to keep him from collapsing. Kelsey saw the worry in her eyes, and she knew something was dangerously wrong.

Ren held his head with his hand, clearly in pain. But in his eyes, she saw only hunger, the hunger for blood. Kelsey watched as Julie exposed the side of her neck, and Ren sank his fangs into her. Julie's once-clear face burned bright red, and a loud gasp escaped her lips. She gripped the back of Ren's jacket tightly, and that's when Kelsey knew it wasn't pain that Julie was feeling; it was ecstasy.

A sharp pain pierced Kelsey's heart. It felt like she'd been stabbed through the chest. Her stomach dropped, and she lost all the strength in her hands. The tray fell to the ground with her stomach, the contents spilling everywhere.

The next thing she knew, she was running; back the way she came, away from Ren. Tears stung her eyes as they spilled over her cheeks.

Ren and Julie heard the tray crash and looked just in time to see Kelsey running away.

"Kelsey!" Ren tried to run after her, but his condition flared. He'd consumed Julie's blood, but it hadn't yet settled in his system, so the effects were still in full effect. This time, he did collapse. When he tried to get up, pain flared through him.

Damn it, he cursed in his head. He couldn't move. As much as he wanted to, as much as he wanted to go after her, his body refused to cooperate. Almost immediately, she was no longer in sight. Now he knew what it felt like. Kelsey was gone.

Twenty-seven

The End of the Beginning

Flip ... flip ... flip.

Kelsey released a heavy sigh and closed the book she was reading. Nothing. She was on the tenth floor of the library now, and she still couldn't find anything on the stones. After all this time, all this searching, all this knowledge, there still wasn't a single thing on these bloody stones. Soon, she was going to have to get Ren to disable the traps and head to the lower floors.

Ren. It had been two days since Kelsey had seen him feed off Julie. She hadn't seen or spoken to him since and practically shut herself away in the library. She couldn't bring herself to be around him. Thinking about the two of them hurt too much. At least there, no one would bother her, and unlike people, the books weren't going to break her heart.

Kelsey pushed the thought of Ren and Julie out of her mind. Thinking about it wasn't going to change anything, and it would only continue to make her feel worse.

Why? Why did she have to fall in love with an idiot like him? Why did he have to be so thick-headed?

"Stupid Ren, stupid Ren, stupid Ren, stupid Ren." She repeated herself as if she were in a looped trance. Finally, she snapped out of it. She needed to clear her head.

Kelsey headed to the stairs, taking them all the way up to the top floor. *This place needs to invent the elevator,* she thought. *This is ridiculous.*

Passing through the labyrinth of corridors, she finally reached the bridge connecting the Eastern and central sections of the palace. Marcus noticed her from the other end as he strode toward her, but she never even noticed him coming. Her eyes were downcast the entire time.

"Hey," he said, but she kept walking, still unaware of his presence. "Kelsey? I said hello." This time, she did stop.

"Oh, Marcus. Sorry, I wasn't listening."

"It didn't seem like you were paying attention to anything." She just stood there, looking at the floor silently.

"Alright, what's wrong?" he asked.

"It's nothing. This is my problem." She started to walk away.

"It's Ren, isn't it?" he asked after a short pause. He asked her the question, but he was almost entirely sure he knew the answer.

Kelsey stopped in her tracks. "I knew it."

"It's fine. Like I said, this is my problem."

"You're right, but he's my best friend. Don't forget, I've known him about eighteen times longer than you've been alive."

Kelsey grabbed her arm, a depressed look on her face.

"Oh, and just for the record, I'm not too keen on her being here either."

"On who being here, Julie?" Marcus never answered. Instead, his expression did it for him. "And, why are you telling me this?"

"Why else would I tell you this, Kelsey?"

"Really? I figured you'd rather Ren be with her than me," she said. "I know you don't like me being with him."

"Who in the hell said that?" he asked angrily.

"You didn't have to say it. I see it in your face when he and I are together. Besides, I think it's fairly obvious that the two of us are just about finished. I guess you'll both get what you want after all."

"Kelsey, if I wanted you apart, I wouldn't let you come anywhere near Ren, no matter how much he pushed back. I'm not stupid. I know you've been making an effort."

"Yeah, well, a lot of good it's done. Nothing goes the way I want it. I've been trying so hard to make things right, but it just doesn't work out. I've tried talking to him, I took care of him when he was locked in his room, I waited all night for him to dance with me at the ball, we went into town together, I even had the perfect date planned. Every time we get close, something gets in the way, something pulls us farther apart. I tried waiting for him, thinking that maybe he would ask to do anything together, but he hasn't. Or, more like he won't."

Marcus released a heavy sigh and leaned against the bridge wall.

"I know. I've been watching. But you know how stubborn he is. When Ren gets set in his way, he digs his heels in and doesn't give up. Never surrender, never show weakness."

The guy was right about that. When Ren was set on something, he was damn stubborn about it and refused to give in.

"Is that why you let him bring me here?"

"What do you mean?"

"You know what I mean. To Nexus. I'm not an idiot either, you know. I know neither of you wanted me here. You only gave in because you had no choice since we can't get the stones off. You had to drag me here. As soon as we get the stones off, I'm sure you'll send me right back to the human world."

"At first … yeah," he confessed. "It's true, I didn't want you here. I wanted you as far away from Ren as possible. Do you have any idea how hard it was for him to be around you? And I had to watch as you constantly tried to get close the distance between you two despite that. But as time went on, Ren started to act normal around you again, so I never said anything, and I let you two be to sort things out yourselves."

"If you hated me so much, then why let me stay? With your power, it'll be easy to separate us. So why let it go? Why keep your opinion to yourself, even for Ren's sake, if you hate me so much?"

"I don't hate you. I've never hated you. I just stopped trusting you. It's pretty difficult to like someone when the girl I thought I could entrust my best friend to … calls him a damn monster."

There it was again. It always came back to that. *Monster.* This was all that stupid ghost's fault. If it hadn't appeared, none of this would be happening. She wouldn't have tried to interact with it, and Ren wouldn't have misunderstood anything. They wouldn't be at odds right now. If it wasn't for that ghost, she and Ren would still be together like before. She was so angry and confused.

Now it was Kelsey's turn to get angry. She balled her fists, her knuckles turning white.

"I wasn't talking to him," she admitted. "I wasn't calling him a monster."

"You didn't call him a monster? I was right there, Kelsey. And even if I wasn't, with my hearing, I might as well would have been."

"No!" Kelsey yelled. "I told you, I wasn't talking to him." She finally faced him head-on, all of her anger gathered in one spot. Then, her focus shifted. Her gaze turned from him to the ghostly figure floating behind him. "Oh great, here we go again! Not you, too!"

Marcus was too confused by her comment to notice her outburst.

"You expect me to believe that? If you weren't talking to Ren, then who?" he asked, intrigued. "You were staring right at him."

"I-I don't know what it is," she said. "I keep seeing this person hanging around him sometimes. Almost like a spirit."

"A spirit?" She nodded. "Why would a spirit hang around Ren?"

"I don't know. I was too shocked to think of anything else. That's why I thought it might be some kind of monster. Watching over him. But I realized he can't see it."

"What kind of spirit was it?" Kelsey was silent. "Kelsey?" he asked.

"The same type you have around you now," she confessed.

Marcus's eyes widened, and he whirled around, searching for the mysterious and unknown specter. He even focused all of his senses on himself and his immediate surroundings but felt nothing.

"Marcus," a voice called to him in his head. He recognized the voice immediately. It was Glorious, the spirit within his heaven's blade.

Marcus looked to his left and saw Glorious appear in a transparent glowing form. An astral projection.

"What is it?" Marcus asked.

"I'm not sensing anything around you," Glorious confirmed. *"There's no presence of any spectral being like a spirit or a poltergeist. Nor any other spiritual being."*

Kelsey was caught completely off guard when Marcus turned to the spirit standing next to him and started talking to it.

"Huh, you can talk to it," she noted. "I've never seen Ren communicate with the one around him."

"Communicate, what are you—" Marcus stopped himself mid-sentence. His eyes almost popped out of his head when he realized what was happening. "Kelsey, what does the spirit around me look like?"

"It looks like a man. He's about your height, with long, red hair that looks like the back has been through an electric theme park. Its eyes are gold, just like yours and the spirit around Ren, and it wears red robes over light golden armor."

Unexpectedly, Marcus burst out laughing.

"Want to explain what's so amusing?" Kelsey asked.

"I can't believe it," Marcus said. Then, to her surprise, he smiled at her. "Kelsey, the 'spirit' you're seeing, it's not a ghost. Nor is the one hanging around Ren."

"If it's not a spirit, then what is it?" she asked.

"It's Glorious."

"What's glorious?"

"No, I mean, what you're seeing is the spirit within my sword, my heaven's blade. More specifically, it's a projection."

"What Marcus says is true," said a deep voice. Kelsey had heard this voice before, and it came from Marcus, but it wasn't his. "Hello, Miss Rose. This is our second meeting. Our first was back in the human world. In Italy, to be precise. I am Glorious. The form you see standing before you is a projection of my physical appearance from within the world of the heaven's blade. We call it astral projection."

"You already know that the spirit within a heaven's blade has a human form and its own world within the weapon. Well, there is more that a heaven's blade can do beyond communicating with its wielder. The astral projection is one such ability. It grants us the ability to manifest ourselves into the physical realm temporarily. Much like how our wielder may enter our world through their consciousness, we may physically project ourselves into your world. However, there is a catch to that ability.

Only the wielder can see the astral form of their heaven's blade."

"Which means I cannot see Shadow Hunter's astral projection, nor can Ren see Glorious's projection," Marcus added. "Unlike when we share control."

"What does that have to do with the figure next to Ren that I saw?" Kelsey asked.

"Everything," Marcus said. "Kelsey, like Glorious said, only the heaven's blade's wielder can see their astral form. But for some reason, you can, too."

Kelsey couldn't understand why she could see something no one else could. Why was this happening to her?

"How is that possible? Is something happening to me, or could it have something to do with the stones? Could their power be causing me to see you?"

"I don't know," Glorious said. "This is the first time I'm experiencing something like this. Nor have I ever heard of it happening before."

"Then, the figure around Ren that I saw after the battle, the one I keep seeing, is the spirit of Ren's heaven's blade?"

"Was it a man have long golden hair, fair skin, and golden eyes?" Glorious asked.

"Yes," Kelsey answered. "And golden clothes. With a black sash at his waist."

"Then yes. That was Shadow Hunter's astral form."

Marcus released another sigh, but this time, it was lighter. It didn't carry any frustration, only remorse.

"I'm sorry. I thought you had rejected him. I had no idea you saw Shadow Hunter, and I just accused you. No doubt you were surprised after seeing him. Now I understand why you've been trying to close the distance between you so desperately. " Marcus put his hands on Kelsey's shoulders. "Kelsey, you have to tell Ren. You have to clear up the misunderstanding before it's too late."

Everything flashed through Kelsey's head at once. All of the attempts, all of the failures. All of the times Ren pulled away. And then, the memory she least wanted to remember pierced her thoughts. Julie overcome with ecstasy as Ren sank his fangs into her. There was nothing she could do anymore.

"It already is," she said.

With heavy words in her wake, she left Marcus standing there in silence and returned to her room.

Don't cry, she thought. *Don't cry.*

That's right, it didn't matter now. It was already too late. There was nothing she or anyone else could do to fix things.

Don't cry. Don't cry.

But she couldn't hold them back. Tears fell down her cheeks as she reached her room. She opened the door and closed it behind her, wanting to just sleep away all of her problems and never leave. That's when she saw Julie sitting in a chair next to the window. As soon as Julie saw Kelsey, she rose to her feet.

"What do you want?" she asked. "How did you get in my room?"

"The maids let me in. I want to talk. But first, I want to apologize."

Kelsey sat on her bed, and Julie moved next to her. "I'm sorry, Kelsey. I'm so, so sorry. I need you to know that. Please, let me explain what happened."

Julie's telling of the story was emotional. But Kelsey only absorbed half of it. The other half of her was in a deep haze. Ren's urges hit him out of nowhere. That's when Julie explained that his constitution still wasn't stable. He still needed time and blood to acclimate completely. The news came as a surprise to Kelsey, but not as much as what came next.

When his urges hit, they went looking for her. The only person Ren wished to take blood from deliberately was her, and Julie knew this. Alas, despite their efforts, they couldn't find her, and Ren's condition slowly grew worse. Julie told her that she called her name, yelled for her as loud as she could, but she was nowhere to be found. If they left it as it was, his urges would start to harm him. So, they agreed to take her blood. That's when Kelsey appeared. Ren tried to run after her, but his condition was too strained, and he collapsed.

Even after her retelling of what had happened, Kelsey and Julie continued to talk for hours. Most of it about Ren, and Kelsey spilled every last one of her stupid feelings.

Meanwhile, Ren lay on his bed after finishing all of his work for the day. It had been two days since he'd talked to or even seen Kelsey. He wanted to, but perhaps this was for the best. Ren had mulled it over, weighing the benefits and losses. Unfortunately, he was unable to counter the King of Dridia. The sly bastard has successfully trapped them in his scheme.

Marrying for politics was something Ren knew he would always have to do, though he'd wished to avoid it for as long as possible. But in the end, what he wanted didn't matter. The kingdom would always come first.

A knock on the door stirred him. "Enter," Ren said. The door to his room opened, and Councilman Sway walked in. Ren sat up on his bed, then swung his legs over and got to his feet.

"Your Highness, you summoned me?" the councilman asked with a bow.

"Did anyone follow you?"

"No, I made sure to arrive in secret."

"Good. As for why I've called you, I've considered our options, but to no avail. So, I am left with only one choice. Send a letter with our agreement to their terms."

"Your Highness."

"Tell the King of Dridia … that I accept the marriage proposal."

Twenty-eight

Realm of the Abyss

Ren sat on his balcony, his chair placed next to the railing. The heat of the sun seeped into his skin, igniting him from within.

Marcus opened the door and sat across from him.

"I've been looking for you," he said.

"What's up?" Ren asked.

"We have a problem. Or should I say you do."

"With what? Did my father say something to you?"

Marcus rolled his eyes. "I'm not talking about your work, ya' moron. I'm talking about Kelsey. You need to talk to her before it's too late." Ren let a sigh escape him. "It's not too late. If you go now, then—"

"No, it is too late," he said, cutting Marcus off. But from Marcus's expression, it was clear that he didn't understand Ren's meaning. "I accepted the marriage proposal," Ren told him.

"You did what?" Marcus yelled. "Why the hell would you accept it? What happened to finding a way out of it?"

"I tried," Ren said calmly. "I failed. Despite my efforts, I couldn't come up with a solution to best him. He's thoroughly trapped us in his scheme. Now, I need to take responsibility. We're not kids anymore, Marcus. We have to make adult decisions."

"This isn't an adult decision; it's just a stupid one! You're just being stubborn and refusing to fight back like you normally would, so you don't have to face Kelsey!"

"I'm not being stubborn. And since when were you on Kelsey's side?"

"I'm on both your sides. Kelsey and I have simply resolved our misunderstanding, something I can't say for you. How could you do this to her?"

"This has nothing to do with Kelsey," Ren said stoically.

Marcus stared at him in shock. He couldn't believe what he was hearing. "Are you serious?"

"There's no peaceful way out of this, Marcus. And I have no intention of going to war with Dridia. Besides, the benefits are extraordinary if you consider them. I'll bring even more prosperity to my people."

"You've been using that same excuse for far too long. Now it's just getting old."

"I'm a prince, Marcus, the same as you are. My people and my kingdom come first. Besides, word has already been sent. It's not all bad. At least I won't be marrying a stranger. Julie is a good girl."

"Yeah, she is. But Kelsey is better."

"That may be, but I've made my decision. You know just as well as I do that what I'm doing isn't what I want. But I don't have much of a choice."

"That's bullshit. You and I both know you're just using this as an excuse to get out. Well, I'm not letting you."

Ren shook his head. "It just won't work. She's not like us after all."

Marcus understood him then. "It's because she's human." Ren nodded.

"She needs someone like her—human. Someone who will be able to grow old with her and share all the experiences that I can't give her."

"You're wrong. And you know it. Kelsey couldn't give a damn about that. If she did, she never would have come on that quest with us. She never would have begged you to spare her memories. And she never would have waited three years without a word, hoping and praying that you'd return to her."

"Regardless, this is what's best for both of us. I will protect my people … and she can move on."

"I don't approve of this. And you can bet that I'll be putting up a fight. I knew you were stubborn, but this is a new low, even for you, Ren. If it's come down to this, it's up to me to find a way out of this mess."

"Disapprove all you want. Moving onto another topic, though, there's something else we have to discuss," Ren said. "As expected, searching the library has been unsuccessful."

"Cole said they're already on the twelfth floor but haven't found a thing," Marcus said back.

"Searching the remaining floors is a waste of time. I've decided to head to the fifteenth floor. It's now or never."

"So, we're finally headed down then. Alright, can I borrow some ink and paper?"

"Go for it."

Marcus headed inside and opened the door to Ren's study. He walked to his desk and grabbed a piece of blank paper and his pen, then began writing a letter to his father, informing him that they were headed to the fifteenth floor of the library. Once finished, he sealed it with Ren's wax and seal.

"My father has the key," Ren said. "Let's go. Oh, and no one but you knows about the arranged marriage, so not a word to anyone."

Ren's father was in his study when they arrived. He sat in his chair, gazing out the window, a cup of coffee in his hand. Outside of Leo's office, Ren and Marcus ran into his personal aid, and Marcus handed him the letter to his father.

Ren opened the door to his father's office. "Dad, we're heading to the fifteenth floor."

That was all Ren had to say. His father nodded, set his coffee down, and walked into the adjacent room, returning moments later with a set of keys in his hand. "Let's go."

Halfway to the library, they ran into Cole.

"Where are you three headed, altogether no less?"

"We're heading to the fifteenth floor," Ren said. "You coming?" Cole nodded and turned right around, following them.

Across the bridge, on the East side of the palace, they met with Julie. She sat on the grass, feeding the birds. As soon as she saw them, she got to her feet. Like Cole, she, too, had a perplexed expression. Seeing the four of them together was a sign that something was happening.

"We're headed to the fifteenth floor of the library," Ren said before she could ask.

Julie's eyes widened, and she stared at Ren for a few seconds. "I'm coming with you," she said. It was clear she wasn't taking no for an answer, not that it really mattered anyway.

"Suit yourself."

Marcus opened the double wooden doors to the library when they finally reached it and walked right into Kelsey. "Whoa! Sorry," he apologized.

"It's alright," she said back. She looked and saw everyone else. Her eyes settled on Ren for just a moment before going around the others. "What's going on?"

"We're headed to the fifteenth floor. Come on." He walked passed her, and the others followed.

"Wait, um, okay." She turned back around and headed inside. Switching to a jog, she quickly caught up to Marcus. "Why the sudden decision to go?"

"There's no point waisting any more time searching pointlessly through the other floors. As we expected, our answers will be on the bottom floor."

They headed to the stairs and took them all the way down to the twelfth floor.

"Why are we stopping here?" Kelsey asked.

"Because the main stairs stop here," Ren answered.

"Then how do we get to the lower floors?" Julie asked.

"There's another set of stairs that are only used for the bottom three floors," Marcus explained. "They're kept hidden since the bottom floors are so dangerous. The traps on this floor are still deactivated, so we didn't have to worry about them."

"Not that it would matter," Ren said. "The traps on the twelfth floor are small in number and relatively easy to counter."

"Unlike the lower floors," Marcus added.

"How do you know that?" Julie asked Marcus.

"Did you forget that Ren and I grew up together?" he asked.

"Let me guess, you were mischievous."

"A little, yeah." Ren snickered.

"You call that a little?" Marcus asked

"Okay, so we were very mischievous, whatever." Ren started chuckling. "Maybe a little too mischievous now that we're older."

"Right, says the guy who swung through a wall of flames on a rope."

Ren stopped and started laughing. "I remember that," he said through his laughter.

Continuing on, they took the steps down to the thirteenth floor, coming out into a stone hallway. It was damp and dark.

"No one move," Ren said. He reached behind him as Marcus reached to his left side and they drew their heaven's blades. The area around them was suddenly cocooned in light.

Ren stepped forward slowly, then again, feeling for any traps.

"Ren, there's a torch to your left," Marcus said.

True to his word, a torch sat in an iron holster attached to the wall. The holster was rusted terribly, and the torch looked like it was about to turn into dust.

Ren grabbed the torch and found that it didn't disintegrate in his hand. He cast a spell, and a fire blazed to life. Then, he handed it to his father.

Unlike all the others, this floor was laid out differently. A maze of stone hallways with massive side rooms covered every corner of the floor. They ran into a number of traps along the way, most of which they were able to deactivate.

Hours passed before they finally reached the end of the thirteenth floor. It was hard to tell how much time had passed, but Ren speculated they'd been gone for roughly six hours. A whole quarter of a day, most of it spent deactivating and passing through the traps along the way.

Ren was the first one to move. He took it slow, his sword ready for anything. Marcus followed behind him and the others behind him, and together, they descended into the darkness.

Twenty-nine

15

"Where are we?" Julie asked.

"I don't know," Ren responded.

Julie grabbed his arm, then, with her free hand, took Marcus's hand. The light from their swords made her brown hair look golden.

Suddenly, Marcus felt another hand on his other arm. He knew who it was, even without the light of their swords; Kelsey.

"We need to keep moving," Ren said. He walked ahead, his sword at the ready.

"Everyone stay close," Marcus added, walking behind him.

They were inside a long circular tunnel made from stone. Moss grew on the floor, and roots and vines grew out of the cracks in the walls. Ren found it strange, considering that no plants could reach as far down as they were.

Ren continued to walk in front. He and Marcus walked with silent footsteps. Ren took a step forward and his foot landed on one of the stones making up the ground. It sank into the floor. *Uh, oh.* He turned and tackled Marcus, taking Julie and Kelsey with him as spikes shot up from the ground and a large square platform of more spikes dropped from the ceiling. The spikes clashed together, making mincemeat out of anyone who would be unfortunate enough to be standing there.

Ren looked behind him at the remnants of the trap. "Well, that was interesting," he said.

"Just like old times," Marcus said.

They continued on through the tunnel. Unlike the other floors, this one had a heavy gathering of functional traps. It had barely been twenty minutes since the first one, and they had already triggered three more of them.

Marcus accidentally lost his balance when he stepped into a small hole while they were walking. He placed his hand on the wall to catch himself. Click! "Oh shit."

"Look out!" Leo shouted.

Marcus pushed Ren in the chest with his free hand as a spear came out of the wall, but it wasn't enough. Ren was about to slash at it when Kelsey grabbed him from behind, wrapping her arms around his chest, and pulled him with her to the ground. The spear struck the wall on the other side.

"Thanks," he said, getting to his feet. He held his hand out, and Kelsey took it.

The trigger on the wall made her curious. It appeared that the triggers were placed inconspicuously. Which meant they had to be even more careful. With no way to tell where the triggers were, they could be anywhere and activated at any time.

Kelsey ran her hand along the wall, feeling the roughness against her skin. A piece of stone slid sideways only a fraction of an inch when she ran her hand over it. Holes opened in the wall, and flames shot out. Her instincts took over, and she tackled Ren to the ground.

Ren looked at her in surprise. "Thanks again."

"Don't mention it."

"Kelsey, you're on fire."

"What?"

Ren pulled her close and wrapped his arms around her tightly, then began patting her hair. That's when Kelsey smelled the burning.

"I guess it's my turn to say thanks."

"Just returning the favor."

"This place is a death trap," Kelsey noted.

"And now you know why I never made it this far," Ren said to her.

"Even with my help," Marcus added. "Come on, let's keep going. We're almost to the bottom floor."

Descending further down the corridor, it didn't take long before the path changed. It split in two directly in the middle.

"Oh, come on, seriously?" Marcus said.

"Can't say I'm surprised," Ren said. "I'll go left."

"Then I'll take the right," Marcus said.

The group split in two when Ren and Marcus headed in the direction they each chose. Kelsey and Julie followed Ren, while Leo and Cole followed Marcus.

Ren and the girls walked along in silence. They hadn't hit a trap yet, and the longer their fabricated peace lasted, the more concerned Ren got.

"Kelsey, get ready to use the stones at a moment's notice," he told her

"Alright," she said back.

Ren felt the bracelet on his wrist go hot when Kelsey placed her hand on the bracelet containing the stones. The stones began to glow, causing his bracelet to glow in turn, feeding them power.

"I wish I could help," Julie said. "My powers won't work down here."

"It's fine," Ren said. "Not getting caught in any traps helps enough."

Kelsey noticed that Ren and Julie were no closer than they ever were. She had expected them to be all over each other, or at least Julie to be all over Ren. Instead, they maintained a clear distance, treating each other as they would working a job at Trinity together. It came off entirely professional in nature. Was it the situation they were in, or had they really not grown closer?

"Just out of curiosity, but what is your power anyway?" Kelsey asked.

"I'm a diwata," Julie answered. "A fairy or forest nymph. I can control animals and plants and summon them to my aid."

After that, the three of them walked the rest of the way in silence. Ren found it unsettling that they didn't spring a single trap along the way either.

Finally, they exited into an open chamber. The chamber appeared endless on all remaining sides. Everything beyond the light from Shadow Hunter was pitch-black darkness.

To their right, another golden light appeared, and Marcus and the others emerged from their tunnel.

"How'd it go?" Marcus asked. "Any traps?"

"No, not a one," Ren answered.

"It was the same for us," Cole said. "Perhaps there's a reason for it."

Marcus looked around, gazing out into the blackness beyond. Even with the combined glow of their heaven's blades, they couldn't see the other side.

Cole looked over the side of the cavern wall, but all he saw below was matching darkness with no end in sight. "Well, that's unsettling."

"This cavern is massive," Marcus said.

"Ren, Marcus, increase the length of your sword's light as far as it can go," Leo said. "I think I know where we are."

Ren concentrated on Shadow Hunter, focusing on the power contained within the blade. He felt the spirit within the sword connect with him and his presence appear in his mind. "Shadow Hunter, give it everything you've got. Light it up."

On cue, the light surrounding Shadow Hunter tripled in size. The glow around Marcus's sword suddenly increased as well, combining with the light from Ren's. It blew away the darkness surrounding them, reaching all the way to the other side of the cavern.

"There, look," Leo said.

On the other side of the cavern, built into the wall, was the front of a temple. The cavern between them spanned a hundred feet across. And yet, even with the combined light of their swords, they still couldn't see the bottom.

"What is that?" Julie asked.

"A temple?" Kelsey guessed.

"I thought we were headed to the fifteenth floor."

"We are. You're looking at it," Leo said. "That is the fifteenth floor. It's another building entirely."

"What?" they all asked at the same time.

"No one ever said it was part of the main library."

Even Ren was surprised when he heard that the building in front of them was the library. He and Marcus looked at each other and shrugged. "Who knew?"

"Ren," Marcus said. He pointed to a bridge off to the right with his sword. The bridge connected their end to the temple. "Looks like that's our way," he said.

"Then let's take it."

"That thing will hold … right?" Cole asked.

"We're screwed if it doesn't," Ren said.

"It'll hold just fine," Leo said. He took the lead, Ren and Marcus following behind.

When the three of them made it a quarter of the way, and the bridge held, Cole and the girls started across. They only sighed in relief when they made it to the other side.

"See, nothing to worry about," Leo said.

Ren rolled his eyes. *Funny, that's what we used to say,* he thought. Nevertheless, they continued on.

Leo walked up the steps leading into the temple. The inside was dark and damp. Cobwebs covered everything.

"*Peechhe hatana,*" Ren said. Kelsey and Cole had no idea what he said until Marcus and Leo moved them back toward the door.

Ren spun Shadow Hunter in circles above his head with his right hand like he was spinning a staff. Then he brought the blade down, the tip pointed toward the ground, stopping just short of impact. A wave of wind shot out, blowing away all the dust, dirt, and cobwebs.

"*Vibhaajit aur khoj.* Marcus, *tum mere saath ho.*"

"*Samajh gaya,*" Marcus said back.

"What did they say?" Kelsey and Cole asked.

"They said split up," Leo translated. "Ren told Marcus to go with him."

"Oh, okay."

They all split into pairs and searched the area. The whole area was open and filled with bookcases ten feet tall. In the back, a set of double stairs led to a balcony with even more bookcases. Shelves were built into the walls, each of them filled tight.

There had to be hundreds of thousands of books and scrolls. So much information to go through, and no one knew where to start. Leo stated that everything was categorized by date, so they began in the area closest to the last known time the stones were seen in the world.

The problem they all unanimously encountered, the stones were so ancient and secretive that any dates they searched were useless. Hours passed without a single piece of information. Not even so much as a sentence.

Ren was on the balcony looking through the books on the second floor. He started down one of the stairs when he noticed Kelsey sitting on the bottom steps, a book in her hands. She sneezed a cute sneeze that made him smirk. Ren closed the book in his hand, took his jacket off, and placed it on her shoulders before walking off.

Kelsey watched him walk off, then wrapped his jacket closely around herself, her heart fluttering in her chest.

The more Ren searched, the worse the situation got. Nevermind that they still hadn't found a single clue, there was so much tainted history, knowledge meant to remain hidden for an eternity, never to see the light of day. Ren had to make sure that anything they learned beyond the stones was erased from their memories.

Some would simply try to learn everything they could and use it, but Ren knew better. He didn't play with things that weren't meant to be played with. When you live for over three centuries, you learn a thing or two, and he'd learned things are kept secret for a reason. Some secrets should remain just that, a secret. And this library and its knowledge would remain just that.

Ren found Marcus sitting and talking with Julie. Marcus walked over when he saw him. Julie waved to him as he left, and Marcus waved back. Ren raised an eyebrow, which Marcus clearly saw.

"Find anything?" Marcus asked.

"Not a damn thing," Ren said back. "Except for all of what I shouldn't."

Marcus nodded in understanding. "Same here."

"I'm okay with you and my father, but everyone else—"

"Let me guess, memory wipe? I agree. It's best that they don't know. You're right; the knowledge buried down here, it's far too dangerous."

"So, you've found nothing else then."

"I assume you mean the stones. In which case, no, us neither."

Us. Ren didn't fail to pick that up.

"We don't have enough information on the stones to give an accurate search, and there's too much knowledge here to search through. Honestly, are we even sure the information is even here?"

"It's here. If it's anywhere, it's here. Let's keep looking."

Ren and Marcus continued walking around, searching previously unexplored sections. The first to find them was Cole. After that, Ren's father appeared, and finally, the girls found them all. Ren, Marcus, and Leo were deep in discussion on where to search next. Searching aimlessly was anything but helpful.

Cole sat down on the ground, leaning against one of the bookcases. He was listening to the three of them conceive a plan when something caught his eye. It was an old flag draped over a bookcase at the end of the row. A flag of their kingdom, the founding flag, in fact. Rumors had said that the original was lost to time or stolen by invaders. But there was no doubt that the flag in front of him was the real one. However, it wasn't the flag that had gotten his attention.

Getting to his feet, he walked to the flag and moved it aside. There was a layer of black books sitting at the bottom row. Behind the books was a string dyed the color of crimson. Taking the books off the shelf, he found the string tied around a piece of black rolled-up parchment. A black scroll.

"Hey guys," Cole said. "I think I found something." They all ran over to him, and he untied the scroll.

"A black scroll," Ren said.

"I've never seen something like this," Julie said.

"And you never will," Leo said. "A black scroll, it's the symbol of darkness, meant for something meant to never be found. It's the highest grade of secret in Nexus. Whatever is within that scroll was never meant to be read."

Ren grabbed the scroll from his cousin and read the contents. "The vein of all legends is only sought through the heart."

"The vein of all legends, what does that mean?" Marcus wondered.

"There's more," Ren said. He continued to read. "For every vein, there is blood, and for every pool of blood, a gift. Gifts untold, gifts forgotten, only to be found at the depths of the soul. The vein will lead the way, but the heart will tell the truth. If you follow the vein, you will find the heart. And if you find the heart …."

"… Well?" the others asked in suspense.

"If you find the heart," Ren read again, "You will find the map to hope. The location of all artifacts, the Records of the Gods."

Ren's face turned white as a paper. Marcus and Leo exchanged nervous glances.

"It can't be," Leo said, at a complete loss for words. They'd never seen him so stupefied.

"What's that?" Kelsey asked, overly curious. She'd never seen Ren go white before, never. Whatever this Records of the Gods was, it was unimaginably important.

"It's an old legend that no one has ever been able to prove true," Leo began explaining. "The artifacts of the gods refers to relics. Ancient and sacred treasures, like the Sun and Moon Stone."

Kelsey looked at the stones on her wrist.

"According to the legends, the Records is ancient magic, a book listing every relic ever created, where the relic is located, when it was created, and more importantly, how to use it."

"That means if we can find the book, we can remove the stones," Ren said. "But no one has ever been able to find the book. Its location is a mystery."

"Let's get back to the palace," Leo said. "We'll take the scroll with us, and only the scroll."

Everyone nodded in agreement and quickly left the library. They made their way all the way up to the first floor of the library and headed to Leo's study. As they approached, Leo's retainer stopped them. He handed Leo a letter with a familiar symbol. The Wolfbane Kingdom's symbol. He opened the letter and read it. Marcus's father was on his way.

Thirty

The Black Scroll

Ren and his father were in the dining room when news of Marcus's father's arrival reached them. Their personal aids waited patiently nearby.

After days of pouring over the scroll, they'd yet to decipher it. Even now, as they sat consuming the day's lunch, their minds poured over the scroll and knowledge it contained. The clue replayed in Ren's mind on a loop.

"Alright, let's go, Ren," Leo said.

Ren and his father were led to the main hall. When they passed through the doors and entered the hall, they saw Marcus standing there with his father and a woman they'd long since become acquainted with.

The woman had long blond hair tied into a rope braid around the back of her head with a short ponytail in the middle. The rest fell flat behind her, reaching her thighs. Her eyes were the color of chestnuts, unlike Marcus and his father, who both had gold eyes. However, her facial features were much more similar to Marcus than his than his fathers were.

"What's she doing here?" Ren whispered to his father.

"I have no idea," he whispered back. "The last time we saw her, your mother was still alive."

"Leo," Marcus's father greeted.

"Kane," Leo said back. They embraced each other for a few moments before separating. "Lycia. I'm glad to see you well again."

"Leo." The woman wrapped her arms around him tightly. "I heard about Eris. I'm so sorry."

Ren noticed the woman embracing his father shaking. *She's crying.* As long as Ren had known her, she'd always been overly emotional. *Damn it,* he thought.

"I know this is just as hard on you as it was for us, Lycia. You never got the chance to say goodbye. The fault lies with me and me alone. I was the one who was never home, and I wasn't there when she needed me. I'm just thankful that I still have Ren."

The woman released her hold on Leo, wiping her eyes. Ren's last memory of her still played accurately in his mind. A memory of her and his mother.

I can't believe it's already been three years, he thought. *Three whole years.*

Ren inclined his head in a light bow in front of the woman. "Queen Allagash. It is good to see you again, healthy. Time and worlds have kept us too far apart."

"Ren," Marcus's mother said. She gently placed her hand on the side of his face. Then, she was crying again. "I can't even imagine—" her voice caught, stopping her mid-sentence.

"Lycia, I know how you feel, and I appreciate that you'd cry for us. However, I'm alright. After all, I'm not alone."

"Not to rush into anything, but did you guys find anything?" Marcus's father asked. "I received Marcus's letter and headed out immediately."

"Actually, we did," Ren's father said. "Follow me." He started walking, ascending the grand staircase. Everyone followed him as he walked to the third story and to his study. "Everyone inside, now. Fetch Lord Vaylor and the rest of our party, please. We are not to be disturbed after that," he said to one of the servants.

"Understood, Your Majesty."

The servant bowed before going to find Ren's master and the others. The next knock on the door came upward half an hour later. The servant had returned with Ren's master, Kelsey, Cole, and Julie in toe. Leo let them inside and locked the door behind them.

"What the hell did you find down there?" Marcus's father asked. The guy was as perceptive as they came. He could practically feel the tension snaking up his body.

Leo walked to his desk and pulled the black scroll out from inside a drawer. Marcus's father immediately put a hand in front of his wife and moved her behind him.

"By the gods. What is *that* doing here?"

"I don't believe it," Ren's master said. "A black scroll. I never thought I'd see another one in my life."

Leo untied the scroll and rolled it out on his desk. "This scroll was hidden deep within the many millennia of knowledge on the fifteenth floor of the Grand Library. And its secret is exactly what we've been looking for."

Ren's master took the scroll and turned it toward him so he could read it better. Once he read the passage, there was silence.

"The Records of the Gods?" Marcus's father asked. "But that's supposed to be a legend."

"Well, clearly it's not. The Records exist," Leo said back. "The question is, where are they? And more importantly, how do we find them?"

Ren took a look at the scroll. It was written in red ink, like blood. Just holding it in his hands felt like he was carrying the weight of the entire world. He swallowed, nervousness wrapping itself tightly around his body, ready to sink its fangs into his neck. Then he felt someone grab his hand. It was Kelsey.

"You've got this," she said. She seemed to know everything he was feeling, and how to help push him forward.

Ren's nervousness slowly faded away. It was always Kelsey that gave them the confidence he needed. She always kept him going.

"Marcus, come help me with this," Ren said.

"You got an idea?" Marcus asked.

"Sort of. Shall we ask for aid? They might just know something we don't."

Marcus knew exactly what he was talking about. They both closed their eyes.

"Shadow Hunter."

"Glorious."

"Switch," they said at the same time.

When Ren opened his eyes, they were the color of melted gold. Marcus's, which were already golden, had a mystical glow to them, emanating power. Shadow hunter appeared on Ren's back and Glorious at Marcus's side. Kelsey saw Shadow Hunter's and Glorious's astral forms appear. They both looked at the scroll, then disappeared.

"We're here, Ren," Shadow Hunter said. "Hmm, a black scroll of confinement, huh? Interesting. It's been centuries since I've seen one of these."

Kelsey saw Marcus look at her. "Miss Rose, tell me, can you see anything?" Glorious asked.

"Why would I be able to see something?" she asked, giving him a look that told him to shut up.

"Umm, woman's intuition?" he guessed, trying to play it off. Clearly, he had got the message loud and clear. Don't say a word, got it.

Kelsey walked up to the scroll. There was nothing off about it. "I'm not seeing anything specific," she said.

"I see."

What was that about? Ren wondered. He took his focus off of Kelsey and focused on the scroll instead.

"Unfortunately, we won't be of much help with this one." Shadow Hunter said. "I'm not seeing anything regarding the future either."

"We could try reading it differently," Ren's father suggested. "Reading it in a different language may trigger something."

"In that case, read it in Lazarus," Glorious suggested. "He's right. Perhaps reading it in the native tongue would spark something."

Leo read the scroll word for word in their native tongue, but nothing jumped out at them. Nor were there any magical effects.

"Anyone got any other ideas?" Marcus's father asked.

"I could try asking the trees and animals," Julie said. "Perhaps they'll know something we don't."

"It's a possibility. I could bring it to someone," Cole suggested.

"No. This scroll does not leave my person," Ren's father said. "No one but the people in this room should even know it exists, let alone read it."

There were sighs all around the room. All these people, and no one had an idea on how to decipher the scroll and find the map. With their first attempts failed, everyone discussed ideas amongst themselves. They shot them out at random, arguing different possibilities and things they could try.

"Ren, try reading it at a different angle," Shadow Hunter suggested. "The future doesn't show anything regarding a map; however, something is present. A ship. I don't know what it means or what to do with it, but I can see it slightly."

"A ship, huh?"

Ren picked up the scroll, turning it in different directions, to no avail. He held it up into the air, letting the sunlight shine down on it. Nothing. He half expected the words to rearrange or for the words to glow, but nothing happened. Wait, glowing words. Something about that seemed to make Ren's brain itch. It was like he had an idea but no clue what kind of idea it was.

He turned the scroll over to look at the back. It was blank. Not even a trace of a clue. Everyone else was still throwing out their ideas in a big landslide.

"Do you remember anything else?" Marcus's father asked.

"No, Ren erased everything we read but the scroll from our memory," Marcus said. "That way, the secrets down there stayed secret."

Indeed, Ren had erased their memories as soon as they'd gotten back. All except for his own, his father's, and Marcus's. The knowledge they read was meant to remain a secret, and it would so long as he could help it.

Ren continued to examine the back of the scroll. "If you follow the vein, you will find the heart," he murmured. Heart, a muscle, life, life … water, ki, plants, fire … fire! His obscured idea immediately realized itself, becoming as clear as day.

He grabbed a candle from atop his father's nightstand. A lantern was placed next to it, still lit inside. He opened the front of the lantern and stuck the candle inside. When he pulled it out, the candle was lit.

"Ren, what are you thinking?" Shadow Hunter asked.

"I'm thinking I hope this works, or we're screwed," he said back.

Ren set the candle on his father's desk. By now, his actions had started drawing attention. His father saw him place the candle on his desk. "Ren, what are you doing?"

God I hope this works.

Ren held the scroll over the fire with the writing facing the fire.

"Jesus, Ren," his father said. That drew the others' attention. He went to grab it.

"Stop!" Shadow Hunter said. Ren's father stopped dead, along with everyone else. They watched Ren, not paying attention to anything else. But while they were paying attention to Ren, he was paying attention to the scroll.

He continued to hold it over the flame, waiting. Then he saw it. A red line appeared on the back of the scroll. And then another.

"I don't believe it," Shadow Hunter said.

In that instant, with those words, everyone rushed in to see what was going on.

Everyone watched as more red lines appeared on the back. The lines glew, like they were magicked, and continued to spread. Soon, the entire back was covered in glowing red lines.

Ren took the scroll off the flames and set it on the table, keeping the back facing up. Long twisting lines made up a border with lines inside that made up clear pictures, indications of markings. One area contained an array of dozens of triangles easily recognizable as mountains. More of them dotted the scroll. Trees covered the majority of the bottom before spreading out. And near the center was an island that floated over the landscape.

Outside the border lines were markings unmistakable as waves. In the top right was a single shape, a book, opened as if it was being read. A series of dotted lines started from the floating island, continuing all the way to the edge of the boundary and across the water until it reached the book.

"It's a map," Marcus said.

"Yeah, the border must be the outline of the continent. It even has a floating island. That's obviously Vesta. There's Darrat, Talos, Veil's to the east, and Cray even further. The ocean over here is the Avoline Ocean. These are the Iron Soul Mountains and the Shadowierre Forest. Just before the pass is your kingdom. So this must be Yamen to the north and Norshire to the south. Which means this spot at the end of the continent before it turns into the ocean must be the town of Seidra."

Ren and the others, as residents of Nexus, knew every single landmark depicted on the map. All except for one.

Ren ran his fingers over the book symbol. There was a small inscription beneath it, just barely visible. He looked at Marcus, raised an eyebrow, and grinned. "Paerlejara," he said.

"The City of Gold," Marcus said back.

"A city made of gold?" Kelsey asked.

"The concept shouldn't surprise you. There are many such myths back in the human realm. No doubt they all take inspiration from each other. But all legends come from a source, even Paerlejara."

"Paerlejara," Ren's father repeated. "It's been a mystery since Nexus first came to be. No one has ever been able to find it. If any did, they never returned."

"It seems that's where the book is hidden," Ren's master said.

"In a legendary lost city?" Kelsey asked.

Ren rolled up the scroll and retied it. "Well, we have a map and a destination. Time to gear up and rock and roll. It's treasure hunting time."

Thirty-one

Necessary Sacrifices

Everyone gathered in the main foyer. Ren, Marcus, and Kelsey had bags over their shoulders and were dressed in their usual outfits they wore when they were at Trinity and Kelsey her first quest.

Ren had his two Beretta-92fs' holstered on the sides of his legs. His grey wooden bow and quiver with a dozen arrows and Shadow Hunter rested on his back. Marcus had his magical ice bow strung over his back, the extra dagger at his right hip, and Glorious sheathed at his left. As for Kelsey, well, she had a dagger and the stones. If need be, Ren would give her his bow. He mainly used it for hunting anyway.

"Everybody ready?" Ren asked.

"Good to go," Marcus said, resting his hand on Glorious's handle.

Kelsey just nodded, never making eye contact. But that was to be expected, especially after what had happened.

It had been beyond surprising when she learned that Ren and Julie were engaged. The news hit her hard. That's when she knew things were finally over between them. Kelsey had never felt that kind of pain before. She didn't even want to see him, let alone talk to him. And Julie, she wanted to unleash the full power of the stones on her. Even as she and Kelsey had conversed after Ren's feeding incident, the two of them had been engaged. It must have been enjoyable for her to mock Kelsey as she did, edging her on, giving her hope when she knew there wasn't any.

The look Kelsey had on her face when she learned of the engagement tore Ren apart, but he had no other options. Just as he had told Marcus, Drida had them cornered. He loved Kelsey, and that wouldn't change. But with no way to turn the tables on them, he had to accept the arrangement.

Needless to say, the others weren't happy either. Marcus and Cole already knew, which he was suddenly grateful for. But his father, man, he was furious with him. Ren had never seen him so angry. The guy nearly smashed his desk in two with his bare hands. Even his master had a few choice words for him, surprisingly, though he at least understood Ren's position on the matter.

Ren remembered everything like it had just happened mere minutes ago. But then again, he didn't think he'd be able to get Kelsey's face out of his head if he tried. They were still in his father's study after discovering the map on the back of the black scroll.

Ren ran his fingers over the book symbol at the far corner of the map. He looked at Marcus, raised an eyebrow, and grinned. "Paerlejara," he said.

"The City of Gold," Marcus said back.

Ren rolled up the scroll and retied it. "Well, we have a map and a destination. Time to gear up and rock and roll. It's treasure hunting time."

"Hell yeah!" Marcus said ecstatically. They were finally going on another quest. The very thought invigorated him.

"Then let's get packed," Ren said.

A sudden knock on the door tore them away from their excitement. Ren's father opened it to see Councilman Sway standing in the doorway, trying to catch his breath.

"Councilman Sway, I've told everyone that we weren't to be interrupted. What brings you here so urgently?" Leo asked.

"My apologies, Your Majesty; however, I have urgent news for Prince Ren."

Ren's father had a questionable look on his face, but Ren knew exactly what this was about, and he wasn't about to have this conversation there.

"It's fine, I'll see what he needs," Ren said. "We've finished up here anyway."

The councilman handed Ren a letter, but before he could take it, Leo snatched it from them.

"What the hell, Dad?"

"This seal. This is from the Dridia royal family." Leo gripped the letter tightly. "I've been hearing rumors of Dridia's activities. And then Julie shows up unannounced immediately after."

"I'm handling it," Ren assured him.

"Prince Ren, after you have read the contents of the letter, please respond immediately to the invitation. I'm afraid we're hard-pressed for time and have been unable to delay any further."

"Invitation?" Leo asked. "Why was I not at least made aware of an invitation?"

Ren grimaced. His father was anything but stupid. With just a few simple words, he knew enough to be suspicious of the letter, its contents, and the plan Ren found himself involved in. Ren reached for the letter, but his father pried open the seal before he could.

Leo's expression grew dark once he read the letter and the invitation with it. Then, it changed completely. No longer simple anger, no longer easily swayed by a simple explanation of words. Now, it displayed only fury.

"You are hereby formally invited to Dridia as an act of good faith and to discuss the following procedures associated with … your union with Dridia's first princess." His father crumpled the note he gripped it so tight. "Ren Nightwalker, you've got exactly three seconds to explain, in very clear detail, what in the hell this is about. You agreed to a marriage proposal?"

Ren's expression changed just as quickly as his father's. He had an ice-cold stare, eyes that could kill just by looking, and he set them directly on his father. They could practically feel the temperature in the room drop.

"I made a decision to protect this country and its people. And not you nor anyone in this room can make me change it."

"Stop," Julie said. She looked at Ren's father. "Both of you. If anyone is to blame for this, it's me. I wasn't able to stop my father from concocting his plan. If I had, none of this would have happened."

"This is not your fault," Ren said. "This is the responsibility we bear as future sovereigns. We do what we must in order for it and the people in it to live happily. And that means we don't have the luxury of freedom. We don't get to choose our happiness."

"Not always, Ren. I did. I married your mother, not for politics, but for love."

"And if I hadn't accepted this arranged marriage, then that very well may not have been the case," Ren said back.

"What does that mean?"

"Councilman Sway came to me because the situation favored it. Even after all these years, I do not have a princess at my side. I fit the conditions needed to satisfy the King of Dridia's plot. But had I not accepted, this offer very well would have been delivered to you."

"What plot?" he asked, still furious.

"Dridia's king seeks a greater alliance of trade through marriage. In reality, it's a way for him to expand his influence and borders. If we deny their request, they've threatened to revoke all trade entirely with our kingdom." Leo's expression changed from rage to surprise, and he wasn't alone. Marcus's mother and father also bore similar expressions.

"If Dridia expands its borders, especially if they cut off all supply lines, it's worse than merely an economic collapse. They could see our refusal as a threat and break the alliance entirely. It could lead to war."

"How long? How long have I been kept in the dark on this?"

"The first proposal came several weeks ago. I deliberated over it for a few days but was unable to find a solution. It left me no choice but to accept the proposal."

"You should have told me."

"If I had, you would have rejected the order from the very beginning."

"You're damn right I would have!" Leo yelled. "Why does it have to be you?"

"Because there's no one else. Cole does not meet the qualifications as he has given up his desire for the throne, and you and I both know that you're not ready to be with another woman after losing Mom."

Ren's father tightened his fists because he knew deep down that Ren was right. He wasn't ready to move on. And now he was going to have to watch his son sacrifice his happiness instead.

"That's not your decision to make!"

"It is my decision! She was my mother! I know exactly how you feel."

"It's my fault that she died, not yours, Ren! It's because I wasn't there when she needed me, when you both needed me."

"And I had to watch her die!" Ren yelled. "It's just as much my fault as it is yours. And this, this proposal, is just that, my burden to bear. Do not mistake my intentions. This is far from over. Just because I haven't found a solution yet doesn't mean I won't. Believe me, if I can find a way out of this, I'll use it. The arrangement hasn't been finalized yet. We have a little time, especially, with this quest added into the mix. But until that happens, this is our only solution."

"I did what I had to do to protect you and this kingdom," Ren continued. "I'm the prince. I have a duty to my people. What I want doesn't matter. So if I cannot come up with a solution to counter Dridia's scheme and get out of this mess, if I have to sacrifice my happiness, what I want," he looked at Kelsey, and her eyes widened, "then so be it."

Kelsey leaned herself into the nearest object, Marcus. Tears fell down her freckled cheeks like a waterfall. Marcus held her in his arms.

"What I want doesn't matter, don't you get that?" Ren said. "The kingdom, will always, come first."

Ren looked at Marcus, who still held Kelsey. "We leave in three days, be ready." He turned and left the room, slamming the door behind him.

Since then, Ren and his father have come to an understanding regarding the reasons for accepting the offer. After reading everything that Dridia had presented, Leo realized that Ren's action had been the correct choice. But that didn't mean he was going to let Ren just go through with it. Someway, somehow, he would free Ren from this plot and this arranged marriage.

Julie approached everyone while they were gathered in the foyer. She was dressed in the usual gear she wore for missions at Trinity. A bow and quiver filled with arrows on her back, a dagger strapped to the side of each leg, and a pistol in the back of her pants.

"I'm coming too," she said. "My accompanying you may give us a little more time since my father can't force my hand. We can use it to figure this mess out. Plus, it's been a long time since we went on a quest together, and I need to let loose once in a while."

Ren nodded. He didn't have a reason to deny her. Having her along wouldn't hurt them. She'd be a good asset.

"Ren!" Ellie called. She came running the steps riding Nidar. "I'm coming too."

Ren knelt down in front of her and shook his head. "Sorry. Ellie, not this time. It's too dangerous. This isn't like our trip here. Remember that first trip I went on, the one that took me to Italy?" Ellie nodded. "This is going to be just like that one. And remember how that one ended up? That's why I can't bring you. Better I get hurt than you. Besides, I need you here. I have a job for you."

"A job?"

"I need you to help my father while I'm gone. He's going to have to do all the work on his own. I need you to look after him. Make sure he eats, drinks, sleeps, gets out of the office, and plays some games. And I might need you to help him look over the documents he's working on. You know, help run the kingdom in my stead."

"But Ren, isn't that your job?"

"It is. Unless I've just made a terrible mistake, and you end up being really good at it. Then I may be out of a job," he joked.

As he'd hoped, his little comment made her and some of the others laugh.

"Before I forget, I have something for you." He reached into his shirt and pulled out the necklace around his neck, the same one Kelsey had seen him first put on when they arrived at the palace. Ren's father's eyes widened in shock.

"Woah, woah, Ren," Marcus said. "That's—"

"I know," Ren interrupted.

The necklace was gold with a pendant that had five different gems in a circle around a large diamond. It was a beautiful one-of-a-kind necklace. He unclasped it and handed it to her, closing her hand over it protectively.

"This necklace is very precious to me," he said. "My mother gave it to me when I was your age. Whenever I felt sad or lonely, I would hold that necklace close to my heart. When I did, I knew that no matter what happened, my mom would always be there when I needed her. That she was watching over me, no matter where she was. And now, I'm giving it to you."

"Ren, I can't—" He cut her off by shaking his head.

"If you ever feel lonely or sad, just clutch that necklace close to your heart. If you do, I'll know you're thinking of me, and you'll know that you're never alone. I'll be with you through the power of that necklace."

He pulled her hair back and put the necklace on her. Then he gave her a long hug before finally letting go.

Outside, the rest of his party mounted the horses prepared for them while Ren climbed on Nidar. He turned to look at his cousin.

"Cole, I expect you to make her a trained aid while I'm gone," he said with a cocky grin.

Cole chuckled lightly to himself. "Understood."

"And Ellie, take care of Leo for me."

"You can count on me," she said with a big smile.

"That's my girl," Ren said back. "Alright, let's go."

Nidar shot forward, running at a reasonable speed. Travel to the port town of Seidra would take two weeks if they went at a steady pace. Where things got complicated was out at sea. They had the map, but who knew how long it would actually take to find the island. No one had ever found it before, after all.

Ren and the others rode until sundown. When they finally stopped, it was in a local town. Ren found a cheap inn to stay at and paid for two rooms. He figured he and Marcus could share one, and the girls could share the other. Instead, they were all surprised when Kelsey grabbed Marcus's hand and pulled him along with her.

"We're sharing," she said to him, and they walked into one of the rooms.

Thirty-two

Off Into the World

Ren and Julie tended to their needs before settling in for the night. Their room had two beds, allowing them to each take one. Julie sat on one, brushing her hair.

Ren laid his jacket over the end of his bed and began sorting his weapons and gear in preparation for the following day. Once he finished, he removed his shirt as he always did at night, giving Julie a mouthwatering view of his chiseled torso.

Julie had seen him shirtless plenty of times during their time together at Trinity, but the view never got old.

"Are you going wear that all night?" he asked. But Julie never answered. She was too busy staring at his abs. "Julie?" he asked again, and this time, she snapped out of her trance.

"Oh, sorry, what did you say?" she asked.

"I asked if you were going to wear your mission outfit all night. Do you need me to leave the room?"

Julie knew he was being polite. She also knew that it was entirely unnecessary. Trinity's missions required one to abandon little things like being embarrassed over disrobing before the opposite sex.

"No. Your sentiment is appreciated, though," she told him.

Julie's mission attire was designed for movement and flexibility. A black one-piece that hugged tight to her body with no right leg. A white jacket with armor plating inside fit over her torso. An armored corset made of black steel fit on top at her waist. And over her hands, she wore pinky-less black gloves.

Below Julie's torso, a black chain draped over her hips. Ren often saw her use it as both a weapon and a belt to attach her gear. It was a rather useful multi-functional tool. And at her feet, she wore black boots with armored soles. However, Julie's exposed right leg had a leg guard over it, clipped together in the back at her calf and thigh.

That particular guard was the reason she left her leg exposed, free from the cover of her one-piece. It required special care when used, making any clothing beneath restrict the joints and her movement. Ren had seen her deflect blades with it, knock people unconscious, and even use it as a shield.

Julie removed her boots and leg guard before getting to her feet and stripping down to her underwear before climbing into bed.

As she settled in, Ren left the room. He returned minutes later carrying a small bucket filled with water. He dumped in his usual herbs, then raised the bucket to his lips, letting it saturate his throat.

"Want some water?" he asked her.

A drink would work wonders right now. The day's travel with the heat beating down on them had left her throat dry. Julie took the bucket, tipping the contents down her throat. By the time she stopped, the bucket was empty. She hadn't realized how thirsty she actually was.

Ren took the bucket back and set it on the small table in front of the window before blowing out the lantern, casting the room in darkness. He climbed into the spare bed, feeling Nidar lying at the foot.

When Ren woke next, it was early the next morning. The first rays of morning sunlight were beginning to shine through the window. A pressure against his chest forced him to open his eyes. Julie lay next to him, her back pressed tight to him.

Ren sat up, using his hand to prop himself up, and looked around the room. He lay in the same bed he chose when he first turned in for the night, meaning it was Julie who had switched places. The thought that she got up during the night and picked the wrong bed on accident struck him.

Next to him, Ren felt Julie stir and open her eyes. They widened when she saw Ren next to her.

"Ren!" she said, shocked. "What are you doing in my bed?"

"I'm not," Ren answered. Then, he pointed to the bed on the other side of the room.

Julie realized it was, in fact, her that was in the wrong bed.

"Oh gods, I'm sorry, Ren. I got up last night. I guess I got the wrong bed."

"I kind of expected that. It's fine. Besides, it's not like this is the first time we've shared a bed."

"Ah, you mean that cheap Texas motel five years ago?"

Ren chuckled. "That'd be the one."

Julie sat up, and Ren got out of bed. Nidar lay sprawled out in the center of the room, still sound asleep. That damn tiger. It was a good thing no one broke in while they slept.

"I'll be right back," he said and walked to the door, grabbing the empty bucket on the way out. When he next returned, it was with a steaming cup in hand and more water.

Julie smelled the familiar scent of coffee. It was a good thing coffee beans grew in Nexus, cultivated after being found and transported from the human world. It was one of the few things that didn't come from Nexus or monsters first. Bless the humans for that, too. She didn't think she could live without it.

Without moving from her spot, Julie held her hands out, a sign that she wanted some. Ren sat down on the bed next to her and handed her the cup. The coffee warmed her as it passed down her throat, warming her stomach to her core.

Ren finished the coffee and threw on his shirt, jacket, and boots. Having finished herself, Julie used the water in the bucket to wash her face before brushing her hair.

For the first time, Nidar got up and followed them as they walked to Marcus's and Kelsey's room. Ren knocked on the door, and Marcus opened it a few seconds later.

"We're ready to go whenever you are," Ren told him.

"Us too. Let's get moving."

Ren and Nidar followed Marcus, Kelsey, and Julie to the stables, where their horses spent the night. Once all three of them had mounted their horses, Ren climbed on Nidar's back. Marcus gently tapped his horse with his heel and took the lead.

They rode until nightfall every day, rising early in the morning, before stopping at another town. After two weeks, they were nearing the port town of Seidra. At their current pace, they would reach it by the end of the next day. From there, all their time would be at sea. Then, they'd put their fate in luck's hands.

Thirty-three
Dearest Friend

R en woke up to Julie lying next to him once again. She had her arm around him and her head propped up on his chest, using it as a pillow. He looked at the bed on the other side of the room and saw Nidar lying on it. The tiger had his head in the air and was staring at them, his tail flicking behind him.

"Oh sure, laugh it up," Ren said to him.

Nidar released a rumbling sound from his throat, which Ren took as the tiger's version of a laugh.

Unlike their first night, this had been the only other time he and Julie had shared a bed. However, unlike the previous, this time resulted from uncontrollable circumstances. Whether intentional or not, their furry feline friend had claimed the second bed the moment they entered the room and refused to budge from his spot, making it impossible for either Ren or Julie to share it with him.

Ren had no idea what time it was since he couldn't see a clock or tell the location of the sun from the bed. He tried to free himself from Julie's hold, but she just snuggled closer after his attempt failed. With a gentle flick on the forehead, Julie moaned rather disapprovingly, and he took the opportunity to escape when it appeared.

A knock on his door appeared as he finished tying his boots, having already dressed himself.

"It's open," he said. The door opened, and Marcus walked into the room with Kelsey behind him. "Yo," Ren said in greeting.

The two of them sat on the other bed while Ren finished up. "We were just about to head out for breakfast," Marcus said, petting Nidar.

"Breakfast huh?" Ren's stomach churned. "You know, I think that's a good idea. Should we wake her up?" He pointed to Julie with his thumb.

"We could always just let her sleep," Marcus said. "Which may or may not piss her off that we left her behind."

"Oh boy."

Julie groaned, garnishing their attention. "Ren, don't put that there. It's not going to fit." Ren raised a curious eyebrow. What in the hell was that?

"Marcus, don't eat that," she continued to say in her sleep. Marcus tilted to look at her, going past Ren. "Bad werewolf."

He and Ren slowly turned their heads to look at each other.

"What kind of dream is she having?" Marcus wondered.

"I don't want to know," Ren said back. A deep sigh escaped his mouth. "Julie. Rise and shine," he said, shaking her. "Time to wake up."

Julie moaned and cracked her eyes. "Marcus? When did you change your eyes?"

"I'm not Marcus, and I didn't change my eyes."

She put her arms around his neck and leaned forward, sending them both tumbling off the bed.

"Oh no! God damn it!" Ren said. They hit the ground with a thud, and he found himself flat on his back. "Julie, get off me." But despite the tumble, Julie was no more awake than previously.

Ren shook her in an attempt to finally wake her. Finally, she rubbed her eyes and opened them fully.

"Ren? What's going on?" She saw Marcus and Kelsey sitting on the other bed.

"Julie," Ren said again. "Get. Off."

For the first time, Julie realized that not only was she riding Ren, who lay on the floor, but she was the only one not dressed.

"Why am I riding you?" she asked.

"Get off of me, and I'll tell you," he responded. "What in the hell were you dreaming about?"

Remembering the events that passed through her head while she slept was an easy task, considering she remembered basically all of it. Her face turned as red as a tomato, and she grabbed the pillow from the bed before smacking him with it.

"None of your business!" she said, embarrassed. "Stupid Ren, stupid Ren, stupid Ren!"

Marcus held his laughter in for as long as he could before he could no longer contain it. Kelsey was the only one not amused with the scene unfolding before her. She kept her eyes downcast, staring at the ground. Her knuckles were turning white she was clenching her fists so tight. But it was all she could do to block everything out. Seeing and hearing would only make things more painful.

Julie threw on her clothes and quickly ran her fingers through her hair. She didn't bother properly readying for the day, only focused on preserving time, given that the others were waiting on her.

One of the reasons Ren and the others chose this inn was it served food to those who stayed there. There was a cost, of course, but the convenience was worth every coin.

As soon as they appeared in the small dining area, noises died momentarily as those present bowed or curtsied accordingly. After one of the female servers greeted them, she guided them to a table. Marcus sat down, and Julie eagerly took the seat next to him, leaving

Kelsey to take Marcus's other side and Ren the remaining spot between the girls. At his feet, Nidar dropped to the ground.

Marcus and Julie talked the entire time, but Ren and Kelsey remained silent. She hadn't spoken to him the whole week since they started their trip, and he didn't blame her. Instead, he focused his attention on Nidar, giving the tiger any desired attention.

Their meal came and went, and with it, so did their stay in the town. Gathering their horses, they headed for the port town.

Night swallowed them after riding all day, casting a dark shadow over the land. Despite that, the whole world was lit up. Stars blanketed the sky overhead, bathing the world around them in light and color. It was the kind of night sky Kelsey had never seen in the human world, especially living in a big city. Even for an outdoor person like she was.

Ren was trailing behind the others at a steady pace when he noticed Julie ride up to Marcus and match his pace. He caught her sneak a glance at him, something he was noticing more of, especially this particular day, and he wasn't the only one. What surprised him was that it wasn't Marcus, despite the guy usually being the first to pick up on situations like this. It was Kelsey who noticed.

Kelsey didn't have a clue as to why, and she didn't really care to be honest. She was still suffering from a broken heart. It made her want to crawl into a dark hole and bury herself. At least she finally knew how it felt. It was the worst.

Ren, however, thought differently. A vague idea floated around in his head, hoping he was wrong, but his instincts and gut told him otherwise, and that made things difficult. If he was right, he would be thrilled for his friend; how could he not be? But that put all of them, with the exception of Kelsey, into an extremely precarious situation.

In the distance, the outline of civilization emerged. It was too dark to make out any distinctive features at their distance, but it was for certain the town of Seidra.

As they neared the port town, they all slowed to a walk. In the distance, they could hear the sound of the ocean crashing into itself and see the sparkle of lights from the buildings. That's how they knew they were getting close. The terrain changed; the once flat ground became mounds and hills. The dirt road snaked up to the top of a hill in the distance, seemingly the largest of them all, like a bridge to the moon. Then, standing at the peak, everything came into view.

In the distance, the ocean sparkled, reflecting the light from the stars. And down below, seemingly within arm's reach, the port town Seidra was cast in a brilliant orange glow. There was no wall surrounding it nor a gate to pass through. Even for a port town, it appeared adequately unsecured, but perhaps it merely did not need it. Too many travelers made checkpoints just as cumbersome as not enough.

Inside the city, Ren split from the others, instructing them to look for an inn while he searched for a ship. That is, should he even be able to find anyone still occupying the docks at that time of night.

Unsurprisingly, the streets were still heavily occupied, even at night. Seidra was a prosperous town, and it showed. Trade never ceased, for money never slept, after all.

The road beneath Nidar's paws was made of stone, as were all the others. And when they reached the docs, it was still wet from the ocean spray.

Ren and Nidar stopped to observe their surroundings. Directly to their right sat the ocean, and to their left, the multi-story buildings that lined the street. He was glad to see that the wooden docks that extended out into the soft ocean waves were just as heavily occupied as the town. Dozens of ships were tied off, their gangplanks lowered. That meant crews were still active. Now, he just needed to get an audience with one.

The first couple they passed didn't meet the requirements Ren was searching for. The ships were too small, indicating that they weren't geared toward long voyages at sea. Others didn't have their gangplank lowered or their questionable. He needed something that could sail well and a crew that he could trust. Of course, he intended to work among them. He rather enjoyed sailing, though it had been many decades since he'd last done so.

When a ship finally caught his interest, he stopped Nidar. The ship itself was nothing special, just like most of the others, but it was large, and its crew diligent by appearance sake. Dozens of crates had been stacked on the dock, quickly and efficiently carried onto the ship one at a time by half a dozen crew members. They were strong, worked quickly and with a goal, and followed orders. That was good. It was a sign of experience, the kind that he was looking for.

Ren dismounted Nidar, and the two of them approached one of the crewmen, a lean man with a light build. Green scales covered his body, with a long snout and tail behind him. A lizardman. They were fairly common around these parts. His black hair was cut short and still wet from the ocean spray. A tattoo rested on his right arm and another on his hand. He was dressed in thin cotton pants with a patch over the left thigh and a white baggy shirt tucked inside his pants. The heavily worn shoes at his feet indicated he wore them often, a sign of continuous work.

"Excuse me," Ren said. The crewman turned to look at him and jumped when he saw Nidar.

"What in blazes is that creature!" he asked, trying to get as far away as possible.

"He's called a tiger, an animal from the human world, and he won't harm you."

The lizardman eyed Nidar. "It looks hungry."

"I assure you, he won't attack you. So long as you mean no harm or try anything funny, you will be perfectly fine."

"And, just what is it that you want?"

"I wish to speak to your captain."

The man eyed him up and down, getting a feel for Ren. "You look like you're on a journey, stranger."

"As a matter of fact, I am. And my next location is at sea."

"Where do you plan on going?"

"I will share information with you and the rest of the crew after I have met with the captain."

"Our ship is not a ferry, nor our crew. We don't transport people. If you're looking for a ride, look elsewhere."

"I know it's not. That's why I've come to this one out of all the others I've seen thus far."

Ren's comment seemed to satisfy the lizardman, or at least make him curious enough to find out how things would play out.

"Alright, follow me. I'll take you to the capin'."

Ren followed the man up the gangplank. The crew was an assortment of different monsters. Taniwha, nachzehrer, lizardmen, beastkin, finfolk, tengu, and other various races.

Most paid no mind to Ren or Nidar, only focusing on their work. However, a few of them noticed them step onto the ship, giving them some curious looks.

They stopped in front of a man who was busy lifting up crates and bringing them down into the hull. He was about six feet tall and covered from head to toe in fur, with two ears on top of his head and a tail.

"Pardon the interruption, Capin'," the lizardman said.

"What is it?" the captain asked, stopping.

"This man is on a journey. He seeks your attention."

"How interesting," Ren said. Ren had a look of pure interest in his eye.

The captain set the crate he was carrying down and turned around. When his eyes found Ren, they widened immediately, and he dropped into a bow, getting down on one knee and lowering his head. Now, they had the attention of the whole crew.

"Capin'!" the lizardman said in shock, but the captain only held his bow.

"Your Highness, it is an honor to have you on board. I am the captain of this vessel. My name is Conrad Rowd."

"Your Highness?" the lizardman asked.

The crew began to gather around.

"You imbeciles, bow, right now! Show some respect!"

The crew was clearly confused, but they had been given an order by their captain and simply followed it, bowing to Ren.

"There's no need for that. Please, rise," Ren said. When the captain rose, the rest of the crew followed. They were a good crew, and he a good captain. Even without knowing them, Ren could tell. "A werewolf. I don't see a lot of you this far out near the border. Being a captain, I think it suits you."

"Your kind words are wasted on me, Your Highness."

"Hey, hold on, I know who you are!" one of the crew members said.

"Yes, and you had better show respect the captain demanded. You are in the presence of Nexus's prince." Hushed discussions began among the crew almost immediately. "Your Highness, what brings you aboard?" the captain asked.

"Captain, I am in need of your ship," Ren said back.

"I would be honored to have you on board, but can I ask as to why? We're currently in the middle of resupplying."

"My team and I are on a quest." When the captain said nothing, Ren explained in further detail. "I am searching for something. An ancient relic, one no one believes exists."

"And you found it?"

"We believe so. We have a location and a map. However, the remaining leg of our quest is out at sea. We need a ship to complete the remainder of our journey."

"I understand the situation. Aiding in your quest is an honor; however, my ship can only handle a few more mouths with all our supplies. Forgive my rudeness for asking, but who and how many will be joining you?"

"Have no worries, I wouldn't be offended by that. I know too well the effect extra cargo and extra mouths have on a ship. There are five of us, including me and my companion here." Ren patted Nidar's head. "The others would be would be Prince Allagash, the Dridia Kingdom's princess, and one more."

"Five." The Captain was silent as he pondered, no doubt running the many variables through his head. "I think we can manage that. Five more should not be too burdensome. Very well, we would be honored to provide you transportation on your quest, Your Highness."

"I'm grateful. Here," Ren said, handing him a piece of cloth. It had a series of numbers on it. "This is the location where we're headed. I cannot give you the map yet since it's currently in the possession of Prince Allagash. However, we can explain everything to you tomorrow."

The captain looked at the piece of cloth. "Understood. Our ship departs at first light."

"We'll be here. And thanks again, Captain."

Ren and Nidar gave their farewells for the night before heading down the ramp. When they got to the bottom, Ren climbed on Nidar, and they headed back into the city. It didn't take long before they ran into Marcus, who had come to find them.

"Did you find a ship?" Marcus asked.

"I did." Ren pointed to the ship they would be taking. "And you? Did you find an inn?"

"Yeah. It's pretty close to the harbor, too. Follow me."

Marcus led the way to the inn. A long silence passed between them before he finally spoke up.

"Listen, Ren," Marcus finally said. He stopped walking, causing Ren and Nidar to stop as well. "It's about your marriage arrangement to Julie."

"What about it?" Ren asked.

"You need to rethink it. The whole arrangement."

"I told you already that I can't. I have no way to confront Dridia's king."

"That's bullshit. You're allowed your own happiness, Ren. Besides, have you even considered Julie's side of this? She was forced into this just as you were."

"What exactly are you getting at, Marcus? That Julie doesn't want this either? Or, perhaps, she does. She's always held a candle for me, after all."

"I know. I also know that she tried to talk you out of it at first, but you disregarded her, as you seem to be doing to everyone lately. Maybe Dridia does have you backed into a corner, I get that. But pushing everything away from you and using the welfare of your kingdom as an excuse is no solution. Especially since you've yet to completely resolve the misunderstanding between you and a certain distraught human girl."

"Misunderstanding, huh? Then what would you like me to do, Marcus? Do you want me to cancel the engagement and risk a war? Or should I just take Kelsey and run away? Is that what you want? I'm afraid that's no longer an option. Not anymore."

"You broke her heart. Do you even realize that, how much you hurt her? You agreed to marry another woman and kept it a secret, knowing she was trying to patch things between you. That girl loves you, Ren. She's always loved you and still loves you, even now."

"Is that why you've been spending so much time together since then? Are you playing Cupid, trying to piece together a broken picture? Are you certain Kelsey even holds any feelings for me anymore? Or are you trying to sweep in and take my place, heal her?"

Marcus gripped his fists tightly, fury quickly threatening to explode.

"What's your play, Marcus? You know where Julie and I stand with each other, but I know nothing of your current position in all of this. How close have you grown to Kelsey now that we're apart? Have you slept with her?"

Marcus snapped. He didn't even think; he just reacted. Then, before he realized what he'd done, his fist made contact with the side of Ren's face, knocking him sideways. Ren stumbled but stayed upright.

"You deserved that. If that's what you really think, you're an even bigger piece of shit than I thought," Marcus said. "And you deserve a hell of a lot more than just one single punch. Do you know what we talk about when we're together? You! It's always about you. And it's not just me she confides in. All the time she spent with Cole, he was telling her stories about you, things you'd never told her yourself. All the things she wanted to ask. I've been helping her to get passed it. She only recently stopped crying herself to sleep."

"At night, when she goes to sleep, I stay awake," he continued to say. "I remember why it is that I fight, why I'm still here, and what I have to lose. And I rack my brain for hours, trying to figure a way to get you out of this."

"Why bother?" Ren asked. "What's the point? Even if I did find a way to avoid marrying Julie, there's no chance she'd take me back."

"Yes, she would. Trust me on that. Despite how you've treated her, what you've done, I know for certain that she would take you back. If you only told her how you really feel. You and I both know that you still love her."

"I don't think I could ever stop," Ren confessed.

"Then stop trying to bear the world on your shoulders and tell her. Be honest with her for once."

"I can't do that! Look at me, Marcus! I'm not even human. I'm a vampire, and she's a human. I'm a killing machine! Besides, I'll outlive her by millennia! Everything she said about me was right. I am a monster."

"Is that why you gave Ellie your mother's necklace?"

Ren's eyes widened. He'd nearly forgotten about the necklace. How could he do that?

"The necklace your mother gave you for your fifteenth birthday? The last memento you have of someone who loved you unconditionally, who taught you what love was. What it meant to live. Do you think she'd approve of how you've been acting? What would she say after seeing what you've become, what you did to that girl?"

Ren said nothing. He only balled his fists tightly.

"I'm done talking about this. I'll be staying at another inn. The ship leaves at first light. This conversation is over. We're done here." Ren turned and walked away, Nidar trailing behind him.

"No, we're not done yet. This isn't even close to being over. I'll get you out of this. One way or the other, I'll stop this arranged marriage."

Marcus watched from behind as Ren walked off, too far away to hear his vow. But the fire had been lit. It showed in Marcus's eyes, and it was a raging inferno.

Thirty-four

Footsteps Found in the Myth

Nidar woke Ren the next morning. It took the tiger several nudges to Ren's face with his nose before he finally opened his eyes.

"Nidar, what is it?" he asked. The tiger looked over at the window. Ren followed his gaze, but except for the darkness that still lingered, there was nothing to note. "There's nothing there, bud."

A paw to the stomach got his attention. The tiger patted him before looking back outside. That's when Ren figured it out. "Oh, right, the ship."

Ren climbed out of bed and walked to the washroom. Filling a bucket of water, he dumped in his usual herbs, letting them blend before splashing the water over his face and running it through his hair.

Gathering his gear, Ren and Nidar headed for the docks. It was dark at the moment, but Ren knew it wouldn't stay dark for long. The sun was just peeking over the horizon by the time they reached the ship.

At the bottom of the gangplank, a small gathering of crew members waited on the dock. Ren noticed one of them had taken on a human form.

"Morning, gentlemen," Ren greeted.

"Ah, Prince Nightwalker, good morning," the one in human form greeted back. That's when Ren recognized his voice. It was the captain.

"That's quite a transformation, Captain. I didn't recognize you."

The captain released a hearty laugh. "I expected that. I find my human form preferable when sailing. You'll see that I remain in it much of the time. Besides, I'm much more handsome this way."

The captain's comment made Ren chuckle.

In his human form, the captain was only a few inches shorter than Ren was. His black hair was cut short at the back and sides, leaving the hair on top long and full. Unlike most other ship captains, Conrad's face was clean-shaven, revealing the patch of freckles on his right cheek. They reminded Ren of Kelsey.

The captain's large muscular arms and thick chest stood out through his clean, beige linen shirt. A long leather jacket sat open on his frame, the buckle of his belt glinting in the light of the sun. Black pants and boots to match fit his lower half.

Ren had to admit, the guy was right. In his human form, he was handsome.

One of the crew members approached Ren and the captain, descending down the gangplank. A man with short ears atop his head and a full beard. He was one of the few beastkin within the crew. Unlike other beastkin, half of his appearance was humanoid. At close to six feet tall, with a heavy build and massive arms, it was clear that he was a seasoned sailor.

"Captain, everything is in order," the man said.

"Are we ready to sail?" the captain asked.

"Yes, Captain."

"Good. All that's left is to wait for Prince Nightwalker's companions. Thank you, Mr. Hawk. Your Highness, I don't believe you've been acquainted yet. This is my chief officer, First Mate Rain Hawk."

"A pleasure. Thanks for having us aboard," Ren said, offering his hand.

"Likewise. Welcome aboard." The chief officer shook Ren's hand.

"Alright, men, all aboard. We set said as soon as our missing companions arrive," the captain ordered.

"Aye, aye, Captain!"

Ren followed the captain and crew members up the gangplank. He and the captain leaned against the port side railing, waiting for the rest of his party while the crew went about their duties.

"Well, look there. It seems your companions have arrived," the captain said to Ren.

Marcus and the girls were just walking up to the dock when the captain noticed them. He moved to greet them while Ren ran off in another direction after someone called for him unexpectedly.

Joining the captain at the bottom of the gangplank was the chief officer.

"A fine morning to you all. You must be Prince Allagash and the other two companions." The captain shook Marcus's hand. "I'm the captain of this ship, Conrad Rowd. And this is my chief officer, First Mate Rain Hawk. Come aboard, and we'll set sail. Mr. Hawk, prepare the ship for cast off."

"At your order, Captain."

First Mate Hawk ran up the gangplank, giving out orders to the crew. At the same time, the captain led Marcus and the girls up the ramp. That's when they finally saw Ren on the deck tying off rope, the chief officer still giving orders.

"Mr. Jackson, rig the foresail. Mr. Wrath and Mr. Kane, untie the ropes. Prince Nightwalker, raise the sails."

"Julie, Kelsey, follow the captain," Marcus told them. "I'll be giving them a hand before we depart."

Marcus approached the chief officer while he was giving out orders in place of the captain.

"Chief Officer Hawk, standing by and waiting for orders."

The chief officer looked at him before speaking. "Prince Allagash, assist Prince Nightwalker with the sails. We'll be casting off momentarily."

Marcus didn't hesitate, heading over to where Ren worked at the sails and grabbing one of the ropes. They exchanged glances, having done the same task so many times before in the past.

"Ready? Pull!" Ren said.

Together, he and Marcus pulled on the ropes and raised the mainsail, then tied the rope off before moving on to the other sails.

"Cast off!" the chief officer said.

"Casting off!" one of the crewmen said.

A gust of wind hit the sails, and the ship lurched forward.

"Well done, gentleman. Mr. Hawk, set a course," the captain ordered.

"Aye, aye, Captain!" The chief officer ran to the helm and took the wheel.

"Your Highnesses, allow me to show you to your rooms," the captain said. "Your companions are already below deck."

They followed the captain below deck to the quarters. Beneath the captain's cabin were two officer cabins. Despite Ren's and Marcus's protests, the captain and chief officer refused their request to sleep with the rest of the crew in their quarters at the bow of the ship, separating them from the private cabins. Ren and Marcus took one cabin, while Kelsey and Julie took the other.

Both cabins had one bed on the starboard side, a desk, a nightstand with an oil lamp, a dresser, and a carpet in the middle of the room.

Nidar plopped down on the carpet, curling himself up. Ren set his stuff down in the corner before opening the door to leave.

"Ren," Marcus said. Ren stopped in the doorway. "Listen, about last night."

"Forget it, Marcus."

"No, listen." Ren turned to face him. "I'm sorry. I went too far."

A heavy sigh passed through Ren's lips. "No, you're not exactly wrong. But at this point, I still don't have a way out of this, aside from destroying Julie's whole kingdom."

"That's because you're going at this alone. Let me help you. You told me you loved Kelsey. Well, it's the same for her. That girl loves you, man. And she wants to be with you. If that's what you really want, you have to be willing to fight. You know better than anyone that if we work together, nothing can stop us. We'll find a way out of this, as a team. What do you say we give it a shot?"

Ren considered his friend's proposal. Marcus was right, about everything. Ren knew that; he'd always known. It was time for him to finally accept that instead of running away. He needed to face what was in front of him, and he trusted no one more than Marcus to help him find a way.

"You're right," he finally said. "Alright, let's do this."

Ren and Marcus embraced before heading up to the deck. Lazing around and doing nothing didn't sit well with either of them. They were too used to work, even when acting as a captain. So, they got to work aiding the crew in their tasks. Now aware of their abilities and experience with sailing, the crew took to them with ease.

Hours passed while they worked, the view of the port quickly fading as they approached the open ocean.

"You're Highnesses," The captain said, getting their attention. He approached while the two of them were busy ensuring that everything on deck was secure. "Lunch will be served soon. Care to join us?"

"Happy to," Ren said back. He and Marcus followed the captain back below deck to the galley.

BAM! A loud crash sounded from the other side. Walking into the room, they each gave a curious look and stepped into the room. Two sets of two large tables butted up to each other at the end filled part of the room. Chairs lined the tables on both sides.

Most of the crew was already present, a few sitting at the tables while the rest gathered around to watch whatever excitement was occurring.

Julie had one of the crew members on his stomach, her knee pressed into the center of his back, one arm pinned behind him and the other to the ground. Kelsey had another on the ground at her feet, her fist raised, the red mark on his left cheek a clear indication that he had been punched.

"What's going on here?" the captain asked.

"Captain!" the crew said.

"Looks like you boys have been having some fun."

"If you ask me, it looks more like the girls are the ones having the fun," Ren said.

The captain started laughing. "So, did you enjoy your playtime?" he asked.

"What do you think?" the crew member pinned under Julie asked. "Just get her off!"

"Julie, finish it!" Ren ordered.

The crewman didn't have time to question or protest before Julie turned to him and punched the ground next to his face, splintering it. His face turned white as paper. Julie released him and stood up, walking over next to Marcus. Kelsey gave one last look at the crew member she punched before flashing a look at the others and went to stand next to Ren.

"So, what happened to you guys?" the captain asked.

"They got a little too wound up," Julie said. "I guess with two women on board, their hands and minds began to wander, thinking that it would be easy."

The captain looked at Ren, who stood there stoically, his arms crossed, gazing out at the crew. No matter where he was, Ren had an aura unlike anyone else. Just standing as he did, the entire crew knew instantly that he was a fight they would not win, even all together.

"You might have just gotten away unscathed had you been up against different women," Ren said. "But you hit on the wrong girls. These two are no match for any of you. Now you know what it means to mess with a member of Trinity."

"Perhaps this was a much-needed lesson," the captain said. "From now on, I want all of you to consider your actions and behave accordingly. There will be no second chances, especially on board my ship. Understand?"

A universal nod spread through the whole crew. There was no chance of anyone else among them making the same mistake again.

"Good. Now, who's hungry?"

Without another word, the crew members took their seats at the tables while the captain walked to the kitchen in the adjourning room beyond. Marcus sat to Ren's left, his right side left open as if reserved for the only missing person.

The captain walked out of the room backward, holding two large plates. He set them down on one table, then returned to the kitchen, repeating the process over a dozen or so times. Each time, placing different food in large portions on the tables at both ends. Then, the tableware, glasses and drinks.

The captain only sat down after all the food and drink had been served, taking the vacant spot next to Ren.

"A captain who cooks for his own crew; I respect that," Ren said. "Now, I do believe I promised you a map."

"An explanation of our voyage would be greatly appreciated, Your Highness. Even more so the destination you seek."

Marcus pulled out a rolled-up piece of parchment from within his gear and handed it to the captain.

"This map is an exact replica of the original we found," Ren informed the captain. "Alas, due to the nature of the source, we could not bring it with us."

"I take it whatever you found the original map in is of unimaginable concept."

"A black scroll." The captain dropped the map out of shock. "The most secretive type of information the world has never known. A secret among secrets."

"Where in the world did you find something as perilous as that?"

"From the lowest floor in the Grand Library, back at Nightwalker Palace."

Once more, taking up the map, the captain glanced down at the contents.

"What we were looking for," Ren started to say, "that is, the initial source that led us to descend the library in the first place, was any knowledge on how to remove the Sun and Moon Stones from their wielder."

"The stones exist?" the captain asked, overcome with surprise. Ren nodded, and Kelsey held up her wrist.

"In the end, we did not actually find a way to remove them, unfortunately. Not as we thought we would. Instead, we found this, a clue to the location of something that could tell us how to remove them."

"Hence the reason for your quest. What you're after, the treasure you seek, is whatever rests at the end of this map. Primary over the removal of the stones themselves."

"Exactly. According to the information obtained from the black scroll, that map will lead us to the divine record of every artifact in existence. The Records of The Gods."

Silence filled the galley. Not even a single breath escaped.

"Even now, the Records are thought to be merely a myth. And, as far as we know, no one has ever found them. However, this map is proof that there is something. Whether it's truly the Records, I don't know."

The captain looked over the map intensely.

"The map identifies the location of the Records somewhere in the middle of the Avoline Ocean. I suspect there's an island or some sort of geography protecting them. We have a name. A city, to be precise. That's where we believe the Records are being kept. Our only hope is that they're not located at the bottom of the ocean."

"A city, in the middle of the ocean? I've traveled these waters almost my whole life, and I've never come across something like that," the captain informed them.

"Well, we should expect that much. The city is a myth in and of itself, so no surprise there. There are many legends about it, even in the human world."

"Huh, is that so? What kind of city is it?"

"It belonged to an ancient people. Legends state that the city was built from precious metal. The walls, floors, roofs, weapons, even utensils, all made entirely from gold." The entire crew had a renewed gleam in their eyes after hearing that. "In Nexus, it's known as—"

"Paerlejara," the captain said, finishing Ren's sentence before he could. "The City of Gold."

"You've heard of it then."

The captain nodded. "It's a legend among sailors. My mentor spent his entire life searching for it. It was his life's desire. A quest to find the legendary City of Gold. But he never did end up finding it."

"Captain," First Mate Hawk said. "You don't think?"

"Ah, you might be on to something, Mr. Hawk. Perhaps, just perhaps, that's what it could be." The captain turned to Ren. "Excuse me for a few minutes. I have something that might just be useful."

The captain excused himself, returning minutes later with a rolled-up piece of parchment.

"I bought this off an old merchant my mentor used to do business with. He found it by chance while exploring. No one who's ever seen it has been able to identify its source. But now, perhaps, I finally have an idea what this is meant for."

The captain placed the parchment on the table and unrolled it. Spread out before them was a map of an island.

Thirty-five

The Monsters That Lurk on the Moon

One week at sea with nothing to show for it was not a good motivator. Not knowing was half of the adventure, but despite knowing what was coming when they boarded the ship, it didn't make things easier as the days passed by ceaselessly.

Atop the deck, all hands were working to maintain the ship's heading with utmost perfection. Lack of care would be the death of all of them, should they let it. Even the hands of two certain princes were being put to work, completing tasks while they were on the lookout for the island.

"Captain, Conrad," Ren said, approaching. "How's our heading?"

"Rock solid, Your Highness. According to the map, we're on route. I suspect it's only a matter of time before we spot our destination."

"That's what I'm worried about. Our supplies are not infinite. And we still need to make the journey back, as do you need to complete your trade. We cannot afford to search endlessly much more."

"Your concerns are noted, Your Highness. However, you let us worry about that. Your fight is yet to come, and it is certainly much bigger than ours."

From the crow's nest, one sailor descended to the deck before running to the helm.

"Captain, ship on the horizon."

"Any markers?" the captain asked. "What does their flag bear?"

"None, Captain. She's incognito and appears to be sailing directly toward us."

"Are you certain of this?"

"Yes, Captain. I counted the paces to confirm it. Its heading has not changed."

"What's the plan, Captain?" Ren asked.

The captain kept his eyes on the horizon while he contemplated their next move. The ship in question was still out of his view. However, his barrelman had confirmed it. Altering course would cost them much needed time and risk them running astride.

"Men, take your positions and ready the cannons. We cannot risk it should the incoming ship be our foe. Hold course, and wait for my signal."

On the horizon, the ship finally came into view from their starboard side. It bore no flag, nor any marker, and was headed right toward them, just as the barrelman had said. Not even a figurehead graced its bow.

At the captain's orders, everyone moved to their positions. Cannons were drawn and loaded, aimed directly at the incoming ship.

When the ship was finally within range of their cannons, Ren felt a wave of ki overcome him. he raced to the bow of the ship as a bullet of air rocketed toward them, parting the ocean beneath it. Gathering his ki, he cast a spell and summoned a wall of wind. The air bullet smashed into his air shield, the impact rocking the whole ship.

"Fire!" the captain shouted.

Explosions of smoke appeared as the cannons were fired. Cannonballs cleaved the water in two but failed to successfully strike the ship.

A ferocious roar filled the skies, and Ren looked up to see the familiar form of a lion with wings, a goat head on its back, and a snake tail flying toward them. On its back sat a lone rider with long brown hair and a mask covering half of his face. Wei Shu, the man who had ambushed them on their trip to the capital.

How did he find them? They left no trace, and on open water, tracking them was practically impossible. The chances of this being a coincidence, however, were nearly zero.

Ren summoned his wings and launched into the air, rocking the ship on liftoff. Drawing his Barettas, he emptied a whole clip from each into the chimera. It reared back and then set all of its eyes on him. In front of the goat head, he saw a sphere of flames gather, growing in size. The fire raged toward him, and he flew to the side to avoid it.

Kelsey and Julie wished they could fly. They all caught the moment Ren launched into the sky to face off against the Chimera and Wei Shu. Were they able, they could help him. Being stuck on the ground was never more frustrating than it was then.

Unfortunately for the enemy, fixed to land or not, Marcus was never one to sit still. He could use wind magic to make himself fly, but before he joined the fight, he was going to make a path for the others.

Putting his ice daggers together at the ends, they transformed into a bow. Marcus drew back on the string and an arrow formed. When he fired, it struck the water, and a walkway made of ice formed, racing toward the other ship. It hit the hull and exploded, coating the entire starboard side.

With one spell, Marcus flew into the air. Julie hopped over the side of the ship and raced toward the enemy vessel over the ice walkway. Kelsey, Nidar, and half of the crew joined her.

Ren summoned flames with magic and fired at Wei Shu and the chimera. The goat head on its back countered his flames with magic, and the snake tail snapped at him. He turned, just barely in time to avoid its fangs sinking into him. The poison contained within it was lethal. Were he to get bit, it was all over. First and foremost, he needed to take care of the snake tail.

Gathering his ki, he cast another fire spell. Only, this time, he cast it on Shadow Hunter, setting the sword ablaze.

When the snake for a tail snapped at him once more, he turned and avoided it. Raising Shadow Hunter above his head, he swung down. The chimera cried out as its tail was sliced in two, and the bottom half with the head of a snake, fell into the watery depths below.

"The rumors don't do you justice," Wei Shu said. "You truly are strong. The strength fit for an S+ Super Monster. It's no wonder you beat Algiroth."

Ren stopped dead in his tracks. This guy knew he had defeated Algiroth. There was no way he would know that unless he were directly involved in the battle, but there was no chance of that. Ren would have remembered seeing him, even among the chaos. The guy's stature was unmistakable. And yet, this was certainly their second encounter, the first just as obscure.

It was impossible for someone of unknown origins to know so much concealed information, let alone carry the strength he did. Unless he worked for someone and was of a certain status.

The realization hit Ren like a truck. Everything suddenly made sense. His presence, his strength, his weapons, and his command; they were the proof of the title that he carried. That meant only one thing, and it sent a deep-rooted chill through Ren's bones. There was no doubt, this guy was one of Verin's generals.

Wei's smirk, evident from the right side of his face, was all the proof that Ren needed to realize he was right.

"You figured it out quickly. I admit, I'm impressed. I may be third among the four, but unlike a certain vampire, I earned my position, as did the other two. Algiroth may have been one of us, but he was a rogue. Without that demonic sword, he was nothing. It's the reason he became a general in the first place. There was no chance you'd have learned how closely we've been watching you with him acting of his own whims. He was both an asset and a hindrance."

"Is that so," Ren said.

Bad. This was very bad. Facing Verin's third-ranked general, in the middle of the ocean no less, was the absolute worst place for it to happen.

Marcus acted quicker than Wei Shu, attacking when he wasn't looking. Wei Shu's instincts took over, and he dodged as Marcus swung Glorious across his body. The golden blade just barely missed him, clipping off the ends of his hair.

Wei Shu forced the chimera back, feeling himself for any open wounds. When he felt nothing, an evil grin formed on his face. Silver ki exploded around him, and he raised his hands. Striking the air in front of him with both fists, Ren and Marcus were suddenly blown clear out of the sky.

Marcus crashed into the ice walkway below, shattering the area around him. Ren slammed into the deck of the ship, knocking it sideways across the waves. They both gasped as all the wind was knocked from them. It was pure luck that Ren didn't land in the water. Fighting out in open water was already dangerous enough.

Ren got to his feet as the chimera unleashed a devastating blast of magic. A column of water smashed into Marcus, sending him barreling beneath the ocean's surface.

"Marcus!" Ren yelled. His body ached from the impact, but he pushed through it. With a surge of ki, Ren unleashed another spell, and a pillar of water shot up beneath Wei Shu and the chimera. But with one punch, the water was blown away.

Being a vampire, as one who was weak to water, his use of magic with it was extremely limited. Though he could use a few basic spells, they were weak and messy. Seeing as it would have no effect on his opponents, he switched tactics. He wasn't as good with this kind of magic as others, but he was no slouch either.

Wei Shu looked around as the air began to shift. When he turned back to face Ren, he found himself no longer in the air. Instead, he now stood on the deck of his hip. To his left, the chimera lay in a pool of blood that dripped through the deckboards. Ren and the others were all gone.

What just happened? Confusion rocked his brain. How had he ended up on the ship? How had the chimera been killed? Where had everyone gone?

Marcus climbed out of the water and back onto the ruined ice walkway, coughing up the water that had entered his lungs. He looked and saw the enemy general sitting atop the chimera in a daze. Looking over at the ship, he saw Ren using his magic. He'd trapped the general in an illusion, which explained his current state. No doubt the guy had no idea what was happening to him. Had he, Ren's illusion would have been broken.

"Marcus!"

Marcus looked to see Julie and the others running toward him. A massive fire quickly erupted behind them, swallowing the enemy general's ship.

Rather than aid Ren, Marcus repaired the damaged walkway, allowing the others to make the way across and back to their ship.

An unexpected fog suddenly rolled through the area atop the vast ocean. It was so thick Wei Shu couldn't see his hand through it. Whirling around, he checked his surroundings, but there was nothing.

Pain shot through him without warning. Blood dripped to the deck from where an arrow had pierced the back of his shoulder. He grabbed it, feeling the blood coat his hands. His mind raced, trying to piece together what was happening. Then, a bright light appeared in the distance.

Raising his hand to shield his face, he focused on the light. How strange it was, and only more questions came with it.

The air around him rippled like the water in a pond. A strange energy traveled through the air, making his hair stand on end. It was a familiar feeling. The energy of a certain blond-haired vampire prince.

Wei Shu looked back at the light when suddenly, a blade of golden energy ripped through the space around him, tearing a hole through the illusion and hitting him dead on. Both he and the chimera were blown clear out of the sky, and fresh crimson sprayed the air like paint on a canvas.

Ren and the others were back in the same spot, all gathered on their ship. His own ship burned in a roar of flames, turning it to ash.

Wei Shu and the chimera crashed into their ship, blowing through the deck. Then, the masts on top gave way, and the whole ship lurched before sinking into the depths.

"Everyone, to your stations!" the captain ordered. "Lower the sails; get this ship moving! I want us out of here yesterday!"

"Aye, Captain!" the crew yelled, getting to work. Soon, they were sailing across the waves, their enemy long behind them.

Thirty-six

Feelings Carried by the Waves

The ship swayed on the ocean waves. A wave hit the hull and splashed back into the ocean. Ren's hair blew about calmy in the breeze, letting it gently kiss his skin.

Except for Ren, Marcus, Nidar, and the captain, the rest of the crew was below deck.
Marcus was up in the crow's nest, looking out at the miles and miles of ocean below. And while Marcus was up above scouting, Ren was down below with the captain and Nidar, his hands on the ship's wheel. The captain stood next to Ren, looking through a spyglass. Nidar sat quietly to his left, looking out at the ocean. His tail flicked back and forth, swaying like the calming breeze.

Ren stared intently at the sea in front of him, turning the wheel ever so slightly as required. He could feel the push and pull of the waves on the ship through the wheel. The ship swayed when a wave hit it, and Ren turned the wheel to steady it. With only the sound of the ocean all around him to fill his ears, a brilliant calm settled on his shoulders.

The long silence finally broke when they heard Marcus shout from the crow's nest. "Ren, hard to port." Ren turned the wheel, and the ship turned to the port side.

Marcus slid down a rope and landed on the deck. "What did you see, brother?" Ren asked.

"Look over there." Marcus pointed to the starboard side.

Keeping his hands on the wheel, Ren and the captain looked to where he was pointing. At first, he saw nothing, but then Ren noticed the slightest jolt of movement beneath the waves. They waited, yet nothing happened. Then, suddenly, something burst out of the water. It had smooth grey skin, a tail in the back with a horizontal fin, and a set of tiny fins near the end of the tail. There was a large dorsal fin on its back with five large spines along its length. Its long snout was partially rounded and on top of its head was a whole recognizable only as a blowhole.

"Iriserie!" Ren said in surprise.

Iriserie were very docile creatures. They always swam in pods and spent most of their time below the water. If you got lucky, you might catch a glimpse of them hopping across the waves like they were now.

Ren wondered if he could get them close to the ship. Besides their docile nature, they were known to be friendly, too. There were many tales of Iriserie swimming alongside ships. He'd even heard of sailors swimming with them, a short few even getting to ride them. They were truly beautiful creatures.

"We see them every so often," the captain said. "They get more frequent as you sail into open waters."

"Captain, your ship. Marcus, go get the girls," Ren told him.

"What are you going to do?" Marcus asked.

"Get a better look."

Ren ran up to the side of the ship and grabbed onto one of the nets connected to one of the masts. He held on with one hand, putting his right foot on the net to steady himself.

Marcus went below deck and knocked on the door to the girls' room. Julie opened it seconds later, surprised to see him.

"Come up to the deck. You might want to see this," he said. "Hurry, before they pass." He turned and ran up to the deck.

Julie and Kelsey looked at each other. "They?" Julie and Kelsey asked at the same time. They ran after him, curiosity now getting the better of them.

Marcus was already at the side of the ship leaning against the rail when the girls reached the deck. Next to him, Nidar stood on his hind legs, his front paws resting on the railing. Then their eyes moved and caught Ren. He was hanging from the cargo net attached to the mast.

The girls joined them, eager to catch a glimpse of whatever was going on. Below the ship, the Iriserie swam next to the hull, jumping in and out of the water.

"Wow! Kelsey said. "What are they?"

"Iriserie," Marcus said. "They're Nexus's version of dolphins and have the same ancestry as the ones found in the human world."

Captain Conrad was maneuvering his eyes back and forth between the Iriserie and the open waters in front of him. Though not frequently, he'd seen the creatures many times and knew there was no cause for concern. They were merely playing with the boat, riding in its wake.

Suddenly, the boat lurched. It was small, barely noticeable, but it was an unusual feeling. The captain had experienced the feeling of a lurching vessel numerous times, but this, this was different. He knew it instinctively. It felt like something grabbed the ship and tanked it.

Another lurch hit them like a storm. This time, it was very noticeable. Gripping the wheel, the captain managed to stabilize the ship.

"What the hell was that?" Marcus asked.

The Iriserie swimming next to the hull quickly disappeared beneath the waves.

"I don't like this," Ren said, climbing down to the deck

A third lurch hit the ship, making them all stumble. The sails suddenly expanded, and an enormous blast of wind caught them. The whole ship shot forward, throwing them all to the ground.

They flew over the waves, the hull completely clearing the water at times. Whatever was happening had them and the ship completely in its grasp, and there was nothing they could do. All they could do was remain at its mercy and hope it ended favorably.

Getting to his feet, Ren headed for the bow of the ship. He climbed on the edge and held onto the rope tying the jib to the bowsprit, hoping to get a glimpse of whatever may be causing this. But, it was to no avail. All he saw was the open ocean.

The ship bounced over the waves for hours until night had almost completely blanketed them. Ren put his hand over his mouth, feeling the urge to vomit. He stood at the starboard side railing. Sailing non-stop as they had been left everyone on board feeling ill, even the captain and crew. Alas, there was no way of knowing when they would stop.

Ren's stomach screamed at him one last time before it gave up. He felt the bile rise, unable to hold it down. Then, just like that, the force driving them stopped, and they slowed to a snail-like pace. His stomach began to settle, as did the others. Unfortunately, some were unable to keep it down after all.

What the hell happened? he wondered.

"What's going on?" Marcus asked, walking over to him. Kelsey, Julie, and the captain followed him, heading to where he and Ren now stood.

"I don't know," Ren said back.

Marcus turned his gaze to the horizon. It was almost dark, so he could barely see anything, but his nose could still pick up what his eyes couldn't. He sniffed around, letting the smell of salt fill his nose. Out of the salt and various other smells, a familiar scent hit his nose. It had a distinctive smell that he couldn't miss. Tiny Sparks of electricity ran through his body and made his hair stand on end. He could taste the humidity on his tongue.

"We need to get below deck," Marcus said. "It's close."

"What's close?" Ren asked. He pointed toward the darkness ahead of them.

BOOM! Thunder suddenly roared through the sky. Kelsey jumped right into Ren's arms.

"Sorry," she said. She attempted to pull away, but Ren kept his grip on her.

"You alright?" he asked.

His eyes mirrored the concern he felt. An affection she hadn't expected to see again. "I'm fine. It just came out of nowhere, is all." He nodded and released her.

"A storm is coming," the captain noted. "Prince Allagash is correct. Let's get below deck. Hopefully, it'll pass over quickly."

Ren returned to his cabin into his room and laid down on his bed, letting the rolling of the waves pass through him. They would hit the storm any minute. He just hoped it wouldn't be too bad.

Thunder boomed overhead. The ship rocked from the intense crashing of the waves. Ren looked out the window to see lightning streak through the sky. It lit up the world within its vicinity.

A knock came from the other side of the door, and Kelsey walked into the room.

"Kelsey," Ren said, surprised to see her. "What are you doing here? Is Marcus in the other cabin still?"

Kelsey nodded silently, but she never moved from her spot. She had misgivings about being alone with him; Ren could tell. But, it was to be expected. He couldn't blame her for feeling the way she did.

"Kells," Ren said, finally getting her attention. "If being here is too much for you, I can leave. I'll sleep with the rest of the crew."

He was being considerate. It was obvious. Talking to each other was like walking on eggshells.

"I wasn't really thinking. My body just sort of wandered here, I guess," she confessed.

Ren held his arms out to her, but she didn't budge.

"I owe you more apologies than I can ever offer," he told her. "For everything that happened."

Kelsey turned away from him, pain stinging her heart with every memory. "It's not like I don't understand why you did it … but still."

"That's no excuse. What I did is unforgivable, no matter the circumstances. But Kells, I want you to understand something. I'm not giving up on you."

Kelsey turned back to face him, a mixture of emotions on her face.

"I know it might seem like I did, and I admit I may have faltered momentarily, but I promise you I'm not about to let you go without a fight."

"And what happens if you can't? What happens if you can't find a way out of the marriage?"

"I don't know. In the worst case, we go to war with Dridia." Kelsey looked at him with wide eyes. "But, I'm not in this alone. Marcus is in this, too, now. He's offered his aid, as he always does."

"I feel sorry for Dridia," she joked.

Ren chuckled. "I won't ask you to forgive me or give me another chance. Whatever happens after this is all over has to be just as much your decision as mine. And if you choose to walk your own path, I promise I will understand."

Kelsey shook her head. "At first, my feelings were different. But the more time passes, the more I start to understand your position and Julie's, especially after talking to her and Marcus. It may take some time for me to fully heal, but if you're willing to go that far, then so

I'm willing to keep trying. Just promise you won't try something like this again. Promise you won't push me away anymore."

"I promise," he said. There was no hesitation, no lack of certainty in his voice.

Ren held his arms out to her once more. This time, she approached him, climbing into bed and lying next to him. When he put his arms around her, so many feelings came flooding back. She didn't even pay attention to the ongoing storm. It simply faded before she even realized it, along with her consciousness.

When Kelsey woke, it was morning. The storm had passed, and the ocean was calm. She quickly realized that Ren wasn't in bed. Instead, Nidar was lying on the bed next to her, having moved from his spot on the floor. A nervous tension filled her frame.

Kelsey gently rubbed the top of the tiger's head before climbing out of bed and heading to the deck. As soon as she walked out into the fresh morning air, her nervousness died. Ren was standing at the bow, holding onto a rope and leaning out towards the water. A sigh of relief escaped her.

"LAND HO!" she heard the captain shout.

The rest of the crew quickly made their way onto the deck, and Kelsey ran over to Ren. Out in the distance, just on the horizon, was a single isolated island.

Thirty-seven

Enemy in the Darkness

Ren saw Marcus and Julie amongst the crew, making their way forward in an attempt to see the land before them for themselves.

"Guys, over here," Ren called. They made their way over to him and joined him at the bow.

The island could be seen on the horizon, getting closer and closer as they approached. Even from the distance they were at, everyone could tell that the island was massive. The coastline was lined with trees, making it impossible to tell how dense the foliage was. Far in the distance, mountains pierced the sky, spanning high above the tree line.

After nearly two fortnights at sea, they finally had proof that the map had been correct.

"There it is," Marcus said. He looked at Ren. "What do you think?"

"I think this is going to be a pain in the ass," Ren said back. "Luckily, we have Conrad's map."

The ship drifted close to the island, coming within three hundred feet of the shore.

"Drop anchor," the captain said.

While the anchor was being lowered, Ren helped Kelsey and Julie into one of the rowboats before Marcus jumped in.

"Best of luck. We'll stay anchored for the next couple of days," the captain said.

Ren hopped into the rowboat, leaving just enough space for Nidar to fill. The tiger leaped over the edge of the ship and landed in the middle of the small boat. Ren and Marcus used the pullies to lower the rowboat down into the water. They each grabbed an oar and dipped it into the water, then started rowing towards the island.

Beneath them, the water was so clear they could see all the way to the bottom. It glew turquoise, like a shining jewel.

The current gave the boat one last push as they neared the island. It rose, and the current retreated, lowering the boat onto the sand.

"We're here," Ren said.

Nidar was the first out of the boat, with Ren and Marcus disembarking next. They set the oars down inside and helped the girls out.

Sand shifted loosely beneath their boots. The grove of trees before them seemed to continue forever. It was a forest, alright, but its true size still remained a mystery. For all they knew, it encompassed the whole island.

Ren pulled Conrad's map out from inside his jacket. The captain and his first officer both believed it to be a map of the island leading to Paerlejara. Now, it was time to see if that was true. If it was, then Conrad could proudly say he realized his mentor's dream of finding the mysterious City of Gold.

The map was a series of pictures drawn at different spots on the island with a dotted line between each one. Ren wondered what the pictures could be, but he was certain the dotted line was the path they had to take. The first picture was drawn at the edge of the island, so their path started somewhere along this beach. It depicted a cat lying on its stomach.

Ren started walking, taking peeks at the map as he went. When he saw a large carving in a boulder, he stopped. The carving depicted a lion lying on its stomach. The cat lay proud, as if guarding the island behind it. It matched the picture on the map.

"This is it," he said. "The first marker on the trail."

"What trail?" Marcus asked. He saw nothing but the statue, sand, and dense wall of vegetation.

Ren walked over to a wall of vegetation next to the statue. He reached behind him and drew Shadow Hunter. "The trail of gold!" With one swing, he cut away the vegetation. It fell to the ground, revealing a stone wall behind it.

Marcus raised an eyebrow at him. Ren turned and pointed to the left. "That trail of gold!"

Marcus slapped his forehead with the palm of his hand. "Ugh." He sighed and followed Ren into the forest.

They trekked through the forest for hours. Ren took the front, hacking away at any vegetation in their way. Marcus took up the rear for defense. They were on enemy territory, as far as they were concerned. Anything could come up from behind them and attack.

The path was not what most people would call a straight shot. It took them through trees, over broken logs, over streams, across a stone pathway in a swamp, and much more. Time had seen it delt plenty of wear and tear. Parts of it crumbled away as they walked. Luckily, the streams and swamp didn't seem that deep, but who knew what was in there.

Ren stood on a massive tree root over ten feet tall at the top. He was staring at the map, unsure of where to go. They had already been to this area three times, going in circles. He scratched the top of his head, trying to figure it out, then cocked his head to the side, trying to look at it from a different angle. In the end, he still had no idea where to go next.

Marcus rolled his eyes and walked over to him. He took the map from him and turned it upside down, pushing it back into his arms. Ren looked at the map again. "Oh~."

After another hour of walking, Kelsey couldn't take it anymore.

"Stop. Stop, stop." She leaned against the trunk of a tree. "No more. I need a break."

"Sorry," Ren said, "I should have stopped sooner."

Marcus jogged over to her while Ren walked a few feet ahead, pushing some brush out of the way. A heavy grin formed on his face.

"You picked the perfect place to stop, Kells." He hacked at the brush and, with one slice, cleared the path. Only ten feet away was a pool of water. It was perfectly clear and only a few feet deep. Steam rose off the surface. "Anyone up for a soak?" Reaching into his bag, he pulled out his herbs and dropped them into the water. It turned green before returning to normal only minutes later.

"Well damn, this is a treat. A natural hot spring," Julie said.

"You want to go in?" Ren asked Kelsey. She nodded.

"Just give me a second to rest my legs."

Ren picked her up in his arms and carried her over to the edge of the hot spring bridal style. He untied her laces and slipped her boots off. Then he gently took her feet and slid her socks off.

"If you need anything else, just let me know."

"Thanks, I will."

He left her alone to take off her clothes.

"Hey, how are you feeling?" Julie asked, coming over to her. She was already undressed down to her underwear.

"My legs are still sore. I'm not used to walking through jungle terrain."

"Yeah, it takes some getting used to." She sat down next to Kelsey, who took her tank top off and set it to the side. "I remember when I had to go on my first mission in Africa. I had Ren train me to handle jungle terrain."

"How did that go?" Julie gave her a look like, *really?*

Kelsey unbuttoned her shorts, then slid them down her legs, setting them on top of her tank top. Last to come off was their underwear before lowering themselves into the spring. It was the perfect temperature. Kelsey let her body sink down to her shoulders, feeling all the fatigue and pain in her legs recede from her body.

"Hey, where are the guys?" Kelsey asked.

"Probably keeping watch somewhere. I'm sure they'll come in after we're done."

"Mmmm," was all Kelsey could say. The heat from the spring was taking control over her body, the relaxation filling her body.

Ren and Marcus ran toward the spring and jumped into the water, splashing the girls with a small wave. Julie pushed her bangs out of the way with an annoyed look on her face.

Kelsey immediately covered herself with her arms. "What are you two doing?"

Ren and Marcus exchanged looks.

"Um, relaxing in the spring?" Ren asked, unsure if that was the correct answer. Marcus just shrugged his shoulders at him.

"No, I mean, why are you in here? I thought you guys were keeping watch!"

"Keeping watch over what?" Ren asked.

"You two are idiots," Julie said, not bothering to cover herself. "She means you just jumped in here while we were bathing."

"Yeah, so what? This spring is big enough for the four of us."

Marcus leaned back and stretched. "Why bother waiting when we can just share," he said. "Besides, it's not like we can't handle anything that comes our way."

"Don't tell me you're embarrassed?" Ren asked. "We're all adults here; we've got nothing to hide. Just relax and enjoy the springs. The water's the perfect temperature." He leaned back against the rocks making up the edge.

Ren, Marcus, and Julie all closed their eyes, letting the heat from the spring take over them. Kelsey was the only one who sat there, still covering herself with her arms. She couldn't tell if she was being too modest or if they were being *too* mature.

They bathed in the spring for a little while before getting out. The sun was setting, and it would be dark soon. They needed to find shelter before it got dark.

Luckily, there was a large hollow in the trees just off their path.

"No fire," Ren said. "We don't want to give ourselves away. Who knows what could be out there."

"I'll take first watch," Marcus said to him.

"Alright. I'll take the second, then. Wake me up in a few hours." Marcus nodded and Ren slowly drifted off into sleep.

Late into the night, Marcus woke Ren, and they switched watch duty. It was better to have someone awake to keep watch just encase anything did happen. Even with Marcus's werewolf hearing, they still played it safe.

Ren woke the others the next morning at dawn. Sleeping in the hollow sucked, but at least they got some sleep. He looked at the map and they continued their path through the jungle. Based on their current location, they would reach Paerlejara sometime within the day.

The final stretch of their journey led them through a large cave. Marcus drew Glorious, using its golden glow to read the map. He and Ren stopped dead the moment they heard a ticking noise coming from ahead of them.

"What's going on?" Julie asked.

"Shh!" Ren responded, shutting her up.

He and Marcus honed their ears and listened. Again, they heard the ticking. This time, it sounded farther away. Whatever it was was moving away from them.

"Come on, stay close," Marcus said.

Ren put the map back inside his jacket and drew his pistols, and they all continued walking.

The ticking started again the farther into the cave they got. This time, however, it sounded right on top of them.

Nidar released a fearsome growl that echoed through the cave.

Marcus turned around, and both he and Ren backed up toward the girls. Kelsey and Julie put their backs to each other, and Julie drew her bow while Kelsey put her hand on her wrist. The stones began to glow slightly as power flowed through them.

Despite the sound persisting, they saw no movement beyond. Ren looked up, and his eyes widened. Marcus followed his gaze to the cave ceiling.

"Oh no, not again."

Kelsey and Julie started to look up, but they didn't get halfway before a large object fell from the ceiling. Ren dove and took Kelsey and Julie with him, avoiding the impact. Kelsey's face turned white as paper as a giant centipede fifty feet in length rose its head into the air.

"You have got to be kidding," Julie said.

Ren released a large grin from his lips. "Hell yeah! Round two, baby!" He pointed his pistols and fired. The giant centipede reared back and let out a horrible screech. "Hahaha!" Ren continued to fire away, pumping the centipede full of holes. "Die, you overgrown caterpillar!"

Nidar charged forward, sinking his teeth and claws into the beast.

My ice bow won't do anything but hinder us in a cave like this, even in dagger form, Marcus thought. His body began to change as hazel fur covered his body. It grew in size, and he sprouted ears and a tail. His nose and mouth elongated into a snout with sharp teeth, and his fingernails extended into razor-sharp claws.

Marcus launched himself at the centipede and slashed at it with his claws. The top half of the creature dropped to the ground and started moving again.

"Come on, let's get out of here!" Marcus said. Inside this dark and cramped cave, there was little they could do to this thing, especially if it just kept multiplying whenever they cut it to pieces.

"What do you mean? We're winning!" Ren said, firing away with glee.

Julie helped Kelsey to her feet, and they ran passed the centipede for the exit.

"Agh, what the hell!" Ren yelled and ran after them.

The centipede was right behind them the whole way. Finally, they saw sunlight ahead of them and broke out of the cave. They stood on the edge of a cliff, a large valley spread out before them, the mountains they had seen from the ship in the background. Nidar let loose a fierce roar.

"Be careful. This cliff could give way at any moment," Marcus said.

Ren stood in front of the others, shoulder-width apart, facing the cave. He holstered his guns and threw his hands down and to the side, a spark of lightning passing between them. The centipede scrambled right out of the cave and leaped toward them. Ren thrust his hands out, and a bolt of lightning crashed into the centipede, blowing both halves into a pile of chunks.

"HA! Ren two, giant centipede zero!"

Crack! They all looked down at the edge of the cliff.

"Uh oh," Ren said.

Crack! The edge of the cliff gave way.

"Ren, you idiot!" Marcus said.

Gravity took hold, and they fell, disappearing into the valley below.

Thirty-eight

City of Gold

Ren, and the others landed on a sloped edge of the cliff and rolled down until they hit the bottom, coming to a stop in a pile on top of each other.

"Ow! Okay, that could have gone better," Ren said.

"Damn, that hurt. Ren, you idiot!" Marcus said back.

"Oh, shut up."

They climbed off each other just as a spear point was suddenly shoved in their face. A man in a loincloth stood facing them. He wore face paint and had a pair of large gold earrings on his earlobes.

Instinctively, Ren pointed his guns at the man, who quickly disarmed him by smacking them out of his hands. He instantly pushed the spear point out of the way and spun around, drawing Shadow Hunter at the same time and placing it against the man's neck. Marcus also pointed his sword at him out of reflex.

The man with the spear looked shocked at the fact that he had just been overtaken so easily, and yet he never lowered his spear point. Even with Ren and Marcus pointing their heaven's blades at him, about to kill him, and Kelsey with her hand on the stones, he didn't back down.

From behind, a group of eight men, all dressed in loincloths or tunics, came running toward them, spears in hand. They circled around the six of them.

Nidar growled before unleashing a hollowing roar that sent the surrounding wildlife fleeing in terror. Julie nocked an arrow, aimed directly at one of the warriors surrounding them. The tension was so thick it could be cut with a knife. They were all ready for a fight.

The man Ren held at blade point held out his hand to his reinforcements. He finally lowered his weapon and looked at Ren, holding his gaze for a few seconds before nodding behind him. Clearly, he wanted them to follow.

Although not completely, the eight warriors surrounding them lowered their spears. As it stood, anything could set either side off, resulting in only a bloodbath on the enemy side. It wouldn't take more than a few minutes to dispose of all eleven of them.

When he noticed no one was following, the man leading them looked back at them and motioned for them to follow once more by waving his spear passed him. Ren and the others followed as he led them away from the cliff, it quickly fading behind them. Puddles of water covered the ground everywhere, forcing Ren to take care of where he stepped. That is, until the puddles turned into a stream ankle-deep. He walked along the bank, paying careful attention to his surroundings.

Silence carried them the whole way until they came to a stop in front of three long canoes, all tied off and matching in appearance. The stream widened into a large river that passed through a cave. Without needing to look, identifying the depth was easy as the river had no current.

Eight of the nine warriors climbed into two of the three canoes. One from each stood in the back, holding a large wooden pole.

The man who had led them this far climbed into the back of the remaining canoe. Ren and Marcus sat opposite each other, with Nidar in the middle. Although the canoe was long, it wasn't exactly wide. Although not ideal in such a small space, they had Kelsey and Julie sit on their lap. Ren put his arms around Kelsey, making sure she was secure.

"Comfortable?" Marcus asked Julie. She leaned against him in response.

"Absolutely," she said back.

The man in the back of their canoe pushed forward using the pole, and they floated down the river. Every so often, he stuck the pole back into the water, the end reaching the bottom, and pushed the canoe forward.

At the entrance to the cave, water fell from above, acting as a gateway to what lay hidden beyond.

"Damn," Ren cursed. Kelsey noticed him start to cover himself with his jacket. She turned and covered him with her body as they passed underneath. It was only a second or so, but she was completely soaked when they came out the other side. Ren, however, was dry except for the little bit that got on his clothes.

He put his hand on the side of her face, rubbing her cheek with his thumb. "Thank you."

"You're welcome," she said back.

He was beyond grateful that she was considerate enough to shield him from the water with her body. She'd protected him, and that meant a lot.

Ren held his hand over her chest and started chanting. When he pulled it away, all the water on her came with it, leaving her completely dry. He moved his hand over the side of the canoe, and the water fell into the river.

They floated down the river in silence after that. There was no knowing how large the cave was. In fact, they had no idea where they were being taken to either. For all they knew, this was a trap.

Minutes felt like hours in that brief span of time. Ren was getting anxious when sunlight started to fill the cave. Thick rays of light pierced the exit from behind a curtain of vines.

"No way," Ren said.

"It's, it's," Marcus started to say. They pushed through the vines and passed through into open air.

"Paerlejara!" they all said at the same time.

Every one of them wore masks of pure wonder. At the mouth of the cave, the river opened up and turned into a lake. Spread out before them were three large stepped pyramids made entirely of gold. Around them, all of the buildings were made from gold and stone.

'*Ho-ly shit,*' Ren mouthed. He looked over the side of the canoe and saw the bottom below the water. A giant sea turtle with horns on its head swam beneath them.

Kelsey tapped him on the arm. He noticed her pointing and looked. On both sides of the lake, people filled the elevated stone roads, dressed in robes and decorated with golden jewelry. Many of them held bowls made from gold with food or golden instruments. Others had whole carts filled with items.

Those who saw them stopped, frozen in place, never averting their gaze. There was no doubt they saw Ren and the others as aliens, visitors of unknown origin.

The first thing Ren noticed was their forms. Their appearances were almost entirely human. Many had wings on their backs, horns on their heads or scales on their body, and some claws or a tail. They were all so similar, but the small differences were so great in variety Ren couldn't tell if they were of the same type of monster or different ones entirely. Either way, these people were an entirely different race of monsters, one completely unknown to the rest of the world.

The canoe stopped at a set of steps in front of the largest and central of the three pyramid structures.

Ren got out of the canoe, offering Kelsey his hand first. She took it, and he pulled her out. Nidar jumped out next, then Marcus and Julie emerged after them, transfixed by the golden ziggurats that towered into the sky behind them. At the top of each one was an enclosed space.

The people of Paerlejara watched them curiously, the warriors who'd escorted them circling behind.

"So, what now?" Marcus wondered.

"No idea," Ren said back. "Let's wait and see what they do."

A thumping sound appeared, drawing closer at a fast pace. Based on rhythm alone, it sounded like the galloping of a horse.

From within the gathering of citizens, a single man appeared. Ren and Marcus instantly realized he was the source of the galloping sound. His bare torso was strong, with large, thick muscles and a hairy chest. He had long hair that fell to his shoulders behind him and a full beard. Below his waist, he had the bottom half of a black stallion. A centaur.

The centaur flicked his head, and his hair flew back behind him, falling back down neatly and out of his face. With his horse half, he was over six and a half feet tall.

When he reached Ren and the others, he crossed his arms, very clearly sizing them up. Behind them, the warriors dropped to one knee.

"My name is Dorair, Chief of Paerlejara. What names may we call you, strangers?"

"My name is Ren Nightwalker. These are my companions, Marcus, Kelsey, Juliana, and Nidar."

"We have not had visitors from the outside world in millennia. Tell me, strangers, how did you get here? What do you want?"

"We come from the mainland," Ren said. "My companions and I have journeyed through much to come here in search of an ancient artifact."

"An ancient artifact, is it?"

The chief continued sizing Ren up. Ren stared back at him with powerful eyes, and the chief nodded, apparently pleased.

"I am the heir to the Kingdom of Nightwalker and Prince of Nexus," Ren said. "That makes me the future ruler of this world."

The chief stood his ground. "And? You think we'll follow you, vampire?"

"I'm not asking you to follow me. I'm asking for your help."

"This is utterly unacceptable!" someone shouted.

A lone man walked forward. He was dressed in a red sleeveless tunic with gold chains on his neck, golden earrings, and golden armbands wrapped around his muscular biceps. Paint covered his face, his hair tied up in a bun on top.

"How could you fools treat our guests with such disrespect. Do you not know who they are? Ignorance!"

The man pulled a tablet out of his tunic and held it high. Kelsey gasped while the others stared in shock. It showed the figure of a man. He had long hair and a set of large wings behind him. Fangs hung down from his mouth, and an immense aura surrounded him. A long jacket with a high collar sat atop his frame. The man's arms were spread out to the side, a glowing sword in one of his hands.

"It's Ren," Kelsey said. But there was one thing that none of them understood. Water surrounded him on both sides, rising up like a wave.

The painted man turned around to face the people. "Citizens! Did I not predict the gods would come to us?" He ran his hand passed Ren and the others. "The gods have finally graced us with their presence!" he went on. "Today is a day of celebration. They have come to liberate us. To vasc in our great city and guide us!" My lords, my ladies, I am Ademar, High Priest of Paerlejara and speaker for the gods."

"Look, dude, I think you've got the wrong idea," Ren said.

The high priest turned around to face him. "What?"

"We are not gods. None of us. I don't know why you have that tablet, but I can assure you none of us are what you think we are. We're just regular mortals here on a quest."

"What kind of quest?" the chief asked. "Does it have to do with the artifact you claim to seek?"

Ren looked at both of them. "Why don't we find a place to talk."

Thirty-nine

The Sanctuary

The high priest stared at Ren with a blank expression. No doubt Ren's words were forcing him to reconsider their whole place in all of this. He was a holy man, and one of extreme faith. The belief that Ren and his companions were gods was literally written in stone. Ren's claim of their mortality questioned his entire belief. It made him unsure if their identities were even true and if they were a danger to the city.

"Very well. Follow me, if you please," the high priest said.

In the end, it appeared that he had chosen to accept them. At least, for the moment. Depending on how the topic of their conversation went, that could change drastically.

"High Priest Ademar," the chief said, suspicious of the high priest's decision. It appeared that the two of them didn't see eye to eye.

The high priest ignored the chief and continued to lead on. They followed him through the city silently, getting curious stares from the citizens.

Finally, they came upon one of the many temples around the city. Like the others, it was made from solid gold and gleamed in the sunlight. The chief and high priest began to ascend the many steps up to the top. Ren and the others followed, and when they reached the top, their legs were on fire.

The high priest pushed passed a purple curtain and walked into the temple. Inside, it was entirely open with the back and side walls made entirely of stone, containing no doors or windows.

There was little of anything inside the room. Only a single pool that rested comfortably in the center, light pouring down on it from the round hole in the roof, and a large rectangular cut boulder in front. The side that faced the pool had been polished to a mirror finish.

"Welcome to The Sanctuary," the high priest said. "It is here that we hold our rituals to the gods. As high priest, you will often find me here in prayer and practicing rituals."

Kelsey was the only one of them that hadn't looked around the moment they entered the room. Instead, she was immediately drawn to the back wall, her jaw going slack. Without a word, she reached up and pulled Ren's sleeve, her eyes never leaving the wall.

Ren, looked at her first, then he turned his head to the back wall, where she was staring. When the high priest noticed their focus on it, he turned toward the wall, drawing the rest of their party with him.

A series of small pictures carved into the face covered it from end to end, taking up half the height of the wall. Carvings just like the tablet the high priest showed them. And at every quarter, a large carving the full height of the wall filled the space.

The first picture was of a baby, still wrapped in a blanket, held in its mother's arms. The next depicted a man kneeling before a pedestal with a glowing sword on it. In the third, the same man held the glowing sword in his hand. That was the moment Ren and the others realized that the pictures carved into the wall weren't random; they were in order. Chronological order, to be precise.

It was the fourth carving, however, that changed things. The scene shifted, now of an entirely different man. One who also wielded a glowing sword and was engaged in battle with a large monster. The fifth scene in the sequence depicted both men. Again they fought, only this time, they fought together.

An army of shadows eerily similar to shades filled the sixth scene. And so it continued, giving picture after picture in each carving. Battles, weapons, death, magic, reunions, and even love. What started as a baby grew into a man, then two, then a woman, and then a third man. At first, they were separate, but very quickly, they joined forces.

However provoking the sequence was, though, nothing stood prouder than the three full-height carvings. Each was as uncannily detailed as the other, but all three transcended far beyond the realm of enchantment than any of the smaller carvings in the sequence did.

Of the three, the one closest to the beginning roared with power. The man they had seen at the start of the sequence faced them, lightning dancing around him. On his back, a set of large wings extended out, and above his head floated his glowing sword.

The second scene was of hope. It depicted all four of the people introduced into the sequence. The three men all had glowing weapons, and the girl bore a glowing bracelet on her wrist. They stood next to each other, the same man who they'd seen continuously taking point. But the third and final of the larger pictures was one of pure courage. The third showed the man with wings and another man with a mask flying at each other with glowing weapons. Two armies clashed beneath them. People under the man with wings and undead beneath the guy with the mask.

As the carvings reached the end of the sequence, they formed a conclusion to what was undoubtedly a legendary tale. The second to last showed the man from the beginning standing on a mound of corpses, his glowing sword raised above his head in victory. And the final picture carved into the wall was an identical replica of the one on the high priest's tablet.

"This is us," Kelsey said. "All of us."

"How is this possible?" Marcus asked. "Our whole story, the war against Verin, it's all right here."

"This wall was carved millennia ago," the high priest said, approaching the wall. "It foretells a legend, one we have long since been waiting for."

Kelsey placed her hand on the picture of Ren that was identical to the one on the high priest's tablet. She moved her hand across it, feeling the texture of the stone. This was Ren. This was his true power.

"Long ago, the high priestess, Kikyo, received a vision from the gods. Kikyo was the strongest priestess in our entire history. No one since since has had the power she wielded. She was a gift from the gods, and in return for sending her to us, she could tell us their wisdom. The gods told Kikyo of this future which she recorded on this wall herself. It foretells of a man with untold power and a war between the living and the dead. He will gain the support of thousands, and together with three companions, he will lead them in a battle to vanquish the undead."

"The man and his companions hold powers unlike anything ever seen before, wielding legendary golden divine weapons. Surely they are gods, scent from the heavens to vanquish a mighty evil."

"I'm sorry to say this, but we are not gods," Ren corrected. "I can understand how you believe that, but I assure you we possess no divinity."

"But you hold the weapons of the gods, don't you?" the high priest asked.

"It's true we possess two of the thirteen weapons said to be made by the gods, but we ourselves are not them. We've come here seeking an artifact that directly ties to the war depicted on this wall."

"And just what kind of artifact would you be looking for? We have many relics, but which of them would possibly help you in your battle?" the chief asked.

"The Records of the Gods," Ren said.

The high priest's expression grew dark. "Is that so? The last one who sought the records was over five hundred years ago. That man did not make it out alive."

"Well, we're willing to take our chances," Ren said.

The chief was about to say something when the high priest held his hand out in front of him to stop him.

"And just why, pray tell, are you looking for the Records?"

"Because we believe they hold the answer to removing the Sun and Moon Stones from their bearer."

Kelsey held up her wrist, showing them the stones.

"Indeed, the girl does possess the stones," the high priest said.

"You don't seem surprised about them," Marcus said.

"Why would we be? The stones were kept in this city for several centuries for safekeeping. Eventually, they were lost. The stones will only follow the commands of someone who is pure of heart and does not waver based on sides. Someone with the will to never give up and possesses vast amounts of love."

"I know how to use them to an extent," Kelsey said. "But there's much I don't know, one of those things being how to remove them. They won't come off my wrist, and there may come a time when I need them off. That's why we need the Records. They can tell us how to remove them."

The high priest shook his head. "We cannot give you the Records."

"Why not?" Ren asked. "They do exist, don't they?"

"The Records do exist. They are kept here for safekeeping, where they have remained since they were created. However, they're impossible to read."

"What do you mean?"

"The Records are written in a language only the high priest or priestess knows. It is taught to all of us, and only us. That is how we keep the Records safe. Even if they were taken, only I can read them, making them useless to whoever does take them."

"Please," Kelsey said. "The Records are the last chance. We have to get the stones off. We don't know any other way."

The high priest looked at her and raised an eyebrow. "Why don't you just ask them to come off?"

They all looked like flies caught in a spider web.

"Ask them?"

"You've never asked them to come off?" Kelsey shook her head. "You need to keep an open mind, my dear. There are things much simpler to do than you think. Go ahead, try asking them."

Kelsey looked at the stones on her wrist. They glowed lightly within the bracelet. Ask the stones? Was that really all it took? No way. No way would that be all it took. Not after they went through so much and so many attempts, and the stones hadn't even budged. What would she even say? Was there a specific way to ask them?

"Um … please come off?" she asked the stones, unsure if that was it or not. The bracelet detached itself at the bottom and fell off her wrist. She caught it with her other hand.

"Are you fucking serious!" Ren yelled. They all looked at him in shock. "We went through all that, came all this way, and that's all it took? I can't believe this!" Man, was he pissed.

"You've been treating them like mere objects. That's your problem," the high priest said. "You can't use the stones without understanding them. No wonder you can't use their power without the vampire." They all looked at Ren. "He possesses the key to unlocking their full power on his wrist, but if you learn how to use them, you won't need the key. It's clear that you have not mentally connected with the stones, as they have not yet imparted their wisdom onto you. Part of that fault lies with your lack of knowledge. You should talk to them more often; form a connection. Without a bond, you'll never draw out their full power."

"But they're just stones. I didn't think anything like this was even possible," she said back.

"They're not just stones, my dear. They are far more than you can imagine. Together, they are sentient. They choose their wielder, their power, and they work together to create miracles. Treat them the same way the vampire and werewolf here treat their weapons. They are something similar to the stones, after all. Do that, and you will connect to them the same way they do their weapons."

Unbelievable. All this time, everything they went through, and it was really that simple.

Marcus remembered something he had almost forgotten. Something only he and Glorious knew about. Kelsey could see the spirits of the heaven's blades. That was supposed to be impossible for anyone but their wielder. Maybe with the stones off, she couldn't see them anymore.

"Glorious, would you mind doing me a favor and manifesting? I'm curious about something," he said telepathically.

"Sure," Glorious said back.

"Hey, Kelsey," Marcus said.

Kelsey turned to look at him, dragging the others' attention with her. That's when a crimson-haired man appeared next to him. She recognized him. It was Glorious, the spirit of Marcus's sword.

Glorious waved at her and smiled, and Kelsey repeated the gesture back to him. She could still see!

"Why are you waving?" Ren asked.

Kelsey realized what she was doing and stopped.

"Perhaps the girl sees something none of us can," the high priest said.

"Ademar," Marcus said. The high priest turned to look at him. "Would you still be willing to let us see the Records?"

"I told you it's impossible."

"I know, I know, but just let us give it a shot. You never know what may happen. Besides, there's another reason we need it."

"Another reason?"

"We think it may hold a way to helping us defeat Verin."

"Who is Verin?"

"Verin is a necromancer," Ren said. He quickly told them the situation.

The high priest and chief looked at the pictured wall.

"So then the legend is true," the chief said.

The high priest said nothing at first. He was taking in the situation.

"Very well," he finally said. "I shall let you look at the Records. But when you are unable to read them, you will return them to us and be on your way." Ren nodded in agreement. "Give me some time to prepare the book," the high priest said. "I will summon you when I am ready."

"You will be staying with us for the night, yes?" the chief asked.

"If you would have us," Ren said back.

The chief gave them a full smile. "Then allow me the honor of preparing a feast for you tonight. Please, follow me."

The six of them walked out of the room, the high priest choosing to stay behind. They pushed open the curtain and descended down the steps.

Forty

The Golden Book

"You can borrow one of the sacred rooms for your stay. Though it is reserved for those of divinity, we shall make an exception this once. Let me show you to the temple," the chief said. He gave them a sly smile.

"Temple?" Ren and Marcus asked. "Cha-ching!"

For the first time since they met him, they witnessed the chief's laughter. He lead them to the tallest temple in the city. It stood proud before all the others, right upon the lake.

Ren's face turned white when he saw all the stairs. He could hear Shadow Hunter laughing in his head. Yet, when the chief started the climb, they were left with no choice but to follow.

It left them exhausted and breathless when they finally reached the top. The chief, however, was completely unfazed. When he looked behind him to see how Ren and the others were doing, they were nearly doubled over.

"Oh, waiter. Check, please," Ren said, and fell face-first onto the ground.

Their reactions solicited a chuckle from the chief. "Come inside. You'll want to take a look around."

Unlike the previous temple they'd visited, this one was open on three sides. Curtains of gold and silk shielded the front and sides from the elements. Inside, paintings framed with gold, golden sculptures, and accessories made of gold filled the space. A large pool lay in the center of the room with seating and a table placed around it. Without uncertainty, the room reflected one intended to be used by gods.

"Your living area is in the back, as is an area where you can clean yourselves," the chief informed them.

"Once again, you have our gratitude for allowing us to stay here," Ren said.

"Of course. I'll take my leave then if you are settled. We shall see to it that you are summoned and guided when the feast is ready." The chief bowed to them before retreating from the temple, making the long journey down.

Marcus crashed on one of the couches, and Julie sat at the edge next to him.

"I'm exhausted. My feet are killing me," she said, removing her boots.

Marcus found himself staring at her legs much longer than he should have when she stretched herself out. It drove him wild when she tucked her legs in beside her. And the worst part was she wasn't even trying.

Ren had to admit that even he found himself staring. Julie was certainly a sight for the eyes, and desirable.

Kelsey glared at Ren with balled fists, but he didn't seem to notice.

"I don't know about you guys, but I'm going to check out this pool," Marcus said. "I'm sure there's something around here we can wear."

"Oh, that's a great idea," Julie said.

Kelsey joined Marcus and Julie in searching for anything that they could wear into the water. Ren had a different desire, though. The pool didn't interest him. Instead, he took his jacket off and laid it over the back of one of the couches. When Marcus and the girls looked over, he was gone. They called for him, but no answer came.

"Where did he go?" Julie wondered.

"He probably went exploring or something," Marcus said. "He'll come back later."

Marcus and Julie didn't seem to mind, but Kelsey was a little worried about Ren not being there. She hoped he didn't get into any trouble. It always seemed to find him somehow.

✦

Ren descended the temple steps until he reached the bottom. There were no citizens in the vicinity, so he just picked a direction and started walking.

The city was amazing, and the people were completely in their own world. But then again, they had lived like this for millennia, isolated from the rest of the world. This city was all they knew. Its people, its culture, it was all they had.

Ren was walking along the edge of a canal when he saw a group of locals. They stopped dead and stared at him. He waved, and they hurried along. Looks like it wasn't going to be that easy for them to accept him.

Making his way through the city streets was like working through a maze. But he didn't care. Everything was so new and unique. Just being in the city filled him with a kind of impassion he had not felt in decades.

A ball crossed Ren's path while he walked in silence. It was about a foot in diameter and made entirely of leather. Several children rounded a corner as he picked up the ball and stopped. It was heavy, like a rock. Ren gently kicked the ball back to them, and they kicked it back once more.

Back and forth their game went, steadily drawing a crowd. When Ren finally noticed the large gathering of spectators, he kicked the ball to one of them, forcing them to join in. And that was all it took. First one, then two, then more people joined in the game.

A sense of joy welled up within him, and Ren escaped from the crowd, running off through the city. He reached the end of a street which turned into a canal. A group of soldiers carrying spears were standing on top of something green. Ren ran to them and they helped him on before they started moving. He realized they were riding on one of those giant turtles he'd seen when he first arrived in the city.

The soldiers smiled at him and nodded. When they reached the other side, he jumped off and onto the walkway.

"Thank you," he said. They waved at him as he ran.

Ren continued to frolic in the city with its people. He played games with kids and drew pictures on the ground using golden paint. He even built a castle out of small golden blocks and anything else he could find.

Rounding the corner, Ren saw the familiar form of a large white tiger. Nidar ran up to him the moment he saw him.

"Hey, bud. Where have you been?" The tiger rubbed his head against Ren's hand, and the two of them journeyed through the city together. They came upon a large square with a fountain in the middle. People were gathered and dancing to a band.

"Whoa," Ren said in excitement. He ran over to the crowd and joined in.

A woman pulled him into the chaos, and he danced with her to the fast-paced music. Then he switched partners and danced with them as well. Partner swapping, he realized, was the main focus of the dance. Even with the music change, the process stayed the same.

Looking over, he saw Nidar jumping up and down, his tail flicking back and forth. His paws darted about, clearly taken by the atmosphere. Then, the music changed once more, and the women retreated, leaving the men to dance among each other. It started off synchronized but quickly turned into a freestyle.

Marcus and the girls saw the commotion first. They were walking with the chief and high priest when the music hit them unexpectedly. Approaching the massive crowd of people, dozens of the city's residents were dancing with each other. It was then that they noticed a familiar face among them. Ren was being pulled around between partners.

Marcus laughed out loud. "So this is what he's been doing. No wonder he left."

Ren ran over to the crowd and pulled an elderly woman into the mix. Then he went over and pulled another woman in. The rest of the crowd started trickling back in and joining the dancing. He was moving to the music alongside Nidar and a group of girls around eighteen in age when he looked over and saw Marcus and the girls. With them was the chief and high priest. The high priest made a sign like opening a book, and Ren knew exactly what he was trying to say.

The chief approached Ren, causing him and those around him to stop dancing.

"Chief," Ren said in greeting.

"Chief Dorair," the teens said to him, giving a light bow.

The chief smiled at them. "You five will have plenty of time to dance later tonight at the feast. But right now, I must barrow our young vampire. We have something of importance to address. I'm afraid it cannot wait."

"I'll see you guys later," Ren said, waving. They waved back.

"Bye, Ren," one of the girls said. He smiled at her.

Irritation shot through Kelsey again. Her foot tapped along the ground rapidly. Why did he have to be so nice around every girl he met? The way he acted just like the prince he was; agh! It infuriated her. She was tempted to tie a sign around his neck that said **I AM TAKEN**, and **PROPERTY OF KELSEY** underneath.

"Hey guys," Ren said, jogging up to them with Nidar. "You alright?" he asked Kelsey, seeing her face.

Marcus chuckled and put a hand over his shoulder. "Come on, bud," he said, taking him with him.

"Someone's jealous," he whispered into Ren's ear.

Jealous? "Oh~," he said quietly in slow realization.

The high priest led them to another temple. One they had yet to visit. It was the second tallest one in the city and designed just like the sanctuary. Three enclosed walls and one shielded by a curtain. Inside, artifacts lay everywhere. They littered the ground and were placed on podiums. A giant hole in the floor with a set of stairs going down displayed the many other levels of the temple below and all the artifacts that were kept there.

"This way," the high priest said. "And touch nothing."

He brought them to a back room, pushing passed a golden curtain. Inside were piles of gold coins and golden artifacts. And in the back, atop a lone round stone table, sat a single golden book. It glew gold, igniting the area around it. Ren recognized it immediately. It was magic.

They approached the book, and the high priest picked it up. It was made from solid gold down to its pages, with an ornate design on the outside.

"The Records of the Gods," The high priest said and handed Ren the book. The moment he took the book in his hands, the weight dropped him. Man, that thing was heavy. He'd expected it, but it still took him by surprise.

Ren opened the book and scanned through the pages, looking over everything he saw. Yup, he couldn't read a word. Oh sure, let us read the book; we'll figure it out. Not!

"I can't read a thing," he confessed and shifted the book's weight for the others to see.

"Neither can I," Marcus said, shaking his head.

"Same here," Julie said.

"I told you you wouldn't be able to read it," the high priest said. "Now do you understand?"

"What do you guys mean?" Kelsey asked them. "It says Alchimax Rope right here." She pointed with her finger. "And this one says Dalwrin's Net."

Bewilderment would kneel in surrender to the surprise plastered on their faces.

"What?" she asked, curious.

"That's impossible," the high priest said.

"You mean you guys really can't read it?" They shook their heads. "But if you can't, then why can I?"

She looked over the book, flipping through the pages and calling out artifacts listed, their abilities, location, and how to use them. It was true; she really could read it. When Ren and the others looked at the book, all they saw were strange symbols. But when Kelsey looked at it, she understood everything, as if she had a translator in her head.

"You've never seen this book or language before?" the high priest asked. Kelsey shook her head. "And yet, you can still read the book."

"When I read it, all the symbols and their meaning flow into my head. Then, they turn into English, the language of where I come from."

"Interesting. Tell me, do you see any strange things? Things that others cannot see?" She nodded again. "And the stones definitely chose you." She nodded one last time. "I can seldom believe it. I thought your kind were extinct," the high priest said in awe.

A sudden rush of fear and confusion spread through Kelsey's very being.

"Extinct? There are millions of humans in my world."

The priest shook his head. "I'm not talking about your species. There's a reason why you can read this book, why you can see things no one else can, and read unknown languages naturally. You, my dear, are a Seer."

Forty-one

The Seer

"A Seer?" What in the hell was a Seer?

"In ancient times, there existed a group of individuals from all different races. They possessed an ancient power, one unlike any other. They were gifted with the ability to see the world."

"See the world?" Kelsey asked. The high priest nodded in response.

"These people could see things no one else could. Spirits, energies, even gods. They could read any language that they came across, use any artifact, see emotions, another's abilities, and things hidden beyond sight, buried deep within the darkness that no one else could. A Seer could see the truth behind the world and all its workings."

Kelse's jaw hung slack. A part of her just couldn't believe she had such power.

"And I'm one of those people? A Seer?"

"You're *the* Seer."

"The?"

"Even in their prime, the Seers were still incredibly rare. There were only several thousand or so. Very few had the gift of All-Sight, and they were revered because of it. Their sight made them legends, at the cost of an immense fear felt by those who did not wield the power. Once, being a Seer was the greatest honor one could hope to obtain. But they disappeared."

"How is that possible?" Ren asked. "How could a whole group of people with powers such as them just disappear?"

"No one knows. How they disappeared has never been solved. They just vanished. The common-held belief is that they died out, and another seer has never been confirmed to exist or been born since then. Until now. You, Kelsey, are proof of everything we once believed in. Perhaps it's your destiny to find out that which has illuded the rest of the world for millennia."

"I bet this has something to do with the stones," Marcus said. "Think about it. The stones chose Kelsey, a human. And now we learn she's the first of a lost power in millennia; a human. She wields power we can't even imagine. Power perhaps greater than even Ren's and mine. Doesn't that seem too suspicious to be a coincidence?"

"That would also explain why she could read the map to the stones," Ren added. "At the time, we had thought it was the power of the map. Now, I'm not so sure. I'm positive that was her Seer powers at work."

"But why only now?" Kelsey wondered. "I've spent my entire life without any special abilities. Why, all of a sudden, do I have this ability? Why didn't it come to me sooner?"

"I believe the answer for that lies in your company, my dear," the high priest said. "You are surrounded by immense magic and even divine energy. No doubt, it was the constant exposure that opened up the inner pathways leading to your ability. Without that, I'm certain your ability would have remained dormant. And the stones recognized that power within you. You have no idea what you are capable of. You're extremely powerful, and extremely dangerous. But you must be careful."

"Careful of what?"

"Of everyone. If word gets out that a Seer has emerged, if they learn of what you can do, what you are capable of, you will be hunted." Kelsey swallowed loudly. "There are few, if any at all anymore, who revere the Seers, which means you will have no support or old allies. Many will attempt to use you for their own gain, to inflict chaos. The ones who fear you and your power will hunt you down to keep you from unlocking your full potential and discovering more of your kind. You must not let anyone find out you're a Seer. No one can know."

Kelsey nodded in understanding. She couldn't tell anyone about what she was. Not her friends, not even her own parents.

"That's not all," Marcus said. "Now we know why you can see our sword spirits. It's because of your abilities as a Seer."

Kelsey could only agree with him. It finally made sense why she kept seeing their astral forms when no one else could.

"What are you guys talking about?" Ren asked.

She and Marcus exchanged silent glances. This was a conversation that would have to happen eventually, but now that it had, they needed to tread delicately.

Marcus finally broke the long silence. "Kelsey … can see the spirits of our heaven's blades."

Ren's eyes widened. He didn't speak. No breath escaped his lips. It was a silent scream of unprecedented shock. When he looked at Kelsey, she nodded in confirmation.

"I've confirmed it, given that she can see Glorious. Earlier, when she waved at me, it was actually him she was waving at."

Ren felt like he'd just been run over by a train.

"Unfortunately, that's not all, though," Marcus continued. "There's … something else you should know, Ren. What really happened that day we fought Algiroth."

Ren gripped his fists tightly, the memory Marcus was talking about resurfacing. He didn't want to remember that day.

Kelsey placed a hand on Marcus's shoulder and shook her head. "You did your part. Thanks for getting it started. Now it's my turn." Marcus nodded back and let her take the reins.

"I'm sorry it's all gotten so messed up," she apologized. "This whole thing has just been one endless downward spiral. We've put this off long enough, and I want you to know the truth. After the battle with Algiroth, I saw something like a spirit hanging around you. At the time, I didn't know what it was. I thought it was another monster. So I asked it."

Ren was quickly putting the pieces of this broken puzzle back together.

"Since then, I've seen the spirit handing around you a number of times. It was only after talking to Marcus and Glorious that I realized what it was. The thing I see hanging around you isn't a spirit; it's Shadow Hunter."

"Agh, I get it now," Shadow Hunter said through Ren's mouth. One of Ren's eyes had turned gold, evident that Shadow Hunter was present.

"You get what?" Ren asked.

"What she saw was my astral form." Kelsey nodded in confirmation. "I thought it was just a coincidence, but I realize that wasn't the case. Since she's a Seer, she can see the spirits of us heaven's blades, like how she sees

Glorious. Suddenly seeing me must have freaked her out."

"You knew she could see you?" Ren asked.

"Not necessarily. I noticed her staring, but I thought it was just at you. I didn't realize she could actually see me."

"These sprits of your godly weapons, no one else can see them I take it?" the high priest asked.

"No," Shadow Hunter said. "Only our chosen wielder can see our astral form."

"Then that is proof that she is a Seer."

Ren ran a hand through his hair with a frustrated sigh.

"Perhaps it would be best if we gave them some space," Marcus suggested.

"Very well. We shall await you at the base of the temple," the high priest agreed. "When you have finished, you may take the book with you. Since the girl is a Seer and can read its contents, you may browse it during your stay here."

"Thank you," Kelsey said, and the high priest nodded back.

Marcus glanced at Ren and Kelsey before leaving with the rest of their group, as if to tell them to settle things between them. As soon as they were gone, Ren and Kelsey stood silently in place.

"I knew it. The entire incident was a misunderstanding," Ren said. "Truthfully, I think I've known for a while now. At first, I wasn't sure. But, knowing how you are, beyond perhaps a momentary lapse, the idea of you pushing me away just didn't make sense. Given how you acted afterward, the possibility that the situation that day was a misunderstanding became more and more plausible."

"I'd never abandon you. I'd never reject you. Never," Kelsey said.

"I know. And I should have known then, too. I think a part of me just expected that, at some point in time, that very notion would occur. So, when it happened, I used it as an excuse. I'm sorry."

"You should be."

The look on Ren's face was a kind of pain she'd never seen from him before.

"Back on the ship, you told me you weren't going to give up," Kelsey continued. "That you wouldn't push me away anymore. Does that still hold true?"

"It does," he confirmed. "Every word."

"Then I have a question for you. And I want you to be completely honest with me." Ren nodded, indicating for her to continue. "Do you still love me?"

Ren approached Kelsey, stopping right in front of her and forcing her to look into those drop-dead gorgeous cobalt-blue eyes of his. "I never stopped," he confessed. "Not for a single moment, no matter how much I tried to or convinced myself to. You're my one and only. And if you should allow it, so shall you ever be."

A lump formed in Kelsey's throat. Her stomach dropped with a sudden bout of nervousness. She never thought she'd hear him say it again. Then, a ghost of a smile formed on her face. "Prove it."

Ren placed his hands on her face and leaned in. Kelsey's eyes closed instinctively, and Ren's lips were on hers. A million tiny bolts of electricity shot through their bodies, and Kelsey wrapped her arms around his neck. Her skin tingled, and a brilliant warmth spread through her. This was the kiss she had waited so long for. The one she had longed for. And for the second time, they shared their first kiss all over again.

Forty-two

A Star Fallen from the Heavens

Even after their lips finally parted, the lingering effects remained. Ren and Kelsey held ech other's gazes, determined to never let each other out of their sight. But, as much as they wished to, there was still much to do, and they needed to look through the Records.

It was true that they no longer needed the Records to remove the stones, but there were plenty of other uses they could get out of the book. To not read through it when the chance was presented to them was a complete waste.

Kelsey spent the rest of the day and the following completely immersed in the Records. During that time, something apparent emerged. She may have been able to read the book, but completely understanding its contents was another story. There wasn't a single artifact listed that she knew of, to no surprise. That made deciphering its contents that much harder.

Ren found her in her usual spot in the temple. Kelsey had taken to claiming the couch as she spent the entirety of her day on it reading. He sat down next to her, and she snuggled up next to him.

"Find anything?" he asked.

"I found the stones. They're the only thing in here I recognize so far. I'm reading about them now. There's so much I didn't know."

Ren nodded in understanding. Even he only knew a small percentage of the artifacts detailed in the Records.

"Marcus and Julie are already waiting. Are you ready to go?" he asked.

"As ready as I can be, I guess," she said. It was a shame they didn't have more time. She wanted to keep reading. But their time on the island had come to an end. They had to return to the ship.

Nidar, the sneaky tiger that he was, gently tugged at Kelsey's shirt with his teeth. Kelsey patted the top of his head before letting him pull her to her feet. The tiger had spent the entirety of the last few days snuggling up with Kelsey, receiving endless head pats and treats. If he kept it up, he'd turn into one chunky kitty.

The three of them gathered their gear and descended the steps, the Records in hand. At the base of the temple, the chief and high priest waited with what appeared to be the entire city, there to see them off. Canoes had been prepared for them, just as when they'd first arrived.

Marcus and Julie had already taken up one canoe, leaving the other for the three of them.

Ren took one last look at the city before placing their gear in the canoe. He was going to miss this place. Or perhaps it was the adventure that he was going to miss.

"Thank you. For everything," Ren said to the chief and high priest. He extended his hand, and the chief shook it.

"You're welcome. Safe travels, mighty prince."

Ren set his gaze on the entrance to the city, far across the lake. The same vines still hung in place, a barrier to the cave and outside world beyond. Far in the distance, smoke rose into the air. Ren followed the plume, watching it disappear into the clouds.

Wait, smoke?

"What the?"

As if on cue, a thunderous boom shook the sky. Ren and the others recognized the sound as cannon fire. It could only have come from the ship.

More cannon fire followed, along with columns of smoke. There was no chance Conrad and the crew would just open fire without reason. Something had to have happened. The ship, it was either attacking or under attack. Perhaps both. But against what?

"Chief Dorair! Chief Dorair!" A single man raced toward them, his feet catching the ground and sending him crashing into the chief's mighty torso. "Chief Dorair!" he said through heavy breaths.

"What is it?" the chief asked.

The man swallowed, trying to catch his breath. "From the north, a group of strangers approaches."

Ren and the others exchanged glances, eyes filled with certainty. The approaching strangers, they were all positive who they were. They'd already had a run-in with the enemy twice now. There was no doubt this was their third. Verin's forces must have followed them. They were probably after the book, just as Ren and the others were.

"Don't worry, they'll never find the entrance to the city," the chief said.

The man shook his head. "They are already approaching the falls as we speak."

"They approach? How did they find the entrance?" the high priest wondered.

"For the record, we found it too," Ren said.

"You were allowed to find it. You had the map and the winds."

"Winds?"

"Were you not propelled by a great wind before your arrival?"

Ren and the others exchanged curious glances. "How did you know about that?"

"Those winds came from the Records. Those who are allowed safe passage with the map are sent the wind to guide them. Without them, you would never have found the island."

"Forgive the foreboding news, but I believe we are responsible for the enemy's arrival," Marcus said. "Our enemy must have followed us, despite our besting them twice."

"If these strangers are your enemy, they must be servants of the great evil who controls the dead, are they not?" the chief asked. He turned to face the people. "Warriors, prepare yourselves for battle!"

"Chief Dorair," Ren said. "You can't fight them."

"We have to."

"You'll be slaughtered."

"Then what can we do?"

"Nothing. Let us handle this." Ren already had a plan formed in his head. It was the worst possible plan, but a plan nonetheless.

"Do you have a plan?" Marcus asked.

"We destroy the entrance," Ren said. "That way, they'll never reach the gates."

"How are we supposed to do that?"

"Just trust me. Come on, get in the canoes."

Marcus and Julie boarded their canoe, with Marcus acting as the coxswain at the stern. Ren and Nidar boarded their canoe next, leaving Kelsey on last to take up the middle.

"Wait, the book," Kelsey said, handing it to the high priest.

"Keep it," he said.

"I can't just keep this. It's your most sacred treasure."

"Don't worry. The Records always has a way of coming back here. It will return eventually."

"We have to move," Ren said. He didn't bother grabbing the pole used to propel the canoe. Instead, he used his magic to cast a spell, and the canoe shot forward over the water.

Kelsey held on tight to the book as they flew into the cave. Ren didn't have the time to brace himself from the rush of the waterfall at the other end. Instead, he drew Shadow Hunter and summoned all the lightning he could, transferring it to the blade. Kelsey covered him with her body as they passed through the falls, and Ren unleashed his lightning with a single devastating swing. The golden energy and lightning crashed into the waterfall, and the entrance collapsed into a massive pile of boulders at the entrance, sealing it forever.

It was a race back to the ship. As soon as they reached land, they all took off running. Every time they had to run, every dash to escape they'd ever faced, Kelsey had always been behind. Being human, she could never hope to keep up with them. But this time, it was different. She didn't know why, but somehow, she was keeping up with everyone.

At the next clearing, all five of them came to a stop. Standing at the far edge was a small group of two dozen, all armed for war. Leading them was the familiar form of a man with long brown hair and a mask over his face, thus confirming their certainties. Verin's general readied his gauntlets with a deeply satisfied grin on his face. Their enemy had found them.

Forty-three

Until It Turns to Strength

"Prince Nightwalker and party," Wei said. Nidar growled dangerously at him. "And pet." Nidar released a vicious roar at his comment. "Thank you for guiding us all the way here. Otherwise, we would never have found the island. Or the magnificent artifact you have on you."

He knew. He knew they had the Records on them.

"Get the book!" Wei shouted.

All at once, the two dozen enemies attacked. Ren drew his pistols and fired. Wei Shu's chimera flew into the air, avoiding the bullets. He continued to fire. He dropped his last empty clips and holstered his guns.

"Damn it! Quick bastard."

Out of bullets, Ren drew Shadow Hunter, spinning it around in his hand. His wings shot out from his back, and he launched himself at the general. Ren was so fast Wei didn't even see him coming. He crashed into him and tackled him clean off the chimera. Wei gathered a hoard of magic in his right gauntlet and struck Ren's stomach. Ren titled Shadow Hunter just in time to block the strike and Wei kicked him off, separating them.

Ren spread his wings and stopped while Wei landed on the ground. The guy punched his knuckles, creating the familiar spark from the clashing of metal. "Let's get started, shall we?"

Ren flew at him and swung Shadow Hunter. Wei Shu raised his arm and blocked the attack, following up with a punch to Ren's stomach. Ren spun in the air, avoiding the punch, and dragged his sword across Wei's arm, slashing at his neck. Wei ducked, and Ren blocked an incoming strike.

"I have to admit, I've grown rather fond of our little get-togethers," Wei said. His next strike released a wave of light with it, aimed right at Ren, who cut it in half with Shadow Hunter.

Wei followed up by striking the air again, this time with both fists, before he punched the ground. Bullets of air rocketed at Ren, and a giant fissure opened up in the ground, headed right toward him.

Ren blocked both air bullets when he was suddenly struck hard from behind. He crashed into the ground and rolled just in time to avoid Wei's punch. The ground shattered beneath the guy's fist, and Ren quickly shot to his feet, putting distance between them.

Silver energy gathered around Wei's body, enveloping him like a cacoon.

What the hell is this guy? Ren wondered. *I've only seen silver ki around werewolves under a full moon, and certainly none like his before.*

Wei didn't give Ren much time to think before charging at him. Shadow Hunter struck Wei's fist in a blast of energy that rocked the battlefield. Ren matched every one of Wei's punches with a slash of his sword.

Unexpectedly, an arrow flew at them from the side. They both dove to the ground as the arrow struck a nearby tree.

Julie dropped into view and fired another arrow at Wei, who deflected it effortlessly. The general unleashed another bullet of air at Julie, who dodged it, then turned and fired at one of Wei's soldiers.

Ren took advantage of the momentary distraction and swung Shadow Hunter, releasing a blade of golden energy that raged toward the general. Wei threw a punch, and his silver energy crashed into it. Ren shielded his face from the explosion when another one came flying at him, leaving him no time to counter.

"Crap!"

He summoned his ki and stabbed Shadow Hunter into the ground. A wall of earth appeared and blocked the attack, but it was easily destroyed, and the force threw Ren to the ground.

Wei charged Julie, who was busy fighting a group of soldiers. She had no room to defend herself when another arrow suddenly flew at him from within the darkness of the forest. A hoard of people rushed out all at once, armed with only daggers and swords. Their loose clothing was unfit for battle, indicating their lack of combat. In a last-ditch effort, half of the crew stationed on the ship crashed into the enemy, taking advantage of the surprise.

Nidar tackled one of the enemies and sank his teeth into them. They struggled only momentarily before their body ceased all movement. Another tried to cut him down with a sword, but the tiger turned and lunged at him, slashing him open with his claws.

A loud cry filled the battlefield and Ren looked over to see one of the sailors get pierced from behind with a sword, then another from the front. Another sailor was cut down after taking out an enemy, and a third defending one of their own.

Ren gritted his teeth in anger. They were losing forces, good, honest men who were merely trying to live the life they thought best. With fury building within him endlessly, he summoned a ferocious amount of ki, the blue energy bubbling off of his skin, and unleashed it, tearing through the battlefield and ripping apart the enemy ranks.

Another blast of golden energy cut between Julie and Verin's general. Wei stopped dead in his tracks as

Marcus flew at him and swung Glorious down on his head. Wei crossed his arms and blocked the strike, but the ground at his feet cracked from the force of the impact.

With a kick to the stomach, Marcus was sent flying. Ren was about to join them when his instincts took over. A chill ran down his spine, and he rolled to the left. A blast of flame struck the ground. Ren looked up and saw Wei's chimera floating above him. It's lion and goat head and serpent's tail staring at him.

That damned beast. It had already caused enough death as it was. He needed to end it, here and now.

The chimera opened its lion jaws and released a breath of fire. Ren rolled and slashed at it, but the beast flew out of the way. It looked like he was going to have to handle this thing before he could help the others. Marcus would just have to handle Wei Shu himself.

Marcus readied himself for Wei's next attack. "We need to get out of here now!" he yelled to the others.

"I'm afraid it's far too late for that," Wei said back.

Damn it. Unleashing all my energy at once is the only thing that will hold him back long enough for us to escape. But if I do, I'll be out cold. He looked behind him at Julie who was still shooting arrows. *More than anything, I need to get her out of here. But how? I need to think of something, and fast.*

"*I think it's finally time,*" Glorious said in his head.

"Time for what?" Marcus asked back. "Do you have a plan? Or did you see the future?"

"Neither. I'm thinking you're ready."

"Ready for what? How about a little clue here."

"You've been the perfect partner, Marcus. More than I could have ever hoped. But you were missing something, something that Ren could never fulfill. Someone you truly want to protect. Someone to give your heart to. Now you have just that. Which means you've met all of my requirements. It's time for you to join Ren and Shadow Hunter in the realm of legends. It's time for you to make your mark on the pages of history. You're ready. Let us become one. Let's show this rabbit the power of a Heaven's Blade."

Marcus took a wide stance and raised Glorious to his eye level. Wei readied himself for an attack. He could feel it. Something was coming.

Golden energy exploded around Marcus. His eyes began to glow as power flooded through them, then shot straight up into the air like a beam, blowing away the clouds.

Ren couldn't hold back his grin, for he was the only other one who knew what was about to occur.

The voice that came out of Marcus was neither his nor Glorious's. It was a perfectly synchronized combination of both.

"Glorious, release!" The golden energy wrapped around him tightly. The first crack formed only seconds later before it exploded like he was breaking out of a shell, a new form and all. His long brown hair had grown even longer, reaching the center of his back, his ponytail shed. The way it stood on end made it look like he'd been caught in a lightning storm.

The familiar black outfit he always wore had been replaced by red robes over light golden armor. And in his hand, he held a new sword. Glorious was now a one-handed long sword with a golden leather-wrapped handle. The crescent moon guard was formed from seven crosses connected at the crossbars, and the pommel a pair of white angel wings.

And just like that, it was gone. The entirety of Marcus's energy had disappeared, undetectable to anyone other than Ren, were he in his released state.

Seeing the state of the fight, the remaining crew members gathered their fallen comrades and rushed into the woods, returning to the ship. They had done what they could, and remarkably so. But now, their usefulness had come to an end, and they knew it.

Wei stared at Marcus with wide eyes. "The release of the heaven's blade." *No, not another one,* he thought. *Not again.*

"*I hope you're ready,*" Glorious said to him, "*because you'll only get one shot at this.*"

Marcus raised Glorious in response, pointing the blade toward the sky. All of his ki, all of his magic, gathered in his sword. Golden flames erupted around it, turning the sword transparent. It was almost as if the sword were made of fire. *Rathos.* "Hellfire."

"Nidar!" Ren yelled. Ren slammed his wings down and flew for the girls. He picked them both up and flew out of the area. The tiger immediately recognized his action and bolted into the forest after them.

Marcus swung his sword down and an ocean of golden flames swallowed the area whole. The fire left nothing in its wake, obliterating all forms of life.

Glorious was right. Marcus only had one shot with that attack. It completely drained the last of his energy. He had just enough to change into his werewolf form, his once brown fur now a brilliant gold, and run after Ren and the others.

Running on all fours, he caught up to Ren and the girls quickly.

"As much as we all have to say, it can wait," Ren said. "With any luck, Wei Shu was killed in your attack. Either way, let's not stick around to find out and get the hell out of here." He slammed his wings down again and shot forward with a blast of speed.

Even in his released werewolf state, Marcus couldn't keep up with Ren. For a race of monsters known entirely for their speed, it was unbelievable.

Ren could see the ship from the air. Below, the rest of the crew that had journeyed to the island rowed across the waves back toward the ship.

Suddenly, Ren lurched, and they were falling.

"Ren!" Kelsey said. He spread his wings, and they crashed onto the sand.

Marcus ran over to him as Ren pushed himself up to one knee. "Hey, you alright? Come on, we can't stop now." Ren was in agreement, but he knew it; he was down.

"I'm out of strength. No more flying for me." His breathing was heavy, too. Now all four of them had to find a way to the ship, with no boat to take them.

Marcus's ears twitched as new sounds hit him. It was easily recognizable. He could hear Wei Shu heading toward them. "We need to get out of here now," he urged.

A sudden splash drew their attention to the water. Something shot out before diving back in.

"What the?" Ren wondered.

The water erupted as something shot out directly in front of them. It was an Iriserie, and not just one. There were four of them. The only problem was they numbered five, including Nidar.

"I've got him, go, go," Marcus said. He put his arm around Nidar and grabbed hold of one of the Iriserie.

Ren ran into the water, and lightning shot out around him. Marcus flinched, but Ren never made a peep. He was sparking up a storm and undoubtedly overcome with pain, but he never his expression never changed. He never faltered, climbing onto one of the Iriserie.

The Iriserie swam forward out to sea and soon they were soaring along the surface. Ren had a lightning field around him, Marcus held on to Nidar with only one free arm, and the girls hung on to their own Iriserie for dear life, but they quickly made it to the ship.

The captain and crew were standing at the starboard side railing, waiting. They quickly dropped a ladder into the water once Ren and the others got close.

"Here, catch!" the crew said. A net was thrown overboard, landing in the water below. Marcus tied it around Nidar, and the entire crew worked to pull the tiger out of the water and onto the deck.

The girls were up the ladder first, then Marcus, and Ren last. He barely made it up; the pain was so intense. But he ignored it and pushed forward, reaching the deck.

"Go, go! Get us out of here," Ren yelled.

"Alright, men, you heard him, turn this ship around!" the captain ordered.

The crew immediately got to work, and soon, they were sailing across the waves.

Forty-four

My Hero

Ren dawned the familiar golden armor he had worn into battle so many times. He had just finished attaching his forearm guards when a knock appeared on the other side of the door.

"It's open," he said.

Marcus walked into the room with Ren's father. "We're ready to go," Marcus said.

Ren strapped Shadow Hunter across his back and walked passed his father and Marcus.

"Let's go."

The three of them walked down the grand stairs in the main foyer. Everyone was waiting for them at the bottom.

"How's the evacuation?" Ren asked.

"Done," Marcus said.

"And our army?"

"We've gathered as many as we could on short notice," Neil said.

"We've fought more with less. Let's get this done. We don't have much time left. The enemy could be here any minute."

"Our scouts last saw Verin's general just outside of Theinsford," Cole said. "Not that it matters, but from what we've gathered, Wei Shu is only the third-ranking general among the four, er, well, now three."

"Soon to be two."

Ren walked outside, where horses and Nidar, all draped in armor, were waiting for them.

"Ren, be careful," Ellie said. She stood in the doorway, clutching his necklace in her hands.

Ren knelt down and hugged her tight. "I'll see you when I get back." Then, he climbed on Nidar, and the tiger shot forward, the others at their heels.

Ren pulled Nidar to a stop at the edge of Theinsford. They could see the incoming enemy force in the distance. Astride a vicious beast, Wei Shu led a gathering of close to three thousand. Somehow, he had survived Marcus's terrible attack in their last battle. Even from a distance, Ren could see a heavy mix of monsters and shades.

Chills shot through their forces when they glimpsed the enemy general's mount. The beast had large webbed wings with a single large claw that dug into the ground. It stood the size of a three-story building, with thick hind legs and a heavy array of thorns emerging from the side of its face, top of its head, and along its spine all the way to its long tail. Two large, thick horns stuck out from the top of its head, and spines extended down its neck all the way to the end of its tail. They filled the gaps where thorns did not. Polished green scales covered the entirety of its body, save for the beast's underside, which was covered in white scales.

Ren and Marcus braced the storm of fear, never moving an inch. They stared ahead, focused solely on what approached. The beast was one they had seen many of, and it was equally worthy of fear. A wyvern, of the Enemara Plains, no less. Alas, such a thing was nothing to them, who had slayed far worse.

How the general had captured or even tamed the beast was unknown. What they did know was that it was far worse than the chimera he previously commanded.

"Let's end this," Ren said. This was to be their last battle. He would not allow a fifth.

Ren slammed his wings down and rocketed into the air. In response, both sides closed the distance until they finally clashed. Ren tackled Wei Shu off the wyvern and they both hit the ground and rolled.

Quickly rising to their feet, Ren swung Shadow Hunter. A blade of golden light smashed into Wei, who guarded it with both hands. Wei Shu struck the ground with his fist, layering it with magic. The earth erupted forth at Ren's feet in the form of massive spikes. Ren easily dodged them and flew at Wei, but his blade bounced off Wei's armor with his next slash.

Ren circled back around and flew back at him. Wei fired off a blast of silver energy, which he cut through with Shadow Hunter. Again with that silver energy. It still bothered him not knowing what kind of monster Verin's third general was.

Before Ren could make his next move, Wei Shu ran at him, sprinting across the air as if there were an invisible platform beneath him. Ren had never seen such magic before. It left him completely taken aback.

Wei moved quicker than Ren could react, appearing right in front of him and striking him in the stomach. Ren crashed into the ground, feeling the wind knocked out of him. His opponent never let up, though. He barely had time to roll as Wei's fist penetrated the ground. The magical energy released threw him through the air, and he landed on his side, gasping in pain.

Using Shadow Hunter as a crutch, Ren got to his feet. He could feel Shadow Hunter supporting him, lending him strength.

"He's coming," Shadow Hunter said in his head.

Gathering his magic, Ren summoned forth a roar of flames in both hands and clasped them together, striking the ground at his feet. A ring of fire shot out, bathing everything in its path. Wei Shu gathered his energy and unleashed it in front of him. The energy formed a wall, deflecting the flames to the sides.

He wasn't done. Ren wouldn't give this guy the chance to even breathe. The moment the flames shot out, he gathered his magic in his hands once more. This time, the energy formed a physical connection and ruptured out, crackling between them. The lightning danced around him before he aimed it directly at Verin's general and unleashed it. The lightning rocketed forward, piercing right through the barrier and striking him.

Wei Shu was knocked clean off of his feet. The lightning threw him through the air, sending him tumbling. Smoke rose from where the lightning struck a hole in his clothes. Ren couldn't believe it hadn't blown a hole through him. This guy was much stronger than Algiroth ever was without his demonic sword. And even then, the difference wasn't too far between.

"You can use lightning!" Wei said, shocked.

His shocked expression rather surprised Ren. He hadn't expected it from the guy.

"What? You didn't know? Then let me show you just how much I can use it!"

Ren threw his hands to his side. Lightning danced between them before he pointed his index and middle finger out, and it flew at the general. The lightning was too fast for him to avoid or counter. His only option was to defend.

Wei Shu crossed his arms in front of him as the intense bolt barreled right into him. The impact sent him tumbling across the ground once more before rolling to a stop. The gauntlet on his right hand steamed where it had taken the full brunt of Ren's magic. Suddenly, a crack formed, and it shattered to pieces.

"Ren, you're using too much magic," Shadow Hunter told him. *"At this rate, you'll run out of strength."*

"I don't have a choice. It seems magic is the only thing that works on him. Just hold out for as long as you can, partner."

One broken gauntlet didn't dare to stop his opponent. The guy raised his fists, ready to continue, then he and Ren threw themselves at each other. They battle it out for over an hour, continuing to exchange blows relentlessly. But with Ren's wings, he had the greatest advantage.

An ear-splitting roar temporarily halted the fighting. They looked and saw Wei's wyvern fall, its body now a lifeless heap. Standing before it was a werewolf brandishing a golden single-edge blade. Marcus always came through.

Ren looked at the fighting below and saw Nidar tearing through the enemy ranks with Kelsey. The tiger tore apart the enemy as he ran across the battlefield. Kelsey summoned all the power she could from the stones, asking them to give her all the power they could muster. They glew brighter than they ever had, and in one single attack, she obliterated the surrounding enemy ranks.

Suddenly, he was knocked clean out of the sky again. Wei Shu flew at him, and Marcus came out of nowhere, swinging his sword. Wei blocked the strike, but the momentum sent him flying.

"Thanks," Ren said.

"Don't mention it. He's a lot stronger than Algiroth." Ren nodded in agreement. "I don't think we can beat him alone right now without releasing."

"Perhaps, but I'd rather save that for an emergency," Ren said.

"Exactly," Marcus said back. "So, let's take him down together."

Ren and Marcus attacked simultaneously. They unleashed a combined fury of attacks and spells. Unfortunately, their team-up didn't prove much use. Wei defended himself against both of them and still somehow managed to push them back.

Wei gave them a sly grin. He was eating this up. They were nothing to him. The cocky bastard knew exactly what he was capable of, and how well he was beating them.

Ren summoned lightning to Shadow Hunter's blade. "Not again," Wei said. He swung, and Wei backhanded with his only protected hand. His gauntlet shattered, and Marcus appeared in front of him, the tip of his blade aimed right at the general's chest.

Wei turned at the last second, and Marcus's blade cut into his armor, missing its target. He spun and kicked him aside.

A sudden laughter emerged from the general. "I haven't had this much fun in ages. It's incredible how strong you two are. You'd give any of us a run for our money. All except for him, of course."

"Him? Who's him?" Ren asked.

"As exciting as this fight has been, I'm afraid it's dragged on long enough," Wei said, ignoring Ren's question. "I'm actually a very busy man, you know."

"You're not going anywhere," Ren said. "We're taking you down right here. And we'll force you to tell us where Verin is while you're at it."

Wei's laughter erupted hysterically. "Tell you where Verin is? Don't be a fool, Ren Nightwalker. Even if you did know where he was, you don't stand a chance against him. Verin has more power than you and all the other Heaven's Blades. Even if you were to all fight him together, you would still die."

Ren and Marcus exchanged concerned glances. That wasn't good.

"Besides, you'll get nothing out of me, no matter how much you try."

"We'll see about that. Everyone has a breaking point," Ren said back.

"Oh no, you misunderstand. It's not that I won't tell you; it's that I can't. I have no idea where he is."

"What?" Ren and Marcus said at the same time.

"You heard me. I've never met him. Not once. None of us have."

"None of you? But you're his generals!"

"Indeed! However, that means nothing to Verin. Not Algiroth, not I, not even our second-ranked general. None of us, except for one. The first-ranked general. He's the strongest of us, with power equal to Verin himself, and only Mr. Hotshot has ever met him. So you won't get a single thing out of me."

"That's unfortunate," Ren said. "But not useless. We got some good information. That means we just have to get stronger. Much stronger."

"I admire your bravado. However, you'll never get the chance, because I'm going to kill you right here!"

The now all too familiar silver energy gathered around Wei Shu's body. Two long white ears sprang up on his head, and a fluffy white tail behind him. White fur formed on his arms, and his eyes turned red. He grinned, and Ren and Marcus saw two long teeth in front. A rabbit.

"No way," Ren said. "You can't be just a rabbit. Rabbit beastkin don't have nearly the amount of strength you have."

"Can't I?" Wei asked.

No, there was no way. Rabbits were a fairly weaker species. No rabbit has ever achieved this kind of strength. And then there was that silver aura. Ren just couldn't figure it out. Silver was the aura of the moon. It only appeared in those who harnessed its power, like werewolves. Rabbits didn't have that kind of power. And it usually only appeared during a full moon. Not at any time like this guy's.

Wei reached behind him and grabbed the weapon he'd kept on his back for the whole fight. A giant war hammer. A rabbit with moon aura using a war hammer, no, there was definitely something else.

Ren looked up. He could see the moon glowing above, hovering in the darkening night sky.

A memory flooded through him. The memory of a legend. Suddenly, everything made sense.

"I didn't think any of you actually existed," Ren muttered. "I've only heard the legends, but in the three hundred years I've been alive, I've never heard of anyone actually seeing one. Born of silver and divinity, the helper of a god. Maker of immortality. A Moon Rabbit."

Wei Shu grinned devilishly. "How very perceptive vampire. Color me impressed that you even know of my kind. There are not many of us left. I am one of the small few remaining and the only one here in the lower realm."

Marcus nearly dropped his sword, and suddenly, Glorious's comment in their last battle made sense. Glorious had called him a rabbit. At the time, he had merely thought it was an insult and ignored it, overcome by the heat of battle, but that wasn't the case. Glorious knew from the beginning exactly what kind of monster Wei Shu was. He knew the guy was a Moon Rabbit.

"Why would a Moon rabbit work for a necromancer?" he asked.

"Because I was ordered to by my master. The Man on the Moon."

Ren gripped Shadow Hunter's handle so tightly he started to bleed. No wonder they couldn't beat him, even together. Against a mythic-level monster, there was no way they were beating a Moon rabbit. Not as they were now. And to make matters worse, the Moon God, a monster herald as the 'Silverlight' and strongest user of lunar magic, had sided with their enemy.

"Shadow Hunter!" Ren yelled.

"Right!" Shadow Hunter yelled back.

Ren's energy exploded. The sudden eruption caught them off guard. Unable to prepare, the force extended beat down on everything in the are. Wei and Marcus held their arms in front of their face to shield themselves.

Marcus knew exactly what Ren was planning. His own energy exploded next. This time, Wei Shu was thrown back. The combined force of their energies ripped apart the area around them, eviscerating plant life and shattering the ground.

"Moon Rabbit or not, now we finish this!" Ren said. "You can tell the rest of your kind to which side to take from hell! Shadow Hunter!"

"Glorious!"

"Release!" they yelled at the same time.

Ren's and Marcus's forms appearance changed with their released forms. Ren's eyes turned gold, and his hair into a long ponytail. He wore a thin golden coat that exposed his chest collarbones with a long tail and wide cuffs, pants to match the coat with a black sash tied overtop at his waist with the ends left hanging, leather shoes at his feet, and a golden gauntlet on his right arm. Marcus in his golden robes over red armor.

Shadow hunter had changed to a single-edge blade with a spiked spine, a guard the shape of a cross, and a white handle wrapped in gold. Glorious a one-handed long sword with a golden leather-wrapped handle, seven cross crescent moon guard, and white angel wing pommel.

Neither Ren nor Marcus took their eyes off Wei Shu. Ren took a single step forward, and faster than the general could register, he was behind him. A horrendous pain pierced through him as his arm fell to the ground.

Wei cried out, overcome by the intense burning pain. *When did he move?* he wondered, shocked. *I never even saw the swing of his sword, let alone him get behind me.*

Marcus swung his sword when Wei Shu reached for his hammer, never moving from his spot. Wei's hammer was sliced in half. It fell to the ground along with his other arm. He rushed in instantly when Ren spun around.

"Raikiri."

"Hellfire."

A massive veil of gold lightning erupted upwards, leaving only a deep fissure in its wake and lighting the sky a brilliant gold before dissipating. An ocean of flames surged forward, consuming everything in its path. When they finally faded, nothing was left of the general.

"The General is dead! The General is dead!" the enemy yelled. Their forces lost their morale and their momentum along with it. They faltered, allowing Ren, Marcus, and their forces to finish them off, leaving none alive.

Their forces roared in victory. Another battle was won, all thanks to Ren and Marcus. That was two generals down, and two to go.

Forty-five

Because of Love

Ren looked at himself in the mirror. He stood in one of the back rooms of the church, dressed in a black suit with a white dress shirt and a black tie.

He leaned his head against the mirror. This is not how he had expected this to go. Any minute now, he would get called out to the alter. Man, things were so messed up.

After the fight with Wei Shu, Ren prioritized the reconstruction of Theinsford. Buildings had been destroyed, livestock lost, civilians injured, and lives uprooted. And he still had to deal with their own wounded and dead.

Then, amidst it all, he was given the news this morning that his and Julie's marriage ceremony was taking place in the capital's cathedral. He hadn't even thought about the arranged marriage with everything going on. Despite the events that transpired, Dridia's king used the battle as an opportunity to set the date and force Ren's hand. Even his groomsmen had been chosen for him. He didn't get to decide who he wanted at his side or his guests. With official procedures completed, he couldn't stop the ceremony from happening.

Ren released a long sigh. This wasn't even an arranged marriage anymore; it was more of a forced one. And one that neither he nor Julie wanted. The plan Ren had been formulating since his time in Paerlejara was now completely useless.

There was a knock on the door, and a man walked into the room. He was dressed in royal clothes with a cape over his shoulders and a golden crown on his head. It was the King of Dridia himself.

"Prince Nightwalker, it is an honor." Ren just glared at him. "I am grateful for you agreeing to this. I apologize for rushing things, but business is essential and best handled early. With the unification of our kingdoms, both countries will secure centuries of wealth and good fortune."

"Cut the shit," Ren said. "You seem excited to sell off your only daughter." The king gave him a nasty look.

"I am not selling anyone. She agreed to this."

"Did she? Or did you force it on her?"

"This wedding will happen, understand that. One way or the other. She has a duty to her kingdom. Something I'm sure you're all too familiar with."

Ren gave him that ice-cold glare that could stop a heart.

"Remember who you're dealing with here. I am not the Prince of Nexus for nothing. If you try anything funny, I'll personally be the one to take your head."

The king could see golden energy flourish behind Ren's eyes, evidence of the raging force contained within him, now surging with his anger.

"Know this, vampire. If, for any reason, this marriage doesn't happen, neither will the alliance. I will personally see to it that all negations between our kingdoms are ceased and take it as an act of agression. You've already got enough on your hands with one war. I'd hate to add another."

Man, Ren really hated this guy. He wanted to rain down lightning upon him. But that was the worst thing he could do.

Without another word, he pushed past the king, bumping his shoulder, and walked out of the room. He opened a side door and stepped onto the altar. Guests were seated on both sides, most of them royal officials and nobles. Even his groomsmen were selected purely for political reasons. Their only real job was to ensure the wedding continued as planned.

Standing next to Ren, the witness playing his best man cleared their throat.

"Archduke Randolf," Ren said.

"Your Highness, it is a glorious day." He had a smile on his face, but the expression hidden beneath was anything but happy.

"Yes, it is. Is everything alright?" Ren asked.

The archduke looked at the rest of the groomsmen. They nodded to each other and quickly huddled together.

"Your Highness, when we give the signal, run," the archduke whispered.

"What?" Ren asked back. "What are you talking about."

"You know exactly what I'm talking about. You can't marry this woman." All the groomsmen nodded.

"I appreciate the sentiment," Ren asked, "but unfortunately, I'm afraid Dridia has us in a bind with this one."

"I'm aware," the archduke said. "The procedure for this event was processed without my or your father's knowledge."

Well, color Ren surprised. That was something he never expected, and was glad to know.

"What are we to do then? I don't have a plan to get out of this. Dridia has been one step ahead of us the entire time. They have threatened war if this wedding doesn't happen. That can't happen. This is bigger than me now. Our whole kingdom is Dridia's hostage."

The archduke grabbed him by the front of his jacket and pulled him in close, looking directly into his eyes. "Screw the kingdom." Ren's eyes widened. "The kingdom doesn't matter right now. You've already done enough. We are not so weak that we will fall from this. You let us handle Dridia."

Ren couldn't believe what he was hearing. For a noble of high rank, an archduke no less, to declare his own kingdom forfeit for the sake of its future ruler, never has there been a situation like it. The mere concept would inspire hysterics in anyone who heard it. But Ren could tell they were all deadly serious.

"And just how—" he was cut off when music started playing.

Everyone turned and looked as the main doors opened, and Julie stood there with her father. She was dressed in a beautiful wedding gown, the veil over her face. But Ren could tell, even with her face hidden, that she wasn't smiling.

Julie started down the aisle, her father's expression unreadable. Once they reached the altar, her father released her and returned to his spot in the front next to his queen. And try as he might, Ren couldn't read Julie's expression behind her veil.

Ren quickly looked at his side of the audience and saw his father seated up front next to his master, Count Vaylor. His father said nothing, only shaking his head. Then he motioned to the door with it, like, *'Hurry up and get out of here.'*

Julie shifted next to Ren, drawing his attention back to her. The priest approached, stopping in front of them.

Ren recognized him, surprised to find that he was the one who would marry them. Adam Blake, a member of Trinity and a Heaven's Blade to boot. Adam ranked fourth among the Heaven's Blades. He wielded the hammer of Mat. A weapon able to control the power of storms and elements.

It was no coincidence that Adam, of all people, was the one chosen to marry them. Ren quickly turned to scan the audience. They blended in perfectly. Were he not otherwise aware, he'd never expected them to be part of a plan he still had no idea about. Mixed in on both sides of the guests were all the remaining Heaven's Blades. All of them except for one.

"We are gathered here today to entwine His Royal Highness, Prince Ren Allen Nightwalker, and Princess Juliana Priscilla Haynes in the ritual of marriage," Adam spoke, beginning the service. "Today is the joining of two hearts and two kingdoms." Adam looked at Ren with a blank stare. Even he knew this wedding was crap. "The perfect marriage is one of commitment and trust. It is the bond between two whose lives entangle each other and seek to become whole through their unification. It is a bond of *love*." He put a lot of emphasis on the word love.

Oh, shut up, Adam. Just get this over with, Ren thought.

"Do you Ren Allen Nightwalker, take Juliana Priscilla Haynes to be your wife? To care for and love, till death do you part?"

Ren was wholly unprepared. The suddenness of everything gave him no time to gather himself or his thoughts. He looked at Julie, hoping for some kind of clue. This time, she actually looked at him, but she had no expression. Ren pleaded with her through his eyes to give him anything, but he only got silence in return.

Silence filled the room. Ren tightened his fists, digging into his palms. Damn it!

"Ren?" Adam asked. Ren remained silent; his mind was far from the church. In that moment all he could think about was Kelsey. She was all he wanted, no one else. But no one was giving him any options. Even his own allies were staying silent. He couldn't risk a war without any certainty of a plan.

"I … do," he said.

Adam turned to Julie. She still hadn't said a word or showed any indication of a plan.

"Do you, Juliana Priscilla Haynes, take Ren Allen Nightwalker to be your husband? To care for and love, till death do you part?"

Julie kept her eyes on him, remaining silent.

"Julie?" Ren asked, but she still didn't respond. Concern was beginning to form within him.

"I'm sorry, it would appear the bride is a little nervous," Ren said, trying to play off her silence.

Adam nodded in understanding. "Then I shall ask again. Do you, Juliana Priscilla Haynes, take Ren Allen

Nightwalker to be your husband? To care for and love, till death do you part?"

This time, Julie looked directly at Ren. "I don't." The commotion that passed through the guests was exactly as one would expect it would be.

Julie's father got to his feet, and Ren grabbed her arm.

"What are you doing?" he asked in a light whisper.

"I have a plan," she said. "You have to trust me."

"Trust you? You've barely looked at me this entire time. No one has told me anything or even given me a clue. You want me to risk everything, the lives of thousands, tens of thousands, on a whim?"

"I do. I know my father threatened a war. We won't let it come to that."

"I can't risk my kingdom on faith, Julie. As a future sovereign, you should know that."

"Well, screw your kingdom."

"Why does everyone keep saying that?"

"Ren, we've known each other for over a decade. We've gone through a lot together in that time, and we've relied on each other more times than I can count. Now, I'm asking you to do it again. I need you to trust me."

"Juliana Haynes!" her father yelled. "What are you doing?"

Ren got in front of her and pulled her behind him. "Back off!" he said.

Suddenly, the doors were kicked clear off their hinges. Marcus stood in the doorway with a horde of armed knights. The Heaven's Blades seated among the guests rose to their feet, drawing their golden weapons.

"I object! Sorry, but this wedding is officially crashed!" Marcus yelled.

Forty-six

Blade vs. Blade

"Marcus? What the hell are you doing?" Ren asked.

"Isn't it obvious?"

Marcus disappeared, appearing in front of him. Ren flew into the wall when Marcus punched him in the face, and the knights behind him charged inside. The whole church was in chaos.

"Guards!" the King of Dridia shouted.

All of the knights the king had brought with him rushed forward to subdue the chaos, and the archduke and the rest of the groomsmen sprang into action. They released a blast of magic, blowing the guards away.

"Oh, I so hate it when a wedding is ruined," Adam said, but the large grin on his face wasn't fooling anyone. A golden hammer the size of his body appeared out of thin air. "Well, what can you do!" He raised the hammer above his head and slammed it down. Lightning barreled into a group of Dridia's knights.

Getting to his feet, Ren spit the blood out of his mouth and wiped his cut lip. If this was the plan, it was a hell of a distraction.

"I think it's about time you fill me in, partner," Ren requested. "How about it?"

Marcus responded by striking Ren in the face once more, then in the stomach. He could feel the full force behind every punch. This wasn't an act. Marcus was serious.

Ren summoned his wings and tackled Marcus to the ground.

"What the hell is wrong with you?" he asked.

Marcus kicked Ren off of him and tackled him outside of the building. They hit the ground and rolled. Marcus punched him again, and Ren kicked him in the chest, sending him flying.

The King of Dridia readied his staff when Ren's father suddenly appeared behind him.

"You've done enough." The king turned in shock, and Leo struck him in the jaw. He fell to the ground unconscious. "That's for my son."

The queen of Dridia stood over her unconscious husband, a furious expression on her face.

"I'm sorry about all this," she said to Leo. "I'll help you get everyone out."

"Mom!" Juliana said, running up to her.

"Julie, you're going to stay with King Nightwalker for the time being. He agreed before this to let you stay until we get things sorted out."

"Your Majesty, we must leave quickly!" the archduke said. "Miss Hayes, please, come with us. You and King Allagash need to stop Ren and Marcus." Leo nodded in agreement.

"Kane!" Marcus's father ran out of the church with Ren's father.

Ren flew at Marcus. Marcus blocked his strike and punched back. Ren knocked it aside and kicked at his head, but Marcus ducked. Ren brought both of his hands up and slammed them down, knocking Marcus to the ground.

Marcus growled and tackled Ren to the ground again. They were both rolling around, trying to pin each other.

"Ren! Marcus!" Leo said.

Marcus got on top of Ren and punched down on him repeatedly. Ren finally punched back, and Marcus landed next to him with a heavy thud.

"That's it, now I'm pissed!" Ren yelled. He flew at Marcus, who changed into a werewolf, and picked him up from behind. They flew into the air, going higher and higher.

Marcus struggled, but he couldn't break free of Ren's grip. Finally, Ren spread his wings, and they stopped. He released Marcus, the momentum taking him higher before he finally started falling.

The ground was coming up fast for Marcus. He had to do something before he became a werewolf pancake. Ren came out of nowhere, and Marcus flew through the side of a building.

Emerging from the hole, Marcus launched himself out of the building and at Ren. He slammed into him and dug his claws into his skin, putting a gash in his shoulder. Ren cried out in pain and was slammed into the ground.

Marcus let out a howl, and Ren hissed at him, bearing his fangs. They launched at each other once more, and blood flew out of their wounds as they fought.

Ren threw Marcus into another building and landed on the roof of a nearby building. Marcus emerged covered in blood, then reached to his side, drawing Glorious.

"No, stop them!" Leo yelled. If two Heaven's Blades of their strength clashed, it could very well destroy the city.

Their swords clashed against each other and destroyed the top of the building. Marcus landed a kick to Ren's stomach and immediately closed the distance. Ren flipped over him and slashed along the length of his back. Marcus howled in pain, and they both turned to face each other. Again, their swords clashed, the energy blowing them apart.

Getting to his feet, Ren's ki bubbled around his body. When he countered Marcus's next attack, his ki flew everywhere, and Marcus hit the ground like a bullet. Ren grabbed him by his face and smashed him into the ground before throwing him across the ground.

Marcus got to his feet, body shaking, and Ren swung Shadow Hunter. Blood flew from Marcus's chest, but he didn't hesitate and howled, infusing his ki into his breath. Ren was blown away with a blast of sound.

As soon as they recovered, they faced each other with fury in their eyes.

"Release!" they yelled at the same time. Two beams of golden energy shot into the air.

"Hurry, we have to stop them. Before they destroy the city!" Marcus's father said.

"And each other!" Leo added.

Golden energy ravaged through the skies as Ren and Marcus fought. They attacked relentlessly, never letting up. But with all that power from their released state, they were so fast that no eyes could follow them save for their own.

"I've had enough!" Ren yelled.

"Then that makes two of us!" Marcus yelled back.

Golden fire gathered around Marcus's blade, and golden lightning around Ren's. Everything seemed to travel in slow motion. It was like the world went silent. A tsunami of Flames shot out at Ren, and a wall of lightning that pierced the sky erupted from the ground, heading right for Marcus. The two attacks collided and held each other in place, neither gaining momentum over the other. Then, a massive explosion blew both of them clear of each other.

They hit the ground and blew it to pieces, landing in a small crater. Despite the wounds, the loss of blood, and the damage, they both got to their feet. Arms grabbed both of them from behind, pulling them back. They looked to see their fathers holding them back.

Ren and Marcus struggled to break free. Ren took a step forward, but his father yanked him back. He and Marcus glared at each other, never saying a word.

"That's enough!" Kelsey shouted, running up to them. She stopped next to Ren and wrapped her arms around him tightly, desperate to keep him contained. "Stop fighting!"

"Stay out of this, Kelsey!" he and Marcus shouted.

"Marcus!" Julie said, heading over to him.

Kelsey grabbed Ren by the front of his jacket. "I said that's enough!" she yelled. "What is wrong with you? You two are going to kill each other if you keep this up! Calm down, now!"

"What's wrong with me? He started this!"

"Oh, bullshit!" Marcus yelled. "This is no one's fault but your own. When are you going to get it? You can't marry her! You belong to Kelsey! You would rather marry Julie over her? Is that what you want?"

"Of course not!"

"Then quit trying to bear everything yourself. Stop being a prince for once in your life!"

"What the hell are you talking about, Marcus? I thought we were supposed to come up with a solution together. So what in the hell was that, huh? The wedding may have been orchestrated without our knowledge, but I know you all had a plan."

"The plan was shot, dumbass!"

"Then what the hell was that, Marcus? Back at the church. All those knights, the other Heaven's Blades, all of it? Why come with a force ready for combat if you didn't have a plan?"

"It was to get you the hell out of there. I thought you'd say no. We all thought you'd say no when Adam asked if you wanted to marry Julie. But you didn't!"

"I didn't say no because no one told me anything! Everyone left me in the dark, even Julie. Dridia threatened war, Marcus. Do you seriously expect me to just go on blind faith with no plan when that many lives are on the line? I figured if I said yes, it would either stall time a little longer, or perhaps even my yes was the signal to start whatever secret plan you had concocted. Julie told me to trust her, and I do, but if you had told me what was going on beforehand, I would have said no and followed whatever was laid out."

"There was no plan, Ren," his father said. "Dridia's Queen has been in contact with us in secret. It started soon after you left. She kept it secret, expressing her displeasure regarding the situation, even volunteering her aid. However, things moved forward without our knowledge. Our only chance was to create a distraction long enough to get you out of there and deal with Dridia afterward. And for the record, despite being royalty, you're still my son. I never wanted you to marry anyone but the woman you chose. All I've ever wanted is for you to be happy. And for you, that's Kelsey."

"Why?" Marcus asked. "Why did you have to say yes? What would have happened if Julie said it too?"

"I told you, I didn't want to. I was backed into a corner and chose the best decision available. I know she didn't want the marriage either. The much was obvious. Once she told me to trust her, I realized she was in on the plan, so I honestly didn't think she would say yes. I—"

Ren stopped mid-sentence when he saw the expression on Marcus's face. Everything suddenly became clear to him. "Marcus."

"You should have just said no, damnit!"

"I'm sorry. I didn't realize how badly it affected you. That's why you punched me, isn't it? You hadn't intended to, but your emotions took over. Your anger and frustration. You should have told me. If you had, I wouldn't have ever considered it, even for the sake of avoiding a war. You're in love with her."

Julie held Marcus tight as he nodded, confirming Ren's suspicions. It wasn't just him. They both did.

Ren looked at Kelsey, and she nodded back. His father released him, and he approached Marcus, pulling him into a hug.

"I need to hear you say it. Please," Ren pleaded.

"I love her," Marcus said to him.

Ren increased his grip, embracing his friend tightly.

"I'm sorry, too," Marcus added. "I shouldn't have punched you. I just couldn't control it. I couldn't hold myself back."

"It's alright. I understand. Why don't you two go have a long talk? I think you owe each other that much. As do I. Besides, I need to have one of my own."

Marcus embraced Ren one more time momentarily. "I'll stop by later. We can talk then."

"I'll take everyone back to the palace. Ren, come back when you're done," his father said.

Ren nodded, and Marcus took Julie's hand, following his and Ren's father.

"Ren," Kelsey said. He turned toward her.

"Kells." She put her arms around him and a loving embrace before he could say anything else. "I'm sorry," he said.

"I know. It's okay. This time, for sure, I can say that what happened definitely wasn't your fault."

Ren shook his head. "That doesn't matter. It shouldn't matter. I keep causing you nothing but problems. I'm really sorry."

"Just shut up and kiss me." She pulled on his jacket, and he lowered his head. She raised to the tips of her toes and crushed her lips against his. Ren put his arms around her in response, letting himself get lost in their kiss.

Forty-seven

Crucifix

S unlight shined through the window. The curtains had been drawn back, letting the morning sky ignite the world. It was just another day back to work, like usual.

A whole month had passed since the wedding incident. An entire month since Ren and Marcus practically destroyed the capital and each other in their fight. Ren still couldn't believe they had gotten into it like that. They'd had fights before, but none like that. For the first time in their lives, it was truly the first time they had actually tried to kill each other.

It didn't take much to recognize that both of them were at fault. If they had just talked to each other, things would have turned out much differently. Unfortunately, terrible timing due to the actions of the King of Dridia made that pretty much impossible. Everyone had their own plans on stopping the wedding, of which no one bothered to tell Ren. And then there were Marcus's and

Julie's feelings for each other, which, although he could sense, had never actually been shared. It's the only reason Marcus got pissed enough to start the fight in the first place, for fear of losing Julie to him.

Ren and Marcus had settled their differences and put it behind them, agreeing to rely on each other more. Marcus recognized that keeping his feelings hidden as he had only made things more complicated. A fight like that couldn't happen again. The repercussions were too extreme, and next time, someone may actually die. In that sense, they got extremely lucky this time.

Of course, they got chewed out for it; that was to be expected. But that they didn't even receive an official punishment surprised them. Even though Marcus was the one who actually started it, they had never intended to hurt anyone or destroy anything. With circumstances being what they were, their punishment was agreed upon unanimously by the powers at be, and they walked away with a simple slap on the wrist. Ordinarily, their punishment would have been severe, so they were grateful for it.

According to Ren and Marcus's fathers, they expected a fight to break out from the beginning. Although they never expected a fight like that, it was guaranteed to happen, given the plan to stop the wedding. It created the perfect distraction.

As for the King of Dridia, according to the report the queen sent, he was currently placed under house arrest until further notice while he reflected on his actions. Forcefully trying to marry off his daughter for the kingdom wasn't uncommon, but that didn't mean it was condoned. The queen was furious, to say the least.

Currently, she was in charge of the kingdom while the king served out his punishment. Her agreement to the parties at be was to maintain their alliance as it stood. Ren would have liked to at least get a mine out of it, but he didn't dare push his luck. An entire mine over a failed wedding that they never caused was too much of a demand. Of course, the wedding and engagement were called off entirely.

Ren and Marcus left the negotiations with Dridia to their fathers while they focused on not only finishing the reconstruction of Axiriles, but the now partially destroyed capital as well. A sort of self-imposed punishment they conditioned themselves with.

Ren felt someone stir next to him. He opened his eyes slowly, letting them adjust to the bright light of the sun. Kelsey was lying with her back pressed against his chest, his arm wrapped around her. At the foot of the bed, Nidar was curled up, sleeping peacefully.

He heard the door open, and someone walked into the room. His first thought was that it was one of the servants. However, the person who'd entered climbed onto the bed, and he felt a pair of small hands on his shoulder, shaking him.

"Ren. Ren, wake up." It was Ellie.

"Mmm," he moaned. "Five more minutes."

"Ren, come on! I'm hungry!"

Ren turned around to look at her. She was still dressed in her pink nightgown.

"Ren, come on! Get up!" She had a pouty look on her face.

"Okay, okay. I'm up, I'm up." He yawned and sat up, and Ellie hopped off the bed. "Kelsey. Come on, Kells." He shook her awake. "Time for breakfast."

"Right now?" she groaned, still half asleep.

"Ellie's hungry. Come on."

"Alright." She sat up and rubbed her eyes.

Nidar's ears twitched, and he raised his head when someone knocked on the door. Cole stood in the doorway.

"Well, it looks like I don't need to wake you up anymore."

"Oh, shut up."

Cole chuckled at his comments, and they got out of bed, dressing themselves in something other than their nightwear.

"Come on!" Ellie said. She grabbed their hands and pulled them along.

Nidar jumped down from the bed and followed them. Cole rubbed the top of his head as he walked by, then closed the door.

They open the doors to the dining hall, only to find it filled with people. Ren saw his father, his father's attendant, Marcus and his parents, his master, Julie, Neil, Archduke Randolf, and the other Heaven's Blades.

"What is this, a hotel?" Ren asked.

His father chuckled. "It's been a long time since we've had so many people at the table like this. Why not enjoy it. This is family, after all."

Ren sighed. "Our family is getting too big." Laughter rolled across the table. He, Kelsey, Ellie, and Cole all took a seat. Nidar sat down next to Ren's chair.

After breakfast, Ren returned to his study. There was still a lot of work to do, and he was determined to see it done. But not so that he would shut himself away again. He only spent a few hours working before taking a break.

Ren headed to Kelsey's room. She was reading through the records with Ellie when he found her. When he asked them if they wished to join him in heading into town, they agreed immediately. Kelsey closed the records before she and Ellie followed him outside.

They took a carriage into town, and Ren watched the world on the other side pass by. He focused on all the buildings destroyed during his fight with Marcus. It made him sick. Walking around the capital proved otherwise, however. Ren and the girls were greeted warmly by the citizens. He'd expected to face at least a little scorn, but got nothing.

A part of Kelsey was still surprised that Ren could walk the capital like he did without being swarmed. He was probably the only one who could do such a thing. But even still, it was a risk every time he stepped out of the palace without guards.

"Shall we stop for lunch?" Ren asked. He pointed to a building with his thumb. A small bakery with a few tables both inside and out. Kelsey remembered this place. She and Ren had stopped here when they were out preparing for the ball.

A bell rang as soon as they opened the door, signaling their entry. "Welcome, how can I, oh Your Highness, Lady Kelsey, welcome!" the woman at the counter said.

"Good afternoon," Ren said. "Might we occupy one of your tables outside? Whatever the two ladies wish, please."

"Ah, spoiling the misses and little one, I see."

Ren chuckled. "Exactly."

"Ren," Kelsey said.

"Kells," he said back. She sighed. "Get whatever you want. You too, munchkin'." Ellie stared at all the deserts and bread.

Once they chose what to eat, they picked a table and sat down. The woman came outside and placed a coffee in front of Ren and Kelsey, along with their order.

"The coffee's on the house. Call it a little something for getting through that wedding fiasco with Dridia. What a miserable pain."

Ren winced. "You know about that, huh? I'm sorry. The situation wasn't handled well, admittedly. And I'm partly to blame for that."

"Everyone knows about it, Your Highness. It's not you we expect an apology from. Well, we should be grateful it ended the way it did. Things would have been even more complicated after the entire city crashed the wedding."

Ren set his coffee down. Even Kelsey was interested.

"What are you talking about?" he asked.

"Oh, you didn't know? When the word spread of your wedding, we all gathered, ready to storm the church at any moment."

"Seriously?"

"Yes. The archduke himself informed us of the wedding and gathered us together."

"Archduke Randolf told you?" She nodded, and Ren shook his head. "That man is going to be the death of me." Kelsey and the woman started laughing.

"Come on, Ren, at least things ended up okay. Think about what I would have had to do to steal you back from her," Kelsey said, taking a sip of her coffee.

"I'm sorry, steal me back?"

"Well, of course. I had just gotten you back, after all. Do you honestly think I'd just let you get taken from me?" She raised an eyebrow at him, and Ren's face turned white the second he imagined it. A chill ran down his spine.

"Remind me to thank Marcus again for crashing the wedding." Kelsey started giggling.

"Well, I'll leave you three alone," the woman said, heading inside the store. "Enjoy your time. It's beautiful outside, after all."

"Indeed it is," Ren said, looking at Kelsey. "Indeed it is."

Kelsey noticed him staring, and her cheeks turned pink. "Who'd have thought," she said, changing the topic.

"Thought what?" Ren asked back.

"That we'd end up like this. From being childhood friends to falling in love."

"You're thinking this now?" She hated the smirk he had on his face at that moment. "But I guess you're right for saying it. You're a human, and I'm a vampire. Had you not been dragged into this world, I would have had to keep my feelings hidden forever. I had intended to."

"You never planned on telling me?"

Ren shook his head in response.

"Then I'm really glad I got attacked by that living shade. And more so that I found out after you returned. Had you looked like this before you left, I don't think I would have stood a chance."

Ren hid a smirk from her. She had no idea how much he loved her.

"Well, you do get jealous easily." He smiled at her, this one unconcealed, and took another sip of his coffee.

Kelsey's face burned red with embarrassment. Damn him!

After finishing their lunch, the three of them returned to the palace. Ellie ran off, leaving the two of them alone. Kelsey grabbed the Records from her room, and they found an empty lounge. With the matter of the stones resolved, they considered what else the Records could be used for. Their first idea was an artifact that could help defeat Verin.

Ren sat in the lounge's recliner, going over a list of artifacts they had read so far. Since he couldn't actually read the book, Kelsey had to pen it all down for him. Kelsey set the book down while he read and left to get a drink. When she came back, she set it on the table in front of him, then positioned herself in his lap on the recliner.

"Find anything?"

"Maybe. We've only gone through a portion of the book so far. Who knows what else we could find."

She wrapped her arms around his neck. "Then perhaps we should take a break."

Ren threw the paper on the table in front of him. "Sounds good to me."

Kelsey leaned down, and they were kissing. They didn't even pay attention to the time that passed, only breaking for air before kissing again.

Ren opened his mouth and stuck his tongue inside Kelsey's. She tasted of cinnamon and chocolate, evidence of her lunch that afternoon.

He felt her body press tight against him, sending heat through his entire being. Kelse's fingers found his hair, weaving their way through it. He wanted nothing but to drown in her.

"Mmm … Ren … wait," she said through kisses. "The iced tea is going to get warm."

"Screw the tea," he said back.

She closed her eyes, getting lost in him. This is what she wanted. No, this is what she had longed for. To be held like this by him, to kiss him like this. It made everything they had gone through these past six months worth it.

Ren moved his hands to her hips, gently grabbing them. Kelsey squealed and broke the kiss. When he gave her a sly grin, she gasped. "Ren Allen Nightwalker!" He grinned and started chuckling. She leaned back against him and crushed her lips to his, shoving her tongue in his mouth.

Someone cleared their throat, and they broke the kiss, looking to see who was there. Marcus stood in the doorway with Cole and all the others. He had his hands over Ellie's eyes.

"Really?" he asked.

"What?" Ren asked. Kelsey's cheeks turned Red as she sat on Ren's lap.

They all walked into the room and found a place to sit.

"So, what's up?" Ren asked.

"We thought we should go over our new game plan. What are we going to do now?" Marcus asked.

"I don't know. I'm still looking for a weakness we can use against Verin," Ren said.

Before they could think of their next move, someone knocked on the door, and one of the servants entered. "Prince Nightwalker, you have visitors." The butler stepped aside as two familiar faces walked into the room.

"What are you doing here?" Marcus and the others all asked.

Arron and his daughter Angela stood in the doorway.

"I thought you might be getting lonely without me," Arron said. "I figured you could use my help right about now, so I requested the help of your beastkin friend, James Wilson. It's good to know that I was right."

"Help with what?" Marcus asked.

"With Verin," Arron answered. "I've been going through the Church's archives while you've been away. While looking through them, I found something that I thought you should see. It fits what you need perfectly." He handed Ren a piece of paper. "There is an artifact that is said to vanquish evil and release tormented souls. A holy sword that repels darkness. And, it's known to have a peculiar advantage, against necromancers." Arron gave him a cocky grin, but Ren figured he deserved it right about now.

"This is exactly what we're looking for," Ren said.

"Unfortunately, I don't know much more about it. I couldn't find anything else."

"That's fine. We have this." Ren showed them the Records and quickly explained is use. "If that sword is a relic, then it's definitely somewhere in this book. We just have to find it."

"And speaking of artifacts, how goes your hunt? Did you find a way to remove the stones?"

"We did," Kelsey answered. "It turned out the way to remove them was anything but what we expected it to be." She looked at the stones attached to her wrist. "Please come off," she said.

The bracelet detached itself at the bottom, and she slipped it off her wrist.

"That's it?" Cole asked. "We went through all of that for you to ask them?"

"Believe me, we said the same thing. It turns out I was misusing them. The key is interacting with the stones. Up until now, I've only treated them as objects. Instead, I need to treat them like the Heaven's Blades treat their weapons."

"So we have the stones, the Records, and now a clue to help us defeat Verin," Julie said. "So what now?"

"We should head back to the human world," Ren's father said. "We're going to be needed back there. And we need to check on the number of shades that have accumulated while we were gone." Ren and Marcus nodded in agreement.

They were going back to the human world. Kelsey was finally going home.

"And then what?" she asked.

"Then? Then it's time for another quest," Ren said. He looked at Kelsey, Marcus, and her. "So, you guys up for another adventure?" he asked. They all grinned in response, and he returned the gesture to them. "Alright then. Let's get started, shall we? It's time to find Verin's crucifix."

Acknowledgements

Here we are. Somehow, book two has come to an end, and I admit, I didn't expect it to turn out the way it did, but I wouldn't change a thing.

Writing a book is a daunting task, especially when you're going at it alone. Unlike Nightwalker, which came to me on its own, The Seer really forced me to plan out the grand scheme of things. Namely the choice to focus on Ren's and Kelsey's relationship. I've never been one for stories focused purely on romance, nor is that what I want this series to be about. So, finding the right balance between that and the main quest was a challenge.

At times, I felt like I'd never get it right and that one would overshadow the other. I really felt the pressure to get this one done perfectly and ready to carry on into the next story. And although things may seem random, I promise you everything has a purpose. It's thanks to the many rounds of edits and inspiration at the most random times that helped me blend everything together just right, and how great it came out. But, that's enough blabbering on about the contents. Let's move into those who helped to make The Seer possible.

To my friend, Josh, for always being there to help me through the gaps in the story, detailing the action scenes, and reading over my many drafts. You were, without a doubt, the reason we were able to finish strong. Twelve years of friendship is a long time and proof of a bond that won't break, even over a lifetime.

Hats off to my amazing cover artist, Dragan Paunovic, for an absolutely out-of-this-world cover that perfectly captures the golden book that has become a pivotal point of the story. I'm blown away by how great it is. You killed it.

Taking a step back, I want to give a shout-out to my friend and coworker, Isaac Hertzson, who created the map for Nexus. You took my dream of a whole new world and helped to turn it into reality. Without you, Nexus would have forever remained an image in my head. I can't thank you enough for your help and hard work.

Special thanks to all my friends who supported me along the way. From reading the book to helping me promote it and get my name out there, you've been invaluable. What would I do without you guys?

To my grandmother, Paula Manioci, who continues to believe in me, even when I don't always believe in myself. And to my grandfather, who was a crucial part of my life and helped me to grow into the man I have become. Thank you for being in my life. Rest in peace.

And most importantly, thanks to all of you who followed along with me in this next phase of the adventure, and for supporting Nightwalker and continuing on this journey with me. Your support and praise gives me hope for the future of this series and more to come. I promise, the adventure is not over yet.